HOLLYWOOD'S EVIL SECRET

By Sally Winter

Published by Edwards and Lillie

First edition published in Great Britain 2018

ISBN: 978-0-9927927-1-8
© Copyright Sally Winter 2018
sally@sallywinter.co.uk

DEDICATION

For my dear old dad, Peter Alexander Edwards, who loved the idea of this story but did not live to see it completed and for my sister Jane who parted this earth the same year as dad. I'm sure you're both catching up with each other somewhere up above. And to my two puss-cats Baggins and Monty, who are now gone, but sat by my feet as I wrote.

INTRODUCTION

If you'd asked me back in 2005 whether I'd ever write a novel, I'd have said absolutely not, simply because I'd run out of ideas after only a few pages.

But then my lovely mum died and I felt lost and unable to do my day job as a Costume Designer. So one evening, I sat and spoke to mum as though she were still here, asking her for inspiration. Out of that came my first novel, *Rhubarbs and Circuses*. Thanks mum.

Since then, it has been optioned by the screenwriter Roland Moore, who is now adapting it for the screen. The chances of that ever happening seem so remote.

I started writing my next novel *Hollywood's Evil Secret*, back in 2016. The idea came to me in a dream and the outline evolved really quickly.

I've always been a Marilyn Monroe fan and cannot help but be wowed by her screen charisma. There are so many theories about what really happened to her. I find it incredibly sad that someone so revered, was in life so deeply troubled, based on the things that have been written about her in the past.

Hollywood's Evil Secret fits into the twisted history genre, a "what if" and is a tribute to beautiful Marilyn.

ACKNOWLEDGEMENTS

A big thank you to the following: everyone within my wonderful family for putting up with my obsessive nature with regards to creativity, Suzie Kennedy who is probably the world's best Marilyn look-alike, for appearing on the front cover, Sophie Drayton for being such a brilliant PA, Simon Scantlebury for career encouragement and for boosting my flagging confidence, Andy Cahill at The Picture House, Bournemouth for the cover shoot, Alan Cooper for the cover design and, finally, my friends and fans who have spurred me on, despite me being a pest when it comes to trying to further myself on social media.

If I've overlooked someone, it's not because I don't care. Creativity is so often accompanied by scattiness. Anyway, you know who you are, so a big thank you (-:

Chapter 1

Faded Grandeur

Olivia stopped abruptly and looked upwards open-mouthed at the most unexpected of sights. She shivered and thrust her hands deep into her pockets. 'What the hell is this place? We're in the middle of nowhere.'

Sam looked down at Olivia from the tree trunk he had been using as a vantage point. He jumped down beside her and adopted a casual stance. 'It's just a ruin. Nothing to get excited about,' he said, shrugging. He began to kick at a pile of dead leaves, but unexpectedly they were whisked away from him in a turbulent flurry.

Olivia turned and glared at him. 'Sometimes, you're imagination is so limited. Aren't you even the slightest bit curious as to what's on the other side?'

'Not really,' Sam replied, shrugging again to compound his disinterest.

Suddenly, an icy chill swept across the woodland clearing and pierced through Olivia's clothes. It made her feel as though she had been speared by a thousand glass splinters. She zipped up her pink hoodie and jumped up and down in an attempt to generate some heat. 'Sheesh, I can't feel my toes.'

Sam contemplated both the rustling undergrowth and the billowing forest canopy high above. Shrieks and distorted chattering emanated from deep within the camouflage. He tried to ignore it. Like Olivia, he had recently cast aside his awkward teens and, being her closest friend, he was trying his hardest to be her protector and not imagine a predator behind every tree trunk. An adult show of strength could also gain him brownie points. 'Give me a minute - I'll just check the map,' he said, jabbing repeatedly at his touchscreen. To his dismay the screen suddenly went black. He pocketed the phone quickly before Olivia could notice.

'I should've known better than to trust your sense of direction Sam. You've got us lost again.' She huffed at his incompetence and the lack of a solution.

'What makes you think that?' he asked, defensively. 'We followed the route planner to the letter.'

Olivia threw him a resigned look. 'Why do I not believe you I wonder?' she said under her breath, at the same time rolling her eyes. She realised the only thing to do was to switch her attention back to more important things, such as what it was that was blocking their way.

Standing before them in the most unlikely of places was a pair of elaborately fashioned fairy-tale gates; their barley-sugar bars spiked with medieval styled arrowheads and heraldic shields depicting feuding dragons and knights. Framing the gates were stately gate posts, their crumbling red brickwork only serving to highlight the splendour of the limestone stags that crowned each pillar. Partially eroded by the elements and the passage of time, the stags still exuded an air of supremacy, squaring up to each other like vying peacocks.

Olivia looked in each direction to see if there was a way that she and Sam, that is if he were brave enough to follow, could pass. She was dismayed to see a high brick wall stretching out far beyond the nearest trees. The approach route to the gates had long ago been reclaimed by undergrowth. Even Sam's boots had failed to uncover any sign of a road surface under the thick sodden forest floor. Olivia wondered how often others had by chance, stumbled across such majesty. In her mind, the scene would be a great location to incorporate into a horror film. Back in the present moment, she realised Sam's hangdog expression was an indication that there was no solution from him, even though he had had plenty of time to come up with one.

She squared up to him with her hands on her hips and her chin jutting in defiance. 'So where to now?' she asked, tapping her foot impatiently, while waiting for another one of his predictable excuses.

He shuffled nervously from foot to foot. 'Let's take a break. We've still a bit of daylight left to find help.'

'Then surely we should get a move on before we lose daylight - if that's alright with you,' said Olivia, more as an instruction than a suggestion.

Sam looked down at her. Her expression spoke for itself. She was far-removed from her normal bubbly self. On top of this, the vast scale of the architecture and gargantuan trees that surrounded them both, created the illusion that Olivia had visibly shrunk, to the size of a small child. He wrapped her in his arms and noticed straightaway that she was shivering. He was uncertain as to whether it was out of fear or from the cold. 'Don't worry, we'll find help soon, I promise.' In that moment, he realised that he loved her vulnerability, but because they had known each other for such a long time, he knew it would be weird to suddenly become more than just friends. He began to stroke her hair to settle her jangling nerves, all the time wishing their relationship were otherwise.

Olivia resisted his efforts and pulled away, preferring to be poised for any eventuality. 'I hope you're right. It's getting dark quickly.'

Sam shot a glance upwards and realised that she had been more observant than him. The canopy was no longer shot through with shades of jungle green backlit by the sun, but with uninspiring shades of muddy brown. 'At least we're away from it all,' he said, trying to find something positive to say about their situation.

Olivia sensed mystery and a double-dose of malevolence. 'Come off it,' she said. 'It's spooky and you know it. Soon as it's dark, we'll be eaten by wolves.'

Sam laughed. 'There are no wolves in England, unless you count those in captivity.'

Olivia took no comfort from him, from the spectacular forest or the breathtaking view glimpsed through the trees of a lilac horizon that was slowly turning purple. Instead, she feared that once blanketed by nightfall, their surroundings would be far less welcoming. She looked down at her bare ankles, imagining lengthening shadows stroking them with vaporous fingers.

Sam shook the rusting gates, showing no respect for their age or possible historical importance. They reacted to his efforts by shuddering within his grasp. Immediately his hands were caked with oxidised metal particles and specks of dark green paint. As though to add to the gates' protest, a dusting of iron filings and dead moths fluttered down from the top of their ironwork, coating his hair with a peculiar cloud of organic confetti. He brushed the debris hurriedly from his hair and his shoulders and checked for spiders, his attempt to fracture the sturdy padlock proving ineffective. Failure embarrassed him. He had wrongly assumed that his rigorous mountain-bike training would be enough to provide him with all the strength he needed. He kicked the gates in frustration, causing them to scream out in protest like a pair of wailing banshees. 'Bastard things,' he cursed, his prime objective to impress Olivia clearly thwarted.

'Be quiet, someone'll hear us,' she squeaked, fearful in case they were being observed from the shadows. 'Let's get out of here and find somewhere a bit more welcoming.'

'Not like you to be so easily spooked,' said Sam. He peered through the bars at fallen trees and rampant weeds that had over time fought their way up through a gravelled drive towards sunlight. Whereas to him the place seemed ripe for redevelopment, in Olivia's mind, the enigma beyond seemed to whisper of faded grandeur and decay, but she was in no mood to explore now that night was nearly upon them.

At the sound of crunching leaves, both spun around. A tall and lean figure had appeared from out of the shadows, walking with a very deliberate stride.

'Ryan mate, you scared the crap out of me,' said Sam, laying out his fear unintentionally for both friends to see.

'Sorry, I thought you would've heard me coming,' said Ryan, with the tiniest suggestion of a Dorset accent in his voice.

Appearing as he had from between the tallest of trees, beating at brambles with a long stick, he had resembled an intrepid explorer making his way through the Amazon rainforest. His knee-length cargo shorts left his battle-scarred shins exposed. An intentional choice as he was proud of his wounds. They spoke to him of heroic action and battles won, rather than the fact that he had fallen off of his mountain bike descending snow-capped mountains too optimistically, on many occasions.

'You should've stayed with the car, like I told you to,' barked Sam.

'Mate, if you think I'm staying on my own now it's getting dark, you can think again,' said Ryan, in an attempt to quash Sam's tendency to take over. He side-stepped past Sam, pulled on a knitted beanie hat and squinted with almond shaped eyes through the gates. 'Too scared to go in?' he asked, directing the question at Sam, while visualising ornamental gardens where multiple molehills now peppered a scrubby lawn.

'Cut it out you two,' said Olivia, fed up with their persistent bickering but secretly feeling marginally better now the three of them were reunited.

'No one's used this gate for years,' said Ryan, scanning the formidable boundary walls, fortified by man but repossessed by nature. Thorny branches had over time overwhelmed the barbed wire's arsenal of miniature steel swords.

'You don't say,' said Sam.

'Straight out of an slasher movie if you ask me,' said Ryan, adding an extra slice of drama to the debate. It was always his style to embellish even the dullest of situations, but in this case he quickly realised he was not helping.

'As it happens, no one's asking you Ryan. So shut up. I'm trying to think,' said Olivia, the sound of her own strident tone making her feel more like her normal courageous self.

'So, are you with us, or not?' asked Sam, verbally slapping Ryan down.

'Of course I am. I'm here aren't I?'

'Then let's stick to the plan, shall we?'

'Yes boss,' conceded Ryan, knowing better than to argue when Sam was in full commando mode.

Their differences of opinion shelved momentarily, all three skirted the intimidatory walls. There seemed to be no perceptible foothold to entice them to climb to the top or a way to conquer the barbed wire so that they could peer over. Trampling on nettles and brambles, all three swore in whispers at the pain inflicted by thorns penetrating their shins at every step. Only Olivia imagined that the wind was calling, advising them to turn around and go back the way they had come.

Suddenly she stopped. 'Hey - look at this.'

'What is it?' asked Ryan.

'I think it's a door,' she said, already attempting to separate climbing plants so that she could take a better look. 'Well don't just stand there you two. Give me a hand.'

As a group they tugged at a matted layer of ivy, until Olivia's discovery had been exposed. She yanked impatiently at a brown Bakelite handle but it crumbled to pieces in her hand.

'Damn - it's locked,' said Sam, putting his shoulder against the rotting oak, still quietly sulking about his earlier lack of muscle.

The door groaned, emitting a sound that resembled a waking giant, insistent that no one could beat it in arm to arm combat. At last, separated from its dry hinges, it began to offer up a small gap.

'You can do all the explaining when we're caught,' said

Ryan.

Olivia began to work out the way to negotiate the narrow opening, her confidence expanding like ripples on a lake.

'What the...are you mad? There might be bloody psychos the other side,' said Ryan.

'Or zombies,' said Sam, pulling a grotesque face and doing his own take on a dance of the undead. He made no attempt to follow Olivia through the opening.

She peered back through the ivy. 'Do you want to find help or what?'

'Yeah,' said both men in lethargic unison. They exchanged concerned looks while Olivia was still working out how to get in without hurting herself.

'Then stop whining and keep a lookout. I'll leg it if need be.'

'Maybe this isn't such a good idea. Perhaps we should go back to the lane and flag someone down,' said Sam, in a last ditch attempt to get her to change her mind.

'Seriously guys, I'll be back before you know it,' said Olivia.' If you're really too scared to wait, go back to the car,' she added, impatiently, having finally squeezed through the tiniest of gaps. Her actions caused the door to give way and crash to the ground. Long grass served to muffle any noise.

Before they could claim to be as brave as she had been, Olivia collected herself up, brushed herself off and made a mental note of her starting point. Suddenly being on her own seemed an advantage, there being no one else to drag along reluctantly. Ryan and Sam's continuing protests were soon lost in the distance as she skirted the edge of the lawns, using the perimeter wall as a guide.

Expecting to find nothing of consequence, she was

totally unprepared when she was confronted suddenly by a run-down Victorian gatehouse. She was even more taken aback due to its state of disrepair to see that it was inhabited. There was a light on inside.

She padded through saturated grass and approached cautiously, until she had positioned herself where she could peer in through a grimy rain-splattered window without being spotted. A state-of-the-art bank of security screens faced her, switching randomly between images recorded by infrared cameras around the estate. Someone had recently been in the room; a steaming mug of black coffee on an ordered desk, testament to this. Normally excited by adventure, she was uncommonly apprehensive. If discovered she would be at the very least challenged, then evicted. Not caring to think of a worst case scenario, she set off in another direction.

Suddenly, the distance between her and her two best friends mattered. The gap between them felt like a piece of elastic stretched to its limit. Before she had time to reconsider what she should do, history chose to repeat itself. Her phone battery died like Sam's had done, plunging her into darkness. Immediately, she doubted the courage she had displayed when entering the estate. Night had thrown on an inky greatcoat, and was marching its way across the landscape in velvety black boots. A feeling of expectancy gripped Olivia, tying her stomach into crampy knots. To run back to the others seemed like the only sane thing to do, but she was not prepared to make a show of cowardice like they had done, or lose her resolve when to find help was paramount. 'Get a grip,' she whispered, to fill the silence.

As she continued on, pinpricks of yellow light suddenly appeared, punching holes through gaps in the dense trees like laser beams. With fresh courage she made her way towards the source, flinching every time the soles of her shoes snapped a brittle twig. Complaining crows scattered from their nests. Olivia forced herself onwards. 'Come on, come on! You can outrun anyone.' Soon she was out in the open and was instantly taken aback by what lay before her.

More impressive than the fairy-tale gates, a Gothic styled house squatted at the end of the drive. To Olivia, it looked more like a mythical creature about to uproot itself from the ground and pounce. All the scary films she had ever seen tripped through her mind, but being a rational person, she immediately tried to block such thoughts. Still she could not ignore Ryan and Sam's comments about psychos and zombies.

More cared for than the outer grounds of the estate, the brick and tiled facade of the house was illuminated by converted gas lamps at the top of wrought iron posts. The house was bathed by the same yellow light she had seen on her approach, whereas a gentler mellow orange glow emanated from a few upstairs rooms. Olivia listened for the sound of guard dogs, pondering the lack of her tree-climbing skills should slavering jaws come for her. There was nothing. Just the occasional rustling of trees in the wind. She was about to step onto the drive when a barely discernible movement caught her attention.

Standing in the shadows on stone steps leading to the front door, was a man dressed in dark clothing. The smoke from his cigarette drifted lazily upwards, towards one of the lamp lights, giving him the appearance of a classic character from an old film noir. All that was missing was a classic trilby. He reached inside his suit jacket and pulled out his phone, but in doing so, he unwittingly exposed a revolver, which glistened menacingly in a black leather holster that was strapped across his white shirt. Olivia froze, uncertain as to whether her imagination was playing tricks on her. She tried to banish the thought of the man reaching for his weapon and opted to remain where she was.

Another man appeared from the house and flicked on a porch light. 'Hey Frank, we gotta problem down at the gatehouse.'

'What's up?' asked Frank.

'Intruders.' He went to take out his gun.

'No need for that. It'll be kids again,' said Frank. Both men ran off, their words and footsteps fading into the distance.

Soon, the only sound Olivia could pick up was the continuing soft whisper of leaves in the trees and the sound of dogs barking far away. She crunched the possibilities. The chance of being invited indoors for tea and cake while waiting for a breakdown truck to turn up, seemed highly unlikely. The three of them were going to die that night. Shot by trigger-happy American gunmen. With little choice of action to consider, she resolved to keep calm as both men would be most likely gone awhile.

Knowing that she had a little time on her side, she sprinted straight towards the house, the thought of dodging bullets still foremost in her mind. She flicked aside such thoughts, hoping that her feet on gravel would not raise the alarm. She was after all, on a mission. Better to be given a ticking off by the owner, who would hopefully allow the use of a land line, than to be left to sit in a freezing car until morning. She climbed the stone steps two at a time. Tripping on the top step, she was catapulted through a stained glass front door that had been left wide open.

Immediately she was inside a capacious entrance hall, which resembled an illustration from within a fantasy comic. She realised that on this occasion, luck was her friend, as on a marble-topped side table very close by, was a telephone. She hurriedly punched in numbers, while listening for someone coming. With her successful call to the rescue services done, she softly replaced the handset and took some deep breaths. Her thumping heart at last began to slow. She was about to retrace her steps out through the front door, when yet another man sprinted down the stairs into the entrance hall. She stepped silently backwards and melted into the shadows behind some heavy velvet drapes, unnoticed as he left hurriedly through the front door. To leave the same way as he had, was clearly foolish. She decided to familiarise herself with the layout of the grand house and hunt instead for an alternative exit.

She tiptoed around the hall, cringing at the occasional squeak of her designer trainers on mirror-finish floorboards. The only other sound was that of a grandfather clock. Her ears were now attuned to every creak and she listened at over-sized doors for any hint of domesticity. Curiosity had caused her to get into all sorts of scrapes since a child. It surfaced like an invisible friend, pushing her all the way up the sweeping staircase with a firm hand on her back. She told herself that if need be, she could escape like in the movies, by sliding down a knotted rope made from bedsheets.

The galleried landing circled around the entire first floor, creating an oval shape. Everything on the ground floor was visible over a highly polished banister rail. The hall was barely lit, giving Olivia the advantage of seeing the men when they returned, well before they spotted her. Knowing this, she allowed her selfish yearning for adventure to lead her on. She would ignore Sam and Ryan giving her a hard time when she recounted her exploits. After all, they were always poking their noses into places that were strictly no-go.

As downstairs, she eavesdropped at closed doors, until on reaching the last one, she found it to be ajar. A muffled conversation was taking place between two women. One spoke in immaculate English, whereas the other was frail and American.

'Can I get you anything?' asked the younger of the two.

'Turn on the garden lights, would you sweetie? I'm worried about my doves. They're not back yet.'

Olivia noted the sound of a single pair of footsteps from inside, but all of a sudden they faded away, making her question whether there was an adjoining room. She took a risk and peered inside. Uncertain as to whether she would be heard, she slowly opened the door for fear of it creaking.

An elegant sitting room greeted her, lit softly by light bulbs inside peach coloured silk lampshades. The room was furnished with an eclectic mix of antiques, mostly from the Victorian era. A fire roared in a large grate, its flames casting flickering shadows on the walls and ceiling. Unseasoned logs fizzed and crackled like fireworks, the sound reminding Olivia of the armed man and the possibility of a bullet meeting its mark. The air was bombarded by the aromatic fragrance of pine from the logs. Two high winged chairs faced away from her towards the fire. One of the chairs was occupied, a halo of silver hair visible above the top of the backrest. A deeply wrinkled hand was stroking the velvet armrest.

Suddenly there was the sound of barking from somewhere on the estate.

The younger woman spoke from the other room. 'I'm going to see what's up. Use the bell if you need me.'

'It'll just be those pesky kids again Mary. Leave them be.'

Another door opened and closed in the distance, warning Olivia that any moment now she would definitely be in sight if she remained where she was. She slipped inside and gently pushed the landing door too.

'What've you forgotten this time?' asked the American, remaining seated in her chair and making no effort to peer round.

Olivia was taken aback by the woman's acute sense of hearing. 'Er - I've forgotten nothing. I was just closing the door - so you don't feel a draught,' she said, not in the least bit thinking she could mimic the younger woman, but willing to give it a try.

'Stop treating me like I'm feeble. And come into the light where I can see you.'

Olivia moved into a position next to the woman's chair, but remained in the shadows, out of her line of sight.

The woman squinted. 'I knew Mary had gone. Is that you Rose? Come at last to avenge your grandmother?'

Olivia struggled with what she should say and the only thing to escape from her mouth was a nervous cough.

The woman began to ramble. 'Your family were corrupt from day one. Too much money, too much power and no common sense for sure.' She sat forward in her chair to try and focus. 'And I know which one tried to kill me,' she added, poking Olivia in the abdomen with a bony finger.

At the mention of attempted murder, Olivia gasped.

'I...I don't know what you mean. I'm so sorry if I scared you.'

The woman gasped. 'You're not Rose. Who sent you?' she accused, sitting back to distance herself from the stranger . A flash of alarm lit up her eyes.

'Nobody sent me. My friends and I are looking for help. My car broke down.'

The old woman hesitated while she weighed up the unlikely explanation, then she switched on a sidelight so that she could see more clearly. 'I can tell when someone's lying. Is that the truth young lady?'

Olivia moved into the light. 'Yes it is. I promise. And I hope it's okay - I used the phone downstairs.'

The woman took a deep breath, dropping her shoulders as she relaxed. 'So that's what all the fuss was about. The suits will be having a lotta fun chasing your buddies.'

'What if they catch them? They won't hurt them will they?'

'Oh no. They'll just holler at them. Just like they always do when kids sneak in.'

'Then what?'

'They'll be sent on their way. With a warning.'

Olivia let out a sigh of relief as she studied the woman in detail. The thought of a chase had clearly amused the woman, a faint smile on her bright red lips testament to this.

She wore a full face of makeup, which made her look like a waxwork. Her skin was translucent and she had overdone her blue eyeshadow and eyebrows, which made her look very dated. A wavy silver bob framed her characterful face. Olivia noted that her clothes were stylish and expensive, but strangely of a different era. Completing her glamorous ensemble were multiple strings of pearls and a huge diamond on her right hand, which was out of scale with her slender fingers.

She noticed Olivia's glance at her neck. 'You like pearls sweetie?'

'I do as it happens. They remind me of my grandmother. They're lovely.'

He gave them to me,' sighed the old woman, with the emphasis on the word he, as she caressed the pearls one by one. For a moment, her eyes misted over as she appeared to reminisce, but as quickly as she had been carried off to her past, her daydream was disturbed by excitable shouting coming from somewhere else in the house.

Olivia shot hurried glances around the room in order to locate the quickest escape route. 'I must go, but it's been so nice meeting you.'

'Likewise sweetie. I don't recall the last time there was a new face around here.'

'I could come again, if you'd like me to,' said Olivia as an afterthought, still hunting for a way out. Despite her predicament, she wished she had more time to dig deeper. 'I don't even know your name.'

'When I was around your age I was known as Norma-Jeane. But oh dear - some days I'm not so sure that's my real name because... '

Olivia stopped her mid-flow, knowing she needed to get away quickly. 'Are you in some sort of danger Norma - a prisoner perhaps?'

'Oh no dear girl. Everything's just dandy. It'd be on their heads if anything happened to me.' She changed the subject, pointing to a tree just beyond a balcony. 'See my lovely birds?'

Outside, a large birdhouse, intricately fashioned into

the shape of a white pillared building, hung from a branch. It was lit by coloured lights strung from nearby trees. Birds were congregating around its entrance, crowding to get in the one entrance hole. Olivia was too concerned to share Norma's enthusiasm for her birds. The voices of her pursuers were getting closer by the second. There was the clamour of multiple footsteps on the stairs. She looked out at the balcony, wondering whether there was an available drainpipe she could make use of and shinny down.

Norma seemed oblivious to Olivia's impending capture. She continued wistfully. 'Only my doves know my secrets.'

There was an urgent hammering on the door, which although anticipated by Olivia, still caused her to jump. Her fascination with the mysterious Norma's riddles had imperiled her.

'Ma'am, if you're by the door, stand well back. We're coming in,' said a macho male voice.

'Oh, give me a second why don't you? At least while I get back to my chair,' said Norma, as a delay tactic, with irritation in her voice. She gestured with a bony hand for Olivia to hurry into the adjoining room. 'Wait in there,' she whispered. 'I'll hold off the goddamn herd of buffalos.'

'Thank you,' said Olivia, giving Norma the thumbs up as she slipped away.

Norma put an index finger to her bright red lips to silence Olivia. 'Sneak out the other door. And remember what I said. My doves know everything,' she said, with a wink.

Olivia waited for her cue. There was the sound of several pairs of feet moving together as though in a huddle as they entered.

'What is it this time?' asked Norma.

'Intruders Ma'am. The dogs have chased them off,' said one of the men, whose voice Olivia immediately recognised as Frank's.

'Are they kennelled now?' asked Norma, as though to give Olivia the heads-up to their whereabouts. 'Every time there's the slightest sniff of a rabbit, I'm woken up by their goddamn barking. '

'Yes Ma'am, they're kennelled for the night,' said a second man.

'If you fed them properly, perhaps they'd not create so. But now you're here, you'd best stay a few moments until I feel safe again.'

Olivia smiled at Norma's chicanery. She crept along the landing, tiptoed down the stairs and out of the front door, her inquisitive mind spinning.

Chapter 2

A Brush with the Suits

Olivia raced down the steps and accelerated away from the grand house, kicking up gravel from the drive in her wake. She felt much like a gazelle being hunted by lions as she slalomed through the trees without daring to look back. Despite her fear being elevated as she ran, she was unable to disconnect her thoughts from her unusual encounter. Norma, if that was what her real name turned out to be, was unfathomable and enchanting. Promptly shaking off such distracting thoughts, she forced herself to concentrate on retracing the path back to where she doubted Ryan and Sam would have the courage to still be waiting for her.

She passed the last of the yellow lights. All of a sudden it was as though she had fallen into a vat of glue, as her feet suctioned themselves to the boggy ground. Her leg muscles began to burn from the effort of making any headway. As well as this, coming from a lit house and driveway into darkness was only adding to her dilemma. At any moment there was the chance that the dogs would be freed again to follow her scent and they would do better in the dark than she would. She stumbled into deep puddles, twisting her ankle more than once, convinced that she was going in circles. The wind began to whistle through the trees like an old kettle on a kitchen range. Twisted branches seemed to take on the shape of beasts reaching out to grab at her. Almost having given up hope, she tripped and fell unexpectedly into Sam and Ryan's arms. Her imaginings evaporated in a heartbeat as they both helped her to her feet.

'You were gone ages. I thought you'd been caught,' said Ryan.

'We heard dogs. They were going mental,' added Sam.

Olivia decided to hide all mention of an injured ankle. 'Had you forgotten I'm a sprinter? Regional champ no less?'

'Please tell us you got to a phone,' said Ryan, ignoring her mention of athleticism.

'Of course I did! Have I ever let you down?'

'You're a star,' said Sam, as they all fist-pumped each other.

'There'll be someone with us soon, so let's get back to the car,' said Olivia, enjoying the praise, as they scrambled through the opening in the wall. She opted to save her story for when they were safely away.

Ryan being the only one with a working mobile, shone his torch, the white beam dancing on tree trunks and the forest floor like a solitary white firefly. They continued on and very quickly were clear of the trees and instantly relieved to be out in the open. Their way was for the first time, lit by moonlight. After they had all got their breath back, Olivia began to recount what had happened, saving the best till last. Ryan and Sam listened with wide-open mouths.

'You really are not going to believe me,' said Olivia finally. 'The place is crawling with armed Americans dressed in sharp suits.'

'You've got to be joking,' said Ryan, Olivia's story kindling his already overactive imagination.

'I'm not joking. It's all true,' she said. 'And the old woman Norma that I mentioned, well she helped me escape.'

'Surely she was just freaked out when you turned up?' questioned Sam.

'More confused than anything. I wish I could've stayed longer to work out what she was going on about.'

The drama of the story was the only thing that day to temporarily silence Sam and Ryan's youthful bravado as they made their way back the way they had come. Finally they reached the car, which they had abandoned in an unmade lay-by. While waiting for the recovery vehicle, they sheltered inside.

'What's bugging you?' asked Ryan finally, sensing Olivia had more to say.

'Norma's a prisoner. I'm sure of it.'

'It'd explain the guns,' said Sam, convinced at last of the validity of her tale.

'We've got to tell the police,' said Olivia.

'Forget the cops,' said Ryan. 'Right now all that matters, is that phone call you made.'

'He's right you know,' said Sam. What if the suits are looking for us? We'll be in big trouble if they find us.'

'And talk of the devil - someone's coming,' said Ryan. 'Say your prayers guys.'

All three snuggled deep into their seats so as to not be visible to an approaching vehicle.

'It's slowing down, said Olivia. 'Can you hear its tyres on the gravel?'

'Oh fuck - it's stopped,' said Sam, jostling with Ryan for the most hidden position.

'What're we going to do?' asked Ryan, his voice having gone up an octave. 'We've no chance in this tin can.'

'Keep your noise down and while you're at it, show a bit of respect for my car,' said Olivia, in an angry whisper. 'If it weren't for me, you'd both be taking the bus.'

Very soon, headlights were shining in. Olivia reached up tentatively and pressed the locking button on the door trim. Despite the battery being flat, there was enough juice to operate the mechanism. She winced at the sound of the button's click, then huddled down again. The only thing in their favour was steamed up windows.

'Oh shit - footsteps. They're coming,' said Ryan.

All three remained as deep in the seat wells as possible, but the unexpected rapping of a fist on the windscreen made them inadvertently pop up like a clan of meerkats from a burrow. A torch was being shone into the interior.

'Rescue services. Anyone in there?'

All three sighed in unison, crawled out from their hiding place and stepped out of the car, too traumatised at first to respond.

'Cold night,' said their rescuer, wondering why they looked like they had been up to no good. 'You don't want to be stuck out here in the dark. You never know what might be hiding in the woods,' he added, not realising how close to the mark he was. He laughed in a demonic way, only to be met with deadpan faces.

'It...it just made a spluttering noise then died,' said Olivia at last, in reference to her car. Instantly she felt as though her statement made women sound incapable of understanding the basics of car engines. Rather than rewording her sentence so as to sound less ditzy, she switched her mind instead to the mechanic's suggestion of armed guards watching them. She scanned the forest trees and the top of the estate's walls but there was no one in sight.

'I'll soon have you on your way. You'd best all sit in my cab while I sort the problem. It's safer there,' added the mechanic as an afterthought, not realising that it probably was. He grabbed a toolbox from his truck and got straight on with diagnosing the problem. All three watched anxiously, wishing he would hurry as he fiddled with connections and spark plugs. Finally he turned on the ignition and the engine spluttered into life, causing a burst of dense black smoke to billow from the exhaust.

Relieved to be leaving such an isolated spot, Olivia signed paperwork while Ryan and Sam watched for anyone who might block their getaway. Soon, they were escorted back to the main road by the rescue truck. Olivia reflected for the rest of their journey about the events of the evening, planning her next move, while the others sat deep in thought. Norma's ramblings had ensnared her so easily. She was surprised when they had reached home without being followed by a fleet of blacked out Secret Service cars.

In her dreams that night, she built castles in the air, in which Norma floated silently through, but by the time that morning had come, the dream had melted away. It was only when there was an urgent hammering on her front door that she woke suddenly, knowing that something was wrong.

Chapter 3

Taking a Chance

Sam and Ryan were worried but it was Sam who spoke up first. 'We've been calling and calling, but your phone just cuts to answerphone.'

Olivia rummaged in her hoodie pockets. It suddenly occurred to her that she had been so overwhelmed the night before by events, that she had failed to put her phone on charge before she went to sleep. 'Damn, I must've dropped it. We'll have to go back to that house.'

'Not bloody likely. Claim on insurance,' said Sam.

'I could do that, but there's stuff on it that I need,' insisted Olivia.

'No way I'm going back there to get my head blown off,' said Ryan.

'Suit yourself. Stay here.'

'Aw, don't be like that Olivia. We're only looking out for you,' said Ryan.

'Then come with me. What else are you going to do with your time? Go find some ridiculously dangerous hill to cycle down?'

Ryan deliberated. 'Point taken. But if you're not out in ten minutes tops, we're calling the cops.'

'That won't be necessary. I can look after myself,' said Olivia.

'Which is why you twisted your ankle,' said Sam. 'You were limping last night but clearly trying to tough it out.'

An hour later, after having taken a detour to Ryan's home to pick up some essentials, they drove to the mansion. Due to the delay, they bickered for the rest of the journey, Ryan insisting however, that all good undercover operatives were always well-equipped. Parking in the same public lay-by as the night before, but using common sense, Olivia thought to face the car so they could make a quick getaway if needed.

'What're you doing?' asked Ryan, sniggering at her precision parking.

'What's so funny? One of us has to use some brain cells, and you clearly don't have any,' she growled.

'You don't seriously think they won't have a performance car to hand should they choose to come after us? You'd need a five mile head-start in this old bucket,' said Ryan.

Olivia squared up to him so that they were nose to nose, although he had to bend for her to reach him. He saw it as just a game, allowing her to think she had power over him. He tried to contain his amusement. 'Do you feel better now you've had a rant?' he asked, when she had finished.

'One more comment about Bessie, and you can walk in future,' humphed Olivia.

'Only saying,' said Ryan. 'But we all love Bessie really, don't we Sam?'

Sam joined in with the sport. 'Oh yeah. She's like my

favourite old hoodie. Warm, cosy...but a bit past her best. In fact, come to think of it, she's got the same qualities as my hoodie all round.' His own joke having got the better of him, he began to laugh out loud.

Olivia swung punches at both men but it soon turned into a play fight. She could never stay angry with either for long. Their child-like attitude to life was a part of their enduring charm. By the time they had reached the fanciful gates, their dig at Bessie had been forgiven.

'Doesn't seem so bad in the light of day,' said Sam, having already reccied their immediate surroundings like a boy scout.

They approached the perimeter walls, acting like casual hikers just passing by. Ryan had thought to bring an army rucksack to add to their disguise. As they reached the door through which Olivia had made her undignified entrance, he pretended to be a nature enthusiast, looking at wildlife through his army surplus binoculars, but in his mind he was undertaking a covert operation. 'Right this is it. Be quick,' he said.

'Are you sure you can do this with a sprained ankle?' Sam asked Olivia.

'What choice have I got?'

'Er - we could just turn round and go home,' suggested Sam.

'I told you - I need my phone,' barked Olivia.

'Maybe the suits are at lunch,' said Ryan, trying to be more upbeat about her tricky dilemma.

Surprisingly, the door in the wall had not yet been repaired. Instead, it had been propped back in its original position. With no phone to keep an eye on time, Olivia set her athletic's stopwatch. With one shove, Sam knocked the door to the ground.

'Don't forget the agreement,' said Ryan, reminding Olivia of her pledge.

'I'll be here, in ten max,' she promised.

She crouched down in predatory cat position to orientate herself, with daylight on her side on this occasion. The imprints from her trainers from her previous foray offered up a ready-made path to follow. Surrounded by the sweet scent of wild flowers and the symphony of birds singing in the trees, this time her trip seemed too easy and quite pleasant under the circumstances. However, she feared that she had already been seen on camera and that an ambush would be awaiting her as soon as she cleared the trees.

When she reached the house there was no one around, which only added to her unease. On this occasion the front door was closed and there was no one keeping watch. She wished she had formulated a better plan, such as pretending that she was delivering a parcel or doing market research. She was considering what to do next, when there were the sounds of male voices and gritty footsteps on the gravel. She stepped back into the trees and waited for whoever it was to pass. Frank and his colleague from the night before approached, deep in conversation.

'We've gotta deal with snoopers. How the hell are goddamn kids finding out about this place?' asked the younger of the two.

'Its kids from the village,' said Frank. They're bound to know about this place. It's an adventure playground.'

'That's as maybe Sir, but it's getting too damn frequent. We've gotta do something, before someone figures out what's going on here.'

'Listen up Dave. We've managed to keep her out of

the public eye for over fifty years, and not been rumbled. What difference will a few more weeks make?'

'Hey, I get your point, but our luck's gotta run out sooner or later,' said Dave.

'She hasn't got long. If it makes you feel better, up security measures,' said Frank.

The men came into sight. Olivia's vantage point meant that she was able to study them in detail. Both men were incredibly fit, their tailored suits enhancing their toned physique. The age difference was significant; Dave being in his thirties but Frank, somewhere between his late seventies and early eighties.

'Do you think upping security will be enough to deter them?' asked Dave.

'God dammit Dave, you've gotta stop stressing. I promised I'd look after her. I know her better than anyone.'

'I know, and I respect that Sir.'

'You weren't even in diapers when he assigned me. It was well before he was assassinated. You got that?'

Olivia stifled a gasp at what was the second mention of murder in only two days. She realised also that Frank had been talking about Norma being at the end of her life.

'Yeah Frank, I got it,' said Dave.

'You call me Sir. Always! And don't you forget it,' shouted Frank.

'Sir, yes Sir!'

Frank softened as though the subject of Norma was too painful for him to discuss. 'How many times have we gotten into this conversation anyway? Bury it. Right now Dave.'

Dave appeared to sense Frank's emotional struggle.

'I'll sort security Sir.' He turned and walked away with a military gait, in the opposite direction, skirting around the side of the house, until he had disappeared out of sight.

Frank stood still, alert, looking up at the house. He was only yards from Olivia. So close, that she feared if he concentrated hard enough, that he might hear her breathing. He lit a cigarette and paced backwards and forwards for a few minutes. Then having calmed down, he sat on a large tree trunk, placed horizontally like a natural bench. After a few speedy drags on a second cigarette, something caught his attention on the dewy grass.

Glinting in the sunlight was Olivia's phone. To her horror, Frank plucked it up and examined it closely then attempted to turn it on. He stood up suddenly, aggressively stamped out his cigarette and scanned the immediate area. Olivia closed her eyes, imagining that if she did so, she would become invisible.

'I can see you kiddo. You're trespassing. And this is yours I guess,' said Frank.

Olivia's heart began to pound. The chances were, that if she ran, Frank would not be able to keep up, despite him being in good shape for his age. But he had a gun. Even a stout stick would offer no defence against that type of weapon. She wanted to stand tall and pull him up for referring to her as kiddo, but she thought better of it.

He second guessed her thoughts. 'Don't be deceived by these old bones. It would be easy as pie to drop you if you made a run for it.'

'Are you going to shoot me then?' she asked.

Frank's eyes narrowed. 'What makes you think I'd do that?'

'I can see the shape of your gun through your jacket,' she observed.

'Is that right kiddo?' He changed the subject. 'You're a bit old to be playing games in the woods. Was it you snooping around last night?'

'Yes,' Olivia said simply. Her expression displayed her fear. She blurted out the account of the car.

'Relax, I'm not gonna hurt you,' said Frank. 'Though I oughta set the dogs on you. Like I said, this is private property.'

'I'm sorry. Truly I am,' said Olivia, meekly. 'Just give me my mobile back and I'll leave straight away.'

'You picked your time well, kiddo. The pack's tucking into nice juicy t-bones. Could've been you instead,' said Frank, taunting Olivia by licking his lips.

She gulped.

Frank laughed at her reaction and tossed her phone from palm to palm, while considering what to do with her. 'How much of our conversation did you hear?'

She knew it was futile to lie. He already knew the answer. 'All of it,' she said.

Frank's demeanour changed. He threw her phone over. 'Skedaddle. The way you came.'

'That old lady...is she...?' asked Olivia.

'The dame is none of your business,' said Frank, interrupting. 'You got that kiddo? Quit with the questions and button it - or else!' His final words were packed with malevolence.

Olivia gave him a twitchy smile and turned on her heels, still imagining that Dobermans would come charging out of the woods or that Frank would fire his gun squarely between her shoulder blades. The trouble was, that despite her fear, she was now even more curious as to what was going on. There was a story to be told, and that need-to-know trait of hers was as dangerous as Frank's loaded weapon.

Once again she joined Ryan and Sam, but she had not forgotten Frank's warning to shut up or else. She divulged only that she had found her phone not far from the perimeter wall.

For the rest of the day she was in a befuddled daze, with no one to confide in and unable to concentrate on athletics. To add to her troubles, she was reprimanded repeatedly by her personal trainer for a lack lustre performance due to her injury. In the end, he sent her home.

Unable to sleep that night, she stayed up until the early hours, searching the Internet for clues about the house. Nevertheless, no matter how hard she trawled through, it seemed like there was little about its recent use. A lack of ready information only served to add to the mystique of locked rooms and probable secret passages. On top of this, she had a strong feeling that Norma had wanted to share her story. It was Norma's fragility in such a hostile environment, that made Olivia realise she needed to go to the police. Straight away the next morning. Without telling Ryan and Sam. They would try to stop her from telling a ludicrous story of armed Americans. And it was the guns that worried her the most.

Chapter 4

In the Light of Day

As Olivia eventually lapsed into sleep after an evening of trying to work things out, she called on the regular characters who frequented her dreams, hoping one might step forward and talk her out of making her statement to the police. Instead, in her restlessness, she was plunged into a lucid nightmare where she was trapped in a rat-infested cellar and tortured with metal implements plucked from a Gladstone bag. Entombed for days with an uncertain fate and only dirty water to drink from a leaking pipe, she endured the stench of the cellar that stretched under the whole footprint of the house where Norma lived. The following morning, with no epiphany moment to point her one way or the other, she decided to stick with her gut feeling from the day before and report Norma's predicament to the police.

By the time Olivia had started on her journey to the police station, she was convinced that everyone she was passing en route had witnessed her nightmares and was judging her to be insane. As well as this, as soon as she arrived, the facade of the police station seemed to take on an otherworldly look. That of the face of a fire breathing dragon with a gaping mouth for a front door. With her nerves frayed, Olivia began to doubt her story, but on entering the car park, she resolved that she should continue now she had come so far. She parked up and in order to gather herself together, talked to her reflection in the rear view mirror.

'You alright Miss?' asked an unfamiliar voice from outside of the car. Standing by her open window, was a uniformed officer, seemingly puzzled by her behaviour.

'Do I really look that nervous?' she asked.

'Well as it happens, yes you do. Can I be of help?' asked the officer.

'I...I haven't done anything wrong. It's just that I've never been inside a police station,' said Olivia.

The officer laughed. 'That's what they all say. But we don't bite, unless you've done something really bad.' He winked, then turned and walked across the car park, whistling as he went.

The officer's words had instantly raised Olivia's anxiety to a new level. She watched him enter the building. The fingers of her left hand were still dancing on the hand brake, while her other hand played with the keys that were in the ignition. She chastised herself for losing the plot for the umpteenth time. It was now or never. There was a need for transparency if she were to save the old woman.

On entering the police station, she was taken aback to see that the foyer was modern and airy. She had imagined instead, a grimy police station with middle-aged men with rolled-up shirt sleeves, working tirelessly in sepia painted offices. However, uniformed officers and several civilians were milling around behind an ultramodern stainless steel front desk, protected by a clear reinforced glass screen, much like in the updated post office in the nearby town. A few people were perched on the edge of chairs in the busy foyer, either reading police advisory posters or looking at their mobile phones. All looked decidedly twitchy, as though they were in a dentist's waiting room terrified of an ordeal yet to come. While waiting her turn to be called up, Olivia tried to imagine why each one of them was there, but very soon she was beckoned forward by a civilian female behind the screen.

'How can we help?' asked the woman. Her stony expression suggested nothing exciting ever happened in this particular neighbourhood.

Olivia stared back speechless, conscious that her own mouth was opening and closing like a cartoon goldfish.

The woman tapped on the glass to jolt her out of her trance. 'Miss - how can we help?'

Olivia put her face close to the window and craned her neck so that she could speak through the gap at the bottom of the screen, rather than into a microphone. 'I want to report men - with guns,' she whispered.

'Say again,' said the woman, clearly shocked at such a proclamation.

'Men. Lots of them. With guns. They've got a prisoner,' said Olivia with conviction.

'Name?' asked the woman.

'I'm not sure of her name, but she's very old,' said Olivia, deciding that as Norma was uncertain of her own name, then she should not put one forward quite yet. I think those men might be after me too.'

'I meant your name,' said the woman. 'And do speak clearly into the microphone.'

Olivia complied and gave her name. In her mind, the woman's downbeat expression had changed to one of suspicion and uncertainty as to the legitimacy of her story. 'I don't want to talk too loudly because of all these other people waiting,' she said, gesturing behind herself to the row of seated people, who now seemed interested in the conversation. 'And I'm telling the truth...in case you think I'm not,' she continued.

'That's not for me to determine Miss White,' said the woman. 'Wait there please.' She disappeared into a side room and returned very quickly with a uniformed officer.

He punched in a code and passed through a door to the left of the desk. 'Sergeant Baverstock,' he said, gruffly. 'Please follow me to the interview room Miss White.'

Olivia found herself sitting alone in an uninspiring space while the sergeant went off to find someone. Detectives would be in Olivia's mind, unravelling gruesome murders on disordered desks in adjacent rooms. She felt as though she had been put on school detention and was waiting for her teacher to arrive and dish out punishment.

The room was lit by a single fluorescent strip light; its diffuser housing a few large dead flies plus a couple on their backs wriggling as they clung to life. Both the ceiling and all four walls were painted a nicotine colour, a shade that would have cleverly masked cigarette smoke at a time when smoking was allowed inside public places. A bare desk and four chairs were the only furniture. The floor was covered with grey vinyl that had been scuffed by rubber soled shoes and chairs being moved around. Apart from a smattering of more police notices, there was nothing to read in order to kill time. Instead, Olivia listened to mumbled voices while wondering whether the oversized mirror on the opposite wall was of the two-way kind. If so, a line of top brass officers might be scrutinising her, laying odds as to whether she was about to tell a bunch of lies or offer up a credible story.

After a few moments, a plain-clothed man in his mid thirties entered, with Sergeant Baverstock in tow. He seated himself at the opposite side of the table, while the sergeant remained silent and began to pace the room. 'I'm DC Taylor,' he said. 'I understand you want to report a serious crime Miss White?'

Olivia felt instantly uncomfortable. The sergeant was now stationary behind her chair and she took a guess that he was trying to unnerve her. 'Yes, that right.'

'I'm all ears. Fire away,' said DC Taylor. He sat back and rocked his chair while twirling a pen between his fingers as he weighed her up.

She noticed a distinctive spark of interest in DC Taylor's bright blue eyes as his intense gaze flipped backwards and forwards between her and the notes he was beginning to write. She hoped he and the sergeant were praying that their day might suddenly become more exciting. Engaging with DC Taylor was not easy. He could not be described as anything other than plain ordinary. His mousy hair hung limply in no particular style, indicating he had no interest in modern male grooming. There was a light coating of dandruff on his shoulders.

Olivia blurted out her story so fast that she doubted any of it sounded genuine. In fact, her entire delivery was questionable. DC Taylor threw in probing questions along the way, making her wonder whether he was trying to trick her into admitting she was nothing but a fantasist. When she had finished, she waited for his reaction, fully expecting him to laugh or scold her for wasting police time. He did neither.

'These are serious allegations Miss White. Are you happy to make a statement?'

'Can't we skip that bit, seeing as I've told you once?' she asked. 'Then you can gallop to her rescue like in the movies. Before something awful happens.'

DC Taylor seemed unmoved by her dramatic take on things. 'The sooner we get your statement down, the sooner we can follow enquiries.'

She felt deflated. Having done as requested, she was dismayed when she was sent on her way. There was the promise of nothing but a phone call if there were more questions to be answered. Her exclusion made her more than ever want to be involved.

With this in mind, she decided to embark on some investigation of her own. Her fitness training would need to be pushed to one side until she was satisfied that she had done all she could to help. Her first enquiry would be to understand firearms law. If Frank was not of military background, he probably had no right to carry a gun at all. Her mind began to work overtime. Maybe the house belonged to a diplomat, or was the backdrop for an undercover police operation of the utmost international importance. Or perhaps Norma had been a spy in her youth. Someone so important, that she had been awarded protection from any foreign threats.

Realising she was losing all sense of reality, Olivia rebuked herself for her wild imaginings and tried instead to relish the thought of returning to a normal life over the next few days, but life suddenly seemed to stretch out before her, with only her daily routine to move it forward in a slow regimental march.

Such negative thoughts were compounded when a

week later she received a call from the police station to thank her for her diligence. The case was being further investigated, but at this point there was no need to question her further. She was instructed to not visit the property again. Under any circumstances.

She considered that her part in the mystery had in all likelihood come to an end. Maybe she should join her parents watching endless detective dramas, so she could fantasise about how the story might have unfolded. But rather than do that, she would visit the property again if she wished. No one told Olivia White what she could and could not do. And anyway, surely the police needed her input. They would not solve the case without the things she was beginning to remember, though as yet they were only grains of thought, lacking in any significant detail.

Chapter 5

A World Apart from the Sticks

While Olivia was reluctantly letting go of a mystery she wished she could solve, Scotland Yard had already received a file from the Oxfordshire constabulary. It had been sent over as a matter of urgency. The file still lay open on Detective Constable Steve Murray's desk, but he was pondering whether the case was too far-fetched to take seriously. On top of this, he was wondering why the provincial police force had handed it on at all. The only possibility seemed to be, that the armed men mentioned might be linked to London's latest terrorist threat. It seemed more likely however, that as he was the new boy at Scotland Yard, he was to be the latest victim of a practical joke, concocted by his colleagues as some sort of initiation. He imagined a group of detectives in a huddle outside the open-plan office, laughing between themselves, while he got drawn into a bogus case.

He crept over to the door and opened it swiftly, expecting that they would all tumble to the floor, but there was no one there. He returned to his desk and read through the notes again.

During the drive to Oxfordshire a while later, he tried to rationalise both Olivia White's statement plus the findings of DC Taylor. There were major discrepancies. Added to this, there had at first been reluctance by staff at Huntley Manor to allow access to DC Taylor. The sloppily dressed civilian who had challenged him had been lolling in a small booth with his feet on a desk. He had been described as a nondescript individual, equipped with nothing but outdated surveillance to keep an eye on comings and goings. Olivia White had chosen to adopt a different take on things. She had been far more melodramatic. She spoke of security cameras throughout the grounds; men in sharp suits, flashy cars and more worryingly - guns. She had gone on to liken the gates to the large house to the entrance of a fairy story castle. The only fact that married DC Taylor's story to hers, was that both had spoken to an elderly resident, who seemed confused as to her own identity and had called herself by several different names during a garbled conversation. Murray wondered whether the old lady was simply experiencing the onset of dementia. Whatever the truth, in Taylor's opinion, the woman's status had not demanded the presence of the high level of security mentioned by Olivia White. As for Miss White, Murray felt she was not to be trusted. He would deal with her with the full force of the law once he had got a firm handle on the investigation.

Despite what seemed like an open and shut case, the further he drove, the more he began to think about Olivia White. Had she been a young teenager, he might have dismissed her story without further ado as that of an adolescent fantasist. But for a twenty year old girl with perfect diction that shone in her statement, something had clearly convinced her that all was not well. He began to quietly question what he could remember from reading her statement. The next day would tell if it had been premature to give her the benefit of the doubt. His first concern was to consider how to get into the house, just in case the small delay Taylor had encountered had enabled a cover up of some sort.

Later that same day, Murray stood at the public bar inside a quintessential country pub called The Lamb. With little time to juggle, getting out of the city was something he did too little of. On top of this, a tight timetable meant he found it hard to switch off. His busy mind was always fathoming out the intricacies of cases other detectives were still battling their way through. He was renowned as being a fixer, which was another word in his mind for being good at solving crime.

The pub was no more than a mile from the estate he was investigating, which at present was nothing but a photocopy of a map in his case file. Old estates had grand names and tall tales attached to them. He hoped that locals had stories they were desperate to tell. So much so, that he half-expected a toothless farmer to stroll into the pub at any second and reveal a tale of intrigue and bad deeds, in exchange for a pint of the best.

The Lamb invited a dramatic entrance like that. Its low beamed ceilings creaked as people moved about in the rooms above. The fires that burned in two hearths at each end of the lounge bar were nothing but glowing embers, so Murray stepped down from his bar stool and picked out a particularly large log from a fire basket and threw it onto one of the dying fires. He prodded the log with a malicious-looking poker. Instantly it ignited, warming his face and body. He sat for a few moments in a well-worn leather armchair and finished his pint while he watched the flames. His beer was to his taste. Dark and creamy. More typical of northern counties.

There was an eclectic mix of people spread throughout the bar. Young couples nestled together in the furthest corners and businessmen were working on wafer-thin lap tops or making calls on smartphones. Being a man of instinct, Murray chose to linger a little longer and was to be rewarded for listening to his inner voice. He turned his attention to three scruffily dressed regulars who were seated on bar stools, chatting to the barmaid. Their conversation was mostly centred on crops and livestock. Murray took time to consider whether he should chat to them as a passing civilian, or adopt an on-duty approach. In his experience, he found people liked to embellish their lives if they were questioned by a detective. Most considered his occupation glamorous. After finishing his beer, he ambled over to the bar and asked for another.

'Not from round here then?' asked the barmaid, eyeing him up. 'Just travelling through?'

Murray found it hard not to laugh at her scripted questioning, which was straight from a TV soap. 'Actually I was going to ask if you had any spare rooms. I'm investigating a case just up the road from here,' he added loudly, to make sure the men at the bar would hear. As he had hoped, all three turned to face him.

'Someone been murdered?' asked one of the bar stool huggers, causing the other two to elbow each other and rock on their seats with laughter.

'You find murder funny, do you?' asked Murray, instantly bringing seriousness back to their ruddy faces.

'They've had a few too many. You'll get nothing out

of them,' said the barmaid. 'You might get more out of me if you play your cards right,' she added, winking knowingly.

Murray grounded the conversation quickly. 'Can you tell me a bit about Huntley Manor?'

'Owned by the same family for well over three hundred years as far as I know. Whoever lives there, they're too posh to grace us with their presence. We all reckon at least one of them's related to royalty, don't we boys?' said the barmaid, turning to the three locals.

All three muttered into their beer, too disgruntled at having been told off.

'Why do you think there's a connection with royalty?' Murray asked her.

'Always swanky cars with blacked out windows coming and going. This is farming country, so they stand out.'

Deciding not to engage her further, Murray stopped at that and booked a room for the night via the landlord. He vacated the bar promptly, as it was clear that the barmaid was keen on him. He put a chair against the inside of the bedroom door, for fear of her letting herself in, so she could wave her pendulous breasts in his face for the second time in one night.

The following morning Murray was at Huntley Manor bright and early, still intending to gain access more successfully than DC Taylor. Though there was nothing obvious to alarm him, from the very second he arrived, something in the pit of his stomach told him that something was amiss. The security hut Taylor had mentioned, was empty. After an icy two-way conversation via the entry intercom to the main house, he was told that someone was on their way. Nevertheless five minutes passed and he realised he was experiencing the same delay that Taylor had encountered. While waiting, he stood with his back resting against the bonnet of his car. He believed that as everyone uses all of their senses at any one time, the efficiency of each one was therefore slightly diluted. Whereas he was practised. Singling each one out at will and fine-tuning it, was child's play.

He closed his eyes and concentrated on his hearing, while allowing his breathing to become deep and regular. Apart from birds flying from tree to tree, beyond that, there was no other sound. That was, until he picked up on the grinding of tyres on gravel. Faint at first but slowly getting closer from inside the bowels of the estate. Taking account of the likely speed that any vehicle would travel along what he assumed was probably a winding drive, he counted in seconds to ascertain how far it was to the main house. Why it should be something to note, he could not be sure, but he methodically stored everything. Just in case.

When the car did arrive, Murray was surprised at its understated design, age and mud-stained bodywork. It turned in a tight circle and came to a stop just inside the gates. He recalled the barmaid's mention of gleaming limousines with blacked out windows. Olivia White had said the same thing too. He was aware that he was being weighed-up from inside the car. Sunlight was reflected off of the side windows, which made it impossible for him to see the driver or anyone else who might be on board.

It seemed an eternity before the door was opened. The delay made Murray decidedly twitchy. He wasn't in the habit of wishing that he was armed, but his right hand began to hover restlessly around his hip area, as though he were a young boy again, acting out his part in a spaghetti western.

The driver however, was cool and poised and did not mirror the vehicle he drove. His suit was tailored and expensive. He walked up to the gates but made no attempt to open them. 'How can I help?' he asked, brusquely, in an American accent.

As was usual, Murray proffered his warrant card.

The man's piercing blue eyes narrowed. 'You're the second cop nosing around. What d'you want this time?'

'And you are?' asked Murray, not allowing himself to be rattled by the man's aggression.

'Deputy head of security.'

Murray shuffled his stance so as to appear more intimidating. 'I'd like to take a look around.'

'Why?' asked the man, playing the same game by pulling himself up to full height. Instantly he dwarfed Murray by at least six inches.

'I'm just following up the case the previous detective was investigating. I'm sure once I've taken a gander, I can close the file.'

'There's nothing to see,' insisted the man. 'Unlike what that kid told you cops. There's no guns - see.' He thrust his chin forward and opened his suit jacket, not realising that although he had removed his leather holster, it had left a sweaty imprint where it had rested against his shirt only moments before. 'The last cop saw everything. He even met the broad who was living here.'

'Was living here? If she's no longer here, I'll definitely need confirmation of that,' said Murray. He realised the man's version of events might be the very thing that gave him a way in.

'She's dead,' said the man, suddenly. 'We're just wrapping things up.'

Murray noticed that the man had barely blinked during the entire conversation, his eyes fixed with an intimidatory stare. 'In that case, I'll need a copy of the death certificate.'

'I guess you've had a wasted journey detective. Give me an email address and I'll see you get a copy.'

Murray was caught on the back foot and he didn't like it. 'I'm afraid that won't be good enough. I'll need to see the original.'

The man seemed to grow another few inches. 'I'm kinda getting fed up with you cops. I was nice to the last one, but if you want to come in, you'll need a warrant.'

'As you wish,' said Murray, turning on his heels. The man was lying. He had not been able to hide the tiniest of twitches at the side of his mouth, an indication that the pressure of being questioned was getting to him.

Murray was about to get back in his car and call up Scotland Yard, when at the last moment he decided to change tack. He strolled back to the gates. 'Tell you what. If you let me take a look around now - and I'm satisfied by what I see, I'll close the case. But persist with denying me access today, and I'll get that warrant. Plus, upsetting me, means you upset my gaffer. He'll see the place is turned upside down.'

The man hesitated then shrugged. 'Sure,' he said, simply, opening the gates remotely. He got back in his car and locked the doors from the inside as Murray approached to get in, but opened his window a crack. 'You'll see more on foot, detective. Isn't that what you British cops do best? I'll see you at the house.'

He drove off, leaving Murray alone. A cloud of dust marked the car's speedy departure, coating Murray's tailored suit. Without considering any possible danger to himself, he decided to leave his car and cut across the grass, glad that he had taken notice of his hearing a few moments previously and measured the distance to the house.

He followed the sound of the car as it snaked up the drive, until there was the sounds of squealing brakes and skidding tyres on gravel. By the time he had reached the house he was convinced that there was a cover up. There was a deep groove in the gravel by the front steps, which he estimated to be at least a metre long. He toyed with the thought of calling for backup, recalling Olivia White's reference to guns. But this was England. Sleepy Oxfordshire. He was uncertain of what he had seen beneath the man's suit jacket, but he would be ridiculed if he made a wrong call to the Yard.

He climbed the steps and rang the bell. Almost immediately a woman's face appeared, distorted by the irregular stained glass as she peered through a spy hole. She took her time in opening the door, a ploy in Murray's mind to stall for a bit of extra time. As soon as he saw her stiff black dress and white frilly apron, he realised she fitted the peculiar housekeeper that Olivia White had mentioned in her statement. He knew a frightened woman when he saw one.

Her manner of speech was as Dickensian as her dress. 'Good morning detective. I was told to expect you. I'm Geraldine. The housekeeper.'

Murray flashed his warrant card and manoeuvred past her. 'Where's the man who came in before me? The man with massive anger issues.'

She dodged his questioning. 'Can I get you some tea or coffee detective?'

'No thank you.'

'Really detective - it's no trouble. Please, come and wait in the drawing room. Mortimer will be down shortly.' She gestured to the back of the spacious entrance hall to where double doors had been left wide open.

'Mortimer's the pleasant individual I met earlier I take it?'

She smiled nervously and shot a glance at the galleried landing, her action telling him all he needed to know. 'Yes Sir, that's him.'

'He seemed in a hurry to get back here. I take it he's up there? Taking care of things, so to speak?'

Geraldine's face turned instantly beetroot red. 'I must get back to my chores. He said you can look around downstairs while you wait for him.'

Murray watched her scurry off. If downstairs was an open book, he wouldn't bother looking around. There would be nothing to see. He climbed the stairs two at a time.

Chapter 6

The News of the Century

Walking straight into his adversary was like crashing into a brick wall at speed. Murray was unprepared for the impact and teetered on the top step. Then time seemed to roll to a snail's pace as his balance slipped away. He was an astronaut floating in space, but he had no umbilical cord to prevent him from tumbling into infinity.

A wry smile instantly crossed Mortimer's face as he stood towering above Murray, but considering the repercussions if he were to do nothing, at the last second he made a grab for Murray's lapels. 'What the hell d'you think you're doing up here detective?' he growled, still holding on. As soon as Murray had found his balance and was clutching the banister rail with white knuckles, Mortimer released his grip .

'Taking a look around, like you said I could,' said Murray, adjusting his tie and straightening his jacket in typical James Bond style. He felt disadvantaged, having already formed the opinion that Mortimer was, after all, just a high-paid thug, pumped up with anabolic steroids. How else could he have reacted so quickly? Had he turned nasty instead of using what little he had of a sensible head, the outcome would have been different.

'Snooping around up here wasn't part of the deal,' said Mortimer.

'But you've nothing to hide, or have you? At least that's what you inferred at the front gates,' said Murray, envisaging himself laying crumpled at the foot of the stairs, a broken and bloody mess.

Mortimer seemed to be evaluating him. All of a sudden he flipped from being aggressive to the perfect host. 'You look like you need a drink after that little mishap buddy. We've got some mighty fine Bourbon in the library. Let me fix you one.' He patted Murray on the back, all the while, flashing a whiter-than-white set of perfect teeth.

'That might be the way you do things in the States, but I'm on duty. So I'll pass thanks,' said Murray, seeing straight through Mortimer's unconvincing show of friendship.

'As you wish, but I'll show you around downstairs first,' said Mortimer. He attempted to manoeuvre Murray back down the stairs without putting the fear of God into him again. 'Sorry I didn't introduce myself earlier buddy. What with the old gal buying it, my mind was elsewhere. Chuck Mortimer.'

Murray stood his ground, ignoring the schmoozing tactics. 'So I've already been told. By the woman who let me in.' He hesitated and then challenged Mortimer with a determined glare. 'Seeing as I'm already upstairs, I will take a look around,' he insisted.

'You're going nowhere buddy,' said Mortimer, his expression changing again to a look of thunder. 'Like

I already said, we're tying up loose ends. It'd be pretty harsh of you to just barge in and disturb the dame's grieving family.'

Ignoring Mortimer's efforts to stall him, Murray skilfully swept past and marched authoritatively towards the first closed door. 'We Brits are known for our sensitivity. You don't need to worry about how I handle things.'

Mortimer blocked his way again, his eyes ablaze and fake smile becoming increasingly difficult for him to maintain. 'Back off detective.'

Murray bristled for a split second, distracted by Mortimer's dazzling teeth. 'Is that a threat? I hope not, for your sake.'

'Listen up detective. I don't wanna report you to your superiors, but I'm mighty pissed with you. I'm showing you around out of the goodness of my heart - with no warrant, remember?' Mortimer reminded him.

Murray weighed up the situation. By the time he could return with a warrant, there would be nothing to see. But if he had misjudged the situation and a grieving family was simply clearing up an old lady's effects, he would be for the high-jump. However, he wasn't one to be bullied. Especially by a Yank in a sharp suit. He decided to play a favourite childhood game and focussed on a point over Mortimer's shoulder, adopting a scared stiff expression as though there was something lurking in the shadows. Instantly fooled, Mortimer turned quickly, only to see an empty landing. Murray darted by and opened the door he had been aiming for.

Back in the moment, Mortimer caught up and followed him in. 'I'm truly sorry Ma'am,' he said to an elderly but curvaceous woman standing by the window, accompanied by a slightly younger man. 'The detective insisted on taking a look around.'

The woman turned and addressed Mortimer. Murray noted her American accent. It's alright Chuck,' she said. 'We can deal with it. You can go.'

Murray turned on Mortimer. 'I take it, this is the person you were trying to hide from me?' The old gal you said had passed on?'

'I was protecting her privacy,' said Mortimer, turning to the woman again. 'I'll be right outside Ma'am.'

'Chuck - don't ever again refer to me as the old gal,' said the woman.

'Sorry Ma'am,' said Mortimer. He backed sheepishly out of the room, his face lobster-red.

As soon as Murray was sure he had gone, he introduced himself to the woman and her accomplice with a brief explanation of why he was not satisfied with the treatment DC Taylor had received. 'Both he and I have met with a lot of resistance,' he said. 'I'm afraid I'll need some convincing answers before I leave.'

'Ask away detective. Although I didn't know I was dead already,' said the woman, referring to Mortimer's lie with a mischievous glint in her eye.

'I'll be brief, as you've company,' said Murray. 'And I'm sorry to trouble you if you are unwell in any way.'

'Some might say that trouble is my middle name,' she jested. 'Lord knows, I've seen enough of it.' She left the panoramic view of the countryside beyond the garden and made her way across the room, to the high winged chair described in Olivia White's statement. The man she had been talking to when Murray had entered, who had said nothing, took up a position next to her. She reached up and touched his arm with a gloved hand. 'Detective, this is Frank. He's my friend of many years and I don't know what I would've done without him. Please detective, have a seat, while Frank rings down and asks Geraldine to make us tea.'

Murray sat down in the other wing chair, thinking that although he preferred coffee, a pot of tea after all, was just as good an excuse to allow him to stay longer. He studied the woman. Despite her face suggesting she was well into her eighties or maybe older, her body suggested she was younger. She made no attempt to hide her well-toned calves. Murray assumed that she must still get out and about regularly for a stroll around the grounds. Her way of speaking confused him, as although she had a strong American accent, she phrased her sentences in a very English way and used very little of what he called American slang.

Frank was still in the room, his body-language suggesting he was not happy with the situation. The woman addressed him. 'Go down and see Geraldine. She always takes too long and on your way out, tell Chuck to stop hovering around outside my door. He's overzealous and he unnerves me to say the least.'

Once Frank had left, Murray pulled out his notebook and got straight to the point. 'The first thing I must ask you is, are you being kept here against your will?' he whispered.

She laughed freely. 'Detective, you've been watching far too many Hollywood movies. I'm being protected, not imprisoned.'

'Why do you need protection? And why was I told that you were dead?' Murray asked.

'It's complicated,' she answered, making him wonder if he was going to struggle to get her to open up. 'How long have you got?'

'As long as it needs. Please - take your time,' said Murray. He started to write in his notebook.

She stared wistfully out at the blue sky. 'I've been here since the early sixties. That's when I came across the pond from the States.'

Murray looked up from his notebook, ready for the ride, feeling like he was about to hear a fantastical story for the first time. The woman had a magnetic charm about her. 'Were you here visiting family, or friends?' he asked.

She raised her over-pencilled eyebrows in response to his comment. 'A vacation? If only. That would've been nice. When I left the States however, I knew I was leaving for good. You see, it wasn't safe there anymore,' she added, nervously screwing up the white lace-edged handkerchief that was in her hands.

'But by all accounts, you clearly don't feel safe in England,' said Murray. 'Even with armed personnel. Which, by the way, is a serious offence in the UK, without a licence or special dispensation,' he added, trying not to appear too bullish.

'I'm not going to deny the shooters detective. I take it the young woman whose car broke down reported that my men are armed? I can't say I blame her. She was scared for sure. What with the dogs on the loose as well.'

'Yes, she was,' said Murray. 'And, I can tell from her statement, that one of your men was less than friendly when she came back a second time to retrieve something she'd lost.' As he said these words he glanced over to the windows and French doors that led onto the balcony, checking to see if they had unnecessary locks to imprison someone as frail as the woman in front of him.

'She came here twice? I didn't know that. There

is however, a very good reason for my mens' covert behaviour.'

'I'm intrigued,' said Murray, trying not to sound sarcastic. 'Is there something else you need to tell me while we're alone?' he asked, checking the room again, only this time for evidence of bugging devices.

'Yes there is… only because of who I am, detective. Or who I think I am on the days my mind is not foggy. I could blow the lid on some very powerful individuals back in California. Hollywood has many evil secrets.'

All of a sudden, Murray felt goose bumps run up his arms, so much so that it was as though he had just received an electric shock. 'So this is when I need to ask you to tell me who these powerful individuals are,' he said. 'And also to ask you to disclose the information you're clearly too afraid to tell me about,' he added, more as a question than a statement. 'If I'm right that you are genuinely afraid - or sworn to silence, please be assured you're in a safe pair of hands.'

While waiting for the woman's response, he fast-tracked his memory of milestone events in early sixties America. The Vietnam and Cold Wars and the assassination of President Kennedy were the first things to spring to mind. He realised however, that he was more familiar with his parent's sugar-coated stories of their English hippy youth, which was a bit later in the sixties. However, he was uncertain as to how much of their lifestyle had migrated from England across the Atlantic ocean and impacted on American youth culture, or whether it was the other way round.

The woman let out a deep sigh. 'You know - you remind me of him. You have his eyes,' she said, seemingly pained by the memory of someone whose identity she had not as yet disclosed.

Murray had no idea if her statement was a compliment or an insult, but the sadness in her expression suggested the former. He was still contemplating her American accent and how it seemed strange against her Englishness. Pinpointing her home state still eluded him. 'Let's get back to why I'm here. This could be your last chance to tell me something… anything, before Frank returns?'

'Frank can hear whatever I choose to tell you. But it's you I wonder about detective...can I trust you?' she whispered, shooting a glance around the room nervously, as though Murray might be right about bugs.

'Without a doubt. I'm part of one of the best police forces in the world,' said Murray, proudly. However, his very next thought was of his grandfather, who had been in Bomber Command during World War Two. Somehow boasting about his own occupation as a detective seemed unworthy of a mention.

Unaware of Murray's self doubt, the woman brushed over his words. 'I've the greatest of respect for British cops, but there are slime balls in any organisation. Though I'm not implying you're a slime ball,' she added, hurriedly, covering her lips with a gloved hand in an attempt to stifle a light giggle.

'Glad to hear you already have some faith in me,' said Murray, sitting forward, with no other intention than to look deep into her eyes. It was hard to fathom whether she was about to spin him a tall story. He was good at reading faces, but on this occasion he was not doing very well. He was plucked prematurely from his unsuccessful analysis as Frank appeared sooner than expected, tray in hands.

'We won't be disturbed from now on,' said Frank, with

one eye on Murray and the other on the elderly woman. He poured drinks, passed them round and then pulled up a chair so that he could be part of the conversation.

'Frank travelled from the States with me,' said the woman. He was with the Secret Service and has never left my side,' she added, proudly. 'That is, apart from the handful of times I absconded.' Her mischievous smile suggested that not only was she about to break out again into a fit of youthful giggles, but that at some point she had enjoyed going awol.

Frank's expression was more serious, suggesting that he was going to keep a lid on things. He intervened. 'Where are we going with this conversation detective? You can see there's nothing untoward going on.'

'It's alright Frank. I told him about the shooters,' said the woman, casually, as though she were used to the presence of guns.

'You shouldn't have done that,' said Frank, throwing Murray a warning look. 'So now you know we're armed DC Murray, what're you going to do about it?'

'We'll get to that later,' said Murray, economically.

'In the big scheme of things Frank, the shooters are irrelevant,' said the woman, shifting the emphasis to other things. 'Time's much more important. We don't know how long I've got.' She took his hand in hers and squeezed it with what little strength she had.

'You know my feelings. Big fat mistake to tell someone you've just met,' said Frank, allowing her to keep hold of his hand. 'You make it goddamn hard sometimes for me to do my job properly.'

'I'm not just anyone,' said Murray, irked at Frank's dismissal of his vocation. 'I haven't as yet got a handle on what your role is in all of this, but I'll take a wild guess that like me, you take a pride in what you do.'

'With all due respect detective, we don't know if you're with us or against us,' responded Frank.

The woman cut them both short before the debate could become more heated. 'Please stop right now. The world needs to know how those two-bit punks treated me. And anyway Frank, I'd like to see the look of surprise on this young man's face when I spill the beans.'

Frank shrugged. 'If I were you detective, I'd leave and forget you were ever here. That is, if you know what's good for you.'

Murray stood up abruptly. 'Well I'm not you...so I won't be leaving until I'm good and ready. Plus that's the second threat I've had since I arrived and I don't like it.'

'Oh sit down detective and ignore Frank,' said the woman. 'He means well. He's just looking out for me.'

Murray sat down again, reluctantly. His pride was bruised but he knew it would do nothing to solve the case if he were to walk away. He looked from one to the other, a second page at the ready.

Between sips of tea the woman began to unpeel the layers of her story. 'You know detective, if you'd asked in high places before you snuck in here, you might have uncovered the fact that I was once protected by your illustrious MI5 and your British government. Though I think they had more pressing issues back then.'

Murray was thrown. He began to twiddle his pen rapidly between his fingers like a cheerleader spinning her baton, which was something he did when he was impatient to get to the bottom of things. He allowed his acute hearing to kick in again, to check out whether Frank already had heavies outside the door, waiting to oust him.

'Let's get to the point detective. I get tired very quickly these days, so what would you like to know?' asked the woman, fixing Murray with an open expression.

His pen was already poised again, ready to record the big reveal. 'Shall we keep it simple and start with your name?' he asked.

Chapter 7

You'll Never Believe Me

The woman watched Murray with a flicker of a smile as he recorded details in his notebook. 'My name is Marilyn,' she said at last, picking her moment.

'Last name?' asked Murray, not noticing her amusement, but in the same breath thinking there was something vaguely familiar about her. Her amusement was not shared by Frank.

'Monroe,' she said, with a flourish of both arms and her head held high.

Murray finished penning the names, taking a few seconds to register their significance when put side by side. 'Named after a film star!' he said, eventually, unconsciously ignoring punctuation protocol and adding several exclamation marks. 'That must've be a talking point with people you've met over the years,' he added, looking up at last.

'No doubt it would've been, if I'd had a life outside of these walls,' said the woman, looking downbeat suddenly.

'Did your parents call you Marilyn as a tribute to

Monroe?' asked Murray, deliberately flattering her by suggesting she was much younger.

'Oh my,' she sighed, not realising that he was trying to reel her in. 'I can see it's gonna be hard to convince you that little old me is the real thing.'

Murray felt fleetingly dizzy. He had begun to perspire heavily and his heart was thumping. He loosened his tie. 'But Marilyn Monroe died last century,' he said at last, wondering at the same time whether he should just humour the woman.

'When you put it like that, I feel positively ancient. Do you see nothing of her in me?' she asked, lifting her chin and looking at him through half-shuttered eyelids. She stopped short of a pout, thinking it might look unsavoury coming from a woman of her mature years.

Murray took a long look at the shape of her face and the style of her silvery bob, hoping for something that might secure her claim, but her youth being long gone meant he was left with no verification. 'With all due respect...I can't...'

'Hear me out detective,' she interrupted. 'I may be old and wrinkled, but I still have all my marbles.'

Murray found it hard not to explode with laughter and as a result, lose all sense of professionalism. The woman's face was as expressionless as Frank's. Murray waited for the hint of a smile from either of them to indicate that they had been playing games, but they both remained deadpan. For the first time in Murray's burgeoning career, his notebook lay idle. His pen dropped to the floor, the magnified sound of it bouncing on floorboards out of proportion for such an insignificant item.

'I don't expect you to believe me,' said the woman. 'Not just yet anyway. It would be hard for anyone to believe such a revelation. I'm guessing you're already thinking I'm a crazy old broad.'

Rather than insult her by confirming her last sentence was close to the mark, Murray turned to Frank for some sort of affirmation. 'I could do you both for perverting the course of justice,' he said to Frank with conviction. 'I've a stack of cases to investigate after this one, so don't waste my time.'

'She's not lying detective, so cut us some slack,' said Frank, corroborating her version of things. 'This is more exciting than any case you'll investigate today, tomorrow, or the next day. In fact, probably for the rest of your career.' He took out a cigarette and lit it, clearly rattled by Murray's disbelief at what he had heard. Then he snapped closed his silver lighter, took a drag and exhaled slowly, as though using the interlude to consider his next sentence. 'You can't tell anyone about this conversation. And I mean anyone.'

Murray's body was behaving peculiarly. In a way that was unfamiliar to him. He was pumped full of adrenaline but he considered that it was due to nearly having fallen down the stairs. He tried to take control. 'No deal I'm afraid. I'll need to update my superiors.'

Frank took a few more drags and then stubbed out his cigarette aggressively in a cut glass ashtray; all the time looking Murray in the eye. 'Just you and him - capiche? And no leaks to the press,' he added, shaking a threatening finger at Murray.

Buying himself a few seconds to think, Murray watched the residual smoke from Frank's spent cigarette spiral lazily upwards, fleetingly forming the shape of a vaporous horned beast. He rubbed his eyes in disbelief, but when he looked again the occult shape had faded to nothing. 'I can agree to those terms in the short term,' he said, annoyed that Frank seemed insistent on having the last word.

Frank stared at him but made no comment.

Murray realised that the woman was plainly desperate to come clean but was under Frank's thumb. More importantly, he was in no doubt that she was delusional with regards as to who she claimed to be. He wondered whether she went by any other name depending on her mood. Also he didn't relish his return to Scotland Yard with interview notes about the madwoman who claimed to be the most celebrated sex symbol of the twentieth century. So far he had escaped an initiation at Scotland Yard, but he could hear the sniggers already.

'So - what's it to be?' asked Frank at last.

Murray opted to try a different tack while at the same time making no pretence of believing the woman's story. He turned to her. 'If what you're saying is true, why didn't you pretend you were someone less famous from that era? It would've been easier to protect you in a place like this and stop rumours at the same time.' At this point he expected her to take the bait and come out with other names she had considered adopting, such as Garbo, Taylor or Hepburn, but she was not forthcoming.

Frank spoke up. 'Because above all else, when Marilyn was young there was no chance of her identity being kept a secret for long if we hadn't had put full security measures in place. She was the world's hottest star and folks aren't stupid.'

Murray felt impotent, but he focussed instead on the enigmatic woman before him. She had seemingly not allowed life to diminish her obvious charisma and she still radiated an air of indefinable beauty despite her heavily lined face. Every sentence she had uttered had been dramatised by a graceful movement of her hand or the quick flick of a finger to remove a stray hair from covering her glittering eyes. He had the most peculiar of feelings that there was a massive story about to be unrolled even though he kept silently repeating to himself that she was a fraud.

She sensed his dilemma. 'So detective, before I get too tired from being interrogated by you, shall we start the story of my chequered past?' she laughed, skilfully drawing him in with a cleverly crafted theatrical teaser. 'And for your notes, why don't you call me by another name until I've convinced you of my colourful background? Maybe that would sit easier with you. Especially, if you think I'm a phony - as I suspect you do.'

Murray wondered whether she had the ability to read minds. 'I'm happy to go along with that,' he said. 'After all, we have no proof of your identity as yet. Do you have a name in mind?'

'How about calling me Norma?' she said.

Already, Murray was certain that at some time in her life she had graced the stage. For a few seconds he imagined that if she were still to have life in her old bones, she might rise unaided and rush to her balcony to reenact the iconic scene from Romeo and Juliet. Choosing to allow her to fill the room temporarily with her bewildering presence, he opted to suppress any sarcasm that might percolate into his questioning. Before he could summon up a polite response, she continued.

'After all, Norma-Jeane was the name given to me at birth.' A shadow passed across her expression as she mentioned her early childhood.

Her dip in mood suggested to Murray that her

childhood had been a dark time. He agreed, raising his empty tea-cup as though proposing a toast while giving her the benefit of the doubt. 'Here's to hoping you'll convince me.'

Her face lit up. 'You bet your bottom dollar I'll convince you. I'm so damn sure I will, that I'm prepared to gamble on it,' she said, certain of herself. 'Are you?' She chinked tea-cups with him.

I'm afraid to say I'm no betting man, apart from an occasional lottery ticket. I'm only interested in facts,' said Murray, waving his notebook enthusiastically, as though to say that whatever he recorded was all that mattered.

'Do you have any vices at all, detective?' asked Norma, with a twinkle in her eye and her tendency to giggle only just kept in check.

'Nope, can't say that I do,' said Murray, preferring to make such an admission sound like a virtue. 'Sorry to disappoint you.'

Norma sniffed her disapproval. 'What a dull life you lead. Life is only worth living if you take a few risks. If I were a younger woman I'd give you a lecture for being so boringly conventional.'

For a second, Murray felt as though his masculinity had just been kicked into touch. But Norma had a point. His life was all work and no play. He cut her short. He was beginning to like her feistiness too much, too soon, which could impact on his judgement. 'Shall we continue with the circumstances that brought you to England - Norma?'

Before she could answer, Frank cut in. 'I helped with the logistics of the journey, if you remember. Shall I continue so you don't tire yourself?' he asked Norma.

'No Frank - it should come from me,' she insisted,

turning again to Murray.

'Please - continue,' said Murray, before Frank could put more pressure on Norma to be silent.

'You know detective, I could tell you about my career, but you might consider I've just read up and watched movies back to back, to prepare myself for an eventuality such as this,' said Norma. 'There's even one movie I can recall about a week of my life. But sad to say, the actress didn't capture the real me.'

'There was only room for one Marilyn,' said Murray, attempting to butter her up.

She smiled, then continued. 'Over the years I've fallen out of love with Hollywood. It's nothing but a melting pot of deception, sleaze and secrecy.'

She had barely begun but Murray was already hypnotised. To him, her irises seemed to suddenly alter, becoming whirlpools shot through with many colours, ranging from bright blue to green to hazel. He felt as though at any second he would be sucked into her world through her eyes, never to return to the here and now.

Oblivious to the effect that she was having on him, Norma sighed. 'You'll no doubt know about my relationship with John F Kennedy,' she said, casually, as though it were of no particular significance.

Murray was jolted back from the top step of his helter-skelter ride into oblivion. At the mention of such an iconic person from the past, he took a deep intake of breath. 'I know a reasonable amount about JFK, though I've heard all sorts of theories about the nature of his relationship with you... I mean with Marilyn,' he said, correcting himself promptly. In his mind, it all of a sudden seemed the perfect time for Norma to be telling such a big story back at the Yard to a captive audience, rather than just to him. He wished he could be a fly on the wall, so that he could witness his colleagues' reactions. Fleetingly, he imagined her seated on his office chair surrounded by an eager sea of detectives and senior officers; some kneeling at her feet and others crowded around, mesmerised by her story-telling.

She tutted at Murray's limited knowledge of the sixties. 'Jack and I were heavily involved. Totally in love,' she said. 'Only those closest to him called him Jack by the way.'

Murray retrieved his pen from the floor and began to write in double-quick time.

'I guess you're already thinking I just had a thing for Jack. Or that I'm a charlatan,' said Norma, pausing expectantly.

'You're story's already fascinating,' said Murray, trying not to patronise, but at the same time dodging an answer. He was not a romantic man, but when it came to iconic historical figures, he could be drawn into a good story as easily as the next man. There was no greater story than JFK and Marilyn, although from his recall it had just been just a fling. What if Norma's tale proved all the theories wrong? He wished for a split second that he had the skill required to write a best-seller, dramatising what he was about to hear.

'Then indulge me,' said Norma. 'Let me tell you more about my Jack.' She smoothed her skirt in readiness with gloved hands, then speedily arranged her hair. It was as though she was wanting to look her best for the ghost in the room that only she could see.

Murray did not believe in spirits but he was suddenly aware that the temperature seemed to have dropped. He scanned the shadows, half-believing that there was one or more souls gathered for the big reveal, like an enthralled audience at the cinema.

'I knew Jack better than anyone,' said Norma, finally. 'We tried to keep our love for each other under wraps of course, due to him being the president, but it was near impossible. Once the cat was out of the bag, those that talked about it, said it was nothing more than a two-bit affair,' she added, compounding Murray's theory. 'However, our relationship being belittled, in a way served our purpose.'

'How so?' asked Murray. 'Surely your relationship being debased was hurtful?'

'If you think I was upset because of snakes in the grass, you're wrong. Back then I sure was a looker, so I just shrugged it off and put it down to jealousy. I bet most of those comments were made by folks with nothing better to do anyway.'

To point out that the younger her still lingered, Norma got up from her chair, Murray noticing that for a woman of her age she did so with ease. Even so, he stood to offer help but she waved him away. 'I'm not an invalid,' she said, irritated, standing in front of an ornately framed mirror. She looked at her reflection and prodded unsympathetically at her deep wrinkles. 'Sadly, I'm not a looker now. I've had my time. If I went outside of these four walls, folks would say I'm just the batty old dame from Huntley Manor.'

'That's bullshit,' said Frank suddenly, forgetting his silence and leaping up. He grasped Norma's hands and led her back to her chair. 'You're as beautiful as the day I met you.'

Murray was taken aback at such romanticism coming from a man who was only there to protect Norma, but he said nothing, preferring to wait for the situation to unfold.

Norma continued, modestly brushing aside Frank's compliment with a weak smile. 'It's true to say I was concerned I'd eventually lose my looks detective. Those close to Jack thought he'd move on at the first sign of it happening. But that aside, let's face it, he could've had anyone.' Settling into her chair again, she repeated the process of preening, smoothing her skirt and hair for the ghosts who were still waiting expectantly for her to continue.

'And did he move on?' asked Murray, intrigued by her delivery of such an unbelievable tale. He felt a sudden pang of sorrow that she had such a low opinion of herself in the winter of her life and that she had to play make-believe to fill what time she had left.

'Did he hell, detective?' said Norma, summoning up some mettle from deep inside her psyche. 'Jack so wanted to step down from the presidency, but with the Cuban Missile crisis going on, talk of that was put on hold. But on a lighter note, we joked that Jack was the equivalent of your King Edward VIII and that I was like Edward's mistress, Wallis Simpson. Though I never much cared for her, even with her being American,' she added, as an afterthought. 'But as for me and Jack, we would've made headlines here for sure, just as much as they did in their day.'

Murray laughed. 'We British are known for making the headlines when it comes to the monarchy.'

'You think your kings and queens could top our love story?' asked Norma, self-assuredly. 'What would you Brits have really thought, if Jack and I'd married and come to live on your little island?' she asked, the mention of marriage causing her face to appear awash with complex emotions.

'I'm sure us Brits would've loved it,' said Murray. A theoretical front page story suddenly blazed across his thoughts, complete with a black and white photograph of JFK and Marilyn stepping off of the president's plane at Heathrow, watched by exuberant well-wishers sandwiched behind barriers.

'Jack would've stood up for what we had done in order to be together, that's for sure. Unlike most of the other men in my life,' said Norma with contempt, still lost in the hypothetical world of wedding bouquets and silver horseshoe tokens.

Murray tore himself away from the thought of fictional newspaper cuttings saved by British sixties teenagers of well-wishers showering Monroe and JFK with confetti. He whisked himself forward to the present, but Norma was still back in the world they had both just manifested. It might be the right moment to catch her out with her historical facts about a string of lovers. He tried to sound matter-of-fact. 'And who were these other men?'

She rallied immediately. 'My three husbands of course. The rest aren't worth a mention.' She went quiet again, seeming to lose all train of thought, making Murray wonder whether she was buying time to remember what she had tried to absorb from factual books. Finally she spoke. 'I had a lousy childhood,' she said, sidestepping. 'My mother was crazy you know.'

For the first time, in Murray's opinion, Norma sounded hauntingly like the real Marilyn Monroe in her delivery. Her fragility was not that of an elderly woman, but more like the troubled icon that the young Marilyn had become in the final months of her life. Meanwhile,

Norma appeared to be stuck somewhere else. For a fleeting moment Murray imagined she missed the arms of someone who would make her feel secure and loved.

Finally she answered his question properly. 'As I said, there were three of them, but the only one to not let me down was Joe. Joe DiMaggio,' she elaborated. 'He came back into my life some time after we divorced. When I come to think of it, I guess he never really went away.'

Murray was beginning to feel awkward asking an elderly woman such probing questions, as he had heard she had at one time supposedly had a huge appetite for men. He tried to position himself in his chair as he wrote, feeling somewhat awkward, his embarrassment causing him to fidget. 'Anyone else worth a mention?'

Norma responded as though sensing his thoughts and awkwardness. 'Why detective - you make me sound like I was a loose woman. But I wasn't. Some say the way to a man's heart is through his stomach, but rather than use food, I used love. Like every other gal, I was just looking for that special something. That special something turned out to be Jack.' She sighed. 'But it wasn't to be. Apart from Frank, one of the most constant people in my life was Joe. He propped me up when I needed it and organised my bogus funeral. Did you know that flowers were laid at the burial site for years? All that to fool the public and the press. Apart from Jack, I think Joe was the only man who ever truly loved me. That was why he delivered me safely to England.'

Murray deviated to save more embarrassment, concerned that his necessary questioning might have dug too deep and offended her. 'So if Jack stood in Joe's way, why was Joe so keen to help?'

'I guess Joe figured that once he got me here and away

from Jack, he could have me all to himself. We'd even been discussing remarrying when we were back in the States. He thought it would give me some security. I hadn't the heart to tell him Jack was to be husband number four instead of him.'

'And where can I find Joe now?' asked Murray, instantly eager to speak to DiMaggio. The key to the truth might be accessible, especially if he were questioned before being forewarned and had no time to construct a story.

'He died back in the nineties. I was devastated. I'll be forever in his debt.'

Murray turned to an empty page, dejected and knocked back by Norma's comment. He tried not to let his disappointment show.

She seemed oblivious to the fact she had just scuppered his next line of questioning and continued. 'Jack was desperately unhappy with his wife Jackie. That much had leaked out to the press. When she found out about me, the threats started coming thick and fast.' She shivered.

Murray sensed there was something as yet not disclosed. 'So how did you know these threats were from Jackie?'

'I don't necessarily think that they were from her, though when I saw her at parties, her eyes cut right through me. I should tell you though detective, there were plenty of people who didn't like me. I'm not proud of the marriages I wrecked. It could've been anyone after me. '

'Well the big question is, if you're not buried back in the States Norma, who is?' asked Murray, hopeful that Frank would not intervene now things were really getting interesting.

Chapter 8

Dead and Forgotten

Norma hesitated. 'Her name was Gloria and she wanted to be me from the start.'

'Who can blame her? You were known all over the world,' said Murray. 'Plus I'm sure you were a role model to young starlets.'

'Well, we were similar I guess in one way, in the sense that we'd both gotten caught up with the Hollywood machine. But the difference was that she was a chorus-line dancer and I'd been a big name for some time. I'm sure you can imagine the sleaze bags that capitalised on her naivety. As for me, I was used to the shmucks. Being famous meant I could be a bit choosy about my lovers. Although to get to the top I admit I did things I'm not too proud of.'

'Where did you first meet this Gloria?' asked Murray, trying to work out how anyone could successfully mimic Marilyn Monroe.

'We met at the studios. Quite by accident we passed each other by on the lot. Immediately, she did an about-turn and came running back. She was like an excited kid, saying over and over how I was her screen idol and begging for my autograph. I'd already spotted the resemblance between us.'

Norma's ability to set the stage had already drawn Murray in. He imagined himself back in the early sixties as a young runner at the studios; by chance witnessing the conversation between the two women as he ferried props to and fro for different productions. 'So you became friends?'

'No, not at all. I didn't see her for awhile after that. Not until after just by chance, I'd dropped her into a conversation with Jack. The second I mentioned our passing likeness, it was like a bright light went on in his head. Straight away he suggested using her as a body-double, so while the press would be chasing her all over town, he and I would be in each other's arms. I sure thought he was crazy to think it could work. But we weren't the first to do it - and we certainly weren't the last. Anyway, Jack and I were desperate to be together. So I hung out with Gloria a bit at the studio in breaks to see if she had what it took.'

'How did you draw her into such an ambitious plan? She must have...forgive me for saying, thought that you were out of your mind,' said Murray, intrigued by the idea that maybe some of his favourite dead music artists and film stars may after all, still be alive, their doppelgängers having been mistakenly bumped off instead.

Norma seemed not bothered by his comment about her mental state. 'Maybe I was a bit kooky, but I was desperately in love. And it was easy to tempt Gloria with big bucks. When she was eventually introduced to Jack, she couldn't refuse. Apart from the money, he could turn any broad's legs to jelly. It was me who was unsure as to whether she could pull it off. Call it arrogance or my self-belief that I was a one-off.' She hesitated. 'There was the down-side of Jack's plan of course that put me off the idea... a teensiest-weensiest part of me worried he might fall in love with Gloria. She was, after all, a younger perkier version of me.'

'I'd argue with that point. Not all men find younger women more desirable,' responded Murray, defending Norma's corner on her behalf. For a second, he thought about his girlfriend, who was fifteen years older than he. He was not romantic by nature, but in his opinion, she had become more stunning as time had passed.

'Why detective - I do believe you might be a dark horse,' said Norma. 'I suspected from the moment you first spoke that there was more to you than meets the eye.' She took a few seconds to recalibrate. 'Now, where were we? Ah yes - Gloria was made to swear on her life she'd never tell.' A frown crossed her face as she realised the relevance of what she had just said. 'Those words have played with my conscience ever since. '

'So how well did she play her part?' asked Murray, still thinking it unlikely anyone could have filled Marilyn's shoes without being rumbled.

Norma laughed, immediately looking twenty years younger. 'Well of course, there was no way she could ever be as talented as I was,' she said, mirroring Murray's thoughts. 'But she wasn't paid to be on the silver screen. That would've been a disaster. But all in all, she was good enough to fool any casual onlooker. That is, as long as they didn't try to get too close up and cosy with her.'

Murray was wishing that everything Norma was manufacturing and glamorising was not fiction. To be the first, apart from Frank, to hear the truth about Kennedy and Monroe's amazing romance would make him the envy of detectives, journalists and members of the public all around the world. 'How involved was the president from then on?' he asked.

'Oh he was straight on it. Everything was planned to the teensiest detail, including Gloria having surgery to make her more like me. I do believe Jack enjoyed the distraction from being president. For sure, he found the deception addictive. But he said whatever the outcome of Gloria's surgery, she could never be me,' she said, smiling at the memory of his loyalty. Her gaze wandered off to the view beyond her balcony.

'Please - continue,' said Murray, urging her on.

'I've always wondered how much the surgeon and nurses were paid to keep their big mouths shut. Anyway, after Gloria was released from the clinic, Jack had her moved to an apartment, where she could recuperate for a few weeks. Then she started coming round to see me. Jack had her disguise all worked out; brunette wig, headscarf and sunglasses. I knew in advance the time she'd arrive. Fortunately, there were only one or two journalists sniffing around outside my gates that first day.'

'How did she slip past?' asked Murray, making a mental note to look at Google images of the home Norma had mentioned, to check for any flaws in her description. He was feeling more and more like a fly on the wall, back in time.

'Jack was so clever. He'd set up some sort of protest rally real close by. That sent the photographers scuttling off. Once Gloria was in, she hid until I was certain no one had gotten into the garden. I hadn't seen her since before the surgery. When she took off her sunglasses, it was such a shock that I nearly fainted. It was kinda like looking in a mirror... but at the same time, it wasn't.'

'I'm not sure I get your meaning,' said Murray, his only yardstick that of identical twins separated at birth meeting after years apart. Only in his mind, Norma's scenario was weirder in every possible way.

She considered her answer. 'Well, I guess in simple terms, there was nothing in her expression that reminded me of myself. Yeah, she looked like me but her eyes were cold and she'd none of what made me tick. It was only much later, that I realised what was so odd about her.'

Murray continued to write, deciding it was better not to interrupt Norma's flow, but his disbelief about Gloria's existence was spilling over so much so, that he was having trouble getting the words down fast enough, so intrigued was he by the mystery of it all.

'Soon Gloria moved in and, that was the beginning of the end. I made a point of wearing the dark wig, so no snooper would see two Marilyns. My voice was the hardest thing for her to master, but in the end she did okay. She was soon confident enough to lounge by my pool and be photographed by those who snuck in and hid behind the palms.'

'Did you fear she might forget her promise to keep quiet about your agreement?' asked Murray.

'Not for a moment. She'd too much to lose. She wanted fame so badly and this was the only way she was likely to get it. That's where we were really different. Fame had led to me being portrayed as a piece of meat and I'd had enough.'

'So once she'd got up to speed with being you, when did everything start to fall apart?' asked Murray, feeling as though Norma's tale was a magnet and that he could not resist the pull. He hoped that once he was back at the

Yard, he could disengage and see her for what she was: an ageing scam artist.

Oblivious to his scepticism, she continued. 'Jack knew someone was out to get me. He told me he rowed with Jackie all the time over me. But she wasn't the only one to be angry. There were others who wanted to give me a good hiding. But not at any time did it occur to me someone had murder in mind. Things really went wrong one night after seeing Jack. I got home and Gloria was in a really bad way. There'd been threatening phone calls coming in all evening. I got real cross and said she wasn't paid to pick up the phone and speak to anyone. She was out of control and demanded more money. Said the job was getting too dangerous and she'd sell her story, as she'd get more than what Jack paid her. I'd never seen her so hostile.'

'What did you do when she kicked off like that?'

'I had to box real clever, so I told her if she promised to keep quiet, I'd get her work as a body double on my next movie. Of course I couldn't really expose her to the public in that way, and when it came to it I'd have to think of a way out of the deal. But I hoped it'd calm her down. Lucky for me it did. She seemed very excited about the idea.'

'Did you tell Jack she was becoming unreliable?' asked Murray, thinking if the story developed any further that he would inevitably run out of pages. He had not come equipped for such an eventuality.

'You bet I told Jack. Straight away. After that things happened real quick. Jack told Bobby our secret.'

'Bobby?' asked Murray, wishing again that his knowledge of sixties history was more extensive.

'Jack's brother, the Attorney General,' added Frank,

suddenly. 'He thought Gloria might be tempted to keep her mouth shut if she could have a piece of the Kennedy action.'

Murray turned to Frank. 'So by this point, you'd become involved in the charade?'

'It wasn't a charade or whatever word you want to use. But yeah detective, I was involved. Assigned by the president himself,' added Frank, proudly. 'Though at first, I knew pretty much nothing, apart from Marilyn was to be moved to a place of safety.'

The mention of Marilyn in peril, seemed to trigger something in Frank's psyche. He began to crack his fingers with the opposite hand as though he were limbering up for a fist-fight.

'Bobby didn't waste any time,' said Norma, taking over from Frank. 'The shmuck started sending her flowers and perfume and ignoring me. Frankly I found the situation pretty lousy. I wasn't used to being put in second place, plus he'd a menace about him that gave me the creeps.'

'So as things were escalating, did things ever settle down to how they were before?' asked Murray, intrigued at how both Frank and Norma were in on such an elaborate fabrication.

'For a while things got better, though the relationship between me and Gloria was never the same,' said Norma. 'She'd gotten above herself. Borrowed my stuff without asking. Worse than that, she began jeopardising all our hard work. She'd been photographed in public when she should've been back at the bungalow.'

Murray imagined the confusion and ripple effect in the tabloids had two Marilyns been spotted in public fifty-five years previously. Twisted history suddenly seemed an interesting genre to write about in his spare time.

'The crunch came one night when I arrived home,' said Norma. Gloria was wearing my favourite outfit and had passed out on my sun bed. When I asked my housekeeper about it, she said Gloria had been drinking for hours and that she'd been in my bathroom helping herself to my Reds.'

'Reds?'

'Barbiturates - to help me sleep.'

'So let me get this right. She was becoming a liability?'

'For sure. But you've gotta believe me, I never wanted her dead. I was getting kinda jumpy too though, because more calls were coming in. Whoever was on the end of the line would breath down the phone, then hang-up. After that, Jack said he'd make sure some of his agents were posted close by, just so I felt safe.'

'That's when we met for the first time,' said Frank, looking across at Norma, with a certain fondness etched across his face.

'Who do you think these calls were from?' Murray asked, breaking up any thoughts of the past on Frank's part.

Norma seemed to crumble. 'I reckon the Mafia were after me. They didn't exactly see eye to eye with the Kennedys and I'd spent a lot of time partying with Sinatra for one. I'd been so naive to mix it up with them. Their tentacles were everywhere. Once they were stuck on you, there was no getting them off. But in the end, it wasn't the Mafia's stooges who turned up at my bungalow.

Gloria and I were both in, when we heard noises outside. As usual, I was wearing the brunette wig, so she could remain in character. She'd been behaving, probably because of the new deal and we'd been getting on well. Suddenly there was this knock at the door. Neither of us knew what to do. I told her to skedaddle into my bedroom. I opened the door and this fella makes a grab for me. Pulls up my blouse. Sees my scar. 'This is her,' he says to the guy with him, then the two of them bundled me into a Sedan.'

'And Gloria? What happened to her?' asked Murray, wishing Norma was not such a skilled fantasist.

'They didn't clock she was there. But whoever had grabbed me, knew there was a second me. Otherwise they wouldn't have needed to check, if you know what I mean. I ended up in the trunk crying and kicking out. I wondered whether Jack had changed his mind about me and I was gonna end up wearing concrete boots. Next thing I know, we'd stopped, the trunk was opened and he was looking down at me. I should never of doubted him.'

Murray felt like he had just gone along for the ride, or had been in an armed convoy watching the black Sedan ahead of him join the freeway at high speed. 'Where had you been taken?'

'I was at a subsidiary airport. Jack gave me the lowdown and after holding me real close, put me straight on a waiting plane.'

'He stayed in the States? Wasn't that his opportunity to leave with you?' asked Murray.

'He was going to go public with his announcement about us first. But he promised he'd join me as soon as he could,' said Norma. 'I'm sure he meant every word.'

Whereas Norma was certain of Jack's intent, Murray smelt a lie. Could Norma have been wrong about Jack in the sense that he had no intention of stepping down from the presidency? It sounded to him more likely that Jack had been simply dealing effectively with the problem in hand. And that problem was a volatile woman who could topple him from his position of power. That was reason enough for her to be taken as far away as possible. But what if the most powerful man in the world at that time had cared for Marilyn as much as she had cared for him?

Norma continued. 'The Secret Service smuggled me out, but what I didn't know back then, was that Joe had promised to see me safe this end. He'd connections in London's underworld you see.'

'So exactly what did happen to Gloria?' asked Murray, several different possibilities circling in his mind.

Norma continued. 'She was simply in the wrong place at the wrong time. But because I couldn't speak direct to anyone back in the States, I couldn't get to the bottom of what had happened until later. Everything I discovered was from Frank and the newspapers.'

'So when you did get to the truth, did you find out whether it was murder?' asked Murray, his heart pounding with anticipation of her reply. These were seriously good scammers, although as yet he could not work out what was in it for them.

'I had no idea at first,' said Norma. 'I waited months to get to the truth. Meanwhile, I felt so responsible for Gloria's death. Talking to you detective, it's like it was just yesterday.'

Chapter 9

The Headlines

Norma began to elaborate. 'This is how I remember things. I'd just put on my favourite capri pants, sweater and necklace. I never went anywhere without my pearls. It was a day or so after I'd arrived, when I heard a commotion outside my suite. I opened my door a crack and peeked out. That was when Frank appeared from nowhere. I was so mad I hollered at him for scaring me. I said I needed to speak to Jack, but he said it was too soon and he'd already gotten a message through to him that I'd arrived safely. That's when Frank told me there'd been an unexpected development.'

'What sort of development?' asked Murray, annoyed with himself for being so willing to hear more of Norma's lies.

'All manner of things flashed through my mind - like Jack'd finally admitted he'd sent me to England to get me out of his hair. Or maybe one of his pretend lovers had finally gotten their claws into him and I was surplus. Frank soon cut those thoughts short, when he presented me with the newspaper headlines.

Marilyn Monroe Found Dead. Suicide.

Next thing I knew, Frank was bringing me round with smelling salts. He fixed me a stiff drink and tried to reassure me that I was in safe hands.'

'So what went through your mind and did you believe Frank could keep you safe?'

'Straightaway I guessed something had happened to Gloria and she'd been mistaken for me. As for Frank, I knew I had to trust him, but I still felt abandoned. But putting that aside, Gloria would never have killed herself. Not with the opportunity Jack and I'd given her. I'm as sure of it now as I was then.' She hesitated. 'Come to think of it, little old me wouldn't have killed myself. I'd turned a corner during those last weeks in LA and was long over self-pity.'

'So straight off, you suspected foul play,' said Murray, captured yet again. 'An intriguing story to say the least,' he added, tempering sarcasm with a deadpan expression.

'Soon as I'd recovered from the shock, I was certain Gloria had been got at. I asked Frank what he thought and what would happen when they found out it wasn't me in the morgue. His face said it all. Then I realised the chance of Jack appearing on a snow white horse and carrying me off into the sunset was zilch.'

'It's just as she says,' said Frank suddenly. 'It'd only be a matter of time, before it would be discovered it was someone else's body on the slab. I had no idea as to whether our tracks getting out of the country were hidden well enough. What I did find out however, came all the way down from the president himself.'

Murray was still thinking he needed another notebook to accommodate such a ground-breaking yarn. 'Even so

Norma, it seems a big coincidence you got away, don't you think?' he asked, looking her straight in the eye.

'To you it might seem that way, but all I knew was that Jack was so keen to have me transported in the trunk of that Sedan. At first I didn't even think he had anything to do with Gloria's death, but if I'd known what was to happen, I would never have agreed to her pretending to be me.' She smoothed her skirt in the same fashion as when she had first sat down, all the time considering her next sentence. 'Then I began to doubt Jack - and I told Frank the second the thought popped into my head.'

Frank thought back to her lightning bolt moment. 'You thought Gloria's murder was intentional, to cover your getaway,' he said.

Norma nodded in agreement. 'Think about it detective, if the very person who wanted to protect me, murdered Gloria instead, it'd be an open and shut case. No one would think twice as to whether it were me and I'd be safe in England forever. I remember Frank staring out over the gardens as though he were looking into the pit of hell at the prospect that his beloved president could've be wrapped up in murder.'

Frank interjected. 'Despite Marilyn's theory, I didn't really buy it, but I think I got to the bottom of it. If the president was involved in any way at all, I believe it was after the event. Once the deed was done and nothing could be done to save Gloria, he instructed Bobby to manipulate the press into printing the suicide story.'

'I even began to wonder whether Gloria's murder had been on the cards from the beginning,' said Norma. 'If Jack were capable of murder, what would've happened if he'd tired of me? And what about the coroner? When he examined every inch of me...I mean Gloria, I'd have been in a fix.'

'He wouldn't have been a problem,' said Frank, with conviction in his tone.

'How so?' asked Murray, wondering whether Frank had been more entrenched in the original event than he was prepared to admit.

Frank seemed to sense Murray's scrutiny. 'The coroner would've been sworn to secrecy as soon as the event happened. The autopsy results went awol too, to hide the truth that the body wasn't Marilyn's. You'll never find any evidence to prove otherwise so don't even bother trying.'

Norma changed the subject to events after Gloria's death. 'I remember when we got here, I was sure there were bugs and cameras in every room. As for Gloria, I couldn't stop thinking about her; even though she hadn't been my favourite person. The thought that she was laid out in some mortuary made me feel real bad. The only thing I was grateful for was that my housekeeper had kept her mouth shut. Only Jack, Bobby and her, knew about Gloria.'

Murray spoke at last, jolting her from a spectacular story. 'There's been a lot of speculation about your...I mean Marilyn's death. Did you get the truth when you finally spoke to Jack?'

'Before I spoke to him, Frank told me Jack'd told him things were not as bad as they seemed. I said it was bad whichever way the cookie crumbled. Gloria was dead and I was drinking champagne every day!'

'Everything we've told you detective, came from the very top,' said Frank.

'Lets run by it all again just so I've really got your take on things,' said Murray.

'This is exactly how it was told to me,' said Frank.

'Turns out Bobby paid Gloria a visit the night Marilyn got away. He was acting under the president's instructions, letting Gloria know Marilyn would be away for good.'

'That's as maybe,' said Norma, butting in angrily. 'But I still wonder what else he told her? That, because I'd quit Hollywood she could become me and take over my life?'

Frank smiled at Norma. 'What good would that've done? Everyone knew there was only one Marilyn Monroe.'

'This is the only time I ever get pissed with you Frank, for making light of what was a big mess. And all because Gloria had gotten greedy and Bobby wouldn't cough up with the extra dough.'

'Do you think there's a possibility it might have been Bobby who killed her?' asked Murray, putting the money issue on hold.

'He wasn't that sort of man,' said Frank.

'But he sure was mad because she was hooched up while they were arguing,' said Norma. 'He wouldn't leave his wife for her. Turns out she told him if he wouldn't do just that, she'd only be a stand-in until she was paid extra, and then she was out.'

'Bobby tried reasoning with her but she having none of it,' added Frank.

Norma interrupted. 'Plus she said she'd read my journal and knew lots of stuff none of the Kennedys would want to get leaked to the press. I was furious. I kept them locked away. I thought it was just my clothes and makeup she'd been helping herself to.'

'Her death was an accident,' said Frank. 'She lashed out at Bobby, he tried to restrain her, but she fell and hit her head. Simple as that.'

'You both really believe that?' asked Murray,

wondering whether the Kennedys had literally got away with murder.

'Bobby was inconsolable when he reported back to the president, having already had Gloria's body removed and the bungalow cleaned up,' said Frank.

Norma plucked herself from the past and looked at Murray. 'Why didn't I see it coming? We should've paid Gloria off sooner. I could've made an announcement that I was gonna quit show business. The studios were used to me stitching them up.'

'You clearly didn't realise how serious your situation had become, ' said Murray. 'It's always easy to imagine what one would've done differently with hindsight.'

'I've come to realise that Gloria was dead the moment she agreed to the whole damn charade,' sighed Norma.

Frank remained silent.

'I think it's important for your investigation that I repeat this again,' Norma continued. 'I was in a good place in the summer of nineteen-sixty-two. Happier than I'd ever been and I definitely wasn't about to end it all. Not this time.'

'What had happened to change your state of mind so radically?' asked Murray, looking up from his notebook, wishing that even the smallest part of what she had said so far was true.

'My acting offers were looking real good. I 'd already signed a new deal. There were two men genuinely crazy about me - Joe and Jack. I loved them both, but still had to tell Joe that I couldn't marry him again. I wasn't looking forward to doing that. Either way, things were looking up, so it seemed ironic that someone was gonna give me a beating.'

'Or kill you,' said Murray.

Norma shivered. 'When Gloria died, I lived in fear that someone would find out I'd gotten away and kill me in my sleep,' she added, drawing a line across her throat with her hand. 'Though I'd been placed with people like Joe and Frank to protect me, when Jack was assassinated, who was pulling the strings with regards to my safety? So I decided to write a fresh journal to replace the ones I'd left behind in my bungalow. I was open about the fact that I was writing again. I made sure everyone in this house saw me writing. My journal was my life insurance if you like.'

'Clever thinking,' said Murray.

'The Kennedys' reputation lay in my hands. While Jack was still alive, there was always the chance I'd fall out of favour with him. His life was continuing in the States. Holed up here, it was easy to forget that I was still Marilyn Monroe, wanted by him above all other women.'

'So when you did eventually hear from him, did you get the impression that his feelings for you were the same?'

'For sure, in fact for a guy he was unusually emotional. He also told me pretty much the same story Frank had told me, but he also mentioned that Gloria was traumatised at the way I'd been dragged out, not because she liked me, which she didn't, but because it could've been her instead. It didn't make any difference in the end anyway. She was dead soon after.'

'So hence the cover up that we know about today?'

'Absolutely. But did you know detective, that the coroner said the body on his slab didn't look much like me and, that whoever it was had let themselves go? It's a shame you can't speak to some of my friends who saw me, just a week before. You could ask them how I looked in comparison to what the coroner saw.'

'Who were these other people you mention?'

'Jack Lemmon, Debbie Reynolds.'

Murray noted their names.

'It's no good. They're both gone. But they'd tell you how I'd bounced back. I'd begun to restyle myself and had ideas for acting roles I wanted. And if you want more evidence, one Hollywood columnist lied and said he'd sneaked into my bungalow. Spread the word he'd seen my body and agreed with the coroner that I had dirty nails and my hair was grey at the roots. Well little did he know, he wasn't looking at me. He was looking at Gloria.'

'I find it hard to believe the truth has never been uncovered,' said Murray all of a sudden. 'No disrespect intended, but I'm a long way from buying into such an incredulous story.'

Although frail, Norma all of a sudden found some anger from deep inside. 'Why would it be uncovered, detective?' she exploded. 'There was never a proper investigation. Plus the key witnesses couldn't make up their damn minds just what happened on the night Gloria died. Some of the people I thought I knew best, turned up during the night to ogle. We could've had a party if I'd been there!' she added, sarcastically. 'Some loyalty. The scum all lied because they were plain scared of whoever did it.'

'So who, Norma, in your opinion did the deed?' said Murray, calmly, thinking that by asking the same questions again, Norma or Frank might slip up and change their story.

'Any or all of them. It certainly wasn't the bogeyman,' said Norma, with reference to the darker side of freemasonry. 'Believe me, I've read all the books about it. If Gloria's death wasn't so tragic, I'd find some of the theories almost funny. But it makes me mad, real mad.'

Murray continued to scribble in his notebook then he looked up hoping for some sort of sign. Finally he spoke. 'I'll come again tomorrow if that's alright.'

'Unless by tomorrow your superiors conclude I'm simply deranged, as you so obviously already do,' said Norma sulkily.

Murray needed time to come to terms with the things that had been put to him. He said his goodbyes and made his way downstairs. In his mind, his notebook was as valuable as Marilyn Monroe's journals. He slipped his hand into his pocket and gripped his notes firmly.

Frank watched from the galleried landing until Geraldine had closed the front door, then returned to Norma's suite. 'Do you want to be alone for a while?' he asked.

'You'd better stay, at least until DC Murray's left the grounds.'

'I'd like to be there when he tells his superiors,' said Frank.

'If they're anything like the FBI, then this place will be swarming with cops within hours,' said Norma, pulling herself up from the chair.

'To see a crazy old dame?'

'No, not a crazy old dame. Marilyn Monroe.' She adopted an erotic pose that was inappropriate for her years.

'Let's hope he buys it,' said Frank.

Norma walked across the room and threw open the doors to her balcony. 'Let's sit out here until we get the all clear.'

Frank lit a cigarette. He took a few drags and followed

her gaze to the horizon. 'You're mighty fine at the play-acting. You were pretty convincing in there.'

'D'you think so?'

'You even had me believing you were Marilyn,' he laughed, taking a drag. 'How do you remember all that detail?' he asked.

Norma laughed. 'It's easy. I've done my homework. If DC Murray's convinced and this story breaks, the press will want to pay serious dollars for the story.'

Suddenly a text arrived on Frank's phone. 'The coast is clear. He's gone.'

Norma laughed out loud. 'Good. I need to get this lot off before I burst into flames.'

She went to the adjoining bedroom and sat at a dressing table. She took off her cotton gloves and silver wig and released the wafer thin prosthetic mask that blended perfectly with the skin around the base of her neck and hairline. Her cheeks and forehead were blotchy where the latex had caused her to sweat. She ran her fingers through her honey-blonde hair. After cleansing her skin, she applied a light foundation and changed into her own clothes. By the time she had finished and gone back into the lounge, Frank had a glass of Scotch in one hand and a glass of red wine in the other.

'Cheers to a good performance Mary,' he said.

Mary chinked glasses with him. 'Bit early in the day.'

'I'm drinking to the fact you remembered everything you'd been told.'

She laughed. 'How could I forget? I've been well-tutored by the best.'

Meanwhile, unknown to Mary and Frank, although Murray had made up his mind early on in the conversation, he was now completely sure that the woman who had addressed herself as Norma, was either an obsessive fan of Marilyn Monroe, or as he had originally thought, part of the scam of the century.

Chapter 10

Reflections

The sun was already blazing down, its beams lighting up everything they touched, as Frank and Mary strolled through the gardens the following morning. Frank was on high alert but covering it well, as from his point of view Mary looked worried.

'Do you think DC Murray will be back today?' she asked, not aware that her nervousness was that obvious.

Frank took off his suit jacket and slung it over his shoulder, exposing his black leather holster against his crisp white shirt. 'Maybe,' he said casually, so as to mask any unease on his part. 'But if he turns up we're ready for him.'

Mary stopped to admire some particularly fragrant roses. 'I'll be much happier when he's off our backs,' she said.

Frank held out a hand to help her step over a fallen tree. 'Let me worry about Murray. Anyway, there's too much at stake to stop now.'

'But what about when the story reaches the States?

How long do you think we'll all be safe here then?'

'It'll all be over by then,' said Frank, all at once deeply saddened by his own comment.

Mary's expression clouded over. 'I can't bear to think about that.' She hesitated then changed the subject. 'I'm feeling a bit jittery being out here. Let's make our way back soon.'

'No one's gonna get through security. Not now Dave's on top of it,' said Frank, authoritatively.

Mary stopped and this time cupped a rose in her hand. It was one of thousands blossoming on untamed climbers around the grounds. 'But they've got in before,' she said suddenly, wincing as she pricked her finger on a thorn. She peered through the trees towards the top of the perimeter wall, half expecting to see someone cutting the barbed wire in an attempt to climb over.

'That was just kids. You've gotta stop acting all het-up,' said Frank.

Mary sat on the same log where Frank had found Olivia's phone and picked up a leaf. She stripped it bare as she had done when a child, until it was nothing but a stringy skeleton.

Frank watched her. 'You're so much like how I remember Marilyn from way back when. It's kinda weird.'

'Well I would be, wouldn't I? Apart from the obvious, I'm a West End actor, remember. I've worked hard to get into the role.'

'Are you missing London?' asked Frank, taking out a cigarette.

'Not while I can be part of this. Plus I hate the press with a vengeance. I get a kick out of knowing they've no idea what's going on.'

'Let's hope we can keep things that way until it suits us

otherwise,' said Frank.

'Challenging to say the least. Especially for you,' said Mary, thoughtfully. She picked up another leaf and repeated the process of stripping it bare.

'Cigarette?' asked Frank, noticing that her hands were shaking.

She took one and lit it from his. Then she stood up and began to walk along the gravel drive towards the main gates.

Frank followed close behind. 'Don't go too far Mary. Can't afford for you to be seen by a snooper.'

Mary ignored his request and continued on, until she came to a fork in the drive. To the left, multiple tyre marks showed it was used constantly. To the right, an abandoned gravel section snaked away into the distance. It was littered with piles of leaves and fallen branches. Mary began to pick her way along it while Frank scanned the grounds nearest to her. The seclusion of this part of the grounds stirred Mary's memory of playing outside as a child. Soon she reached the perimeter wall. She could hear the drone of cars in the distance, travelling on the dual carriageway to and from Oxford, but noticed that other than that there was little noise pollution. 'I can't hear any traffic in the lane,' she said, thinking it strange.

'No one can pass this way anymore. I've blocked off both ends of the lane,' said Frank, now on high alert with Mary being so far from the house and with only him to protect her.

'You can't just go round decommissioning roads Frank. Before you know it, the council will be here investigating as well as local residents,' said Mary, vaguely amused at his audaciousness.

He laughed. 'Get real, Mary. Have you noticed the state

of British roads? Anyway, the public have been easy to fool. We put out roadworks signs.'

Mary nodded her head in disbelief at Frank, as they approached a pair of ornate gates sandwiched between two massive gateposts. The bars of the gates were strangled by brambles and more climbing roses.

'Keep out of sight,' said Frank, his hand reaching inside his suit jacket as a precautionary measure.

Mary peeped through the bars at the unused lane. 'A shame such beautiful gates aren't used anymore. They're the stuff of fairy tales,' she said, romanticising about who might have used the entrance when the manor house was first built.

'Quit with the schmaltzy stuff. We should head back,' insisted Frank. He turned about and beckoned for her to follow. A that precise second his phone bleeped, making Mary jump. He read the new text and reacted instantly. 'Mary, move yourself. Murray's back. Get back to the house while I hold him off.'

She floundered, looking in every direction like a panicked fox being pursued by the hunt. She was uncertain of the quickest route to avoid being seen when Murray's car swept up the drive.

'Go. Now! They've not let him in yet.' Frank turned and walked briskly out of sight. He made his way across the grass, keeping the high wall to his right. Not far away was the gatehouse that Olivia White had stumbled across, hidden behind rhododendron bushes. Through the windows multiple screens flashed images of the estate.

Mary criss-crossed the grass and gravel drives, picking out the most secluded route, glad of her flat shoes. By the time she had climbed the stairs to the galleried landing, she was so hot that she doubted she would be able to don a disguise and carry off a convincing act.

She reversed the process of the day before, dressing first and leaving the prosthetics and wig until last to allow her face to cool from her exertion. She was adept at applying her stage face in double-quick time, having practised it for such an event many times over.

It seemed like no time had passed when all of a sudden, there was the sound of voices from the hallway. Frank's voice was much louder than Murray's, warning of their approach. There was an urgent knock at the door. Mary settled herself into a chair by the hearth, glad that Geraldine had not made up the fire. Her face was flushed and the prosthetics she had applied were already making her feel uncomfortably claustrophobic.

Frank entered with Murray in tow. 'You have a visitor,' said Frank, checking Mary's appearance discreetly.

'Hello again detective,' she said, trying to sound welcoming while struggling to keep her breathing relaxed. 'I wondered if we might see you today.' She gestured for him to sit in the other wing chair.

'Good morning - Norma. How are you today?' Murray asked. 'You sound a little out of breath.'

'I am ninety-one detective,' she replied, to hide the fact that she had been rushing. 'But thank you for asking how I am. Have you or your superiors already made a decision?' she asked, steering him away from her symptoms.

'Not yet,' said Murray, economically. He sat down and took out his notebook and pen, noticing suddenly that Frank's normally highly polished shoes were splattered with mud as was the hem of his trousers. He decided not to challenge Frank immediately as to the reason why.

'So it's just your curiosity that brings you here again?' asked Mary, fanning her face with a delicate silk fan.

'You could put it like that,' said Murray, conscious that she did not look as highly groomed as the day before. Her complexion was somewhat waxy and her hair less coiffured as when they had first met. 'Are you well enough for a second interview?'

'If you mean I don't look myself, I didn't sleep too well,' said Mary, inwardly worrying that she was about to be rumbled. 'The dogs were barking for most of the goddamn night.'

She need not have worried as Murray was satisfied with her response, although he was still pondering over Frank's less than pristine appearance. 'Once I've finished here, I'll be heading back to London.'

'So, what would you like to know today?' asked Mary, finally recovered from rushing in order to disguise herself.

'I'd like you to tell me more about your journey to England back in sixty-three.'

'You mean sixty-two,' Mary corrected him, already one step ahead.

'Oh yes - sorry. My mistake,' said Murray.

Mary studied his expression. 'I wonder, was it a mistake, or were you trying to trip me up? I'll warn you, setting traps won't work, because everything you've heard so far is the absolute truth.'

Murray wasn't the type of man to blush, but he could not determine whether it was the heat from the day or how critical his questioning was that was making him overheat. He had planned the tripwires and already he had been caught out. Before he could gather his thoughts together, unexpectedly a fresh voice joined the conversation, coming from the adjoining doorway to the bedroom.

'Why don't you let me tell the story?'

Mary, Frank and Murray turned in unison. Murray's head began to spin as he looked first at the woman he had all along called Norma, then to the elderly woman standing in the doorway leaning heavily on a stick. They seemed to be twins. 'What is this?' he asked, continuing to look from one to the other.

'Mother, what are you doing out of bed. We can handle this,' said Mary. Her voice had suddenly changed from American to that of someone English and much younger, which made her elderly appearance seem all the more odd to Murray.

'Stop fussing Mary! Go and remove that ridiculous mask and wig, then come sit by me,' said the woman, still standing in the doorway, but looking as though she might fall.

Frank leapt from his chair and took her arm. 'Ma'am, you shouldn't be out of bed. You should be resting.'

Mary stood up with no further comment and left the room, no longer pretending to be infirm.

'Frank, you might want to fix the young detective a stiff drink. He looks very pale,' said the elderly woman.

'What's going on?' asked Murray finally, anger clear in his voice to everyone present.

'And you are?' asked the woman with a weak smile as Frank seated her on a third chair and went over to her cocktail cabinet.

'DC Murray. From Scotland Yard. And I'm the one asking the questions around here,' said Murray. To say that he was confused was an understatement. He forgot his work ethics and readily accepted the offer of Scotch.

Frank kept an eye on the unfolding situation as he poured drinks and passed them around.

'What sort of scam is this?' continued Murray, snatching his Scotch from Frank. 'Can anyone tell me their real name?'

'There is no scam,' said the woman, with a broad smile crossing her face. 'Mary is my daughter. She was disguised as me and is the one you've been happily calling Norma. She did it well don't you think?'

'I for one, do not find this anything to be amused about. I need a genuine explanation right now,' said Murray, his anger rising to another level.

'Of course,' said the woman. 'But you might not make it back to Oxford today.'

'Why's that - are you going to set the dogs on me? The Yard knows I'm here.'

She laughed. 'Why of course we won't set the dogs on you, detective. We're not crooks or murderers.' She introduced herself properly. 'Detective, I'm the one you need to speak to. You see, Mary and Frank were simply protecting me.' She went off at a tangent. 'Coincidentally, my housekeeper in LA was named Murray. I trusted her. Let's hope as you have the same name, you manage to continue that trend.'

Murray took a few gulps of his Scotch. He was as hot and waxy as Mary had been a few moments before due to her complex disguise. He emptied his glass and held it out for Frank to refill it. 'Get to the point quickly Miss... whoever you are.'

'Really detective, you may be angry and I understand why, but please show me a little respect. I am after all, the real Marilyn Monroe. It's as simple as that.'

'Really?' answered Murray, sarcastically, refusing to be taken in.

'Yes - really. So now I've come clean with no hesitation,

I would be most grateful if you let us off our... shall we say... our little performance and not tell anyone you've met me. Until after I'm gone?'

Murray was beginning to gain his composure as the whisky coursed through his veins. He toyed with the information he had surrendered to Scotland Yard overnight and the fact that this woman was as anglicised as Mary had been, despite the remnants of an American accent still evident when she spoke. He was used to negotiation, but he had never come across such well-practised scam artists. He had been fooled the day before, and now he had to watch their play-acting all over again. It was becoming tedious and he was having trouble getting his head round the ins and outs.

He sat for a few seconds looking at the woman while she looked at him, trying to see something that would convince him either way of her true identity. But no matter how hard he tried, it was the same as when he had looked at Mary in her clever get up. All he could see now was a withered old lady. He would not be made fun of. The law was the law. 'Any more lies and I'll charge you all,' he said at last.

The woman sighed openly. 'Everything you've heard so far was not manufactured in any way, but just told to you by the wrong person. Mary just happens to be well tutored. But as for me, you have no idea how much information I have on the Kennedys. I know too much for my own good. Now my life is nearly over, all Frank and Mary want for me, is that it will end peacefully and that the truth will eventually come out.'

'And what if I was to agree to your request?' asked Murray, pretending, in order to draw the woman out, knowing full well that he in reality he could not promise anything. He made a mental note to not forgive any of them for wasting his time.

'We'll comply,' said Mary simply, appearing through the doorway without a disguise.

Murray was immediately taken with her likeness to the Marilyn Monroe he knew from decades old photographs, despite this woman Mary being in her fifties. He was clearly transparent, as his current thought percolated across to the elderly lady.

'So detective, call me Marilyn from now on,' she said, beckoning Mary to her side.

'I prefer Norma,' said Murray, still angry and fed up with all the confusion and lies. 'After all, Mary was happy to adopt that name, so you can carry on where she left off,' he growled.

'As you wish,' said the woman. 'So to be clear for all our sakes, I'm to be Norma from now on, that is until I convince you of the truth.'

Murray pressed on. 'I'm going to need you to start from the beginning so I can cross check your stories.'

Norma hesitated before beginning her version of things. 'I've spent many happy years in England detective, with Mary and Frank and other friends I'd rather not involve in this conversation. People I can trust. But let's make one thing clear from the start. I didn't want to come. I was beginning to get my life in order and looking forward to a lucrative deal with the studios.'

'So I've already heard from Mary. I don't how long it took to teach her all these details, but why let her pretend to be you?' asked Murray.

'Believe me, we argued a lot about that. I was totally opposed from the moment the idea was put to me. Since she was a teenager and understood what had happened back in the States, she'd feared someone might find out I was alive and come for me.'

'So as her mother, you let her be the target for would-be attackers,' said Murray more as a statement than a question, bewildered as to why any mother would risk her daughter's safety in such a way.

Offended by Murray's take on her actions, Norma defended her corner. 'You've seen how good security is. Frank had hoped we'd get adequate warning of a serious breach. None of us expected Mary would need to use the disguise. And if you want to argue about it, let's not forget - you were fooled,' she added, smiling.

'It was still a ridiculous gamble,' said Murray, not used to being deceived so effectively. 'How can you be sure Mary wouldn't have been hurt before security could stop any intruders?'

Frank jumped in. 'We're all on the same page detective and...'

'And it scares me rigid thinking of what might happen,' interrupted Norma. 'But I'm old and Mary's a force of nature. I can't stop her from doing what she wants. Not anymore.'

'It's not much of a life, being holed up here is it?' asked Murray, changing the subject.

'I've grown to love it, although the first two years were difficult. I take it Mary has already explained why,' said Norma.

'Yes, she has, but I'd like to hear it from you,' said Murray.

'At first I just wandered corridors, trying locked doors, peeking through keyholes. When I tired of that, and not being allowed in the gardens so soon, I spent time in the library. Fortunately it was well stocked. As time went on, I ventured out, first just in the gardens, then further afield. When I was younger I quite enjoyed disguising myself so folks wouldn't know who I was. I guess Mary inherited the desire to act. Anyway, I visited the ocean many times. It reminded me of home. Frank always came with me, but sometimes I found ways to slip past him, usually while he was buying train tickets. On one occasion he found me before the train set off, so we spent the day in London together. After that he always stuck close.'

'Why use the train instead of driving into town?' asked Murray, looking for any holes in Norma's story that might differ from Mary's.

'I'd have thought the answer to that was obvious. Frank couldn't defend me at the wheel of a car.'

'What did you do in London?' asked Murray, trying repeatedly to think of a tripwire question as she dished out cleverly prepared answers.

'It was just the one time. We had what you Brits call afternoon tea. At The Ritz. Then we went to a department store because I wanted to buy perfume. I still remember it vividly. The shop assistant tried to sell me Chanel Number Five. She couldn't understand why I got the giggles when she sprayed it on my wrist.'

'What was it about buying perfume that was so amusing?' asked Murray.

'I made Chanel what it was. Even fifty years later they used my name in their advertising. Poor girl, if only she'd known who she was serving.'

Feeling foxed, Murray turned his attention to Mary. It made him feel better to be right about some aspect of the unfolding case. 'Your accent and lack of American phrasing let you down at least once,' he said, for a second feeling as though he had the upper hand.

She came straight back at him. 'I was ready for you if you'd queried it detective. Remember, I've been in England all my life. Plus we weren't expecting you so I had no time to rehearse,' she said, inwardly cursing her acting skills.

'She was born here,' clarified Norma. 'Seven months after I arrived. So you see it wasn't just me that needed protection. I had her to think of.'

Murray continued writing. 'I see,' he said, not at first grasping the importance of her statement.

'Do you really see?' asked Norma.

'Of course. You wouldn't want your child mixed up in the potentially dangerous situation you were in,' said Murray.

'You're making light of the facts. It was far more serious than that. Mary was the daughter of my darling Jack. The president of the United States.'

Murray looked up from his notebook in disbelief, stunned into silence.

Norma's expression changed as she reminisced. 'It was the saddest moment of my life leaving Jack at that airport. I knew I was with child, but I decided to keep it quiet until we were safely away. I had no idea where we were going until we landed and Frank told me where we were.'

'So when did you plan to tell the president?' asked Murray.

'Firstly, I didn't want him to know until I was well into the pregnancy. I'd had many miscarriages. And also I didn't want to tell him on the telephone. I was so scared someone might be listening in. In the end, I didn't tell anyone it was his, not even Frank, until after she was born. When Jack was assassinated, it was Mary that kept me going. She was part of him - all that I had left, so in a sense he lived on.' She looked wistfully out of the window to her favourite hills. 'Jack did meet Mary though. Just the once, when he came to England in nineteen-sixty-three. He was murdered only a few months later.'

'Tell me about that,' said Murray.

Norma hesitated and gathered herself up. 'When you get back to Scotland Yard, find some old film footage of Jack's visit. You'll see how unhappy he looked. He came across with Jackie after their brief stop in Ireland. He'd tried everything to stop her coming to England with him so that we might meet up somehow.'

'How did you get close to him on an official visit?' asked Murray, finding the thought that she could have slipped through tight security, ludicrous to say the least. He might already have found a yawning chasm in her storytelling.

'I must admit detective, I found it a bit of a thrill. He knew his itinerary well before he came of course. It was going to be difficult, but I received intelligence that he would be attending a Catholic service not far from Brighton. I'd gotten right to the front of the crowd by the time he arrived at the chapel. I thought he might leave as soon as he came out, but knowing I'd be there, he insisted to his agents that he wanted to speak to the people who'd been waiting outside. His agents were mad when he broke protocol. It was a hoot watching them bristling with testosterone. Anyway, he shook hands with people and accepted flowers from young children. To this day, I still can't believe his agents didn't spot me even with my disguise. But then, why would they? I was dead to them.'

'Did Jack acknowledge you?' asked Murray, still convinced that such a story was too far-fetched and more befitting to a conspiracy novel.

'Not at first, but as he walked along the line of people I winked at him. That was when he saw Mary for the first time. Despite trying to act normal, I could see it was difficult for him. She was asleep in my arms despite all the villagers shouting out. He kissed Mary's forehead. I could feel him trembling as his hand shook mine so tightly. That's when he gave me a piece of folded up paper.'

'A note?' asked Murray.

'Yes. It was his way of saying goodbye after the night before. He'd been staying at Macmillan's house. I have the note still if you'd like to see it,' said Norma.

Murray decided to make it a priority to organise a handwriting comparison as soon as she had given it to him. 'What about the night before?'

'I met up with him,' said Norma. 'I don't expect you to believe me, but it's true. He got me in. Though I had to be incognito at three in the morning. His agents thought I was just a floozy.'

'But didn't you say his wife Jackie was with him?' asked Murray.

'Sometimes they had separate suites because of his back problems.'

Murray looked to Frank for confirmation.

'It's all true detective,' said Frank. 'You have no idea how difficult it was to plan. But then what the president wanted, the president got, and I organised it from this end.'

'We had twenty minutes together,' said Norma, a smile lighting up her face. 'Mary was with Frank. It was enough to show each other how we felt. We couldn't use Jack's suite in case the housekeeper got wind of me being in the house. It was extremely undignified. There's not much room in a broom closet and poor Jack's back was particularly bad on that trip, so I had to be gentle.' She smiled an all-knowing smile. 'That was the last time I saw him apart from on TV. Don't you think it ironic detective, that he had a daughter waiting for him in England but he and Jackie lost a baby in the August of sixty-three?' Her expression changed from the joy of the memory of a few snatched moments to desolation. 'After that, he continued with the charade that was his life. He had other affairs.'

'Why would he have other affairs if he was so in love with you?' asked Murray. 'And if what you say is true, why would you want to be involved with such a man when you could've had anyone?'

'His affairs were a smokescreen. When we were seeing each other, we both agreed that we should be seen with other people to throw the press off the scent. I did the same with Bobby although nothing happened between us. We let people believe what they wanted to believe.'

'Who were some of Jack's affairs with?' asked Murray, making a mental note to check out the finer detail later.

'Mary Meyer and Judith Exner,' said Norma, recalling exact names with ease. Mary Meyer was murdered in nineteen-sixty-four. Don't you think that's a bit of a coincidence after what happened to Gloria? Both in the space of two years? '

'And how about you? Who were you seeing?' asked Murray.

'There was no one once I came to England. Mary and Jack were my life. When Jack was murdered I swore I'd never fall in love again,' said Norma with conviction.

Murray turned back the pages in his notebook and thumbed through Mary and Norma's statements to see if he could see a discrepancy. He changed his line of questioning. 'So let's recap. Although you came to England before Gloria's murder, you clearly had fears for your own safety before that happened.'

'That's right, but not for one moment did I think I'd be bumped off. As to whether it was fate intervening that made Gloria the victim, I don't know. It could've been planned all along. She spent more time at the bungalow than me, while I was out and about. It was only towards the end that things heated up, when she told Jack about the threats. I think she was preying on his manliness, hoping he would charge in and protect her. In retrospect I think she wanted him to herself. It was very soon after that, that I was on a plane to England.'

'Tell me your version of that flight and the plane you flew in,' said Murray, aviation history a subject he was expert in.

Norma suddenly seemed more frail. 'I'm not sure I can talk anymore today detective. The memory even now breaks my heart in two.'

Murray suspected she was stalling because she probably could not accurately name an aircraft type from that era. 'Frank was with you. Do you mind if he gives me his version?'

'Yes Frank, you tell it,' she said, sitting back and closing her eyes so she could picture the scene.

Frank began discussing the itinerary. 'The first part of our journey was planned so we could arrive at dusk and have less chance of being seen. We used Hollywood Burbank rather than the main airport for security reasons. We made a couple of stops, refuelling at Chicago Midway and then went on to Newfoundland. It was morning by then so I insisted on staying there, so we'd all grab some shut-eye. In the end Marilyn couldn't sleep, despite being exhausted. We flew direct from there to the UK.'

'Was she told the destination?' asked Murray, trying to recall whether it was Mary or Norma that had mentioned they were in the dark with regards to that.

'No, she was told nothing,' said Frank. 'Me and the hostess were the only ones to talk to her. The hostess had been briefed to keep her mouth shut if Marilyn started asking questions. But there is something else you should know detective.'

'And that is?' asked Murray, wondering why all of a sudden Frank was so forthcoming.

'I heard later that the hostess died soon after that trip. I've often wondered whether she was silenced to prevent her from blabbing to the press.'

'I'll need specific details of the flight and all the crew,' said Murray.

'You won't find it on any aviation records. I'm sure of it,' said Frank. 'But what I can tell you is that the weather was something else when we approached the UK. We nearly had to find somewhere else to set down due to one helluva cross-wind. When we did touchdown we were all mighty relieved. The rest is history. A car was waiting, and we came back here.'

'Had my future not been determined for me detective, I would have ordered the captain to turn around,' said Norma, having opened her eyes suddenly. 'Believe me, I wanted nothing more than to sit on a Malibu beach with the sun on my shoulders.'

'Along with the rest of us,' said Murray, his quip an attempt to keep her lifted and willing to continue for a while longer so that he could catch her out.

'I need to rest now,' she said. 'If there's nothing else,

please remember my request to keep this under wraps.' She stood up, aided by Frank and Mary. 'I've told you all there is. I doubt we'll meet again.'

Her directness concerning imminent death made Murray feel inclined to stand to show respect as she left the room. Whoever she was - he was fascinated, despite her willingness to dismiss him in such a matter-of-fact way.

Chapter 11

A Storm is Coming

As she nestled under her candy floss pink satin eiderdown on a sumptuous four poster bed, Norma thought about her last few hours of interrogation at the hands of the young detective. She closed her eyes so that she could concentrate. For the moment she felt safe from the outside world, but she could not help but mull over whether she had just revealed her past just a little too theatrically to DC Murray. He had explained with clarity the reasons for his visits, but questioned her relentlessly. Now he had gone, leaving suddenly, as though there were no tomorrow. She wondered whether he would return. She hoped that if he did, he would accept that she was indeed the celebrity she had claimed to be. She sighed. Even she knew that her story was far-fetched. Whatever the truth, it was more likely that however hard she tried to convince him, DC Murray would continue to call her Norma, a name she did not care for, even though it resonated with her some days more than others .When she had unrolled her story in glorious detail, the look on Murray's face had suggested that he had concluded she was either deluded, or worse still an out-and-out liar. His attitude upset her, but he was not the only one to doubt the legitimacy of her ornamented memories. Now she was into her nineties, her mind was fragmenting, making the past appear to her like an incomplete jigsaw puzzle. More recently, she had accepted that most of the time she was forgetful. She told herself repeatedly that it had to be something to do with getting old. Despite this, and with no warning, her mind began to buzz and fizz until a scene popped into her head with razor sharp clarity.

She was a young woman again, on her last ever flight out of the United States to England, only hours away from when Jack had held her so tenderly at the airport. It seemed as though it had occurred a matter of days before her first encounter with DC Murray, even though in truth, it must have been fifty-five years ago, at the beginning of the nineteen-sixties. How she missed those times, when fashion, music and conversation was so much more colourful than in the twenty-first century. Back then, people as a rule readily engaged with each other without texting instead and would talk and debate face to face for hours, about things that really mattered.

Norma felt as though her heart was in a vice like grip, so much so, that the urge to order the captain to turn the plane around made her want to leap up from her seat and demand it of him.

She concentrated on relaxing so she could hold on

tightly to the images that were dancing across her retinas, and was soon midway between wakefulness and sleep. She willed her mind to stay in the past for awhile. It was a game she enjoyed, pretending to be a transcendental traveller. She had the urge to escape old age and feel the force of youth pulsing through her arteries once again. She took a few deep breaths and waited, not knowing what to expect.

Within seconds, she felt her invisible form land noiselessly, her toes cushioned by a luxurious soft carpet. Straight away it was clear that despite the pleasant sensation, she was not where she wanted to be, which was back at Hollywood Burbank in the arms of the one man she loved so much, that it hurt. Her dream had deposited her instead as an elderly will-o-the-wisp passenger into a luxuriously-appointed cabin of a DC6 airliner, flying high above the clouds. She knew instantly by the body language of the cabin crew and other passengers, that none of them could see her ethereal form or sense her presence. But then there was no reason why they should, as they were part of her dream too. She could do with these people whatever she wanted. Hang them upside down from the ceiling or make them appear naked if she so wished, but as she was not feeling mischievous she decided to leave well alone. On this occasion, from her viewpoint it was as though she were looking through a broken telescope. The edges of the scene were blurred, the peripheral detail such as the night sky outside the cabin out of range.

She stood mesmerised, gazing down at a sensuous woman who was seated by the window all alone. Norma was almost certain that it was her younger self. Marilyn Monroe, beautiful, curvaceous but unusually pale and rather like Snow White in her famous glass coffin. Only there was no doubt that this woman was very much alive as her chest rose and fell with every breath. Dropping in and seeing herself asleep on the right side of forty with curves in all the right places, was a cruel tease for Norma, especially as in reality she knew she was fast approaching death. She flicked such a morose thought away and instead again studied the sleeping woman.

There was a distinct lack of unsightly liver spots and pronounced veins on the backs of Marilyn's hands. Her fingernails were painted bright red, the same shade as her glossy lipstick. Her complexion was flawless and her lips were full, but a furrowed forehead suggested that in sleep she was troubled. Strands of bleached hair were trying to escape from under a brunette wig and headscarf. Marilyn was no doubt, dreaming of her lover, the invisible bond tethering him and her together stretched to breaking point the further the plane travelled. As though that were not enough, betrayal by those in high places had accompanied her like a Judas, all the way from Hollywood Burbank, leaving her pondering whether she had ever had a real friend, or, if she ever would in the future. The light sedative that had been slipped into her cocktail by a stealthy agent, would have failed to diminish her constant yearning for John F. Kennedy, the president of the United States of America.

Usually obsessive of how she looked even as an old woman, Norma continued to look down with envy, imagining how it would be if she could melt into Marilyn's curves and be young again. It would be like sliding into a favourite made-to-measure cocktail dress and doing up the zipper. Marilyn had been writing on a napkin. Norma moved closer still, unseen, so as to see what it was that she had penned.

Somewhere over the ocean. Day one of the rest of my life! What have the agents given me? I'm feeling pretty woozy and what's more, I can't think straight!! I've sorta lost track of the time and the day, and why the heck is it still so dark? I sure as hell don't know where I'm going!

There's music piped into the cabin just for me. What's the betting most folks would think I hadn't heard of Gustav Mahler? Well I have and I just adore him.

Jack's joining me soon, so I'm gotta stay upbeat and not drink so much, or use Reds. Who needs 'em anyway? Not me for sure!!! Every time I think of Jack, perfect Jack, I tingle in places I daren't mention. I can still feel his last kiss. So passionate. So urgent.

Anyway, I've gotta go now. It's getting a bit stormy out there and more than a bit bumpy in here - and I'm kinda finding it hard to write.

See ya.

Norma left the napkin where it was. As seconds ticked by, her mind began to fragment again. She could not remember writing those words and with every passing second, she began to feel unsure of whether she and Marilyn were one and the same person and yet she knew that Marilyn had been a big part of her life. Incapable of body-snatching wizardry, Norma decided to make do with having to cast her mind back. She was sure she was recalling an actual event rather than playing make-believe.

At the time, the flight had seemed to have taken forever, despite her having slept restlessly for a good part of the journey. When awake and with nothing else to do, the magazines on the seat next to her flicked through, she had glanced out of the window at the night sky.

It was crystal clear over the ocean, a large scattering of candy-floss clouds lined in silver suspended between layers of deep blue, putting on a show. She had been drawn to one cloud in particular that bore an uncanny resemblance to a huge white dragon. Even though it possessed hollow sockets for eyes, she imagined it watching her as the plane glided by. As it dispersed, she turned her attention to the moon, which was shimmering like a mystical orb. Lights were twinkling on ships, mirroring those in the heavens.

Norma had the urge to laugh out loud at her poetic memories of long ago, but instead she remained silent, reliving how she had felt at the time, as though she were God sitting up on high, examining his handiwork. Indeed, she wondered whether if he had been able drop in for the ride, he would have been disappointed by what man had done to the planet. It was so goddamn fragile, rather like her - then, and now.

The memory of Jack's tenderness at the airport engulfed her again. She wondered fleetingly whether he meant more to her than she did to him, but the doubt passed before she had time to let doubt settle in and eat away at her. Either way she looked at it, she had been a willing victim, sucked in by the charisma of an elusive man who was larger than life, but swathed in political shadows. Had he told her to throw herself off the Golden Gate Bridge to prove undying love for him, she would have done it, in the blink of an eye. Nevertheless, cruising twenty-five thousand feet above the ocean, nothing seemed certain. He would not be exclusively hers until a wedding band was on her finger.

She switched her thoughts instead to the day when he would join her. Until then, she must wait until the heat died down, as instructed by him, before venturing out to mingle incognito. Her protest at the time scale had fallen on deaf ears. As a lover she could risk defying him if she so wished: tease him, tantalise him, even argue with him, but when he put on his president's hat, she knew she must agree to obey. She was grateful he had sneaked her out by a back door; the undignified escape from her bungalow put into place so quickly. It came at a price however, meaning they would be apart for an equivocal amount of time. Even so, his carefully orchestrated plan would have quickly come apart had she flown from LA International. The press camped out there, like a pack of hungry hyenas, drooling at the prospect of a mouth-watering kill.

Being held captive for her own safety was a new experience, completely out of her hands. It worried her how long she could endure near solitude. What would it be like wherever she was going, away from the limelight that was Hollywood? But tired of being a commodity, she would endeavour to embrace it as a new chapter. She needed time to adjust. But, if something stopped Jack from joining her, life would suddenly stretch out like a grey-slabbed sidewalk disappearing towards the far horizon. How many other icons had chosen to go into hiding, mourned by unsuspecting fans, only to find that solitude was no better than the world they had left behind?

The DC6 had made its difficult descent hindered by a storm that arrived with a fury, making the plane buck and weave. The land beneath had disappeared, masked by a thick blanket of angry-looking cloud. The cabin had vibrated and groaned as the pilot battled with the controls. The elements were stirring things up as a welcome party, distracting her from her thoughts as it beat on the fuselage with giant clenched fists, brandishing its raw beauty in her face.

The agent who had been across the aisle observing her behaviour throughout the flight, sensed her fear. He moved across to sit with her while the storm was at its worst. Having left her seat belt slackened to avoid pressure on her abdomen, she hoped that he would not notice that she was pregnant.

As the DC6 descended through low cloud, she closed her eyes and hummed long-forgotten lullabies to her unborn child. By the time the plane had touched down and taxied to a halt, her sedatives had lost some of their potency.

She descended the slippery metal steps from the plane and stepped onto the runway, only to be greeted by a torrential downpour. Although inwardly broken, she felt safe, cocooned by the Secret Service bodyguards that flanked her as she dodged puddles. As a group they walked briskly across a rain-drenched relic of an airfield that had once seen active service in World War Two. She shivered from the cold biting gusts and icy sideways rain and pulled her cream summer coat around herself for warmth.

For a second, the wind seemed to relent, as though it realised she needed gentle coaxing into her new life. It wrapped itself around her curvaceous form like a protective cloak, shielding her from the storm and from unwelcome glances as it propelled her towards the waiting Jaguar parked outside an insignificant terminal building. She wiped the rain from her sunglasses with the back of her cuff, instantly smearing the lenses and rendering them useless for anything other than masking her identity. Re-tying her silk headscarf, she already resented the fact that her once iconic platinum hair was flattened, hidden by the hated brunette wig that had become her daily camouflage. To add to her misery, her coat belt had come unfastened, causing the metal buckle to flail the back of her legs while she was making a dash for shelter. She yelped in pain as the buckle mercilessly pounded her calves.

By the time she had reached the car, she was soaking wet right through to her silk stockings. Her feet squelched uncomfortably in her kitten heels. The DC6 was already being towed into a hangar, possibly in hiding like her from hostile forces in hot pursuit from the United States of America. The bodyguard who had sat with her on landing, addressed the driver of the Jaguar, but their conversation was instantly carried away on the wind.

He opened the back passenger door and helped her in, sandwiching her between himself and another agent. He offered her a slug from a hip flask that he took from his pocket, expecting her to refuse something that had been drunk from by someone else. It was already laced. She downed the contents while listening to the agent's explanation of what would happen next.

When she woke up, the hedgerows were nothing but a blur, trees and shrubs the shade of a pan of overcooked mushy peas. The weather was worse; flashes of lightning illuminating the sky. She sat up, at first still unable to focus and was told she was in Oxfordshire. The car pulled up at a T-junction, opposite which overhanging trees and large shrubs encroached on what looked like what was once a narrow lane. Although the way seemed blocked, the driver drove the Jaguar straight on. Its suspension bumped and groaned due to potholes disguised by deep puddles. After having made some headway, the way was suddenly barred again, this time by a pair of imposing iron gates set between two high brick pillars. Each pillar was topped by a crumbling stone stag. The driver braked and flashed his headlights. Seconds later, yellow torchlight flashed from behind the gates, mimicking his signal.

The agent she had rested against reached inside his jacket and took out a high calibre gun, before getting out, sheltering himself behind the open door and shouting a nonsensical code to whoever was the other side of the gate. Satisfied with the verbal response and backed up by a few more flashes from the torch's owner, he returned to sit by her side.

The nausea brought on by her alcohol induced sleep was passing and as a result her sense of humour was returning. She remembered thinking of the car as not offering much protection as it was not what she was accustomed to. She had referred to it as a rust-bucket, despite being reassured by the agent next to her that it was as safe as the president's. In her mind, adding a few bullet-holes would have made it more like travelling in a watering can.

As the gates were heaved open by two pairs of strong hands belonging to broad-shouldered suited agents, the driver opened the window and spoke to one of them. He leaned in through the open window and glanced curiously at the scared woman in the back seat, then patted the roof of the car and waved the driver in. The gates were closed again, their bars illuminated by more flashes of lightning. A black car that had been parked unobtrusively by a nearby gatehouse was ready to follow behind. As it pulled away, another man came out of the building accompanied by two large dogs.

This was it. This was gaol.

After travelling along the twisty shingle drive, which was lined by an avenue of mature oak trees and rhododendron bushes, a large house began to emerge, lit only by a few lights visible in the central section. The car circled a large stone circle, in the centre of which there was an impressive fountain, illuminated by the moon, which reflected on the surface of the water. The black car that had followed behind, pulled up.

She was helped out by her personal agent who by now had introduced himself as Frank. The others clustered around her like a colony of penguins sheltering from an Arctic storm, as she moved towards a steep flight of marble steps to the large house. The door was opened by a woman resembling a character from an old black and white movie. Her face had an unnatural and sickly pallor, her age hard to define due to the fact that her hair had been scraped back so tightly into a grey bun. It gave her the appearance that she had indulged in a brow lift. Her plain black calf-length dress, starched white apron and flat black shoes placed her in decades gone by. She excused herself with a bow of her head as though the younger woman was of royal descent, then melted into the shadows like tumbleweed.

Once Frank had flicked a few switches, the grand house was clearly nowhere near as sinister as she had first imagined. Taking time to familiarise herself with her surroundings, she quickly realised that she had underestimated the size of the building as the car had approached.

A splendid oak stained staircase dominated the hallway, sweeping upwards in a majestic curve to the first floor. Its barley-sugar banisters and highly polished handrail were testament to tasteful architectural design. The house overall, was an eclectic mix: oak panelled walls covered with oil paintings, flagstone floors adorned with expensive and richly coloured Persian rugs and unfamiliar plants in oversized ceramic pots adding a touch of the exotic. Doors led off from each side of the staircase. A large Art Deco glass and steel chandelier dominated the centre of the vaulted ceiling, casting a comforting orangey glow over everything beneath.

The storm was still at full strength and was battering the windows by the time she had been shown to her bedroom. After having checked they were secured against the gale-force wind, Frank adopted his ready-for-action bodyguard stance by her open bedroom door. Knowing the effect she would no doubt be having on him, she faced away and bent over to smooth the satin bedcover, knowing full well that he would probably be studying her curves. She gave him a few seconds to take in her outline then stood up again.

For a second, their eyes met, and she thought fleetingly how much more uncomplicated it would be to love a regular guy like him rather than Jack. His glamorous career would attract most women, but to her, he did not possess anything like the charisma of a Kennedy. Knowing this, she felt vaguely uncomfortable with the knowledge that she could ensnare him with one click of her fingers. He would give up his life for her should the occasion arise.

He left the room, closing the door firmly behind him. Unknown to her, he had several issues. His immediate concern was how to maintain a professional distance. She seemed intent on manipulating him for her own purpose, in any way possible. Now that she was out of sight his heartbeat began to slow and the sensation in his groin diminish.

While he had been gathering himself up, she had flopped down onto the deep marshmallow bed. The mattress undulated like a sea swell and instantly the motion caused her to fall asleep; a rare occurrence without a massive cocktail of drugs. She began to dream of suffocation at the hands of a masked intruder with her own pillow. As she was about to give up the struggle, a faceless agent pulled the intruder off and fired a single bullet into his chest. The sound ricocheted around the room as he collapsed dead onto the floor. A pool of blood began to spread out rapidly covering the entire bedroom floor. When it had reached all four corners, it crept up the walls and formed crimson demonic shapes.

As quickly as the dream had formed, it dissolved, until the pool of blood was nothing but tiny red pieces of her familiar jigsaw puzzle floating around on the surface of Norma's eyes. As she opened them and blinked a few times, she realised that she was back in her bed as an old woman again. She cursed the sound of a modern airliner approaching Heathrow airport that had woken her from her dream, then sighed, reluctantly far removed from her memories of Jack, so much so that she was uncertain as to whether she had witnessed a dream-scape described to her by someone else.

More realistic and embedded in her mind were the few months in nineteen-sixty-two spent with Gloria. Or as Gloria. Or was she someone else completely? Now that she was approaching death, nothing seemed certain anymore. She closed her eyes again, praying that not only would she not be subjected to any pain, but that she would fall asleep again and not wake up.

Chapter 12

Realisation

Murray had inadvertently had a positive effect on Norma. So much so, that she awoke refreshed and free of her persistent demons the next morning. It was a beautiful day, evidenced by sunlight filtering through a gap in the curtains accompanied by the sound of cheerful chirruping of birds in the trees near to her balcony. She was instantly glad that her wish had not come true and that she was still alive. Added to her feeling of well being, the aroma of fresh coffee and cookies left by Geraldine shortly before, was beginning to tease her senses. She shook off the dusky pink satin sheet and matching eiderdown that she still cherished from the sixties. Her metaphorical storm had done its worst and her body felt strangely stronger. The promise of a walk in the gardens willed her to get up and embrace whatever time she had left.

As she ran a bath, she thought about the insatiable curiosity that had led her to read everything she could about the iconic Marilyn Monroe. Could it be possible that she had simply taken on the life of someone she admired so much because of her own life being lack lustre? If so, it made no sense for her to be surrounded by armed men. Her very valid point seemed to ignite the voices in her head and all of a sudden they began to argue between themselves. She resisted being drawn in and pushed their chattering to one side and, in order to keep them at bay, she reminisced instead about a trip to the United Kingdom with her third husband, Arthur Miller. Her arrival at London airport had been more public then. She had been greeted by Sir Laurence Olivier, Vivien Leigh and a strong police presence. But before she could enter the terminal building, the image began to flicker and break up as though she had been watching someone else on an old cine film.

She was left instead with the reminder of her final arrival in England, which had been and would continue to be, a far less positive experience. Her incarceration had forced her to get used to feeling far less of a star. The tumble into oblivion had been rapid. It had seemed to her that the press had tired of the suicide of Marilyn Monroe and, that no one outside of Huntley Manor mourned her once other headlines attracted their attention. On top of that, among the conspiracy theories, no one seemed to have thought it possible she could still be alive. As far as the world was concerned, there would be other starlets to take her place.

Pushing such negative thoughts away, she sprinkled rose petals onto the surface of her bath water. She recalled the memory of Jack tenderly washing her back and how the first time he had seen her naked she had tried to conceal her body in luxurious bubbles. He had been the only man whose opinion mattered when it came to examining her so intimately.

Now that she was frail, she stepped guardedly into the turquoise and marble bath and lay back so that she could admire the bathroom's exuberance. It had remained unchanged since her arrival back in the sixties but unlike the Victorian decor in the rest of the house, it was a fine example of the symmetry of Art Deco. The bathroom suite was embellished with fittings of turquoise and stainless steel. Caramel coloured tiles covered the walls, floor to ceiling. Despite her surroundings however, Norma was unable to distract herself for long enough to cast off memories of a harrowing past. Solace came only in the form of the show of strength outside her bedroom door. She wiped a tear away and concentrated instead on how back then, Jack had taken care of everything, hoping that making her feel at home might diminish her ordeal.

Duplicates of all her favourite beauty products had been waiting in the bathroom, lined up on frosted glass shelves. She still had the empty bottles somewhere as a reminder, but she could not remember where they were hidden. At some point before she awoke from that first night in England, a bottle of champagne had been left in a silver ice bucket by her bedside, accompanied by a message, saying: *To a new beginning. I love you. J.*

She had known that the card had been written by another hand than Jack's, but nevertheless she had placed a gentle kiss on the words, knowing that the sentiment was indeed his. How she had loved him and loved him still, on what would have been his hundredth year.

As soon as the water began to cool, Norma stepped out of the bath, patted her body dry and splashed her favourite Floris eau de toilette liberally all over. Her senses were instantly bombarded by the scent of geranium and rose with undertones of cedarwood and citronella. She smiled at the thought that it was Frank who took notice of her preferences these days. He chose not to rally with the public who believed the Chanel ads were an indication of which fragrance she preferred.

When Norma finally arrived downstairs, Frank was waiting for her in the breakfast room. He was seated by the French windows, a lit cigarette in his hand and several burnt out stubs still smoking in the ashtray beside him, suggesting he had been there awhile. He went to the sideboard, poured her a coffee, then sat down opposite her.

'How did it go, after I left you with Murray?' asked Norma.

'Boy, was he a tough nut to crack? But I think he's finally on our side,' said Frank, sounding encouraged.

Norma laughed. 'Are you surprised he was difficult to win over? After all, he's met several versions of me in two days.'

'I'd be confused too if I were him,' said Frank.

So, do you think we've convinced him and that he'll close the case?' she asked, hopefully.

'I think he's gonna be more involved if anything. I think he was trying to hide he's excited who you might be,' said Frank, wishing that he could warm to Murray.

'But then you've always had a persuasive nature Frank,' said Norma, laughing again.

To Frank, the situation was serious. 'What's important is that he trusts no one. Not even cops at Scotland Yard. I still wish you'd not opened up. But now it's done this is our only opportunity to prove who you are.'

'And who am I Frank? Some days I don't have a clue what day it is, let alone whether I'm Marilyn or Gloria.

I've lived with them both in my head for so long, that I can't tell one from the other anymore.'

'You're just tired,' answered Frank, which at that point seemed not to answer the question that Norma asked him every morning.

She looked across at him and for a second doubted him. She wondered whether it mattered which one of the two women she actually was. Either way, Frank stood to make money out of either revelation once she had gone and he could finally sell her story. She decided to let it go. In the next heartbeat she would remember exactly who she was. 'I like the young detective. He has something old-fashioned about him,' she said, changing the subject.

'I'm not paid to like him,' said Frank, aggressively.

'Why - I do believe you're jealous,' said Norma, touching Frank's hand as though to reassure him. 'But whether you like him or not, this whole situation has gotten dangerous. I'm feeling mighty twitchy.'

'It'll all be fine, as long as you don't tell him where the journals are stashed. They're your only genuine security to deter anyone from harming you,' said Frank.

'I won't tell him. Even you don't know where they are.'

Frank loosened his tie a fraction. His neck was red from where his collar had rubbed. 'I don't like that you don't trust me.'

Norma bit into a slice of buttered toast, giving herself a few seconds to contemplate his comment and thinking about the pang of doubt she had just pushed away. Such feelings had become more frequent and she also had her doubts about Frank's feelings for Mary. They often walked in the grounds together. 'You know I trust you with my life. I always have done,' she said, telling herself that she meant it.

'You sure about that?' asked Frank, sensing something had changed between them.

'I swear. And anyway, I was careful when I wrote my journals. I always suspected someday they'd be found,' said Norma.

'Do you want to tell me now where they are?' Frank asked, suddenly.

For a split second, Norma saw something in his eyes that suggested imminent betrayal, but she flicked the image away. She dabbed at the melted butter on her lips. 'You'll find them soon enough, along with my secrets. Everything I've written since I came to England,' she said, looking away.

'If you must keep them from me, why keep the truth from Mary?' asked Frank.

'It's not about Mary - or you Frank,' said Norma. 'It's more about if someone snuck in and forced either or both of you to reveal their whereabouts. The less you know the better.' She hesitated. 'Anyway, I've put a clue out to the universe. It probably hasn't been picked up yet, but it will be, in time.'

'What are you getting at?' asked Frank, worried that she may have been too forthcoming with the wrong person. Try as he might, he could not think of who that person might be within the household.

'Do you remember me telling you about me being pursued by that cult?' asked Norma, changing the subject to something totally unrelated.

'Uhuh. And I had to reassure you that you weren't the first Hollywood star they'd tried to brainwash. They're probably still at it too.'

Norma buttered another slice of toast. 'I'm sure they are Frank. But they tried to turn me into a puppet. Control my mind. Just to get to Jack.'

'You didn't mention any of that to Murray. Why not?'

Norma wrung her hands together. 'Isn't it obvious? Not only will he think it's all hocus-pocus, but I'm scared. If they were to find out I'm still alive, it wouldn't matter how good a cop he is. They'd come and murder me in some sort of twisted ritual. Just like they did to that young jazz singer a few years ago.'

'That was self-inflicted alcohol poisoning,' said Frank.

Norma checked the room for visible bugs before continuing. 'You think? Alcohol poisoning is what the press were paid to say. You know that. What about the fact that the poor girl's neighbours reported hearing tribal drums the night that she died?'

'C'mon,' said Frank, suppressing a laugh. 'All that cult stuff you're worried about, happened years ago, before you even came to the UK.'

'C'mon nothing. Now I've off-loaded all the past on that young man, I keep thinking about the conspiracies around my... I mean Gloria's death. They may have had Bobby under their control,' said Norma. She shaped a symbol in the air with her forefingers and thumbs. 'I'm not naming them. They're probably hiding in the grounds waiting to get to me.'

'So what other fantastic theories have you come up with?' asked Frank, pouring more coffee and seating himself by the window so he could keep one eye on the grounds. He was enjoying Norma's make believe when all of a sudden, a shadow flitted through the trees, followed by several more. He leapt up and scanned the area with his hand on his holster.

'What is it Frank?' asked Norma.

'Just buzzards,' said Frank, returning to his chair.

'What were you saying?'

Norma tried to regain her train of thought. 'Well there's Bobby. What if I've been wrong about him all these years?'

'I can't see where you're going with this,' said Frank, still checking outside, uncertain of what he had seen but not wanting to alarm her.

'Hear me out. What if Bobby arrived at my bungalow after Gloria was murdered? Or worse still while they were doing it,' said Norma.

Frank stood up and started to pace the room, irritated about revisiting the past every single day. 'Why all this now, after all these years?' he asked.

'You told me that Bobby was scared that night,' said Norma.

'Not scared, traumatised, because of Gloria's accident. He had to report back to Jack remember. He was worried about what would happen as a result.'

'There's something I've been missing all these years and now I'm near the end I'm desperate for answers. Surely you get that Frank? I'm beginning to think Bobby was on our side after all and that he cleaned up quickly before the real murderers discovered Gloria wasn't me.'

'What if you're right? How does any of that matter now?' asked Frank.

'It might mean I've got a lot more people to hide from - people I've no clue about.'

She suddenly looked more frail to Frank. 'Let 'em come,' he said, firmly.

She ignored his bravado and went off at a completely different tangent. 'My regular makeup artist did Gloria's makeup after the autopsy. Then Gloria was dressed in my green Pucci dress.'

'What has that got to do with these people you're

thinking about?' asked Frank.

'Listen up. Joe demanded to handle the funeral arrangements and requested I was made look half decent. He knew it was my wish should anything happen. He'd have paid the makeup artist and his assistant to keep their mouths shut about the body not being mine. They would've realised straight off anyway, and because they loved me they wouldn't have taken much persuading. If anyone was going to make Gloria look exactly like me it would've been them.'

Frank went back to standing by the window. 'Some story but like I said, what does it matter now?'

'Sure is. None of this has occurred to me before. I guess it's because I hated Bobby so much. But now I think Bobby and Joe hid the truth together.'

'Murray's got his work cut out for him. You've lost me already.'

'You know one of the things that really upsets me when I think back? Jack and I had to make do with some pretty unusual places to do...you know what. At the time, it all added to the excitement. Closets, washrooms, you name it, we used it. Then later I hear that when poor Gloria's body was taken to Westwood Village mortuary, she was stashed in a cleaner's closet because the press were screaming to get in. How ironic. Didn't stop one photographer though. He snuck in somehow when the others had given up.'

Chapter 13

Ring of Deceit

On leaving Huntley Manor, Murray had found a quiet spot outside the perimeter wall with a spectacular viewpoint and waited for the effects of the whisky to wear off before making his way back to London. It had given him time to think while Norma's words were still fresh.

Once he arrived back in town, he dropped his suitcase off at his immaculate contemporary flat in Clapham and mentally mapped out how he would continue his investigation into Norma. He showered, thinking back to the en suite at the Oxfordshire pub having not measured up to his stringent expectations of cleanliness. For some reason he felt as though germs had accompanied him home, so he spent an unusually long time washing himself down. Although still as he had left them, he refolded unused towels on his chrome towel rail and rearranged his toiletries on the shelf above his washbasin so that their symmetrical positioning pleased his eye. He knew in a smug way that his glossy bathroom would defy any forensics team to find a stray hair or clipped fingernail on any surface.

Taking care not to leave visible fingerprints on the sliding mirrored doors to his twin wardrobes, he ran his fingers affectionately across the shoulders of too many pressed white shirts and four charcoal-grey suits that hung like a line of shiny sardines. He dressed with military precision, then made his way into the office. His compulsion continued at Scotland Yard. It helped him think clearly, if he rearranged his papers and pens into perfect order, stopping short of using a ruler to measure the distance between each item. After having done this numerous times, he settled into his usual daily routine, irritated by the slovenliness of his counterparts. He would think long and hard about Norma for the rest of that day and the next. She had him hooked.

Once darkness had set in there was only a skeleton crew of detectives at their desks that were meant to be handling urgent cases. Their idle nattering and pen-tapping irked Murray and distracted him from the task at hand. In his opinion, casual talk clouded the mind and he had yet to finish his report. His desk was orientated in such a way that his back was against a wall. He liked it this way as no one could breathe down his neck and see the subject of interest on his computer screen. To shut out the gabble, he put on his old-school headphones so he could concentrate on an old film clip of Marilyn Monroe at Madison Square Garden. His headphones also served another purpose; preventing other detectives from hearing what it was that he was so interested in analysing. Sometimes clues were in the less obvious places, so he listened to the audio crackles that accompanied the grainy black and white footage, with that in mind.

Marilyn was singing happy birthday to John F. Kennedy. Murray looked again for subtle clues, such as mannerisms that would make her personality reveal itself to him. Standing at the lectern, she seemed delicate and unsure, flashbulbs reflecting off of her transparent gown making her appear iridescent and ethereal in her bejewelled near-nakedness. It was difficult to not stare at her magnificent curves, although it occurred to him that despite her obvious beauty she was as fragile as the old lady he had been interviewing for the last few days.

He felt like he had inadvertently flown back in time and was a voyeur witnessing her making love to a hungry audience. Studying more footage and photographic evidence of that evening, he observed a swarm of bees around the glistening honey pot that was Marilyn. Middle-aged men seemed turned on by the experience of being so close to her. Strangely, the more Murray studied the males clustered around Marilyn, the more he sensed menace in the expressions of some. Less than three months after that event, the news of her sudden death would swiftly send shock waves around the world.

It was clear that Marilyn was kept separated from the president that evening. Was this because she was becoming extremely volatile? Might she run to him, throw her arms around his neck and declare undying love? Or could the president's wife Jackie be present, hatred for Marilyn boiling beneath the surface?

Murray replayed what he had just seen, acquainting himself with Marilyn's characteristics, such as the way she lowered her eyelids when she posed and how she smiled. Her persona was lodged firmly in his head. He logged off. He was disappointed. The footage was poor, plus there were no close ups of anyone in the audience.

There was no way of telling whether there were murderers in Marilyn's midst. He rearranged his desk and turned out his desk-light.

It was only when he had stood up, buttoned up his jacket and locked his desk drawer, that something made him stop what he was doing. Giving time for a thought to mature, he replaced his jacket on the back of the chair and smoothed an imagined crease before logging on again. He had been so engrossed in Marilyn's charisma, that he realised he had overlooked some subtleties of the commentary from Peter Lawford and the president. Was it just coincidental on introducing Marilyn, that Lawford had emphasised the word late when he had mentioned her delay before arriving on the stage? The devil echoed in the use of that singular word. Murray tried to rationalise why he should hear such malevolence in what was after all, just a joke to amuse an expectant audience. Was he also reading too much into John F. Kennedy's mention that since he had heard Marilyn sing, he could now retire from politics? Was he being cryptic in his verbal caressing of her; hinting perhaps that he would be joining her soon in another country, his intended message? The clues were enticing but Murray knew he should not read too much into them.

This was the indeed the most thought-provoking case he had handled by far. He wondered fleetingly how Frank could have knowledge that there were those at Scotland Yard who could not be trusted. He shot a glance at the few detectives still remaining, wondering whether one or more of them were known to Frank, who clearly knew more about intelligence than he was going to disclose. Suddenly he grappled with the possibility that he was surrounded by subterfuge and slipperiness amongst his colleagues, some with feet on desks showing little respect for the furniture. He glanced over to his DI's office door. The room was in darkness, but he imagined the red eyes of Lucifer glowering at him through the partially closed blinds. Something was amiss.

In relation to demon worship, little did Murray know that Marilyn and Frank had been discussing the dark arts. Had he been aware of their conversation, he may have thought that the cults that had perpetrated the lives of Hollywood's finest actors and musicians had followed him back to Scotland yard. He shivered. The office suddenly seemed several degrees cooler.

What to do about Norma? If he sought authority to investigate officially, he would be laughed off of the force. But now, to his own surprise, he was adamant that he had to follow his instincts. He could not let it go. He had been won over, schmoozed, and endeared by a bunch of wackos at a secluded country estate. And quite by accident, he had just stumbled across a new Marilyn Monroe novel while researching her online. It seemed like an unexplainable gift to him and one that might be a fortuitous find judging by the author's claims.

Murray worked as one of a pair, but Judy Phelps, his partner, was still away on annual leave with her husband, daughter and two young sons. Had she been in the office, Murray knew that he would have had no hesitation in sharing his findings. He needed her opinion and he trusted her. They had always looked out for each other even though they had only recently become partners at Scotland yard.

He plucked a novel from her desk, which was adjacent to his and read the synopsis. The well-thumbed pages centred around the cover-up surrounding the death of an ex KGB chief. It confirmed what he already knew, that Judy was interested in subterfuge. She had an eclectic personality, which made her a top-class detective, as she could pluck clues from the most unlikely of places. She was also a creative who thrived on solving a good mystery and saw drama in everyday situations. He was convinced. Back tomorrow, relaxed and refreshed, she would be the only person he would share his knowledge with. He quietly cursed Frank for having managed to spook him. Frank and he would have to disagree when it came to whether Judy was trustworthy.

Before he could get wrapped up in more compulsive behaviour that would delay him further from getting home, Murray left the office quickly, this time not allowing his habit to drive him to reorganise his flat when he got in. He would stall his report, at least until he had spoken with Judy. He flopped down on his bed with a single malt whisky and began to read the novel that he had downloaded onto his tablet. Though it grabbed his interest, by the time he had read several pages, he had lapsed into a restless sleep, one where in his dream he was suited, booted and muscle-bound like Schwarzenegger. He had been helped by Secret Service agents with Frank at the helm of the operation, to pluck a young Marilyn from the sacrificial altar of a satanic ritual.

He woke with a start early morning, to the sound of a lorry backfiring on the street outside. His bed was wet from perspiration and his jaw hurt from clenching his teeth: an all too familiar habit when something big was about to erupt at work.

It suddenly occurred to him that there were hundreds of books and articles written about Marilyn, all considering her fascinating life or digging into her likely suicide or possible murder, but he was not aware of any that had suggested she may have staged her death. Maybe that was because such a notion was clearly ridiculous.

Chapter 14

Judy in Disguise

Judy Phelps was seated opposite Murray in Scotland Yard's staff restaurant. He had already briefed her on his trip and Frank's idea of how to prove Norma was indeed Marilyn Monroe. Judy was gripped, eating faster and faster, as she voraciously tucked into a full English plus extra toast. He on the other hand, was trying not to be sidetracked by wondering how she stayed so trim.

'Oh wow Steve, is this for real?' she asked, between bites. 'It can't possibly be true.'

He shushed her enthusiasm and discarded his apple half-eaten, by lobbing it accurately into an open bin yards away. 'Well, that's the problem - it sounds ludicrous doesn't it? Until we dig deeper I don't have the slightest clue what's real and what's just fantasy in the old dear's mind.' A bewildered expression crossed his face. 'Before you arrived Jude, I had the strangest of early morning calls.'

'Who from?' she asked, buttering another slice of toast.

'From Frank. He's done a complete turnabout with his

side of the story. Says Norma isn't Marilyn after all,' he added, dejectedly, meticulously lining up unused cutlery as though having some sort of order might help clarify his thinking.

'What the...why would he do that? Who does he say she is then, if she's not Monroe?' asked Judy.

'He said she was in essence what I had thought all along - a batty old woman, and, he kept saying the same thing over and over. Something's not right. It sounded to me like he was being prompted,' said Murray.

'Did he say anything else to give you a clue as to why he's changed his story?' asked Judy.

'Only that she's obsessed with Marilyn and that he was humouring her in her last days. Which to be fair, is what I've thought all the way along too.'

'Even so, he can't be stupid,' said Judy. 'He must've known about the penalty for wasting police time when he first met you.'

'I did warn them all about those consequences. But now I've had his call, I don't know what to think. All my questioning seems to have been a waste of time and, we're back to square one,' said Murray, dejectedly.

'Come on Steve. You're smarter than that. What does your instinct tell you?' asked Judy.

Murray straightened the salt and pepper pot so that they were dead central on the table. 'It's too early to say, but it's one of two things I reckon. It was either a scam from the beginning to extort money out of the tabloids, or, as Frank said, he was just keeping her happy. I get the bit about coming clean while I was there. It might've been too distressing for her.'

'Well I don't believe either of those two scenarios,' said Judy. 'None of what you've just said is enough reason for them to spin such a yarn and then about-turn overnight? Then there's the armed presence to consider.'

'Maybe whoever she is, she has money or she got cold feet and decided she couldn't make money out of it,' said Murray, trying to rationalise what he knew.

'Or maybe someone or something scared her,' declared Judy, with a touch of theatre in her voice. 'Have you told the governor anything yet?'

'No, you're the first,' said Murray. He took a second apple from his pocket and polished it with a paper napkin, before taking a bite.

'Er - and why haven't you?' asked Judy. 'This is truly amazing. I've never heard anything remotely like it. Come to think of it, it'd make a great movie.'

Murray finished chewing. 'Whoever she is, her and her entourage had such a gift for spinning a yarn, it was seamless. They clearly did their homework. Added to that, the security setup is something else.'

'Well from what you've told me, I believe it's Marilyn. And so do you, otherwise we wouldn't be having this conversation,' said Judy, eyeing up fresh doughnuts at the counter.

'You've read too many conspiracy novels Jude. Your head's in another world,' said Murray, laughing at her appetite.

'Listen Steve, I'm open to any possibility, no matter how unlikely. I bet she's not the first celebrity to fake death. '

'Back in the real world,' said Murray, sarcastically, trying not to become drawn in by Judy's fanciful notions. 'Some other time you can tell me your ridiculous thoughts on their deaths.'

'You're such a cynic,' Judy responded forcibly. 'And even if you've not reached a conclusion yet, you've still got to file a report. I'll fight your corner if the guv's in two minds as to whether to let us investigate further.'

Murray told her his fears based on Frank's warning statement to trust no one.

Judy scanned the restaurant, suddenly feeling as suspicious as Murray had the night before. 'Blimey Steve, who can we trust?' she asked, quietly, clearly revelling in the subterfuge.

'I don't know. I'm flummoxed. The moment I run it by the guv, the moment our mystery woman becomes endangered.'

Judy was now wide-eyed. 'What - you don't trust him either?'

'That's just it. I'm so on tenterhooks Jude. Feels like everyone's involved,' said Murray, despairingly.

'Well, I'm flattered you trust me,' said Judy, wiping her plate with her last piece of toast. 'Thanks for sharing. It means a lot.' She pushed her sparkling clean plate to one side and continued to eye-up the doughnuts.

Murray hesitated. 'I came across something yesterday that might help us. A new docu novel. Apparently the writer knew Marilyn really well. Has some things she gifted. Lives in Ireland. We should look at DNA, if this guy has something. You never know what it might prove.'

'Whatever he has, it'll have been handled hundreds of times,' said Judy, suddenly thoughtful. She changed tack. 'Have you taken any time off sick this year?'

Murray added his empty plate to hers and dropped sugar cubes into his coffee. 'No, I haven't. Why d'you ask?'

'I've an idea,' said Judy. 'And by the way, you might not be able to drink that coffee. You've stirred in at least ten cubes if my adding up's right.'

Murray despondently pushed the cup to one side.

'Okay, hit me with it. I'm all out of ideas, so what's your suggestion?' he asked, for some unknown reason, expecting a ridiculous idea from Judy on this occasion.

Instead, she smiled as though she were a young child who had just found a favourite lost toy. 'You're going sick, so you can investigate while I hold the fort. All unofficial of course, and hush-hush.'

'And just how am I going to do that?' asked Murray, tucking into his apple again.

'Tomorrow you'll have food poisoning, then get the first flight or ferry you can.'

'And where am I going exactly?' asked Murray, feeling vaguely amused.

Judy leant across the table and whispered. 'To talk to that author. You never know, he might say something that'll convince you either way.'

Murray was unimpressed by her suggestion. 'What about my report?'

'Hand it in on your return. Say you've been dealing with a time-waster and that's what held it up,' said Judy, her excitement now obvious.

Murray thought for a second. 'So it wouldn't be a complete lie.' He retrieved his cup, took a few sips, grimacing at the sickly sweetness, but feeling the need for the buzz that caffeine and sugar would give. 'Ah one problem - then I get a bollocking.'

'Nah, you're the guv's favourite,' said Judy. 'Just tell him you think we shouldn't prosecute because the old dear's doolally, is about to pop her clogs and you need one more visit out of respect.'

'Uh. You've completely lost me. You're going much too fast,' said Murray.

'Pay attention. All we're doing is buying us some time.

147

You'll just change the name of who Norma claims to be to a B-lister, so you don't raise the guv's curiosity about her being such a big star. We don't want him paying her a visit.'

Murray loved it when Judy came up with something quirky. 'That might work. I'm liking where you're going with this Jude,' he said, letting her know he was pleased.

'Neither of us know what that author has of Marilyn's. Could be nothing, could be something. When was the book published?'

'Only a few days ago,' said Murray.

'Then chances are, if anything underhand is going on, no one has got to the author yet. Even if multiple prints are all over whatever it is Marilyn gifted him, we have to take a look.'

'I'll lose my job for investigating elsewhere when I claimed to be in bed,' said Murray, trying to bring Judy back down to earth.

'Fired for uncovering the story of the century? At most, you'd get a disciplinary,' she suggested.

'But it was the guv who handed me the case in the first place. He'd have read DC Taylor's findings,' said Murray.

'What if he did? Is Marilyn mentioned by name in the original file? From what you've said, Taylor didn't get that far with her,' said Judy.

'You know, I'm pretty certain you're right. But it's still taking a gamble,' said Murray, thinking that sometimes she was cleverer than he.

'I can check on that this afternoon,' she said. 'Meanwhile you just go sick in the morning. I'll stall the guv while you do what you need to do. He's wrapped up in a new terrorist threat anyway. '

'What about if we need DNA testing done in a hurry?

Norma only has days to live. With everything else hotting up, it's hardly the guv's priority, ' said Murray.

'I'm owed a really really big favour,' said Judy, a mischievous smile crossing her face. 'Soon as you're back from Dublin I'll get straight on to the lab.'

She collected together their crockery and cutlery and piled it on a trolley, trying to not look too eager to return to her desk and get started on covering Murray's back. She spent the rest of the day commenting out loud that he looked pale to other colleagues, to lay footings for his excuse for being absent the following day.

When she slipped outside into the car park to call him the following morning, she had already told the DI that he had phoned in with a bad case of food poisoning. The DI made no mention of the findings of Steve's excursion to Oxfordshire, or of his report not having landed on his desk as yet.

Whilst she was making his excuses for him, Murray had already arrived at City airport early, opting to fly rather than travel by ferry to get to the author quickly, as time was so critical. Fearing a luggage check for fear of an enthusiastic baggage checker going through his neatly folded shirts, he tried not to draw attention to himself. As he passed through the airport, he noted the armed police presence due to the terrorist alert that both Judy and Austen had mentioned. He checked in and killed time by watching planes and discreetly observing other passengers he would be travelling with.

He had picked up a paperback copy of the new Marilyn Monroe book on his way to the airport, but he could not settle and read it. He wondered about the authenticity of the content and whether the author, Michael Dogherty could prove that he knew Marilyn well. He suppressed a smile, knowing that he was on an unusual mission. He might prove over the course of the next few weeks that most of what had been written about Marilyn in the past was rubbish. He reprimanded himself fleetingly for allowing himself to be so unsure of the end result. Nevertheless, he wished that the elaborate piece of storytelling by Norma was the truth. Also, Judy's love of mystery had rubbed off on him, he realised. She would be calling him, day in, day out, to hear what he had discovered.

Once settled into his seat, he waited impatiently for take off, glad that it was a short flight to Dublin. Flying was not a favourite pastime, especially as in his opinion, airport security was lax. It would be ironic if he became embroiled in terrorist activity on a short haul rather than back at Scotland Yard where terrorist investigation was a priority. He flicked idly through the book, scan-reading the short paragraphs attached to black and white Marilyn images. Some he had seen before, while others were unfamiliar, claiming to be the property of Dogherty, taken while in Marilyn's company. The back of the book's fly cover sported predictable comments by tabloid papers promoting the author's links with Hollywood and the suggestion of fascinating reading within its cover. As online, nowhere in his scanning of the book did it list specific details of what Marilyn had gifted the author. Inwardly Murray cursed Judy's suggestion that he make an unannounced visit to a writer now in their mid eighties, who no doubt had a ghostwriter to aid them with putting their memories on paper. More than this, Murray feared that he may might become victim to the same resistance he had received at the gates of Huntley Manor. Nevertheless, he began again at chapter one, quickly finding himself drawn into the intrigue of the author's supposed life.

Chapter 15

Just in Time

Norma's sleep pattern was normally peppered with fear, her dreams often spiralling into something darker due to the spine-chilling scream of vixens in the woods on the estate. In the hours of daylight as a rule, she felt differently, as despite her lingering fear of intruders, it was a time when staying close to Frank made her feel safe. Added to that, he cared for her welfare. Nevertheless, more recently, she had begun to wonder whether Frank's fitness would stand the test if he were to challenge an attacker, even though he worked out and had the body of a much younger man. What she did know, however, was that he had grown to love her over the years, although due to his role, the words had never passed his lips. She wondered whether his adulation had ever been a romantic love, or whether it was a love borne out of compassion and familiarity. Either way, Frank was Frank, and she could not do without him, despite her occasional doubts.

Time was running out much like sand passing through

an egg-timer, but strangely Norma had been calm over the last few days, knowing that once she passed on, her journals would fall safely into the right hands due to a clue of their whereabouts having been put out there. With that in mind and with time of the essence, she waited for news from Murray, anxious that he was keeping her in the dark. As she strolled the gardens on this particular morning, she wished Frank were with her, either telling her there had been developments or simply just enjoying the day with her. She tried instead to forget Murray and look forward to a picnic later under the hot summer sun.

Due to the gardens sloping gently away from the main house, she could stroll alone with little risk of falling. She walked unaided most of the time, more by choice than need, preferring to keep her pride intact and to not allow her legs to get too lazy. Nevertheless, she discreetly carried a foldaway stick in a velvet dolly bag, preferring to use it only when uneven ground challenged her. On this day, she had started her walk at the back of the house as she so often did, leaving by the French doors from the library. They led her to the Victorian orangery, which was constructed from glass and cast iron. Its deep pitched roof sat immediately beneath the balcony that led from her lounge, offering some protection from intruders reaching her suite. The orangery was one of her favourite places, along with the tranquil lake at the far end of the estate and a swimming pool that had fallen into disrepair that still evoked many memories. The scent of potted plants; citrus fruits, herbs and spices planted in the orangery by the gardener, manifested a mental picture of how Norma imagined Indian markets to be. So powerful was the exotic cocktail that at night its heady fragrance found a way into her rooms, even when her windows were closed against the outside world.

She particularly liked the fact that shrubs and trees had been left unattended in some parts of the garden, allowing those areas to fall into spectacular utopian decay. No one ever seemed to go off the beaten track apart from her. The only thing to interrupt the natural beauty had been an early addition of electric fences and CCTV cameras, placed so they would deter anyone trying to cross the vast expanse of lawn in order to gain access to the house. Olivia White and DC Murray had quite by chance emerged from the woods just at the point where the electrified fencing stopped short either side of the gravel drive, saving themselves from an unexpected electric shock. Frank was dealing with the weak link by installing a motion detector under the gravel, which in Norma's mind would no doubt be troublesome every time a car came and went.

These days she rarely visited the lake unless she had Frank or Mary to accompany her. It was a good round mile trip around its uneven shore back to the house. When they did venture out that far on a hot day, she would stop occasionally and rest on the wooden benches that had been placed at regular intervals round its banks for her benefit. In her younger days, she had regularly rowed to the natural island in the middle of the lake and lay in a rope hammock strung between two weeping willow trees. There, she had rocked Mary to sleep in her arms on many occasions, reading books out loud that she had taken from the library and imagining mermaids beneath the surface of the water.

On this particular day, she had cut short her visit to the orangery, the sun's heat making it too unbearable to stay under the glass roof for long. Instead, she had turned left and was very soon outside the boundary walls to the swimming pool. It had been constructed solely for her as soon as she had arrived in the sixties to placate her yearning for a Malibu beach. As she walked on, she considered how English summers had seemed hotter back then.

The cast iron gate to the pool area mirrored the main gates but unlike the grand entrance could easily be missed due to the weeds that had wound their way through its scrollwork. It tussled for space, sandwiched between yew trees and overgrown privet that had formed a natural arch overhead, planted against the pool's perimeter walls decades before. Norma lifted the latch but was instantly met with resistance due to the bindweed, which had over the last few weeks created a natural chain and padlock against visitors. She pulled away as much as she could and once inside, trod carefully as the narrow path that led to the pool undulated, each paving slab outlined by slippery tufts of moss.

There was a haunting beauty in how nature had snatched back the very place where she had spent many lazy summer afternoons with Mary. The stylish pool that she had languished beside, was neglected and forgotten by everyone apart from her. She sat down gingerly on a wooden-slatted seat, afraid that in its dilapidated state it might collapse beneath her. Ghostly reminders of fun-filled days littered where she had once sunbathed. The stagnant pool no longer reflected an azure blue sky, but instead the slow passage of time. The surface of the water was a floating carpet of thriving algae and weed, on which danced pond skaters and dragonflies. Dotted around were sun loungers and coffee tables, damaged beyond repair, most upturned and abandoned where they had last been used. A single wine bottle sat forlornly on the one table that was upright, the remains of the bottle's contents the colour and consistency of congealed blood. Apart from a few smashed wine glasses, a couple remained intact, full to the rim with dirty rainwater, in which small dead insects had sunk to the bottom after a futile struggle. The mosaic tiles that decorated the pool area were mostly unbroken, but their original vibrant blue and green colours had faded due to relentless sunshine and inclement weather.

Norma reflected on her second year at Huntley Manor. Once her baby bump had shrunk to a respectful size, she had not been afraid to reveal her body by the side of the pool. The act of her bathrobe slipping to the ground had been a teaser for Frank and other agents. She realised nevertheless, that her figure had never returned to how it was before she had given birth to Mary, not that it had mattered, as at that time she had been still grieving for Jack since his assassination.

Twenty minutes later, the warmth of the sun had lulled Norma into a light sleep. On this occasion her dreams at the start were pleasant. The cork from the wine bottle beside her had just been popped. There was the gurgle of wine as it was poured into a sparkling clean glass by Frank. She had forgotten everything from her later years so was not surprised to see Frank much younger, leaning over to wake her. As always, the pool area back then was in immaculate condition. She was surrounded by a small group of party-goers drinking champagne in celebration of a whisper that Jack was stepping down from the presidency within the month. The sun was a magnificent fiery orb, as though it was putting on a display to celebrate the news. She should have been delirious with joy, but somehow, something felt not quite right.

Just as she was revelling in the thought that Jack would be with her soon, an indefinable change in her immediate surroundings made her shiver with morbid expectation. Threatening shadows began to form, triggering her already fertile imagination. There was an unfriendly visitor named menace lurking somewhere close by. She scanned the faces of the people she had grown to know so well and found herself staring at someone she felt she had come across before she had escaped to England. His presence was a mystery and she did not remember Frank recruiting him.

The sun dipped behind a solitary cloud, making Norma stir, but she was still in that place where sleep meets wakefulness. She recalled that she had been dreaming of a party long ago. Nevertheless, though she was back in the here and now, something was still not right. Someone from her dream had wakened with her, blackening the blood in her veins with their poison. She sat up and tried to pull herself from out of the chair so that she could make her way out of the pool area. She needed to seek help from Frank or his colleagues to get her to the house safely. The trouble was, she had not told anyone where she was going. She knew that until someone noticed she had been gone awhile, she would need to rely on all of her senses to deal with whatever threat was close by.

To fool whoever was stalking her into believing she was fitter than she was and not in the slightest bit afraid, she stood and began to walk round the pool, masking her arthritis with her best effort. She hummed a favourite melody, feigning interest in the wild roses that had over time spilled like a waterfall over the top of the pool's boundary walls. Holding the oversized blooms close to her nose as though to savour their scent, she glanced discreetly through their unusually large petals into all corners of the pool complex.

She saw sense in being able to defend herself should someone appear suddenly and try to make a grab for her, but she had nothing to hand. She reached inside her dolly-bag for her fold-away stick and used the opportunity to allow her fingers to remind her of the few other contents she carried, should one of them make a suitable weapon. Her hand closed around her metal nail-file, perfume and lipstick. The three things she considered a woman should carry at all times. It was a long time since she had also carried a bottle of prescription drugs to dull her emotions. Removing the nail-file, she hacked at a few roses and wrapped her cotton handkerchief round their lower stems to protect her fingers, having picked the variety possessing the most lethal thorns. She was ready, but how effective she could be, she dare not think. There was a time when her body was her deadliest weapon. One glance at any time would have floored any man.

Armed with her thorny whip, she backed against the boundary wall, so that she need not fear an attack from behind. She doubted she could get close enough to inflict an injury with the nail file but thought that should the roses be swung with enough force, she could inflict enough lacerations with their thorns to maybe scare someone off.

To her left was the changing room. The doors hung loosely on broken hinges, swinging slowly in the soft breeze like those in a Western saloon. The pool was directly in front. She closed her eyes and listened, not realising that she possessed the same gift as DC Murray. Despite her age, her hearing was acute. She concentrated and detached it from her other senses. Her heart thumped in her chest; its irregular beat a concern to her right now and potentially to her doctor later. It seemed like she had been standing there for an eternity, rather than just the short time that had passed when the stench from the pool began to make her feel nauseous. She found a partial solution beneath a particularly large cascade of fragrant yellow roses, drawing in their scent. She was about to reprimand herself for allowing her fertile imagination to get the better of her, when all of a sudden there was a faint rustling noise close by. She recognised it as the sound of bushes being parted. Her assailant was clearly not concerned as to whether his approach had been heard. Perhaps he thought it would intensify his terror tactics because he was dealing with a defenceless old woman.

Norma half-opened her eyes, ready to take aim with her roses, but the thorns had pierced through her handkerchief, making her fingers bleed. Her mouth was dry. She edged to her left, slowly covering the distance between the perimeter walls and the changing rooms, not wanting to go inside for fear of others waiting in the darkness to ambush her. There was no time to reach the path to the open gate. With few options to consider, she suddenly remembered the alarm that Frank had given her and had instructed her time and time again to use should she get into difficulty. She reached inside her bag and pressed down hard on the button. A shrill note filled the air and echoed in the distance. Her assailant emerged from the hedging to her right and looked her straight in the eye. She froze, expecting to be knocked to the ground.

'Don't move - stay right where you are,' came an authoritative voice, all of a sudden from the other side of the pool.

At that precise moment, Norma realised that more than one person had been sent to kill her. She closed her eyes and braced herself, hoping for a quick and painless death.

The threats continued. 'I mean it. Don't move a muscle. Or you're a goner.'

The rustling had stopped but it did not make any sense to Norma that she was still alive. Suddenly, it dawned on her that she knew the voice. The fog cleared in her head. It was Frank.

He knelt down and clicked his finger and thumb several times. A powerfully built guard dog turned and snarled at Norma, revealing teeth that could make short work of any meal. Then it trotted over to Frank who hurriedly attached a lead to its collar.

Norma sank to the ground and wept openly. As she did so, Chad appeared, out of breath. He took the dog's lead and led it away, so as to allow Frank the opportunity to comfort Norma.

He sprinted round the pool and gently swept her from the ground where she had been crouched and trembling. 'You could've been ripped to pieces,' he said.

She melted into his arms remembering a time from long ago when she had been swept off her feet by someone else. Her tears fell freely as he carried her away from the pool area. 'How did the dog get out?' she stammered.

'One of the men hadn't secured the gate to the pen. I'll find out who it is and discipline him straightaway.'

'No don't do that - I'm okay now you're here Frank.'

For a moment knowing looks were exchanged. Looks that suggested nothing more than - another life, another place.

Frank carried her back to the house, her head resting

on his shoulder, wishing he had told her how he had fallen in love with her long ago.

Chapter 16

The Emerald Isle

By the time Murray's plane had touched down at Dublin airport, he had already scanned through the Marilyn Monroe book he had purchased en route and scribbled extensive notes in the margins. Nothing Michael Dogherty had said however, made him any closer to unravelling what was going on at Huntley Manor. In his mind, the contents were far-fetched and he wondered whether he had just made a wasted journey. Dogherty had claimed that he had stumbled into Marilyn's life quite by luck rather than by planning, back in the early sixties. Fortunately, his adopted pen name had not held Murray from finding his whereabouts due to some rigorous internet searching. He hoped no shady characters were on their way too, as if that were the case, it was touch and go as to who would get there first.

Murray hurried through arrivals and glanced at the other passengers rushing through, wondering whether any of them were onto him and had the same destination in mind. Having successfully grabbed a taxi outside the terminal building, he laid out his case file on the back seat and began to thumb through what he would need. Once they were out of town he found it hard at first not to be seduced by the beautiful counterpane of Ireland's countryside rather than compose his questioning tactics. He also began to be concerned that he was out of his jurisdiction and could land himself in a lot of trouble. He tried to remember a time when Scotland Yard had become involved in a case that affected both sides of the Irish Sea but nothing sprang to mind. His biggest hope was that Dogherty was ill-informed about police procedures and would not report him to the Garda.

When the taxi finally pulled up outside a modest cottage tucked away by the side of an ancient church, Murray paid off the driver, adding enough to hold him in the vicinity until he had finished his questioning. He knocked on the door of the cottage but at first there was no response. Before he had had the chance to walk round the back to seek access another way, the peace was shattered by the sound of a speeding car. He spun round just in time to see an immaculate black saloon with tinted windows sweep too fast round a bend and disappear into the distance. He noted that it seemed out of place. A cloud of dust had risen up in its wake making it impossible for him to record its number plate. He knocked on the door again and glanced in through a window while he was waiting, but his view of the interior was hindered by lacy nets. Two cats had wriggled their way under the curtains and were sitting like identical bookends, blinking lazily at him from the ledge. Just as he was thinking he should have arranged his meeting with the author rather than making a surprise visit, the door opened a crack. It was restrained by a security chain.

The craggy face of a woman peered round. 'Who are you? What do you want?' she asked, suspiciously.

Murray hoped that she had no idea of how police would normally identify themselves, so he chose to withhold his warrant card and smiled broadly, acting more like a door-to door salesman. 'Detective Constable Murray. Sorry to disturb you Madam, but I'm looking for Michael Dogherty - the author.'

'You're English,' the woman said, accusingly.

'That I am, but I was born here,' said Murray, feeling uncomfortable with lying. 'Although I'm back for now,' he added, underpinning a fictional Irish heritage.

The woman grumbled and huffed under her breath. 'Wait there,' she said, shutting the door in his face.

While she was gone, Murray took in his surroundings. The cottage, along with a hotchpotch of properties form a similar era, formed a triangle around a manicured village green on which a handful of kids were kicking a ball around. Modernisation did not seem to have reached this far, as most properties looked as though they had barely changed in two hundred years. For the best part, owners' cars were parked on the road, meaning that the majority of gardens had not been demolished in favour of a drive. Instead, cottage gardens competed for the best show of flowers behind stone walls.

Murray was beginning to think he was locked out for good, when there was the clink of metal as the security chain was released.

The craggy face peered round again. 'Still here? I hoped you might've gone,' said the woman, brusquely. 'You can come in now. The author will see you briefly,' she added, loftily.

The door was pulled open barely enough for Murray

to slip through the gap and it was impossible to squeeze through without making uncomfortable body-contact with the woman's low-slung bust.

'Outside, writing as usual,' she complained, pointing down the passage to an open door leading onto a garden. 'I'll make some tea.'

Murray was glad that he had not alienated her further by confessing that he was not local and had just come from the airport. He had already noticed the redness of her large hands, which were heavily peppered with scars. He imagined she was made of tough stuff and at one time could have won a fist fight and it seemed likely that she had worked on the land when much younger. Somewhere in her mid to late seventies, her rosacea complexion suggested that she was either a heavy drinker or had never bothered to use suncream. She shuffled off in ill-fitting slippers leaving Murray to make up his mind about her origin and whether she was the author's wife.

Once in the garden, Murray was immediately welcomed by well-stocked flower beds and orchard trees heavy with apples that looked fit to fall. Strewn underneath was more fruit than was on the trees, suggesting that neither occupant was a keen gardener. Beyond the orchard, fields rolled away like a billowing green and yellow patchwork quilt, equally as stunning as the view from the taxi. The hills in the distance were not dissimilar to those near Huntley Manor.

Murray turned his attention to the woman seated at a round table under a fringed parasol. A scattering of papers covered the table, weighted down by large polished stones. Murray was confused. At first the woman continued writing on a laptop, seemingly oblivious to his presence, but after a few seconds she looked up from her work. 'Have you never seen a woman before?' she asked, with a touch of sarcasm, seeing the obvious surprise on Murray's face. 'And more than that, do you have a name?' she added, slamming down the lid to her laptop so that he could not see what it was that she was writing.

'DC Murray. I'm sorry if I appeared rude - but I expected a man,' said Murray, surprised that the internet or the novel's foreword had not revealed the true gender of the author.

'And why would that be? ' asked the woman, inviting him to sit.

'Your book - the name on the cover,' said Murray.

The woman instantly opened up. The subject of gender seemed to irk her. 'If you knew as much as me about the literary world, you'd know that even these days women are overlooked. I've had far more success since adopting a pen name.' She fondly patted the freshly printed copies that were stacked on her table. My real name is Aileen Dogherty. Michael Dogherty was my uncle,' she added, crossing her chest in respect for his passing.

As Aileen tidied her chaotic scattering of notes into one reasonably neat pile and weighted it down with the largest of her polished stones, Murray studied her face. She was of the age he had hoped for, meaning had she could have known Marilyn when she was a young woman. She had clearly lived abroad at some point in her life as her accent was an odd mix. So much so that Murray doubted that she had spent much time in Ireland at all. Her hair was tied back in a loose bun and was predominantly silvery-white, but it was streaked through with a tinge of ash blonde. Her complexion could not have been more different to that of the woman who had let him in. Her skin was smooth, pale and surprisingly wrinkle free for a woman in her eighties. Her eyes were an unusual shade of green.

She was astute. 'Margaret and I aren't related,' she said all of a sudden, reading Murray's mind. 'And we're not lesbians, just in case you were thinking that we were. We're just very old friends and that's all there is to it.'

Murray was taken aback. 'I apologise if you thought I was staring, but I wasn't making any assumptions, I promise - especially with regards to your private life.'

'Of course you were. That's your job,' said Aileen.

Murray felt the colour rise in his face. He was momentarily lost for words and knew that he must not rile Aileen. as she might send him on his way with no information at all.

'Well - cat got your tongue? What is it you want? You're not the first to visit me this week. Seems like everyone's come out of the woodwork,' she growled.

Murray was instantly alarmed as to just who that might be, but before he could ask the question, Aileen continued in more detail.

'All of Ireland want to know me now I've a potential best-seller out. Journalists turning up at all hours. I should never have done that TV interview. I even have relatives and friends I never knew existed,' said Aileen.

This was Murray's opportunity to draw her out with flattery. 'I saw you on TV. It was a great interview Miss Dogherty. That's why I'm here,' he said, schmoozing her.

'I've not done anything illegal. And I've certainly not plagiarized anyone,' she answered, defensively.

Murray stopped her short, seeing the worry in her face. 'I don't doubt you. I'm just enquiring about your relationship with Marilyn Monroe.'

Aileen seemed to hold her breath, as she considered

what questions she might be asked and what she should say in response. She fixed her eyes on Murray. 'You've already read about it in the book. So why would you want to ask me something you already know?' she asked, having noticed he had a copy of her novel poking out of his jacket pocket.

He was unprepared for such a direct response. 'I'm an ardent fan.'

Aileen burst out into laughter, but stopped as suddenly as she had begun, fixing Murray again with an intimidatory stare. 'You're not a fan are you? If you were, you wouldn't have said you're a detective. And you've come all the way from England.'

Murray faltered. He was in a quandary. Cornered. How could he discuss Norma aka Marilyn with such a savvy woman?

'Show me your warrant card,' Aileen insisted, suddenly. 'I need to know that you're genuine.'

'Of course,' said Murray, opening it and holding it up for her to see.

After nothing but a glance, Aileen waved it away. Unexpectedly, she reached out and grabbed Murray's free hand. She began to examine his palm, while he wondered about Irish folklore and whether she was about to put a hex on him. Instead, she interpreted his hands in a different way to how he had judged her ageing friend's hands.

'The hands tell everything about a person,' said Aileen, running a finger along Murray's life-line. 'But right now I must warn you. I see darkness and devilry ahead. Be very vigilant.'

'A fortune teller too,' quipped Murray, trying to make light of her prediction, but slightly alarmed by her reference to the devil. Also he was not sure whether her comment was a threat. 'Let's get back to why I'm here, shall we?' he suggested.

'Don't make light of my gift DC Murray. I'm never wrong. You will need strength to deal with what's coming,' said Aileen, releasing his hand. 'You shouldn't have come here. I don't have to answer your questions.'

Murray thought quickly. He had definitely riled Aileen, so he opted to display some professional naivety, hoping it might make her think she had the upper hand. 'You're right of course. You don't have to answer my questions. But it's true that I volunteered for this case because I am a fan of Marilyn.'

'Well we've something in common then,' said Aileen. 'Though I'm curious as to why you're investigating her.'

'I'm hoping some new facts might help,' said Murray, tailoring his words carefully.

'Might help with what?' asked Aileen, narrowing her eyes.

Murray knew he had to give Aileen something to stop her from adopting such a defensive stance. 'There's some doubt about the authenticity of some items that are supposed to be hers. They've found their way to England and I'm simply following every lead by talking to those that knew her best.'

'I see,' said Aileen, Murray's lie enough to convince her to cooperate. 'What do you want to know?'

Murray took out his notebook and began to write. 'What were you doing in America in the early sixties for instance?'

'Surely you've read that in my book? I was there with my mother,' said Aileen.

'To be honest - and no offence meant, I've only read the

very beginning. You only came to my attention yesterday,' said Murray.

'Well now you've come all this way, I'll try and give you what you need - within reason. I'll begin by telling you that back then, there was already a big Irish community in the States. We went out there to see an aunt, my mother's sister.'

'How long were you out there?' asked Murray.

'My mother returned to Ireland a few weeks later, but I'd already persuaded her to let me stay out there. I wanted an adventure you see,' said Aileen.

'Whereabouts in the United States?' asked Murray, remembering what he had underlined in Aileen's book.

'Right on the outskirts of Hollywood. My aunt was something of an entrepreneur. She'd seen a gap in the market so set up a business designing and making handmade shoes. She was well-known among the stars and supplied footwear for some big films of the time.'

'So is that how you met Marilyn?' asked Murray. As he waited expectantly for Aileen to answer, he could not understand why she was slow to reply. For a fleeting second he thought she had changed her mind, but was instantly relieved that she had only stalled because Margaret had appeared with a tray. Aileen took it from her and waved her away impatiently so that they could continue in private.

'You were telling me how you first met Marilyn,' said Murray, helping Aileen to get back to where they had left off.

'Where was I? Oh yes - I'd become my aunt's apprentice in order to pay my way, delivering sample fabrics to the studios and helping out in her workshop. Other times, I'd go with her when she was measuring actors' feet or delivering shoes.'

'Tell me about your first meeting with Marilyn,' said Murray, noticing that his writing hand ached from the last few days of intense notation.

'I didn't know who we were going to see that day,' said Aileen. 'We were shown straight to Marilyn's dressing room, me carrying my aunt's equipment. She said it helped make her look professional if she didn't arrive looking like a pack-horse. It was a big shock to walk in and see Marilyn laying on a sofa. She looked like a reclining goddess, especially as she was dressed in a silver gown.'

Murray imagined the moment and the impact it would have made on someone of any age. 'Apart from how she looked, what did you make of her as a person?' he asked.

'In a word - kind,' said Aileen. She asked me to sit by her while my aunt was getting everything ready for a fitting. There was so much I wanted to ask her, but she was more interested in my life in Ireland and how my aunt came to be so clever. She asked if I could deliver the finished shoes, but my aunt said no.'

'Why do you think she wanted you to deliver them?' asked Murray.

Aileen thought hard about Murray's question before answering. 'There was a certain sorrow in her eyes. She reached out and stroked my hair, saying she wished she didn't have to dye hers to make it the same shade as mine. She went on to say, that had I been a few years younger, we could almost be mother and daughter. So in answer to your question - I think she was lonely.'

'Why do you think she was lonely?' asked Murray.

'As I got to know her I found out that she was fed up only mixing mainly with people that had an agenda. Nice to her because of who she was,' said Aileen. 'She got more pleasure from locking herself away and reading a good book.'

'So you saw her often?' asked Murray.

'About once a week. She made excuses that she wanted more shoes and she'd change her mind about colours all the time, sending me backwards and forwards for fresh samples.'

'And you met no resistance from security at the studios? After all, she was a big star,' said Murray.

'My aunt was well-respected and she didn't need ID to get in through the main gates. It wasn't long before I didn't either.'

'So Marilyn must've satisfied her appetite for shoes,' said Murray.

Aileen laughed. 'What women ever does detective? I certainly don't think Marilyn did. As well as that, I felt like she'd adopted me, plus she kept my aunt sweet by introducing her to rich friends. You could say it was Marilyn that gave my aunt's business the extra push. Orders were coming in thick and fast. So things were great, I had an excuse to stay, but then everything changed...' she said, stopping mid flow.

Murray let Aileen mull her thoughts over and said nothing, hoping for a big reveal.

She poured two cups of tea, and seemed to be considering her next sentence. 'I didn't put everything in my book that I found out about Marilyn, out of respect for her memory. Because we had got very close. We talked about things I daren't discuss with my own mother. Like men, sex, drugs and more importantly why I shouldn't get wrapped up with any of them. It was a shame that Marilyn couldn't follow her own advice,' said Aileen finally, laughing at the hypocrisy of Marilyn.

'Yes, if she'd followed her own advice she might still be alive today,' said Murray, watching Aileen closely for a reaction to his words. She showed none.

'So what's the real reason you're so interested in Marilyn after fifty-five years?' she asked, suddenly suspicious again. 'I don't believe it's because of a few possessions.'

Murray was scuppered again. Under scrutiny and face to face with Aileen, he felt as though they were like pieces on a chessboard. She was the queen and he was a lowly pawn. 'I've told you why. It could compromise the case if I were to discuss it in more detail. You know that surely, judging by your crime-writing history.'

'That's as maybe,' said Aileen. 'But I have to know I can trust you before I tell you anything else.'

'You can trust me one hundred percent,' said Murray with conviction. 'I mean to look after Marilyn... I mean Marilyn's possessions.'

Aileen looked deep into his eyes before continuing, but failed to pick up on his near faux pas about Norma. 'You're an honest man. I can see that.'

Her statement made Murray feel instantly guilty, although he had only bent the truth to suit his questioning. If she were ever to have the opportunity to cross-question him, he was fairly certain he could wriggle out of his white lies. 'There are those of us - the majority in my opinion, that are honourable,' he said.

Aileen ignored his defence and continued. 'I can prove I knew Marilyn. I've something really precious to me that will undoubtedly convince you.'

Murray's heart began to beat faster as he thought about the possibilities of trustworthy evidence.

Aileen disarranged her pile of papers again. Underneath

was a bunch of faded photographs held together with an elastic band as well as a beaten-up album. She began to turn the album's dog-eared pages. 'This is a year by year record of my every birthday including when I went to America,' she said.

Murray decided to go along with her to win complete trust, sharing moments of humour with her over specific photographs. 'They're a wonderful record, but I still don't see what they prove,' he said, finally, not spotting anything of use and frustrated by her detour from her story.

Aileen pointed again to the penultimate page in the album. 'This is me on my nineteenth birthday - taken here in the garden.'

Murray looked around for confirmation of the location and was instantly satisfied to see nothing much had changed as far as the cottage was concerned. Other than that his interest was fading. 'I can see that it's here, but how is this proof?'

'Now take a look at this one,' said Aileen, turning to the last page of the album. Would you say this is me?'

He compared the two. 'Why yes - undoubtedly. You haven't changed that much,' he said, feeding her ego.

'So bearing in mind, I can prove I was born here, and the picture is clearly of me, what do you make of this?' She moved her thumb to one side to reveal the remainder of the black and white photograph. With an arm wrapped around her shoulder, was Marilyn Monroe, barefoot and smiling, holding a pair of kitten heels above her head.

Murray gasped. 'Some photo,' he said. 'But all it proves is that you posed for a photo with her.'

Aileen humphed. 'This was taken at my aunt's house in the States. It was the one time Marilyn visited us there.

It was my twentieth birthday.'

It suddenly occurred to Murray that Aileen's unusual background made a story in itself. Ever thought of writing a sequel?' he asked.

Aileen laughed. 'There's not much more to say about me, but there was a lot of mystery attached to Marilyn that would make a great read. I must admit I've toyed with the idea. But as it's facts I have to be careful when it comes to Marilyn's estate. I could be sued if they don't like what I've got to say.'

Murray had not really heard the last part of Aileen's explanation, as the mention of mystery had instantly drawn him in. 'I'd really like your take on her last few months,' he said. 'And then perhaps we can talk about how you think things ended for her. Like whether it was suicide or murder.'

Aileen put on her glasses and moving closer, looked at him through thick lenses. 'Don't try and fool me detective. The Irish have many gifts apart from reading palms. I can see right inside your mind. The cogs are spinning fast. So I'm right there is more to your visit than you've told me.'

Murray took a gamble and imparted the smallest of details to Aileen. 'There have been some developments,' he said, watching to see if she was hooked by such a simple statement.

'Developments? Bejesus, I'm in no doubt that you've stumbled across much more than that. I can feel it in my bones. You just want me to ratify what you already know,' she barked.

Again Murray felt like he was on the receiving end of the questioning. He was getting nowhere, so without a second thought, he bent police protocol. 'Okay Aileen, I can see you're a highly intelligent woman, so I'll tell you this much. A new witness has come to light, with a different version of events of the night that Marilyn died.' Instantly, he was taken aback that Aileen did not bat an eyelid to such a bold claim.

Instead, she looked out over the orchard while she reviewed their metaphorical game of chess. Suddenly her eyes seemed to sparkle, making her look jubilant as though she were about to make the winning move. Murray held his breath expectantly.

'Glory be... or should I say Gloria?' Aileen said, cleverly, playing with her words while at the same time watching for Murray's reaction.

Murray gulped and his words stuck in his throat. 'What the ...?'

'Shush for a second,' interrupted Aileen, fumbling through her papers until she had reached the bottom of the pile. She slid a Polaroid across the table. It was faded and dog-eared but showed Marilyn next to a woman who was her double in appearance, with a wine glass in her hand.

Murray was beginning to sweat. He discarded his jacket. 'How did...how do you know about her?' he asked.

'Gloria's the only person who's not ever come to light. Only the president, his confidantes and Marilyn's housekeeper knew about her. It wasn't difficult to guess who you were talking about,' said Aileen.

It was obvious to Murray that Aileen took great delight in having the upper hand. 'Even so,' I didn't expect you to know her, and if you did know her, I'm surprised you've told me so willingly,' he said, feeling a little bruised that he had been rumbled.

Aileen chose to side-track. 'I thought that Marilyn's possessions were why you came to see me. But that's not the case is it? Is Gloria the real reason? Because if she's still alive, senile, disabled or otherwise, I'd like to give her a piece of my mind?'

'All I can say is I'm looking into a possible scam,' said Murray, still astounded by Aileen's intuition, but keeping the rest secret. 'So what makes you think she's still alive?'

'I always thought she might surface. After all she's a few years younger than Marilyn. Is she after these possessions you've mentioned? If she is, it's just to make money. She was a gold-digger from the start. I always had a bad feeling about her. '

'Why - something she did?' asked Murray, saying little in order to draw Aileen out.

'Sometimes I feel her still watching me from wherever she is. She hated anyone who got close to Marilyn.' She trembled and then abruptly switched the subject. 'Did you see a black car outside the house?'

'With tinted windows?' asked Murray.

'That's the one. Anything to do with your lot back in England?'

'No, not at all,' said Murray, making a mental note to check if it was there when he left for the airport.

'It's been hanging about for a few days. I'm followed wherever I go. I'm sure it's because of the content of my book. If Gloria's not read it yet and is concerned about the content, she could have something to do with me being followed.'

'Why didn't you go to the Garda? They could've investigated,' said Murray.

'I don't want to add even more attention to myself plus there's been more happening,' said Aileen, becoming edgy. 'That's all I'll say on the matter. And if you know what's good for you, you'll get back to England as quickly as you can DC Murray.'

'I really need some more answers before I head back,' said Murray, sensing he was about to be blanked.

'I've given you plenty to be going on with. You've been here a while now. Enough time for whoever's in that black car to think you're just a journalist. Before their suspicions are raised I'd rather you go. Leave me your private contact details, not Scotland Yard's and I'll be in touch,' insisted Aileen.

Despite Murray trying to open up the conversation again, Aileen was having none of it. But somehow, when she was showing him back into the house, he managed to walk far enough behind her, to be able to discreetly pull the photo of Marilyn and Aileen together from out of the album and pocket it.

The taxi driver was asleep in his car by the village green. Murray roused him but chose to sit in the back again so that he could think through his conversation with Aileen, undisturbed by idle chatter.

As they pulled away, he looked over his shoulder and noticed what looked like the same blacked out car entering the village. He opened his window to get a better look, but his obvious scrutiny caused the driver of the other car to speed off. Murray took one last look at Aileen's cottage. A feeling of trepidation gripped him, but he pushed it to one side and concentrated instead on the evidence he had gathered. He wished he had managed to re-engage with Aileen further, but she had clearly been frightened by the end of their conversation. He took out the photo he had borrowed, feeling guilty that he had just confiscated such a special memory. He hoped however, that as Aileen read people's fortunes, that she would imagine that the photo had been spirited away, rather than confront him.

He woke suddenly to the voice of his driver, surprised at first that he had dozed off so easily.

'Do you know the people in that car?' his driver asked.

Murray looked out of the passenger windows either side of him. He had been asleep for some time and they were already driving through a built up part of Dublin on their approach to the airport. He could see nothing untoward and he knew better than to spin around as to do so would most likely turn an untoward journey into a drama. He feigned indifference. 'I doubt it. I'm not from around here.'

'Well they seem to know you,' said his driver. 'They were circling the village green while you were in that house. They've been behind us all the way from Carlingford.'

'How far are we from the airport?' asked Murray, weighing up the situation.

Ten minutes or thereabouts. Five if I step on it.'

As they passed shops, Murray tried to use their display windows as mirrors, but to no avail. 'Make it five minutes then. Gives me time to freshen up before my flight,' he said.

The driver seemed to think it time to familiarise himself with Murray. 'My names Darragh,' he said, realising that talk of freshening up was a ploy and that something was amiss.

'Good to meet you Darragh, now step on it,' said Murray.

'As you wish,' said Darragh. He took immediate and decisive action, seeming to revel in the chance of a chase. Murray could see his steely expression in the rear view mirror as he gripped his steering wheel with firm determination. He suddenly took a sharp turn to the right, crossing oncoming traffic.

Murray slid involuntarily across the leather seat, barely preventing his one piece of evidence from disappearing down into the foot well. He used the opportunity to take a quick look out of the rear window. The pursuing car was stationary, held up by the same oncoming cars that Darragh had narrowly missed. Darragh seemed practised at the art of being a getaway driver and although the streets were narrow and cobbled, he was not put off by obstacles such as dustbins cluttering up pavements outside cafes and slot machine arcades.

'Are you sure we can get through this way?' asked Murray.

Darragh seemed unflustered by the chase. 'You'll not be getting away without help from the likes of me. I'll get you there in time for a shave and a haircut as well as a freshen up if you like,' he added.

Murray took another furtive glance behind. The other car had turned into the same street and was gaining ground. 'There'll be extra money if you make it to the airport unaccompanied,' he said, taking several notes from out of his wallet.

'That's settled then. Hold onto your hat,' said Darragh. He made another turn into what seemed an even narrower street than the one before. 'You don't want to come down this way on your own at night - copper or no copper,' he laughed. 'You'll either get beaten to a pulp or catch something nasty in a brothel.'

'I'll remember that next time I'm in Dublin,' said Murray, wondering whether his profession was transparent or if Darragh had just made a lucky guess. He wished he could treat the chase with the same mirth that Darragh seemed able to adopt. Glancing at the shops, which were for the most part boarded up or victim to vandalism and graffiti, he gathered his paperwork together. He could then make a quick exit once they reached the airport. But then, he reminded himself that he still had to retrieve his case from the boot of the car.

The pursuing vehicle was losing some ground, its stylish but exorbitant width causing its tyres to screech as they came into contact with the kerb stones each side. Darragh reacted inwardly to the situation, acting as though he was a character in an American gangster movie, being aided by the underworld. Several cars seemed to have come to his aid, scuppering Murray's pursuer, having pulled out right at the opportune moment behind Darragh's taxi.

Finally, they turned a corner and were instantly back in the flow of normal traffic on the main road to the airport. The other car was nowhere in sight. In Murray's mind, it had been ambushed and dealt with by characters from Dublin's ghetto. He breathed a sigh of relief as they pulled up by the airport's drop off-zone.

Darragh jumped out and grabbed Murray's case from the boot. Murray held out a generous wad of notes, which Darragh hid quickly in his trouser pocket. 'You won't need to worry about them,' he said, handing over a tatty business card. 'In case you need me again.'

Murray adopted a stoic expression in order to give the impression that he neither approved or disapproved of whatever measures had been taken by Darragh's less than savoury friends back in the narrow streets. So as not to seem ungrateful, he shook hands firmly and headed off into the departure hall, still on alert for anymore unwelcome attention. By the time he was seated on his plane and taxiing out to the runway, his nerves were jangling. London suddenly seemed a peaceful destination, though in the corridors of his mind, he knew that whoever had nearly got to him, would most likely already have arranged an unpleasant reception for him at the other end. He messaged ahead for Judy to meet him, omitting any reasoning other than he would rather discuss his initial findings out of earshot of anyone at the yard.

Chapter 17

A Close Shave

As Murray made his way through arrivals, he received Judy's text. She was already outside waiting, armed with coffee and cake as usual.

Within a few minutes, he was sitting next to her. 'Let's get out of here a bit sharpish. I was tailed to Dublin airport,' he said, checking outside the car for unwelcome attention. He realised that Darragh's love of melodrama seemed to have rubbed off on him and travelled with him all the way from Dublin to London.

Judy put on her shades and pulled away, tyres skidding on tarmac as she accelerated, causing passers-by to turn and stare. 'I have to say Steve, there's never a dull moment with you. I love a good car chase,' she said, taking corners like a Le Mans driver.

Murray clutched his steaming hot coffee with both hands to prevent it from spilling. 'You know me. I like to keep things interesting, but would you ease off just a bit or I'll be wearing this coffee?'

After a short drive, Judy slowed down and swung

the car into a parking space overlooking a boating lake, which was one of her favourite spots. She undid her seat belt and turned to face Murray. 'I only want to hear the exciting bits,' she said, thrusting a box of doughnuts into his free hand.

'No thanks - I feel sick,' he said, pushing them away. 'I think I'm going to throw up.'

'It was you that told me to get a move on. So get over it and tell me about Ireland and about being followed,' said Judy.

Murray rolled down the window and gasped for fresh air. 'At least I got to meet the author, Dogherty, but that meeting's made the case more complicated.'

'You must've got something out of it that will help us. And you being followed means you've rattled someone's cage,' said Judy.

'I couldn't catch their number plate so I couldn't run a check. I'm waiting for Aileen Dogherty to email me what she was too frightened to discuss in person.'

'I'm confused,' said Judy. 'You said the author was a man.'

Murray explained Aileen's pen-name and filled Judy in on his trip, while he allowed himself to drift and think about how he was due for a holiday. In between sipping his coffee and considering his love for his job, he wistfully wished he were with his compliant girlfriend, Jane, drinking Chablis and feeding ducks on the grass bank in front of Judy's car. More recently, his relationship with Jane had been challenged, the gaps between seeing each other widening with each passing week. He pushed thoughts of his ailing love life to one side, relieved that his nausea was beginning to pass.

He looked out across the boating lake, which was

busy with families in rowing boats, despite it being mid evening. People were having fun, but their lives were a world apart from the mystery that he and Judy were investigating. He felt fleetingly robbed, in the sense that he had so little time for leisure activities. 'I did get this,' he said as an afterthought, remembering the Polaroid photo in his pocket. 'Aileen with Marilyn. Seems they were very good friends until the night she died.'

Judy studied the photograph of the two women. 'You're making me doubt everything. Could this be Gloria rather than Marilyn - and Aileen's in on the scam?' she suggested.

'Gloria's beginning to fascinate me as much as Norma does,' said Murray, sidestepping the question.

'Why's that - got a hunch?' asked Judy.

'I'm not sure yet but something's niggling me. I think it's to do with Huntley Manor. A mystery we've yet to unravel.'

'Well don't keep me in the dark,' said Judy, excited by the intrigue.

'Whereas Aileen was reluctant at first to talk about Gloria, counting Mary's performance out, Norma was quite the opposite,' observed Murray. 'I'm thinking I should have been persistent and stopped over in Ireland longer. I might have achieved more clarity.'

'Well, you've still got the next two days off. Follow your instincts. Go back if need be,' suggested Judy.

Murray looked down at his phone thoughtfully. 'I need to head off home. Grab a bit of shuteye and wait for Aileen's email.'

'I'll drop you at the station then,' suggested Judy, quickly tidying the mess in her lap.

She pulled away to join processional traffic, noticing

that Murray seemed preoccupied with his thoughts. She glanced across at him. He had that faraway look about him, signalling that he was onto something meaningful. She knew better than to try and draw him out, while his brilliant mind simmered. Whatever he came up with next would be worth her patience. She dropped him in Lower Marsh.

'See you in the morning,' said Murray, jumping out and closing the door before Judy could respond. He walked briskly away.

She watched him disappear along a cut-through to Waterloo station, mingling with a few late commuters, thinking that one day he could make Commissioner if he wanted.

Murray meanwhile, was dealing with a whole new set of emotions. His nerves were frayed and he was tired. After having purchased a ticket to Clapham Junction, he looked at the departures board. With time to spare, he sat on a bench and picked up a dog-eared newspaper that someone had discarded. He glanced up occasionally, finding himself suspicious of everyone, so he flicked idly through the newspaper in order to ground himself.

Just as he was about to go to his platform his phone lit up but before he could answer, it stopped ringing. He did not recognise the number but the caller had left a voice mail. The message was from Aileen and not only was her voice very shaky; she had followed him to London. His battery was low so for fear of his phone cutting out when he called her, he scribbled her number on the back of his hand. He had only just put his pen away when she called again. She sounded even more overwrought and her tone was urgent.

'I had to come. Soon as you'd gone I got a bag together

and got the next flight.'

'But why are you here? You were going to email what I needed to know,' said Murray.

'Listen - I daren't talk now. I'll explain when I see you. Where can we meet?' whispered Aileen, suggesting she was surrounded by people.

'Clapham Junction, in half an hour? There's a cafe called the Birdhouse a stone's throw from the station. I'll wait for you there,' said Murray.

'On my way,' said Aileen, hanging up with no further explanation.

Suddenly Murray's screen went black. 'Fuck it,' he uttered, gaining a few disgruntled looks from passersby. Worse than that, without it, it was harder to throw Aileen a lifeline should she suddenly need it, or call Judy and ask her to join them to get up to speed. Instead, he sat on the train from Waterloo to Clapham Junction tapping out an impatient rhythm on the table in front of him as he looked out of the windows at graffiti and grime. The middle-aged couple seated opposite looked irritated by his habit and spoke to each other in whispers in between fixing him with stony stares. He imagined they thought better of complaining as most likely in their minds they did not know what this young man was capable of. He could after all be a mugger. Aware that they were looking down their noses at him, he smiled as he left his seat, getting not the slightest acknowledgement in return.

Soon after, Murray was seated in a booth drinking whisky ahead of Aileen turning up, his phone charger plugged into a socket at fingertips length away. There were no new missed calls or texts from her. The Birdhouse was a favourite haunt of his. Open from early till late, it was the place for tip-offs to police by London's undesirables.

He and Judy frequented the place often when there was talk of something kicking-off or when a serious crime had just been committed. Murray had opened his wallet many times and offered up its contents to his regular informers in the very booth he was now seated in. The cafe owner, Mike Higgins lived upstairs. He generally pretended to know nothing and to have seen nothing, but was happy to stay open even if the closed sign was on display, in exchange for a generous tip.

The cafe could be easily missed by anyone passing, due to its nondescript appearance and unappealing menu. Murray had never thought to ask Mike how it got its name, but he had been told by an unreliable source that the cafe used to be a strip joint where the dancers had performed in over-sized bird cages to prevent the punters from feeling them up. Mike Higgins had no interest in drumming up new business, so since taking the place over, he had chosen to leave both exterior and interior shabby, to encourage passing commuters or business people on lunch break to stay away. His was a cafe of the old sort, a dubious stopping place, where people met to make deals in whispers. Out the back, accessed by a cobbled alleyway, was a meeting room with blackout curtains reserved for those who wielded power in London's underworld and wished to remain completely anonymous. Mike made more money by accepting the wads of notes that were shoved in his back pocket as he cleared tables, than from the food and drinks purchased there by the punters. His attractive much younger wife, Angie, asked no questions as to why the takings differed from the till record, preferring to keep both Mike and his racketeers sweet by serving cheap but good fry-ups and strong coffee, while looking seductive in low-cut tops.

Murray had no need to ask for another drink. Mike was at the ready. He kept cheap spirits under the counter and had no intention of paying a licence fee that could be anything up to a couple of grand. Murray was treated no differently to any other customer. His glass was always full, but only because Mike was far too generous with the ice, a habit that Murray frowned upon. At home he drank alone, savouring a single malt with a few drops of water in a tulip glass. Either way, on this occasion, he could feel the whisky working as the tension began to diminish in his shoulders and neck.

He slipped off his coat and jacket and loosened his tie. It was at that precise moment that he had a thought. Could it be possible that Joe DiMaggio had at one time frequented the Birdhouse? It seemed an obvious conclusion to make, bearing in mind the rumours that back in the fifties and sixties he had hung out with the lowest of the low in London's underworld. In the same breath, Murray dismissed the possibility. It would have to be an amazing coincidence if it were true.

He looked at his watch and then out of the window for any sign of Aileen. The weather had closed in. Rain was falling hard, but the dirt on Mike's windows refused to be shifted. On top of this, a drain in the road was blocked. As a result, the contents of a puddle were being deposited all over the shop front every time that a car passed by. Murray had just checked his watch for the umpteenth time when at last he spotted Aileen, encumbered by a suitcase on wheels, that was slowing her pace as she made her way along the pavement on the other side of the street.

Finally, she reached the kerb opposite the cafe, only to step into the road without checking for traffic. Several passing motorists hooted in anger. For a few seconds she disappeared from view behind a slow-moving bus. When it had moved on, Murray realised that she was nowhere to be seen. He scanned the street in both directions, fearful that she had been followed and snatched, or hit by a car and dragged along the road. He was about to run outside, when she flung open the door.

'Jesus, Mary and Joseph,' she uttered. 'I must look a sight.'

'Come in, come in,' said Murray, pushing the door closed behind her and shooting a glance to check she was completely alone. 'While you get your coat off, let me get you a coffee or tea.'

'Nothing for now thanks. Give me a minute to catch my breath,' she said.

Murray took her things and held out a chair for her. She was drenched and the worse for wear. She removed her headscarf, which was so old-style it had aged her twenty years.

'I'm too old for all this malarkey,' she said at last. 'But I was too afraid to stay at home. I've sent Margaret to stay with a cousin until I get back.'

'Afraid - did something happen after I left?' asked Murray.

Aileen lost her cool. 'Don't downplay the situation detective. Remember that black car I mentioned to you? Margaret was watching through the net curtains after you left and saw it take off after you. Like a bat out of hell according to her.'

Murray tried to make a joke of it. 'It followed me all the way to the airport. Luckily my driver fancied himself as a bit of a Steve McQueen and lost him.'

Aileen smiled despite her anxiety. 'That'll be Darragh

- am I right? There's only a handful of drivers ever come out our way. You were fortunate it was him.'

'Surely me being tailed wasn't the reason you came all the way to London,' said Murray. 'You could've emailed like you said you would.'

'I got frightened about being watched all the time. Is that a good enough reason?'

Murray recalled Norma telling him a similar story about Gloria being tailed. But I wish you'd told me you were this scared. I might have been able to help.'

'I doubt that. If the Garda had got to hear you were sniffing around on their territory, things would have gone from bad to worse, believe me,' insisted Aileen.

Murray tried to reassure her. 'Well you're here now, and while you're in London, nothing's going to happen. I'll make sure you're well looked after,' he added, wondering how he was going to progress with the case now it had gathered a more sinister momentum.

'You'd better keep to your word,' said Aileen, poking Murray in the arm with a bony finger. She pulled out a hip flask and took a swig. Then she spoke again in a whisper. 'I realise I've no choice but to spill what I know about Gloria - before someone gets to me.'

Murray felt like all his Christmases had come at once. 'Before we start, I'd like my colleague Judy to be here. Anything you tell me is safe with her. Are you okay with that?'

With Aileen agreeing to his suggestion, he called Judy. She had made little headway due to heavy traffic near Waterloo so did an immediate turnabout, probably in Murray's mind, in the most dramatic way possible. With a view to keep Aileen exactly where she was for as long as it took to squeeze out every last drop of information out of her, he ordered her a meal of her choosing. Mike appeared promptly with a couple of lagers.

'I'll not be drinking that,' said Aileen, pushing hers away. 'Pond water, that's what it is. I'll be downing the black,' she added, pulling several bottles of Guinness from her hand luggage.

Murray gave Mike a discreet wink to ignore Aileen's disrespect. 'Perhaps some of your amazing bread pudding Mike?' said Murray to placate him.

Mike sloped off, his hackles up.

Aileen rummaged in her bag again and pulled out a multi-tool, which resembled a fat penknife. She flicked off a lid effortlessly with one of the many threatening metal implements hidden within its casing. 'I'd use this if I had to,' she said, brandishing it freely. 'No one starts on the Irish and gets away with it.'

'I have to say Aileen, you're not typical of a woman your age. In fact you're showing me a completely different side to when I first met you,' said Murray, laughing. 'But maybe keep those comments to yourself and don't go assaulting anyone while you're in London. We need to be on the same side and not draw attention to the fact you're here,' he added.

'Agreed,' answered Aileen, taking a generous slug from her bottle.

By the time Aileen had sampled Mike's bread pudding and congratulated him on his successful recipe, Judy had arrived, having parked her car a few shops down so as to have clear vision of the area outside.

She sat down and introduced herself to Aileen and then whispered to Mike. 'Close up shop will you? I think I was followed here.'

Chapter 18

Now You See Me, Now You Don't

Mike jumped into action, locking and bolting the front door and closing the blackout blinds in super quick time, as though he were practised at lock-downs. Any regulars picking that time to arrive, would know immediately that if the cafe were closed at this hour, there was a very good reason and, they were not to ask questions later.

Murray watched the process then turned to Judy. 'How long were you followed?' he asked, peering through a small hole in the blinds. There was no one in sight and no parked car apart from Judy's. Murray looked around to check they could not be overheard. The only people of concern were a handful of doubtful looking characters seated at tables at the back of the cafe, but they were well out of earshot and the types to be expected at the Birdhouse.

'Don't worry. I lost them,' said Judy, casually. 'We

must've been followed to the boating lake when I picked you up at City airport. After I'd dropped you at Waterloo, a couple of guys approached my car as I was pulling away.'

'Did you recognise them?' asked Murray.

'No, but they were bloody careless. They walked right into view of the CCTV cameras. I'll request the footage later,' said Judy.

'Bejesus, you've got me wondering what I've got myself into,' said Aileen suddenly. 'Maybe it was safer in Ireland after all.'

'There's nothing to worry about. It happens all the time,' said Judy, shooting a concerned look at Murray. 'We're safe here,' she added, avoiding any eye-contact with Aileen that might give her personal doubts away. She took out her notebook and pen.

'Judy's up to date on what we discussed back in Ireland Aileen, but she'll record everything you tell me from now on,' said Murray. 'We need to get to the bottom of why all of us have been followed.'

'Let's get on with it then before I change my mind. All the shenanigans has made me lose my thread,' said Aileen, opening another bottle.

'You'd just started telling me about Gloria,' said Murray, willing her on.

'Oh yes - and I think one of the last things I said, was how she scared me,' said Aileen.

'Can you enlarge on that for my benefit?' said Judy.

'Well, I met her a few times and it didn't take me long to work her out. In my opinion she wanted to be Marilyn. And I mean, really be Marilyn, not just a highly paid stand-in.'

'Let's backtrack to where you met her the first time so

we can pinpoint the exact moment you got an inkling of that,' said Judy.

'It was round about the spring of nineteen-sixty-two. By then, I'd been to Marilyn's a few times. On one of those occasions she introduced me to Gloria,' said Elaine.

'This was at her bungalow in Brentwood?' asked Murray.

'That's right. Marilyn set me up meeting her, treating it like a joke, so she could see my reaction. I'd been let in by Gloria - me thinking all the time it was Marilyn. At first she'd fooled me, as we had a hug and I hadn't spotted anything different at all. All of a sudden, out popped the real Marilyn from her bedroom. I nearly fainted. Anyway, once I'd recovered and the situation had been explained, we all had a laugh about it. Marilyn in particular found it hilarious. But in answer to your comment about when I first felt something wasn't right, there was something about Gloria that got to me. I disliked her from the start. You see, Marilyn was mostly like a playful child, whereas Gloria had a built-in smugness about her. As far as personalities were concerned - they were like chalk and cheese.'

'So if you could see the differences how do you think Gloria managed to carry off the body-double act?' asked Murray.

'Physically, they were very similar, so in public and not too close up, Gloria was amazing. She could turn on everything that Marilyn had taught her at the drop of a hat. She had everyone fooled. That's what worried me,' said Aileen, her face clouding over at the memory.

'Why was that?' asked Judy.

'There were always Gloria's dark sideways glances at Marilyn. Gloria didn't think I'd noticed. She was obsessed with Marilyn in a very unhealthy way. Insanely jealous. It got worse,' added Aileen, finally, shivering at the memory.

'Tell me more about that,' said Judy, realising all of a sudden that she had been totally sucked into Aileen's story. The chink of teacups and incessant buzz of conversation throughout the cafe had become nothing but a distant murmur.

Aileen continued. 'Much as I loved being with Marilyn, I was back and forth to the studios for my aunt plus learning to make shoes so that I could stay on long term. I couldn't protect Marilyn at the same time.'

'You felt she needed protection from Gloria?' asked Murray.

'Without a doubt,' insisted Aileen. 'Marilyn was so sweetly naive. I was so worried that in the end I concocted a lie to free up time to be with her. Told my aunt I'd injured my thumb hammering leather. Lucky for me she didn't think to examine it. She cut my working hours to give it time to heal. By the end of April I was managing to see Marilyn, and Gloria most days.'

Judy looked up from her writing, imagining the idea for a Hollywood movie unfolding due to Aileen being such a good storyteller. A tale of two Marilyns seemed much more intriguing than the story that had been put out to the public for decades. She continued with her notes.

'Would you say that by that point you were a close friend to Marilyn? asked Murray.

'I think so. I was her biggest ally for sure, though to most people I was just a silly kid. Marilyn told me so many secrets. During one of our conversations I suggested she told fewer people, especially Gloria, about her innermost self.'

'How did she react to your suggestion?' asked Judy.

'She laughed and at first didn't take me seriously. But then I decided it best to tell her that Gloria was jealous. We were by the pool when I told her. She was wearing a dark wig so she looked just like a regular visitor, in case any photographers got into the garden. Gloria was always in character, dressed and made up as Marilyn. On this particular occasion, Marilyn was painting her nails, only half-listening to what I was telling her, when she noticed her favourite shade of nail polish was nearly empty. Just as she was figuring out why, Gloria appeared, in one of Marilyn's favourite bikinis. Marilyn completely lost it. I'd never seen her get angry before. She tore a piece out of Gloria, saying she had no right to help herself to anything without asking first.'

So real was Aileen's description of events, that Murray imagined himself in the moment, just as he had when listening to Norma's accounts of President Kennedy. He looked across at Judy only to see that her eyes were glazed, as though she too were in a far off place. He could practically feel the heat on his skin as he lay on a sun lounger next to Marilyn, he and Judy, as a pair of time travellers, lapping up the sun while watching a past argument unfold. He allowed himself to be sucked further into Aileen's storytelling, so much so, that he felt as though he was on the brink of being in two places at once.

'That's when I saw the real Gloria,' Aileen continued, allowing her writing skills to describe the scene in full Technicolour. 'She dived into the pool and slithered silently under the water like an Amazon river snake. Finally, she came up for air. Her eyes were just above the surface; cold and fixed on Marilyn. I'll never get that image out of my mind. As she reached us, she pulled herself up on the side of the pool, mimicking Marilyn's voice to a tee, as though she were in front of a camera. I could almost imagine her winding her coils around Marilyn. But the problem was, that as usual, Marilyn was so trusting. She seemed to think that by putting on such a fine performance, it was Gloria's way of apologising. Just like that, Marilyn had forgotten their argument. She was lovely. Couldn't see the bad in anyone. Gloria however, saw it in a completely different light. As for me - all I could see was pure evil. Gloria was a brood parasite - the cuckoo in the nest.'

Murray shivered as the temperature seemed to drop from a hot summer's afternoon in LA to the rainy day that had fallen on London. He jolted himself back to the conversation. 'So after that incident, did you continue to warn Marilyn of your suspicions?'

'Of sorts. Like I said, Marilyn always saw the best in everyone so I thought she'd brush off whatever I said. That was what made her so vulnerable. Even though I was only twenty at the time, I was smart enough to have spotted what Gloria was up to. She wanted...to get rid of Marilyn.'

'Please don't take offence at the next question,' said Judy, expecting to witness an outburst from Aileen. 'On reflection, have you ever thought all this might have been in your imagination?' she asked. Aileen did not bite back.

'No offence taken. I did question myself at first. After all I'd been dropped into a glamorous world, miles from what I was used to back in a sleepy village in Ireland. But Gloria was very transparent. That performance in the pool convinced me she was up to no good. I realised I was right when something even more sinister happened.'

Judy shivered, caught up in the mystery. 'How can it have got worse?' she asked. Realising her statement might have misconstrued as sarcasm, she carried on writing.

Aileen took another slug of her Guinness and composed herself. 'I was at Marilyn's one evening. She'd popped out to the studios for a costume fitting but told me to wait for her to return. It had been another hot day so I'd found a secluded spot in the garden and was flicking through a magazine. Gloria appeared from the bungalow, not realising I was there. Call it intuition if you like, but something told me to remain silent and watch what she was up to. At first, she stood by the pool, seeming to enjoy the cool breeze, but then she flopped down onto a pool side chair. She was very pale, which was unusual. All of a sudden, she lifted up her top and peeled away a dressing that was taped to her abdomen. What I saw next I couldn't believe. There was a large wound. Even from where I was sitting I could see it was fresh. She winced as she replaced the dressing. I realised immediately what she had done.'

'Why would she do that to herself?' asked Murray, noticing that Judy had turned grey.

'Marilyn had an operation scar on her stomach,' said Aileen. 'Gloria was putting the finishing touches to her likeness to Marilyn. She would clearly do whatever it took. The trouble was, she hadn't done her homework as far as recovery was concerned. The wound would take some time to heal, so she wouldn't be able to get rid of Marilyn before that had happened. Anyway that aside, I think I must have made a noise without realising. Covering my tracks, I pretended I was still reading. Then all of a sudden, Gloria was towering above me, her shadow blocking my sun.'

'What happened then?' asked Judy, slightly recovered.

'Gloria asked me how long I'd been sitting there. I said I'd been there ages reading. She asked me if I'd seen her come out and I said I'd been too into a story to notice her.'

'Did she believe you?' asked Murray.

'No she didn't, because she said if I did see her by the pool, I'd better put it out of my mind and keep my mouth shut. She was intent on scaring me,' said Aileen.

'Did you think she was capable of violence?' asked Judy.

'I was certain Gloria had inflicted that wound on herself, so definitely yes. From then on, she filled me with terror every time our paths crossed. We'd a secret that I was desperate to unload but she was desperate for me to keep. She was unhinged.'

'How have you kept quiet about such a story?' asked Judy, finally having lost all professionalism. 'It'd make a fantastic novel.'

'I've already made that suggestion,' said Murray. 'Not meaning to take anything of what you've said lightly Aileen, but Judy's right.'

Aileen suddenly looked offended. 'Meaning it's just a story I've invented to make money? I know it's far-fetched, which is one of the reasons I'm having to work so hard to convince you.'

'If you were us I think you might feel the same,' said Judy.

Aileen humphed then continued. 'I thought Gloria was mad but she wasn't the only one. Poor Marilyn was troubled too. She'd inherited some of her mother's madness for sure.'

'How do you mean?' asked Judy.

'When I'd known Marilyn a few months, she confided in me that sometimes she couldn't think straight because of all the voices in her head. I played it down and told her it was a typical symptom of stress, but she told me she'd suffered from it since she was young. I think I must've reassured her as for a while the episodes stopped. But just when I thought she was in a good place, the voices returned, tenfold, only this time she insisted they were warning her about the people who were following her.'

'So did you think she was crazy?' asked Judy, suddenly feeling terribly sad about Marilyn's vulnerability.

'I don't think she was crazy, just extremely troubled. Not a day goes by when I don't think I should have seen what was coming. When she died, I couldn't bear to be anywhere near her home or the studios. I was devastated so I came straight back to Ireland. You can check on my whereabouts if you want.'

'Don't worry, we will,' said Murray.

Judy shot him a warning glance to be more considerate of Aileen's feelings.

'I did a lot of thinking on my return,' continued Aileen. I for one, never believed Marilyn killed herself. Those last few months, she was reaching out for new opportunities.'

'So what's your theory on her murder?' asked Judy.

'It's no secret she was madly in love with President Kennedy. She told me he'd said they'd be together one day. Her ex, Joe DiMaggio was back on the scene too. I told her not to play with fire as it might cause rivalry, but she ignored my advice. On top of this, she knew too much for her own good. So although her lovers had good cause to shut Marilyn up, I don't think it was any of them. I lay money on it being Gloria in a fit of jealousy.'

Judy looked up from her notebook. 'You think she

secretly administered the cocktail of drugs that killed Marilyn?'

'Without a doubt. She could have just spiked Marilyn's drink so she passed out and let someone else do the rest,' said Aileen.

'If that's the case, why didn't Gloria just assume Marilyn's identity after the murder and cash in on her fame?' suggested Murray.

'Someone wouldn't let her. She'd become too greedy. I think it was a double killing that night in August. Unless of course, Gloria got away and there is an empty grave.'

Judy gasped at Aileen's twist in the tale. Her head was overflowing with the new information.

Murray too was overloaded with fresh possibilities. He needed time to think it through, so stepped away from that fateful night by changing the subject. 'Your book claims you have something of Marilyn's,' he said.

'That I do,' said Aileen, quickly undoing her luggage and taking out a small box. 'I also had a photo of me with Marilyn , didn't I detective?' she added, looking Murray straight in the eye. 'Could I have it back now?'

He placed it on the table. 'I'm sorry. I couldn't leave with nothing.'

'If it kept you interested, then I can forgive you,' said Aileen generously. 'Now take a much closer look,' she said, pointing to the identical necklaces worn by herself and Marilyn. 'Back then it was the equivalent of friendship bracelets.' She opened the top button of her blouse. 'The very same one.' She unfastened the chain and handed it to Murray.

Murray felt as though he had just recovered sunken treasure, but he decided to withhold his enthusiasm. 'What else do you have of hers?'

Aileen reached inside her bag again and pulled out a delicately carved box, inlaid with mother of pearl. 'This too.' Inside was some jewellery. 'Marilyn said that when she died the vultures would tear her place apart and take everything. She went on to say that these were the bits she would have saved for a daughter if she'd had one. You can see some of the pieces in old photographs.'

Murray examined the items inside, thinking that Norma's daughter Mary would probably love to see the pieces after all these years. He was also surprised that by touching the very things Marilyn might have worn, he felt as though he was reaching out to her lost soul. He scolded himself. He did not like being ruled by emotion rather than logic and decided instead that there just happened to be more than one scam artist cashing in on Marilyn's fame. 'When did she give you this?' he asked Aileen.

'Ironically only a few weeks before she died. For once, Gloria unintentionally did Marilyn a favour by allowing herself to be seen very close to the gates to the bungalow. The press were all over her. While the commotion was going on, Marilyn pulled me into her bedroom, thrust the box into my hands and told me to treasure it as it would serve me one day. She was really upset and said she would rather I had everything before it was too late. With hindsight I wish I'd asked her what she meant. I think she knew the odds were against her and that she was going to die.'

Murray halted Aileen's thought processes. He had been sucked in enough. 'I'd like to hold onto these items for now. As well as the photograph albums if you have those too,' he added.

Aileen swiftly pulled the jewellery box back to her

chest. 'I'd rather not. They're irreplaceable.'

Judy stepped in, in order to show a sympathetic approach. 'They'll be kept secure at all times. We'll return them in person if you prefer,' she said.

'And risk coming to Ireland? I can't believe you've forgotten what's happened,' said Aileen, inwardly wishing she had not revealed her precious gifts.

Murray suddenly asked himself who he could trust with the evidence should Aileen agree to release it.

She spoke again earnestly. 'When the evidence reveals the truth about Marilyn's death, there'll be those who'll wish I'd not come forward. Telling you what I have, is like disturbing her peace.'

Murray's mind was reeling. If he were to become convinced that the woman he had been calling Norma was actually Marilyn and, if he could prove beyond doubt that Aileen was indeed a friend of hers, he would happily reunite them before Marilyn slipped the bonds of earth forever. But he was not happy. He felt as though his logical way of thinking had been hijacked and that the case was spreading through his very being like dandelion seeds on the wind. Who was it at Huntley Manor - Gloria or Marilyn? If it was Gloria who had made her way to England, he could not fathom how had she managed to spin such a complex web of deceit. Maybe she was so well rehearsed that she had learned the skills to pull it off.

Chapter 19

Who is the Enemy?

Aileen said her goodbyes to Murray and Judy at the airport the following afternoon. 'All I have left of Marilyn is what I entrusted to you. I expect everything to be returned to me as soon as a week's up. Is that long enough for you to examine it all?'

'Of course - and thank you for your cooperation,' said Murray.

'A week then,' said Aileen, hesitating, seemingly having trouble leaving.

'Judy or I will oversee the whole process,' said Murray, although he was uncertain of how he could honour such a promise with so much else on back at the Yard.

'I'll meet you at Dublin airport for the handover seeing as you're happy to risk the trip,' said Aileen. 'I'll have Darragh drive me so he can give anyone the slip. There'll be less chance of you being followed if we do things my way.'

Judy placed a friendly hand on Aileen's shoulder as she turned to leave. 'We'll talk about a day and time to suit sometime during the week.'

Aileen disappeared among the throng of other travellers, leaving Murray wondering whether she was genuine or as he had already considered, part of the scam. On their way back to Scotland Yard, he said little of consequence to Judy, spending more time summing up what was going on at Huntley Manor. When they finally did speak, the invisible connection that made their crime solving ability second to none, kick-started into action.

'We will get to the bottom of things,' said Judy, determinedly, as they parked up. She turned to Murray, all the time wondering whether this particular case was beating him. So she was not surprised to see that he had a deep frown etched across his forehead.

'The way I see it, we have two problems to iron out,' said Murray. 'Frank's sudden turnaround for starters is really getting to me. I need to have it out with him.'

'And secondly?' asked Judy, as they got out of the car.

'Secondly, it's just such a fucking ridiculous story Jude. Don't you think we should wrap it up right now. Bury it before we become the laughing stock at the Yard?'

Judy laughed. 'Er - how about no. And if I thought you meant what you just said, I'd find a new partner. One with more imagination.'

'The only person with too much imagination is Norma,' said Murray, not meaning to be disrespectful to a woman of her age. 'I can't help it if my head says it's all bollocks, even if a piece of me says we've discovered a massive cover up.'

Judy locked the car and gave Murray an encouraging pat on the back. 'Good man. I knew you had instinct. There's hope for you yet,' she joshed.

They made their way to Detective Inspector Austen's

office, both feeling as though they were going to get slapped down before they got past the first sentence of their cockamamie findings.

'Come in,' came a gruff voice from the other side of the opaque glass.

They entered and stood close together with their forearms touching, as though some sort of bodily contact offered moral support and comfort. Austen took his time to finish what he was writing, put the cap on his fountain pen, blotted his notes as he was old school, then finally looked up. He was well-renowned for being astute and immediately picked up on Murray and Judy's body language.

'What am I about to hear I wonder?' he asked. 'Either you two are up to no good, or I'm about to be bullied into something. Which is it this time?' He looked from one to the other impatiently. 'Feeling better Murray?' he added, sarcastically.

Whether it was something in Austen's tone or his own guilt, Murray feared that his sick leave excuse had been identified as a ruse. 'How shall I put this?' he said at last, coughing nervously and wishing he could be swallowed up.

'For God's sake Murray. Spit it out. I haven't got all day. It feels like I've been trying to single-handedly stop a terrorist attack on London while you've been on a jolly.'

Whereas Judy was mindful that their explanation might come apart at the seams, she too remembered Murray's warning about enemies in the camp. 'You remember the Huntley Manor case Sir?' she said, helping Murray out. 'Handed to us via Oxfordshire constabulary?'

'Yes, what of it?' growled Austen.

'Backtracking for your benefit Sir, a young woman

claimed to have seen an armed man on the premises,' said Murray, finally feeling his courage return.

'Yes, yes, I know. Clearly rubbish, and you've been down there already. Find anything?'

'Well yes Sir,' said Judy. 'There's a reclusive old woman. Thinks she's Marilyn. . .'

Murray stood on Judy's foot so forcefully that she struggled to suppress a yelp of pain.

She turned to look at Murray for a sign of what she should say, but feeling another gesture in the form of a sharp dig in her ribs, she faced the front again. Taking heed of his fierce warnings she declined to comment further, hoping that the web he was about to spin was better than anything she could weave under such pressure. She felt like a teenager being reprimanded in class, on the cusp of being put on detention if she said a wrong word.

Austen's iciness and lack of a response made the silence in the room seem like a vacuum. For a second Murray's heart did a flip when he thought he saw a flicker of red in Austen's pupils. It reminded him of Frank's words to trust no one but either way he had to say something. 'In her youth the woman we're talking about was an obsessive fan of certain film stars of the day, Sir.'

'Yes - and?'

'She changes her mind all the time as to who she is,' said Murray, recalling Judy's suggestion to tweak his statement. 'I haven't as yet witnessed any armed men on the premises though, but I'm on it as a priority.'

'Deal with it quickly if you get a sniff of that evidence being correct. I need you on this terrorist case pronto,' insisted Austen.

'I could do with another day or so to wrap things up Sir - and as today's my day off, I'd like to take another look, in case I've missed something and there are firearms. There's always the possibility of a terrorist link to what you're investigating.'

'I see your point,' said Austen, changing tack due to Murray's lateral thinking.

'And it actually rather nicely ties in with my plans. I've family down that way overdue a visit,' added Murray.

'Alright, you've twenty-four hours. And DC Phelps, you stay at the Yard. The last thing I need is Starsky and Hutch upsetting the locals with you at the wheel.'

'But Sir...' Judy protested, as eager as Murray to get down to Huntley Manor.

Austen looked down and continued writing. 'That will be all.'

Both Murray and Judy knew better than to challenge such a fearsome personality, so they closed the door quietly as they left.

'You're damn good,' said Judy, with a triumphant smile as she and Murray walked briskly away from Austen's office.

Murray felt strange. In his mind, the heat from the devil's den radiated down the corridor and burned the skin on his back. At the same time it made him shiver as though he were freezing cold. He only began to feel normal again when they had turned a corner into the hubbub of activity that was the open plan office. 'Twenty-fours?' he protested in a whisper, in reference to their deadline. How are we going to close the case in that time?'

Judy was clearly thinking ahead and had already decided that Murray needed to adopt a more aggressive stance when it came to dealing with Frank so she told him so. In her mind Frank was the first thing to deal with.

With her words in his mind, Murray elected to arrive

without notice at Huntley Manor, as there was always the chance he could catch security off guard. This time however, he chose to park out of sight and inadvertently ended up in the same lay by that had been used by Olivia White and her friends. He decided to check out her statement with regards to the door in the wall, although her description sounded more like an extract from a fairy story. With that conclusion in mind, he was extremely surprised to be greeted by the same door, sheared from its hinges in Olivia's attempt to get through. Considering the lengths Frank had gone to when securing the rest of the estate, Murray was perplexed as to why the door had been repaired so shabbily. He pondered on what he should do next. Without a warrant he was out of bounds the moment he entered without permission, so he decided to do just a localised sweep.

Within a very short space of time, while following the perimeter wall inside the estate, Murray realised that Olivia's statement was accurate. Her description of the bank of security cameras located within a Victorian gatehouse was beyond all doubt not a figment of an overactive imagination. Keeping low, he peered through a rain-spattered window much as she had done. All of a sudden there was the sound of laughter. He drew back.

Now there was disparity between what had been offered up on his previous visits and the reality, Murray had enough to encourage him on. Rather than explore further and risk being apprehended, he retraced his steps, collected his car and drove up to the main gates, wondering whether his movements had been caught on camera. He had no need to surprise Frank anymore and Frank's dogged evasiveness was in his mind an inviting challenge. Now it was just a matter of using all the artfulness his training had given him.

He spoke into the intercom, making no attempt to appease the voice at the other end by being particularly civil. Expecting to be delayed or sent away, he stepped back quickly as the gates opened promptly. Before Frank could change his mind and lock him out, he got back in his car and made his way up the drive. He knew that he was drawing attention to himself by driving fast. Frank being forewarned was now unavoidable. As before, Murray felt disadvantaged with no weapon to defend himself with. Nevertheless, he took courage knowing that Frank and his heavies would most likely hold back, now that the goings-on had been brought to the attention of the Yard.

By the time Murray had climbed the front steps, Frank was already standing by the open front door, but he was a different man to the one Murray had first encountered, his hangdog expression making him look years older. He appeared to be carrying the weight of the world on his shoulders. Murray wondered whether his expression was an indication of torment or merely the expression of a man who knew he was about to do time.

Frank made no eye contact. 'Come in detective. I was wondering when you'd return.'

'You've got some explaining to do,' said Murray, aggressively. He had no sympathy for Frank's hidden dilemma.

Frank dejectedly led the way. 'Come into the library.'

'How's Norma - or would you prefer me to call her Liz Taylor or Audrey Hepburn?' asked Murray.

Frank turned on him. 'There's no need for sarcasm detective. And I'm afraid you can't see her. She's fading fast and I don't hold out much hope she'll last the day.'

'You expect me to believe you?' asked Murray, taking a

seat opposite him.

'No, not really. But that's your prerogative.'

Just then there was a knock at the door.

'Come in,' said Frank.

The door was opened by a plain woman in her fifties, with nothing about her that would make her stand out in a crowd apart from the fact that she was dressed in a generic nurse's uniform.

Before Frank could introduce her or she had the chance to speak, Murray spoke first. 'Enter actress dressed as nurse from side stage.'

'I beg your pardon,' objected the woman, fiercely, turning immediately beetroot red.

'That's enough Murray,' said Frank, sternly.

Not a man to stop when he was enraged, Murray continued. 'So tell me, did you pick up your uniform from a fancy dress store?'

'How dare you?' said the woman, so red now that she looked fit to burst. 'I'm nurse McCall and I'll have you know, that I'm fully qualified,' she added, puffing her ample chest out in defiance. 'I've been caring for the lady upstairs for the last ten years.'

Murray reined himself in, realising that his frustration had got the better of him.

'Who is this person?' the nurse demanded of Frank. 'I have never been so insulted.'

'This is Detective Constable Murray. It's my fault he's suspicious Linda, but I'm sure he'll apologise.' Frank presented Murray with a steely expression. 'Won't you Murray?'

Murray looked from one to the other, suddenly uncertain of the truth. 'If I'm wrong, you have my humblest apologies Miss McCall,' he said, backtracking and feeling caught off balance. 'But I'll need proof of your identity before you leave the premises.'

'Give us two minutes Linda?' asked Frank. 'So DC Murray can see for himself?'

'One minute only,' said Linda, clearly still enraged by Murray. 'No conversation mind. She's very weak.'

Murray was of the opinion that had it been fifty years previous, he would have been doffing his cap to Linda as though to take the rap, as he left the room backwards. However, feeling humiliated by his abnormal lack of control, he smiled limply and followed Frank.

He coughed nervously. 'I might have been wrong about her,' he said, trailing Frank up the stairs, while trying to think of a way to regain the upper hand. 'However, I'm not wrong about you. It's my opinion you've held up this investigation right from the start.'

'Cut me some slack detective. Save it until you've seen Marilyn. Then I'll come clean,' said Frank.

'You mean Norma don't you? Nothing's been proved as yet.'

'Whatever,' said Frank, leading Murray straight into Norma's bedroom.

Murray was instantly so taken back by Norma's appearance that he had to suppress a gasp. For a second he thought that she was Mary in her full prosthetics and had to stop himself from reaching out to check. She looked more like a waxwork than a real person. Her health was discernibly failing and she was either unconscious or in a sedated state.

'We moved her bed to the window,' said Frank, mournfully, as though Norma had already passed. 'She likes to see the gardens and hear the birds.'

Murray suddenly felt acute sorrow, a feeling that

until now he had reserved only for the passing of his grandmother, but thinking quickly, he used Frank closing the window, to pull the high lace collar of Norma's nightdress to one side. She was wearing an identical necklace to the one that Aileen had entrusted to him.

'She'll know you're here,' said Frank, turning to look down at her. Apparently the hearing is one of the last things to shut down.'

Murray turned to him and for the first time both men sensed they were at least temporarily on the same side. 'Let's have that talk,' said Murray, sympathetically. 'I'll try and speak to her when she wakes.'

They moved through to Norma's adjoining lounge, the place where Murray had first interviewed both her and Mary. Frank closed the door between the rooms and gestured for Murray to sit while he poured them both what was becoming a regular drink.

'With things as they are, you're welcome to stay tonight detective. Geraldine will make you up a room in the summer house.'

'Thank you,' said Murray lost as to what to say at first and still wondering why Frank had adopted such an amenable attitude.

Frank sensed his bewilderment. 'So I lied on the phone. That sucks I know. But when she became poorly, I was just trying to keep everyone away.'

'Listen Frank, I'm here not just because I've been allocated this case,' said Murray.

'What do you mean?' asked Frank, sitting down opposite.

'Well, my DI has given me one day to close it down. This is actually my day off. I could be playing golf, but I opted to come here instead.'

Frank looked nervous. 'Who is your DI?'

'Is it relevant?' asked Murray, wondering why it should be of interest to Frank.

'You might not like me that much detective, but trust me on this one. It's very relevant under the circumstances.'

'His name's Austen,' said Murray.

'Robby Austen?'

'You know him?'

'Of old,' said Frank, smiling widely but economical with his answer as he tapped on his whisky glass.

'In that case, surely he knows about your presence here.'

'He does,' admitted Frank.

Murray was suddenly sucked into a whirlpool of doubt, angry that Austen and Frank had kept him in the dark for some hidden purpose. As well as not being given the full facts by both men, he wondered why he had been told to close the case promptly.

Frank interrupted his thoughts. 'Robby's damn good at his job. But you need to watch those above him.' He downed his whisky in one gulp.

'What are you insinuating? That Scotland Yard is corrupt?' growled Murray.

'Come on. You're not that green behind the ears,' said Frank, pouring another whisky.

Murray teased the amber in his own glass with his tongue, tempted to mention the look of the devil he had sighted in Austen's eyes. Frank seemed ingenious at second-guessing his thinking.

'Hey, like I said, Austen's clean. Don't you get it? He's closing it down to save Marilyn from being discovered. He wanted you to find nothing.'

'I can see why he might want that, but why not mention

you when he assigned me to this case?' Murray quizzed him. 'Or shut it down sooner.'

'That's simple. He and I go back a long way. His father Douglas was very senior at Scotland yard and it was he who set in motion Marilyn's protection package when she first arrived. Her case got handed down to Robby.'

'If all this is true, why are you concerned about corruption amongst senior officers?' asked Murray, defensively.

'Robby's never gotten promotion beyond Inspector. Haven't you ever wondered why?'

'Not really. I presume he hadn't put forward for it.'

'He wanted to be more in touch with the core of Scotland Yard,' said Frank. ' Plus until you came along Murray, there was no one he trusted Marilyn with.'

'But like I just said, it was Austen that told me to close the case,' said Murray, that very fact making him feel confused. He wondered whether it were possible that Gloria's play-acting had been so convincing that she could have fooled everyone. After all, it was unlikely that Austen or his father had ever visited the States and seen Marilyn in the flesh. None of what Frank was saying proved who Norma was.

Frank continued. Robby knows you've been captured by Marilyn's magic, which is why you've played down your findings to him. You've been prolonging your investigation for that reason. Am I right?'

Murray decided to keep his doubt close to his chest even though his anger was rising to challenge him again. 'Your attitude is a bit different to the first time I visited.'

'I'm sorry we led you up the garden path,' said Frank.

'So what about the twenty-four hours I've been granted,' said Murray, more certain than ever that something was amiss.

'He's trying to keep this low profile, in case anyone above him sticks their nose in. You've as long as you need. All I need to do is ply you with more evidence in order to convince you of Marilyn's legitimacy.'

'The term ply - smacks of deception, but I'll consider it nothing but a poor choice of words,' said Murray. He removed the photo he had taken from Aileen from his file and handed it to Frank.

'Who's the other girl?' asked Frank, taking his time in looking the photo over.

To Murray, Frank's reaction seemed genuine. There was no flicker of recognition in his eyes. 'I'd have thought you knew everyone she's been acquainted with, both here and in the US,' he said, choosing to drip feed information until he was really certain of Frank.

'Over here, yeah that's about right. But in the States things were different. I was only consigned to Marilyn a week or so before we got her out. I only met DiMaggio the day before we flew out of US airspace.' He lit a cigarette and took a deep drag. 'So is this girl someone I need to know about?'

Murray was economical with his response. 'In essence - yes. She's an Irish woman. She went out to the US and ended up working in her aunt's business. That's how she met Marilyn.'

A light seemed to go on in Frank's head. 'I think Marilyn's mentioned her in the past. Her aunt owned an upmarket shoe company.'

How Frank could have known such a pivotal piece of information escaped Murray, but this was something that both Gloria or Marilyn could have told him. He dug deep to think of something Marilyn had shared with

Aileen, that she would not have shared with Gloria. He had bought copies of the photographs Aileen had handed over while her originals were being examined back at Scotland Yard. None of the photos had ever been in the public domain. He selected a couple and handed them over to Frank. While he was preoccupied with examining them, Murray placed Aileen's necklace gently on the table. 'Recognise this?'

Engrossed in the photographs, Frank did no more than glance at first. Finally he picked it up and examined it closely. 'This is Marilyn's. She must've dropped it. Where did you find it?'

'A favourite of hers?' asked Murray, thinking that Frank's statement did not prove anything except that the duplicate was the same as either Marilyn or Gloria's. Gloria could easily have stolen it from Marilyn in the US or the woman in the photo with Aileen could have been Gloria all along. There was also the vague chance the necklaces were not made especially at Marilyn's request, but were instead commonplace back in the early sixties, which was something Judy would check on.

'Yes, for sure. She wears it most of the time.'

Murray toyed with revealing that Aileen was still alive, but she was already vulnerable back in Dublin. There was also the fact that he should speak to Austen again to verify all that Frank had just told him about their long-standing relationship. He now had an added problem to consider. If Frank pocketed the necklace with the intent of returning it to Norma, his promise to Aileen to keep it safe would be compromised when Frank realised Norma was still wearing hers.

'So where are we at, detective?' asked Frank all of a sudden, seeming to forget the necklace. 'I realise I've messed things up with the way I've handled things. What do you want from me?'

'The truth from now on for starters. I suppose the big question I need answered, is why, if that is Marilyn next door, does she want to expose the Kennedys now?'

'You know the answer to that question. To do so before now, someone might have come after her.'

Murray changed tack. 'There have been whispers of something going on up here. I was told in the local pub.'

'We've come close to being discovered a few times, but only because of media hype. Then it's yesterday's news. The trouble is that every time Marilyn's gotten to hear about it, it's convinced her someone's after her.'

'Has that ever been a possibility?' asked Murray.

'If you mean, does anyone know she escaped the States and might come after her, then no. The murder and suicide conspiracy theories have kept people busy for years. Speculation has kept the heat off her.'

'Odd that no one seems to have considered she might have escaped,' said Murray, wondering why he had found no evidence of that theory on the internet.

'The press coverage the days after she was supposed to have committed suicide stopped those sorts of rumours from ever taking off,' said Frank. 'Her past addictions were common knowledge.'

'There is another option to consider,' said Murray, looking straight into Frank's eyes.

'Is there one? Throw me a line here detective.'

'That Norma isn't Marilyn at all. That she's her body-double Gloria, who quite frankly sounds like she had the motivation to bump Marilyn off back in the sixties.'

'I can see Mary's play-acting has really gotten to you big time. But whoever you think this scam artist is, it suggests you're implicating everyone in this house.'

'That's right,' said Murray, setting his glass down authoritatively.

'What will it take for you to trust me detective?'

Just as Murray was wondering what that might be, the nurse popped her head round the door.

'Excuse me Mr. Hayworth, but the lady only woke for a few moments. Enough time for me to get her to drink some soup. I'll be in the cottage should you need me.'

Having said her goodbyes to Frank, she left, offering Murray a frosty look.

'She lives in?' asked Murray, wondering why he had not seen her before.

'Yes, and she's paid a helluva lot to keep her mouth shut.' Frank drew a line across his throat.

'We don't tolerate murder in the UK,' said Murray.

'Let's get back to the important question,' said Frank, sidestepping any incriminating answer should he be forced to comply. 'How do I convince you that the woman sleeping in the other room is Marilyn?'

Murray thought for a few seconds as he looked out of the window. Linda was crossing the lawn. 'I'm not sure you can. You see, we have a dilemma. Not only were there no DNA facilities in the sixties, but practically everybody that knew Marilyn as a young woman is dead. Even if they weren't, too much time has passed for a reliable identification.'

'I love her,' said Frank suddenly. 'And I'll do whatever it takes to protect her.'

Murray turned from the window. 'That much was obvious from the start,' he said.

Frank sank into a chair and put his head in his hands while trying to regain some equilibrium. 'At first it was the love you feel when protecting a child. She was so damaged. I didn't even trust DiMaggio near her.'

For the first time Murray found himself believing him. His normally muscular body seemed to have folded inwards under the weight of the knowledge that his love was nearing the end of her life. Finally he spoke. 'To be honest, with her time running out and nothing more to hide, you might be better hanging around. There are plenty of remote parts of the estate for you to explore if you need thinking space.'

Murray was beginning to understand Frank's complete turnaround. His grief was eroding away his hard edges. Might he also be considering Murray's Scotland Yard lineage might come in handy if something untoward was about to kick off? Whichever way Murray viewed it, there was nothing like being on the inside when it came to flushing out truths. 'Okay I'll accept that offer thanks,' he said quickly, just in case the offer were snatched away.

Not long after their conversation, Murray had found the lake and was strolling round it deep in thought. Frank was right about head space. The mist that lay low over the water was like a cotton-wool barrier cocooning him from the outside world. It could also be said that his dilemma had been softened by the knowledge that DI Austen was not on his back. But if the red in Austen's eyes had been real and he was part of the devil's work, that could only mean one of two things. He may be working under instructions from someone who may not have the real Marilyn's interests at heart at all. On the other hand, he may be one of Gloria's disciples, keeping snooping eyes and ears away from the ultimate truth. Murray's mind wavered between the possibilities, the only certainty being that those above Austen should be treated with caution, whereas Frank had been expeditiously demoted, becoming nothing more than a puppet, manipulated by something far more sinister than a clever pair of hands.

Chapter 20

The Devil's Darning Needle

Murray sat on one of the benches by the side of the lake and looked out towards the island Norma had loved as a vibrant young woman. Her name was beginning to sound alien to him, but he refused to allow himself to use the alternative option until he had proved her heritage either way.

Secure in his case were the photos that Aileen had entrusted to him. He badly needed somewhere where he could continue with his work and not meet eyeball-to-eyeball with Frank, Frank's agents or an unexpected antagonist. He had also thought better of using the room that Geraldine had hurriedly prepared for him, in case he should fall victim to hidden cameras.

He continued on, embracing the solitude as it was something he did too little of. He glanced at his phone every now and then but there were no voice mails or texts from Judy. Ignoring his frustration, he began to think instead about how inviting the prospect of working in a provincial force could be if places like Huntley Manor were on his turf. He also wondered fleetingly whether DC Taylor felt the opposite way, wishing he were high-flying in the City.

The route Murray had chosen skirted the lake between a line of forest trees and the shoreline. Before long, his way was blocked by an enormous uprooted oak tree. Its redundant roots towered above Murray like a giant outspread hand reaching up to the sky. Some of its upper branches were partially submerged, but in other places some branches snaked across the surface of the water, creating a sanctuary for nesting birds and camouflage for herons. It took considerable effort from Murray to clamber over the tree trunk, but once he had, he continued around the perimeter of the lake in an anti-clockwise direction. To traverse it this way was an essential urge that he had been unable to shake off since childhood. Squabbles in the playground had been commonplace when friends had forced the roundabout to spin the other way.

There was no obvious evidence to suggest that anyone had walked this far for some time. Kept damp by the water from the lake, the grass grew prolifically, untrampled and sprinkled with meadow flowers mingling seamlessly with rushes and yellow irises on the water's edge. Nettles outlined a narrow footpath that had for the greater part been reclaimed by nature.

Murray looked around for somewhere dry to lay out his things. He had just selected a fallen tree trunk that would serve as a table, when out of the corner of his eye he spotted a rowing boat tethered at the lake's edge. He poked at the boat's wooden hull with a stout stick to check that it was watertight and, reassured that it would not sink to the bottom, he stepped in. Though he did not pride himself in being the best of swimmers should the boat spring a leak, he took the oars in his hands and looked towards the island. He set off, occasionally checking the depth of the water with one of the oars but then he began to panic when it became entangled in pond weed. He pulled it free but fearing it might happen again and before he could make a sound decision on whether to go on, he had the strangest sensation that the island was calling out, inviting him to explore.

His panic disappeared as though it had been spirited away, replaced instead by the memory of being a young boy. He was on a family holiday with his best school friend, racing hired pedalos close to the shore on the Isle of Wight. As the moment evaporated, he resumed rowing, soothed by the memory of happy times. By the time he had reached the island he was already relishing a short power nap in a hammock he had spotted hanging between two mature willows. He took off his shoes and socks, rolled up his trouser legs and stepped from the cool water onto a man made shingle beach. He was not used to going barefoot and winced as sharp stones dug in.

He knew that he had the luxury of the afternoon to come up with a light bulb moment, but he still resisted the hammock even though his best revelations normally bombarded his brain at that point where sleep and wakefulness jockey for position. Added to this, the sudden thought of Judy, head down at her keyboard in the office made a power nap seem unfair. Instead, he opted for a comfortable spot where he could seat himself on the ground against a tree. He took a bite out of a highly-polished apple that he had liberated from a fruit bowl on his way out of the main house and closed his eyes. The sweet juice slipped down his throat making him instantly long for an ice cold cider. With sleep calling, he forced his eyes to stay open.

He removed Aileen's photos from his case, using a few large sun-bleached stones to anchor the corners of the album. Without her lengthy explanations for each image distracting him, he was able to concentrate and look for signs of forgery. Most of the photos were black and white but some were in colour and as vibrant as the day they had been taken. At first, the quality made Murray doubt their authenticity, but he considered instead that they were simply treasured memories.

He began to think about Scotland Yard's security measures knowing there were always competent hackers trying to get into their system. For this reason he feared scanning the images to his office computer. The album seemed safer in his briefcase, which he took everywhere with him. The internet and its terminology in his opinion, was a hostile force and he did not trust it one bit. It would be the ruination of man one day, but he would thrive in the workplace when all others struggled with basic skills. He dismissed the thought that his old-school way of doing things provoked laughter among colleagues. He was old-fashioned and had no intention of changing.

Having finished his apple, he tossed the core into the lake and watched it bob about. The distraction of nature at work was hard to resist. It was such a contrast to city life. Murray watched as ripples disappeared, the surface of the water becoming a flat green mirror again now that ducks had lost interest in his apple.

Nearer to the shoreline, dragonflies darted here and there, similar in colour to rainbow bubbles created by blowing through a plastic bubble wand. Less than keen to have their egg-laying interrupted, female dragonflies spiralled upwards to avoid the aggressive males interrupting their egg-laying. Damselflies were plucking juicy spiders from gossamer webs. Murray began to reflect again to evenings during school holidays spent at his late grandfather's allotment next to a small pond. His grandfather had referred to dragonflies as the devil's darning needles.

The mention of the devil made Murray think back to Scotland Yard again. Whereas until recently he had considered it as a pretty safe haven from the darker side of mankind, in his mind, it was beginning to morph into something otherworldly that might harbour disciples of the occult. He wondered whether Mary's casual mention of the evil side of Hollywood might not be a myth after all. He forced himself away from such a ridiculous notion. He was losing all rationale and turned his thoughts instead to the physical evidence spread out on the grass.

From all he had read about Marilyn Monroe, the photos of her last year in Los Angeles taken by Aileen or another family member, conflicted with the general consensus that she had been deeply troubled. There was nothing to see but happiness in her expression. Murray took out his father's magnifying glass and held it so he could look deep into her eyes for signs of anything other than that, but could see nothing but a sparkle. He closed the album and put it back in his case, pushing it under a nearby palm to prevent the heat from the sun from frying its contents. He was dejected. There might be no fingerprints to tie Norma to Aileen in any sense of the word. Added to this, there were no existing fingerprints from Marilyn that he knew of. He would follow that up.

It was then that he heard someone approach but before he could react, it was followed by the agonising crunch of a blow to the back of his head. His world began to turn upside down, his lakeside view becoming a kaleidoscope of embracing insects and turquoise kingfishers. He felt as though he were on an undulating fairground carousel having indulged in too much alcohol. As he lapsed into unconsciousness, the sight of spinning elder trees above caused him to recall another tale told to him by his grandfather. If elder wood was burned, the person who set the fire would see the devil. But if they were to instead plant elder by their house, they would keep the devil away. Despite not being a religious man, Murray clutched at a twig beneath his twitching palm as everything turned to black, praying that it would protect him from evil.

When he began to come around, he had a throbbing headache and was completely taken aback to see Judy and DI Austen leaning over him. He felt the back of his head for evidence of a bump, then tried to sit up, but thought better of it as his head began to spin again.

'Here - drink this,' said Judy, holding a silver cup to his lips, her voice as distorted as his eyesight.

He drank from the cup, expecting it to be water, but it was warm and had a flavour much like mulled wine, laced with a bitterness that he could not distinguish. 'What is it?' he asked, swallowing it quickly to get rid of the taste.

'A tonic. Elderberries. You'll be as right as rain in no time,' said Judy.

'Stay where you are,' said Austen. 'We're waiting for help.'

Murray tried to move again but paralysis seemed to have taken over, affecting not only his body but some of his thought processes too. He lay and looked upwards at Judy and Austen's faces, which kept dipping in and out of focus, behind which the sky was shot through with shades of claret and blood orange as though it were about to be the most spectacular of sunsets.

'What time is it?' he asked. 'It was sunny only a moment ago.'

'It's late,' said Judy. 'You must have been out for a few hours.'

'What are you doing here?' asked Murray, trying to fathom their presence, and how they had found him so easily.'

'Come to cut you into little pieces,' said Austen suddenly, laughing, at which point he exposed a mouth full of yellowing serrated teeth. Murray's rational world had gone, replaced by a cacophony of strange images and sensations, including Austen's head distorting into that of an enormous goat with bloodshot eyes. Judy was laughing too, her head thrown back like a wolf baying at the moon.

Whatever he had drunk, Murray knew it was doing its work. Either that or he had a serious injury to the back of his head and was experiencing something resembling a hallucinogenic trip. At any moment, he expected to plunge down a rabbit hole into an alternative world. The only thing was - he was certain that Judy and Austen were really there, but why Judy was finding Austen's suggestion of dismemberment funny, he had not the slightest idea. He was aware of having been manhandled onto a stretcher, while he was trying to get a handle on his thoughts. As well as this, he could hear hear the distorted sound of an orchestra comprising of screaming violins, an out of tune piano and rhythmic bongos. Soon he was lifted from the stretcher and laid out on a cold surface and tied down. His clothes were cut away from his body and he was surrounded completely by unfamiliar faces looking down at his nakedness.

A young woman dressed in a transparent white robe stepped forward and began to smear him with more of the liquid he had drunk from the silver cup. 'Where is she?' she asked, hissing like a snake.

'Who?' he could hear himself asking, involuntarily.

'That bitch Marilyn. My master has been looking for her since last century. She made a pact and now she must honour it.' The woman began to draw symbols on Murray's body with her fingers, chanting in an unrecognisable language. The other revellers began to disrobe and dance clockwise around the raised slab.

'Anti-clockwise,' screamed Murray, trying to escape his bonds. 'You must always go anti-clockwise.'

'The woman let her gown fall to the floor and began to climb on top of Murray. Even in his hallucinogenic state he noted that she was stunningly beautiful, her long raven black hair a contrast to her pale skin. She straddled him and writhed around on his stomach, clutching a sharp blade in her right hand. Had he been single and the circumstances different, it occurred to him that he would welcome the attention from someone so sensual.

The music gathered in crescendo as the dancers spun faster and faster like whirling dervishes. Beyond the out of focus figures was nothing but blackness. Judy and DI Austen were nowhere in sight. Murray squirmed around as he struggled to pull himself free, but the rope dug deeper into his body as though it were tightening like the coils of a snake.

The woman raised the knife high. 'Tell me where she is or I'll rip out your heart,' she threatened.

Speechless with terror, Murray anticipated a violent

death, but at the last second, he heard a more familiar voice.

'Murray,' said a voice all of a sudden. 'Murray, wake up, but don't try to move.'

His arms were no longer paralysed but he had pins and needles in his fingers and toes. He opened his eyes and clutched at his chest for evidence of a knife wound. There was nothing. He was fully dressed and all his clothes were in tact. Time had lapsed again. It was getting dark and someone was shining a torch light in his eyes. He pulled himself up onto his elbows.

'That's far enough. Stay still,' said Frank.

Murray felt the back of his head. There was a large bump, but no blood or sign of a severe injury. 'What happened? Where are Judy and Austen?'

'There's no one else here,' said Frank. 'It's just me and Dave. You must've fallen and banged your head. We only found you because we noticed the boat had been moved.'

Murray pulled himself up to a sitting position. 'Christ, that hurts.'

'Do you reckon you can make it across the lake?' asked Frank.

'Yeah, I think so. I'll give it a go.'

'Here, let me help you up.' Frank put both of his arms underneath Murray's armpits. Dave had been standing close by. He shared Murray's deadweight with Frank, and they manoeuvred him into the boat and rowed back to the other side of the lake. While they were rowing, Murray pondered how they had reached him without a second boat, but still dazed, the thought slipped from his mind before he could ask.

'We need to get you checked out,' said Frank, his tone suggesting to Murray that he was genuinely concerned.

'That won't be necessary. I'm feeling better by the moment. Too much sun has done more damage than a bang on the head.'

'We'll get the nurse to take a look at least,' insisted Frank.

'Do you think she'll care one bit after the way I spoke to her?'

'Linda's off duty. One of the others will look you over,' said Dave.

As they made their way back slowly along the path, Murray supported still by both men, the thought of a stroppy matronly nurse with no good looks to shout about, seemed very inviting, compared to the dagger-wielding woman who had straddled him so erotically in his drug-induced state. As he considered the lesser of two evils he began to notice that his wrists were stinging. He still found it hard to focus, but on first examination, both displayed faint red lines. It made no sense but he ignored the memory of being tied up and instead, put it down to sunburn. He pulled his cuffs down to cover the evidence and was glad to be soon back in his room.

Chapter 21

Lock Your Door

The shock of his fall had caused Murray to drift off again. When he finally awoke it was daylight and he had no concept of exactly how long he had been asleep. He glanced at his watch and was surprised to see it was already mid morning. He had been undressed by someone while he slept. He got out of bed, but found himself unable to move at anything other than a snail's pace. His head began to thump again. There was the sound of muttered voices coming from somewhere in the building. He opened the door to find Frank and Judy deep in conversation.

Judy took one look at him and stopped mid sentence. 'Christ Steve - you look awful.' She took his arm and led him slowly back into his room.

Frank turned on his heels and disappeared out of the guest apartments and across the lawn, before Murray could drill him about the previous night.

'Sit down before you fall over,' said Judy, easing Murray into an armchair.

'I'm alright - stop fussing,' he said, resisting any body contact.

'You don't look alright,' said Judy, continuing to examine him for signs of injury. 'You're grey and you're still in shock,' she said, finally.

'Why are you here?' Murray asked, unappreciative of her concern. 'The guv told you to stay at the Yard didn't he?'

'Well that's being grateful for you,' said Judy, handing Murray his phone from the bedside table. 'Here, take a look. When you didn't reply to my calls and texts, I got worried, so I snuck off without telling him. I got here this morning and Frank filled me in on what had happened.'

Irritated at having lost valuable time, Murray checked his phone. Judy was right. He had been bombarded with calls and texts.

'You don't have the monopoly on everything that's been happening you know,' said Judy, still defending her corner.

Murray opted to ignore all the nagging doubts that were creeping into his bruised head about Judy and DI Austen, or their fictional doppelgängers that had morphed into satanic creatures. He tried to smooth things over. 'Sorry if you got the impression I was lording it over the investigation. I'm glad you're here.'

'Good, because I was beginning to think you weren't, quite frankly. I'm going to stop over as you're below par. Frank said I could use the room next to yours so I can keep an eye on you.'

'How are you going to convince the guv to let you do that?' asked Murray, wondering about Judy's reasons for keeping an eye on him. In the same breath he chastised himself for getting sucked into the content of his nightmare.

'I'll find a way. Anyway, it shouldn't be a problem now Frank's filled me in on everything. I tell you what Steve. This case is turning into a blockbuster of a story.'

'Well that's the whole point isn't it? It's just a story,' said Murray, feeling distinctly unsure of what he thought anymore. Also his hallucination from the night before seemed much more than a hippy trip. But it was against his nature to believe in witches and demons. He turned his attention instead to the taste of a strange cocktail that still lingered in his mouth. He went to the mirror and stuck out his tongue. It was stained deep red.

'You know, you're behaving very weirdly,' said Judy, joining him at the mirror. 'What's on your mind?'

He thought quickly. Judy was as intuitive as him. They knew each other's thoughts before words had the chance to pass their lips. If he denied the whole episode, she would know he was pretending and that he was trying to shut her out.

'What do you make of this?' he asked, sticking out his tongue again, this time for her to see, but also so he could judge her reaction.

'Ew, what on earth have you been eating?'

'Nothing that would turn my tongue that colour,' he suggested, watching for the flicker of a giveaway expression on her face.

'I bet you've pigged out on blackberries again. There'll be tons of them in the woods.'

'Too early for them. I think I was drugged,' he speculated.

'That bump on your head is making you a bit whacko. And anyway, since when did you become an expert on seasonal fruit?' Judy teased.

Put down by her take on the previous day, meant that Murray had initially failed to notice that at some point, any blood and dirt had been washed from his skin. He was also wearing someone else's vest and shorts and wondered whether his own clothes would reveal the truth of what had happened to him. The bouquet of exotic spices and incense still lingered about his body. He ran his fingers through his hair. It had been washed and was still vaguely damp. Without warning, he broke away from Judy's side and began to feverishly turn the room upside down.

She looked on aghast. 'What are you doing Steve? You'll get us thrown out.'

'Where's my briefcase? They've taken it - with all Aileen's photos in it.'

Judy leapt into action, by grabbing Murray by the arms and pushing him roughly back down onto the bed. 'Get a grip Steve. No-one's taken anything. Do you think I'd let that happen?'

'Where is it then?' he asked fighting back against her hold. Her grip reminded him of being bound tightly with rope and he was surprised at her strength.

'It's under your bed. Right where Frank left it after he found you. He told me if you asked, to tell you where it was.'

'Has he looked through it?' asked Murray, getting on his hands and knees. The room began to swim.

'How would I know? I've only been here and hour or so. And so what if he has? We're all on the same side,' insisted Judy.

'Look at this,' said Murray, standing up slowly and holding up his exposed wrists right in front of her face. What do you see?' he asked in reference to rope marks.

Judy took his hands in hers and examined his wrists gently, taking her time to be thorough to appease his anxiety. 'It looks like you grazed your arms when you fell. What's with you anyway?'

In response to her too casual notion, Murray abruptly pulled his hands away and examined them as closely as she had. There was nothing untoward to suggest anything other than what she had concluded. Though he had no recall, he accepted finally that she was also right about the berries having stained his tongue. Nevertheless, despite him trying to regain some sort of equilibrium when it came to thinking things through logically, he could not help but think that Huntley Manor was getting to him. It was like a parasite burrowing into his train of thought, altering his perspective on everything.

'Oh well, maybe I have just had too much sun,' he said, shrugging his dreams off. 'I suppose we ought to get on with the investigation before the guv hauls us both back in.' Deep inside a second voice was telling him something, but he could not work out what it was trying to say. 'Where are my clothes?' he asked, suddenly, glancing round the room.

'Must've been taken away for laundering,' said Judy.

A flash of being meticulously prepared as a human sacrifice tripped through Murray's thoughts. 'If I didn't know better, I'd think someone's tried to clean up a crime scene.'

He picked up the change of clothes that had been left on the end of his bed and went into the en suite bathroom and slipped them on. His personal belongings had been removed from his dirty suit and left on his bedside table. Knowing the order of everything within his wallet, he cast a cursory look over the contents. If someone had rifled through he would know it. Finally, he put on his shoes, which had been highly polished by someone practised at the job. He checked himself over in the mirror, happy with his appearance but surprised that the suit fitted as though it were his.

Judy and he walked across the lawn in the direction that Frank had taken. Murray was still exhausted from his ordeal, but he began to talk about the bare facts of the case. 'Norma hasn't got long. Could be any day now. We'll need to find some items from her past, otherwise a DNA match won't be possible.'

They entered the breakfast room from the garden. 'Can't we just call her Marilyn from now on?' asked Judy, frustrated by Murray's insistence to do otherwise. In her mind, he still seemed detached, seemingly more interested in the continental breakfast that had been hurriedly laid out. It was unusual to see him load his plate in such a gluttonous manner.

'No we can't call her Marilyn,' he said, simply.

Judy thought better of arguing and moved on. 'Regarding something from her past, I think I've come up with something,' she said, all of a sudden animated. 'I'd have told you as soon as I got here, but you were out of it.'

'Well I'm all ears now,' said Murray, buttering and tucking into a croissant like there was no tomorrow.

'The guv called me in before I left to come here, otherwise I'd have got here sooner. That's when he told me about his connection with Frank. I kept quiet of course about the fact I couldn't get hold of you.'

'I could've been eaten by guard dogs in the time it took you to get here,' said Murray, beginning to regain his sense of humour, now food was inside his belly.

Judy laughed. 'If anyone can handle themselves, it's

you. Anyway, if I hadn't found you straight off, I'd have raised the alarm.' She took a few sips of her coffee, as though using the time as she always did to add dramatic tension to her news. 'Guv thinks the less we know, the less we can be pumped for info if things turn nasty.'

'So what's his priority then? Originally all we were interested in was proving the old dear is or isn't Marilyn.'

'This is much bigger than that. If it is her, you'll want to know as much as the next man what she's got on the Kennedys. Plus whoever she is, I think you actually care about her welfare now you've got to know her a bit better. Am I right?' asked Judy.

Murray refrained from giving a direct answer. 'If she is the real thing. It'll take a lot more for me to believe it's not a scam. In this particular case she's guilty till proven innocent.'

'I saved the best bit till last,' said Judy. 'The guv has given us a massive lead. A connection to Joe DiMaggio.'

'That would've been really exciting if he weren't long dead,' said Murray.

Not allowing his lack of enthusiasm to get her down, Judy continued. 'Our biggest clue was right in front of our eyes, but we just didn't see it. At the Birdhouse.'

'Now you've lost me,' said Murray.

'Have you ever wondered why the Birdhouse hasn't been closed down?' asked Judy.

'No, not at all. We get a lot of leads from there. It's a valuable asset to the Yard.'

'That's as maybe, but apparently it's used pretty much now as it was way back in the fifties and sixties. Not only that, Joe DiMaggio used to hang out there whenever he was over.'

'The guv told you that?' exclaimed Murray, finally

wanting more. He remembered that it had already occurred to him, that Joe DiMaggio might have frequented the place.

'That's not all. It was the equivalent of an operations room for the worst of the bad guys, such as the Krays and the Richardsons,' Judy continued.

'So, now you've got my attention, where's this all leading re DiMaggio?' asked Murray.

'The point I'm trying to get at, is that there's a couple of Joe's younger cronies still hanging out there. They might be able to tell us what he was up to back then.'

'Get real Jude. What can we offer crooks like that in return for that sort of information? They'll want top dollar.'

'If the price is right - they'll take the bait. I'm sure of it,' insisted Judy.

At that moment Frank walked in and handed Murray his freshly laundered clothes in a suit bag. He sat down between them both.

'Does a place called the Birdhouse mean anything to you?' said Judy suddenly, trying to knock Frank off balance.

'No, can't say that it does. Should it?'

Judy studied his expression for tell-tale signs of deception, but was convinced that he was being honest. 'It's not important,' she lied. She changed tack, standing up urgently. 'We've got a lead to chase up, so we'll be back later. Call us if there's any change for the worst.' She ushered Murray away from the table before he could argue against her making the decisions on their day's movements.

'Did I miss something?' he asked, as they drove down Huntley Manor's drive a while later.

'No, not at all. I just want to keep Frank out of this.'

'So what else has the guv told you that might be of use?' asked Murray.

'He said information about DiMaggio filtered down from his own father while he was still in the force. Apparently DiMaggio wasn't too convinced of where the Secret Service's loyalty lay, after JFK was assassinated, so he hired henchmen to keep watch over Huntley Manor twenty-four seven.'

'How could they have done that effectively from London?'

'That was simple. They bought up a few local properties and moved in. Forcibly. Must've been a few scared landowners booted out at the point of a gun. Also, despite DiMaggio being disillusioned with the Secret Service, he had something else up his sleeve. There was an unspoken agreement between him and JFK. If anything happened to Marilyn, then DiMaggio would expose all of the Kennedys' dirty-dealings.'

'So he had the Kennedy family wrapped around his little finger?'

'Pretty much,' said Judy. 'Plus she agreed to keep her mouth shut if Joe promised to stick by her.'

'I'm sorry to bang on about this, but you still refuse to believe there's the possibility that Gloria got her claws into DiMaggio as well as Bobby and Jack,' said Murray. 'What if he fell for the younger version too?'

Judy bit back. 'There are rumours Joe and Marilyn had booked a date to remarry while she was still in LA. It was to be two days after the news of suicide broke out. Even if it was JFK she really loved, marrying Joe made certain that her and Mary would be looked after for the rest of their lives.'

'Then why didn't the Kennedys bump off both her and DiMaggio, just to be safe?'

'Maybe they weren't sure killing Joe would stop his associates spilling the beans,' suggested Judy.

'That adds up,' said Murray, noticing that Judy seemed suddenly thoughtful.

'There's another strange coincidence regarding JFK, that I think proves the Kennedys were paranoid. The guv told me that twenty years after JFK's assassination, there was an attempt on President Reagan's life,' said Judy.

'Where's the connection between Reagan and the Kennedy family?' asked Murray.

'Only three days earlier, DiMaggio had visited Reagan at the White House. It's a known fact Reagan admired JFK's economic policies, but that doesn't mean he liked the man himself. Maybe DiMaggio and Reagan talked about other issues. If that's the case then maybe Reagan's new knowledge also became an instant threat to the Kennedys, meaning their past misdemeanours might get out,' hypothesised Judy.

'Well done Jude. You've uncovered a hornet's nest for sure,' said Murray, proud that they were a relentless team.

Chapter 22

Not Long Now

A s they made their way out of the heart of Oxfordshire and headed back towards London, Murray took out his old-school pencil case. He had a particular way of doing things that included scrawling elaborate diagrams in green ink. He prided himself in solving convoluted cases this way. Within a short time, his scribbling had begun to resemble a spider's web, featuring all the possible characters that could be involved in the mystery surrounding the elusive Norma. He had considered as he sketched, that everything Austen had told Judy could apply to either Gloria or Marilyn. He studied the intricacy of his artwork as it grew, wondering who the powerful malignant owner of this particular poisonous web would prove to be.

Judy drove without speaking for most of the journey, Murray having made it clear on many occasions that he hated to be disturbed when weighing up the bad guys. From time to time, she glanced across at his sketches, in awe of his unorthodox but highly effective method of brainstorming. By the time they had reached Waterloo, the web had grown so large, that Murray had ripped pages out of his notebook and taped them together, creating an art piece that would later be his foundation for an explanation to Austen. Judy bit her tongue, knowing that her more conventional approach, in the form of excel spreadsheets and photos, seemed more appropriate to present to the team back at the Yard. Despite this, she quietly envied Murray's lateral thinking. As they approached the Birdhouse, he folded his masterpiece lovingly and stashed it in a zip pocket deep within his battered briefcase.

Ignoring double yellow lines, Judy parked right outside the Birdhouse. She was nervous and for some unknown reason felt that being able to make a quick getaway was important. She followed Murray in, compelled to look over her shoulder for signs of having been followed. As she turned to check out who was in the cafe, all conversation stopped as heads turned in their direction. Their presence seemed to have been elevated unexpectedly to being the key actors in a Western shoot out movie scene. As though to break the invisible tension and signal his patrons that all was well, Mike shouted a welcome from behind the counter. Immediately, the air was alive once again with vibrant chatter, as though neither Murray or Judy had ever been there in the first place.

Heavy tobacco smoke hung low over tables like a thick smog. Mike broke smoking restrictions because he knew that he could get away with it and it brought in the punters. Murray and Judy squeezed through narrow gaps between tables to the only free one right at the back. The others were occupied by workmen and a generous lacing of London's underworld. It was difficult to tell who was in a trade and who made money in other ways. Judy's unease had increased tenfold, as apart from Angie she was the only other woman present, the difference being that Angie moved from table to table comfortable in her natural environment.

Mike approached immediately with two mugs of coffee. 'Didn't expect to see you two trouble-makers back here so soon. What can I do you for this time?' He set down the coffee, sat down and looked guardedly from one to the other waiting for an answer. 'Well I guess it must be important otherwise you wouldn't be here again. But you'd better remember - there's only so much I'm prepared to tell you.' He draped his tea towel over his shoulder and gestured with a quick nod to Angie to mind the front counter. 'Is it worth my while?' he asked, rubbing his finger and thumb together to suggest ready cash.

'Isn't it always?' asked Murray, sliding a twenty pound note across the table. 'DiMaggio,' he added, with no further embellishment.

The side of Mike's mouth twitched several times telling both Murray and Judy it was a sure sign that he knew something, but he shrugged as though to say the name meant nothing.

Judy was impatient, unlike Murray who liked to slyly reel people in. 'DiMaggio. You know who he is, so stop playing us.'

'We've been told by a very reliable source he used to hang out here,' pressured Murray.

'Maybe, but would've been before my time,' offered up Mike, begrudgingly.

'That's easy to check out, or you could just furnish us with details of anyone still alive that knew him,' said

Murray.

'Principally the ones that hung out here. And still do,' said Judy, fixing Mike with a stony stare.

'It'll cost you more than a score,' said Mike thrusting the twenty pound note forcibly back into Murray's hand. 'But I'm not greedy when it comes to you two or your guvnor.'

Judy ignored Mike's fake compliment. 'Our guvnor?'

'Yeah, DI Austen.'

'For a second, the devil reared its ugly head in Murray's mind, with regard to the possibility that Austen might indeed be on the wrong side of the law if he mixed with the likes of Mike.

'Don't worry yourself about him,' said Mike, appearing to read Murray's mind. 'Straight as a die. Him and me - all give and take.'

'How d'you mean?' asked Judy.

'When it come to fuckwits like rapists and paedos, I won't harbour them. Austen asks and I hand 'em over, for cash in hand.'

Murray could feel his shoulders drop in relief. 'Fair enough but how much do you want this time?'

'A ton will do it, but before you cough up, give me a mo. I'll be back in a jiffy.' He leapt up and disappeared behind a curtain that obscured the corridor that led to the infamous back room.

'What's he up to?' asked Judy. 'I don't like it. Do you reckon he's gone to fetch some of his heavies?'

'Not if I know Mike. He's probably making some quick calls on our behalf.'

Judy's anxiety was getting the better of her. 'I need to splash some water on my face but I'm not keen to use the cafe loos. Someone might corner me.'

'Give over Jude. You're safer here than anywhere in London.'

He stifled a laugh as Judy crossed the cafe clutching her handbag close to her chest. As a rule, she exhibited a tough demeanour, but on this occasion she had surprised him. While she was gone, he took the time to study various individuals eating all-day breakfasts or drinking from pint-sized white glazed mugs. He could not help but be amused by the thought that the Birdhouse was a perfect setting for a TV drama, so much so that he wondered whether its appearance had ever been duplicated brick by brick for that purpose. He now knew from what Judy had said earlier, that the darkest elements that make up London's crime faction were present at that precise moment.

Mike suddenly appeared from behind the curtain. He beckoned to Murray to follow him.

'Have you got a contact for me?' asked Murray.

Mike smiled, showing rotten yellow nicotine teeth. 'Have I ever let you down?'

'Come to think of it, you haven't,' said Murray, thrusting the ton that Mike had requested into his hand as Judy appeared and joined ranks.

Although the cafe was known as the local greasy spoon, Angie prided herself in doing her best to keep it clean. However, the narrow corridor Murray and Judy had to negotiate as they followed Mike, was a different story. His territory was unwelcoming and filthy, lit by a solitary light bulb that flickered and fizzed. Aging anaglypta wallpaper hung in frayed ribbons, saved from total detachment from the walls by cardboard boxes stacked high against them. The carpet was greasy and threadbare, held down with gaffa tape, much of its original pattern long since faded away. It stretched away into the darkness at the end of the corridor like a rippling muddy stream. Unlike Judy, Murray was not fazed by unwelcoming surroundings. These were the places he liked to frequent in order to get information. Nevertheless, he sensed her anxiety and reached behind to take hold of her hand, excusing his unusual behaviour in a whisper, by saying that he was guiding her in the near darkness. She held on tightly like a frightened child, nestling in as close as she could without causing them both to trip.

'The ton will buy you ten minutes,' said Mike, as a prequel to pushing open a door to the secret world of hardened criminals. 'But *they* might want more, depending on what you want,' he warned.

At first, neither Murray or Judy could see anything apart from gargantuan silhouettes of two men, due to the blinding sunlight piercing through a large picture window. However, as their eyes adjusted, the figures came into focus.

'Ring the bell when you want 'em out,' said Mike, dissolving back into the shadows.

Murray felt as though he had just stumbled into a band of gorillas. The men loomed larger than anyone he could remember dealing with in the criminal fraternity. Each possessed a partially shaved square head with an overhanging forehead and jutting chin, but one looked more intimidating as a part of his ear lobe was missing and he had a deep scar on his cheek. His injuries gave Judy the impression that he had been bitten by a ferocious dog. Both were missing any sign of a neck, their heads squatting on top of ridiculously broad shoulders. Their fat hands were completely covered in tattoos making their fingers appear a peculiar shade of indigo contrasted only by gold rings. In Murray's mind, the rings had been selected for the amount of grievous damage they could inflict. Due to their obvious brawn, he immediately formed the opinion that these were DiMaggio's aged henchmen, impressive in stature for men in their later years.

Murray stood motionless, Judy likewise, rooted to the spot where Mike had left them, both fearful of saying anything until invited. The silence seemed to stretch out like an elastic band about to snap, as the two silver-backed gorillas weighed them up.

'Sit down - you're crowding the place coppers,' said the one with the injuries, at last, stubbing out a half-smoked cigar in an already full ashtray.

'Don't mind if I do,' said Murray, adopting a chipper attitude in order to hide his apprehension. He had forgotten that he still had hold of Judy's hand. As he sat, he pulled her down onto a neighbouring chair and released his grip.

'Thank you for seeing us,' said Judy, hoping that a courteous approach might win them over.

'You interrupted our favourite sport,' said the second, looking over at the TV, which was airing horse racing. 'Lucky for you we just won a fucking grand,' he added, displaying his toothless grin primarily for Judy's benefit.

There was awkward silence again, neither party opting to get on with discussing the business in hand. The first man clasped his hands together and cracked his knuckles, as though to draw attention to his arsenal of nine carat gold jewellery, before flicking off the TV with the remote. Mike had clearly primed them for Murray's questions. 'Yeah, we knew DiMaggio. What of it?' he offered, aggressively. 'Like a father to us, so you'd better not fuck about with his memory.'

'You look too young to be his sons,' said Judy, trying to lighten their mood with flattery. She sank lower into the chair's sagging upholstery for safety, knowing full well that if she spoke one wrong word she would be out of the window in double-quick time. Her fawning delivery had fallen on deaf ears.

'He looked after us, like we look after our own,' said the first man, this time clicking his nonexistent neck as he touched his head to his shoulder. 'By the way, you can call me Bill, darlin', he said to Judy. 'And he's Ben,' he added, in reference to his brother. 'And I'm guessing you're the fucking flowerpot men,' he added lastly, in reference to Murray and Judy. Both he and his brother dissolved into broken rasping laughter, which reflected years of chain-smoking.

'Sorry - I don't understand,' said Judy.

'Bill and Ben's an old kids' programme from the fifties,' said Murray, irritated by the men's sarcasm.

'Bill and Ben it is then. I quite like it,' said Judy, going along with their humour and deciding to ask for real identity might just be a step too far.

'Like we already said, we won't be dissing DiMaggio, if that's what you're hoping for,' said Ben.

'You needn't worry about that,' said Murray, adopting his professional head.

'Stop wasting our fucking time,' said Bill, as he lit another cigar. 'Get to the point. Time is money and you're already beginning to bore me. '

Murray was floundering, but at the same time knowing he had to put some of his best cards on the table to draw them out. 'We're protecting someone that was once very dear to DiMaggio. The word's out to the wrong people that this person's still alive.'

'Which means this person's in imminent danger,' added Judy. 'That's why we're here.'

Bill seemed to be considering them both as he began to blow smoke rings that floated in perfect symmetry up towards the ceiling.

'What's this bleedin' well got to do with us?' said Ben, speaking at last.

'We know DiMaggio entrusted you both with this person's safety, and since his death, you've continued to do so,' continued Murray. 'Am I right?'

Bill whispered in Ben's ear.

'We protect a lot of people, and we hurt those that get in our way,' said Ben, threateningly. 'Why should we talk to you, copper?'

'Well the thing is, before we can offer this person - your friend even, continued police protection, we have to prove who they are,' said Judy, cleverly. 'We believe DiMaggio - and his accomplices, may be able to help us with that.'

'It's a woman,' said Murray suddenly. 'And she's very ill. We just want her last weeks to be peaceful.'

'Tell us about these fuckwits who are after her,' asked Bill, standing up all of a sudden, as though to intimidate by blocking out most of the light from the picture window.

'We can't be sure, but we think most likely someone close to the Kennedys or the Mafia for a close second,' offered up Murray.

Bill lowered himself back into his chair and leaned across the table so that his jutting chin almost met with Murray's. 'How come you know this, copper and we don't? I like your girlfriend, but I'm beginning to think I don't like you that much.'

'You'd only know I suppose, if you already knew the woman we're trying to protect,' said Murray, taking a chance with an impertinent response despite Bill's last comment.

Judy turned on him. 'Steve, do you want to get us killed?'

'You're girlfriend's right,' said Bill. 'Watch your step copper. But now we're all clear on that, the woman you're going on about, I'm guessing you think is Monroe,' he added suddenly, grinning at his brother.

'Nothing's as it seems,' said Ben, touching the side of his nose cryptically, smiling as though he harboured a secret.

'What do you mean?' asked Judy.

Bill ignored her and side-stepped. 'Look, normally we'd want a wad for information, but as this is to do with Joe, we'll settle for something else.' He scribbled a few lines on a piece of paper, folded it and thrust it into Murray's hand. 'Read it when you're out of here. Go back on your word and you'll be missing something that matters to you.'

'Like my fingers?' asked Murray, making light of the threat.

'For starters. But you might have trouble fathering kids once I've finished with you.'

Murray gulped while Judy began to feel sick at the thought of having parts of her hacked off if they did not comply with Bill's wishes.

'Let's talk about the proof before we go,' insisted Murray, dangerously pressing them for more.

'Your proof's in a vault,' said Ben. 'In town. Not been touched since Joe pegged it.'

'Do you know what's in there?'

'Yeah course we do, down to the last itty-bitty bit of jewellery,' said Bill. 'Joe's fucking blood-sucking lawyer wanted control of it, but Joe was smart. Put his trust in us.'

'We'll need access straight away. Times running out,' said Judy.

'If your boyfriend does what I ask, you can have the key straight away sweetheart - and anything else if you play your bleedin' cards right,' said Ben, looking at her cleavage.

Judy checked that the top button of her blouse was done up, looked to Murray then back at Ben. 'Why would you give the key up so easily?'

Bill chipped in. 'Joe would've wanted it.'

'I'll carry out our part by the end of today,' said Murray, handing his card to Ben. 'How do I get word to you I've done as you asked?'

'We'll know,' said Bill, ringing a brass bell on the wall that neither Judy or Murray had noticed when they arrived.

Murray knew what he meant. The brothers would have eyes everywhere. Once he and Judy had left the room, he began to compartmentalise everything the brothers had said, whereas all Judy could think about was that the walk down the corridor seemed more oppressive than ever. It seemed as though the walls were closing in and would squash them both before they reached the other end. Due to the sunlit room they had just left, the silhouettes of Bill and Ben were etched on her retinas. She clung onto Murray for a second time, until they reached the pavement outside.

She took a few deep breaths in an attempt to regain

some equilibrium and disperse the panic attack that was rising in her chest. 'What did Bill ask you to do?'

'Authorise a couple of cell doors to be left open tonight?'

'Whaaat? Whose cells? You can't do that?'

'The doors in question are no doubt often left open. Accidentally of course,' lied Murray. 'The prisoner's a serial rapist. His last victim was a girl of thirteen. The brothers know her father, so are asking us to do a favour for him.'

'And the other cell?' asked Judy.

'The person who will carry out the punishment,' said Murray.

'Even so...' protested Judy.

Murray interrupted. 'This rapist only got three years for messing up the girl's life. Before he'd finished with her, he beat the crap out of her too and left her at the side of the road naked. Call it justice.'

' He should get the full force of the law, but I don't want to have any part of what you're going to do. I don't want to know if you've done it either,' said Judy, surprised at Murray for being prepared to break the rules.

'As you wish Jude, but as far as I'm concerned he's a waste of taxpayers' money. He deserves to have his balls removed with a rusty knife.'

'Let's change the subject. The less I know about it the better, especially if word gets out about what you've done.'

By dawn the next day, Murray had received word where to pick up the key from for DiMaggio's safety deposit box. He retrieved it before commuters began to make their way to work, from a deep hole in the corner of a crumbling brick wall of a cemetery. He considered the collection point to be a morbid message from the brothers.

He was walking for once with Judy, rather than driving, to Michael O'Flannagan's security services in a hidden part of London, sandwiched between some of its oldest buildings and the river. At the same time, he was still wondering whether the pick-up point for the key was a metaphorical warning. A vivid image of Judy and himself flashed through his mind, as they hung from two of the oak trees in the middle of the cemetery being pecked at by crows, the ropes constricting their neck having turned their faces a blueish-grey. He was about to be cut down by officers when Judy spoke, jolting him out of his macabre daydream.

'You kept your side of the bargain then? Was he roughed up enough to satisfy the brothers?' she asked.

'I thought you didn't want to know. But in answer to your question, he got what he deserved. He'll survive minus the use of his crown jewels.'

'Still, I don't like it,' said Judy.

Murray stopped in his tracks and faced her. 'You've got a daughter,' he said, sternly. 'She might only be seven now, but imagine her in six years. Girls of that age are prime targets for paedophiles like him. We should bring back hanging.'

'Point taken. When you put it like that I get why you agreed to get it done,' said Judy, shivering at the thought of her beautiful, perfect daughter being defiled. She shook the thought away by taking in the view of the river Thames as they made their way along a cobbled path, sections of which dated back to the latter part of the seventeenth century. 'Why are we coming this way?' she asked. 'Couldn't we have driven?'

'We could've. But the brothers will have their side-kicks out to keep an eye on us.'

'All the more reason to use the car then, surely?'

'Quite the opposite. I want to keep the brothers sweet. At least, to start with.'

'What are Bill and Ben's real names?' asked Judy.

'The Gator Brothers to you and me.'

'Can't say that name means anything,' said Judy, glancing over her shoulder. She was instantly dismayed to see the only other people using the little-known path, were two slightly scaled down versions of the brothers.

'You must know them. Gator - as in alligator? They got that name from all the bodies fished out of the Thames missing arms and legs.'

Judy shivered and glanced again at the winding expanse of unwelcoming grey water, expecting at any moment to see a line of torsos bobbing by on the current. 'Weren't you scared yesterday if you knew who they were?'

'I might of thought twice about Mike introducing us if I'd known up front.'

'So if what you say is true, how d'you know all the bodies fished out of the river are their handiwork?' asked Judy.

'I'm not saying every single body is their handiwork, but most are. They want to rid London of what they see as scum. They leave clues relevant to whatever crime the person they've murdered has done.'

'Give me an example. I'm almost beginning to respect them,' laughed Judy.

'Well for example, there's the Glengorm case,' said Murray. 'Twin girls, snatched from hospital just after they were born. We got a tip off about the girls and recovered them, but we never found the abductor, alive that is. A week after the girls were recovered, a body was fished out near Canary Wharf. It was clearly dumped in such a way it'd be found rather than sink to the bottom. It was the Gators' handiwork.'

'How did you know it was them?'

'The body had a dummy in its mouth and was wearing a baby's bonnet and had been wedged inside a pram.'

Judy gasped.

Murray continued. 'Mike and the Gator's have one thing in common. They all have a great aversion to crime against women and kids. The body found in the pram was unusually a woman. On examination it looked like Jack the Ripper had butchered her. The Gators were proud of their handiwork and always leave a calling card. The woman was wearing a necklace with an alligator charm.'

Judy tried not to retch and at the same time sound unbiased. 'The child abduction is just terrible, but bearing in mind the twin girls were found unharmed, what had she done to deserve such a death?'

'We'd been looking for a serial child abductor for nigh on three years. She was taking kids and selling them on to a paedophile ring right under our noses.'

'Why weren't the brothers questioned about their link to her?'

'Ask yourself that Judy. Why d'you think? I'm all for justice and doing things the correct way, but between you and me, everyone they've dumped in the river is one less scum bag for the Yard to deal with.'

'You'll be telling me they've got hearts of gold next.'

'Well, in an abstract way, they have as it happens. Think of all the kids they saved.'

'You're sounding more and more like a vigilante than a DC. What about the judicial system? Don't you believe in that anymore?'

'Sorry to backtrack again, but what would you do if it were your kids taken?'

Judy stopped and turned to face the river again. It seemed to swell and boil. She thought about Scotland Yard's stretched resources. Murray stood next to her and allowed her a few moments to reflect, nodding his head in pretend respect to the two men who had also stopped thirty yards behind, but at the same time working out how he could lose them without them knowing it was deliberate.

'Without a doubt, I'd go straight to the Gator brothers with my life savings,' she said suddenly, her love for her family evident in her wildly staring eyes. As she uttered these words, she knew that Murray was not only sound in every way, but that he was more than that: a man prepared to go a step beyond what was legal and decent in order to get a fair outcome. She stepped back onto the path, feeling changed in some way, but uncertain as to whether she liked the new reasoning that lurked within. 'How long until we're there?' she asked.

'Not long now, but I should tell you, we're heading into a rough area,' said Murray, sensing that his background story to the Gators had touched Judy in such a way, that she had deliberation in her stride.

The bigger part of their journey lay within metres of the river. The cobbled path that for the most part followed the edge of the Thames had in places fallen into disrepair, patched up unsympathetically with modern paving stones. The connection between old and new continued, where buildings damaged by bombing during the London Blitz had been stapled shabbily to modern blocks, or torn down and replaced altogether. From time to time, Murray and Judy were both forced to stoop low under modern engineering, which supported the oldest of buildings, the worst of which threatened to topple into the Thames. Murray pointed out shrapnel damage, in an attempt to distract Judy from revisiting scenarios of her children becoming victim to an abductor.

The path was empty apart from an occasional cyclist and the Gators' heavies. Attuning himself to the echo of the men's hard soles on the cobbles, Murray determined they were keeping pace but making no attempt to close in. Judy seemed to have accepted his explanation that the men were not enemies. With this in mind, Murray still increased the length of his stride, hoping their followers would not notice a gap opening up. As he and Judy rounded a curve in the path, he used the moment to pull her brusquely down a flight of stone steps, along a narrow alleyway sandwiched between high brick walls and into a street full of late commuters. He stepped into a newsagents with Judy behind and pretended to read the headlines on a carousel, all the time watching the street outside.

'I thought you'd no problem with those guys,' said Judy.

'They're just an irritation, that's all. We've carried out our part of the agreement, so I don't quite get why we're still being tailed,' said Murray.

'They're going to be pretty pissed off we've given them the slip.'

After a few moments Murray led Judy back to the riverside path. The Gators' muscle was nowhere to be seen. Murray closed his eyes and stood silently in one of his hypnotic-like states, listening, having studied the nature of their particular footfall before he had darted down the steps. 'They're about eighty metres ahead, walking quickly away from us.'

'How can you possibly know that? I can't hear anything but boats on the river and car horns,' said Judy.

Murray honed in again. 'The shorter of the two walks with a limp, exaggerated when he speeds up. The other guy's sole is coming loose from his shoe. It rubs on the pavement every time he lifts his foot.'

'Sometimes you amaze me Sherlock. But which shoe has the loose sole, clever dick?' she asked.

Murray concentrated again before answering. 'The left one. There's a channel of water collected along the path's camber, where it joins the wall next to the river. Every now and then, I can hear the noise of his loose sole rubbing on the cobbles, but it disappears when he steps in a puddle.'

'You can't possibly know that for sure.'

'Can't I? Well, I can't hear either of them now. They must've cut through to the main street like we did. Come on, we'll catapult past whilst they're going round in circles. We should reach the vaults ahead of them.'

Judy could not imagine being partnered with anyone other than Murray but nevertheless, she struggled to find the right words to accurately define him. She imagined him in a different era, with quill and ink, plus an oversized magnifying glass, specialising in gruesome crime scenes and reporting his findings on parchment pages within a dusty ledger. She thought better of asking him what qualities he admired in her for fear of being found lacking. She felt ordinary and easy to read. Whereas she used by the book methods, Murray could find clues in a simple house fly that had coincidentally died a few feet from a murder victim. He revelled in the unusual. Feeling dull as she did in that precise moment,

she walked on ahead, hoping that he would not trade her
in for his perfect Watson.

Chapter 23

More Valuable than Gold

A s they drew nearer to O'Flannagan's vaults, Judy was distracted about her job security by the possibility of opening up a treasure trove deep below one of London's murkiest streets. Her excitement about Marilyn's personal belongings were beginning to take hold. Nonetheless, when they eventually reached O'Flannagan's, her zealousness was quashed, when she realised that the heavies had closed in on her and Murray again. However, just as she thought they might be forced into an argument as to how they had been given the slip, the heavies turned back and disappeared back the way they had come without so much as a second glance.

The door to the premises was locked, so Murray rang a bell and spoke into the intercom, while Judy stood back and looked the building over. For a place that housed thousands of security boxes within its vaults, it could easily be missed by the casual passerby. She instantly took the view that its muted and peeling paintwork might be a deliberate ploy. It blended into the background like a piece of rancid meat, sandwiched between a foul-smelling butcher's shop and a greengrocers displaying limp vegetables and overripe fruit. Above the row of shops were shabby flats, most with their windows open, through which a mish-mash of reggae and hip-hop music could be heard behind greying net curtains that flapped in the breeze. The squeal of council trucks was testament to it being rubbish collection day. Overflowing wheelie bins lined the pavements, doubling the stench already prevalent in the air.

'It's no picnic here is it?' said Judy, clasping a clean white tissue tightly over her nose in an effort to shut out the stinking odour of rotting meat. 'Surely this can't be the place,' she protested. She peered in through gaps in the posters and billboards that covered fifty percent of the shop window, at the same time trying not to allow any part of her face to come into contact with any of it. All of a sudden, the intercom buzzed in response to Murray ringing the bell and the door clicked open.

'Sorry to break this to you Jude, but this is it for certain,' said Murray.

At first appearance, O'Flannagan's seemed to be a run-down betting establishment, but Judy instantly concluded that due to its state of decor, business was on a downwards spiral. Two thirds of the shop's interior was nothing but an empty space with a badly scuffed linoleum floor in need of a good clean. The place stank of beer and cigarettes. Around the edge of the room were mismatched chairs, upon which were slouched a handful of undernourished and drugged up men watching a TV that was secured by a chain to a bracket high up on the wall. At the end of the room was a caged counter, much like that in old-fashioned post offices, but this one had been installed to protect cashiers from being attacked by the betting fraternity.

A man so true to the image of Ebenezer Scrooge was inside the cage, watching Judy and Murray cross the threshold. The tip of his nose resembled molten wax, hanging down almost to his top lip. He had pinpricks for eyes and his hair resembled a badly tended haystack. Only visible from the waist up, he was dressed in a holed brown jumper and shirt that needed a good boil wash.

Silently, he beckoned Murray and Judy forward. 'Fuck off you lot,' he shouted to the seated men. 'Come back in an hour. If you're lucky I might be open.'

The men scraped themselves unwillingly from their chairs and left the shop in single-file, moving like emaciated zombies, but not daring to argue with Ebenezer. He pressed a button and the front door clicked closed behind them.

'DC Murray, DC Phelps?' he said under his breath.

'And you are?' said Murray, both he and Judy giving a quick flick of warrant cards.

'Jimmy. This is my gaff.'

'You were expecting us?' asked Judy, surprised.

He ignored the question. 'Put those away, ' he said in reference to the warrant cards. Walls have ears and I can't be seen talking to the fuzz.' He went to the front window and took a furtive look outside through gaps in the posters. Then he put the closed sign up, bolted the door and dropped the blinds.

'Let's go out the back. Never know who's snooping about outside.'

For the second time in two days, Judy felt as though she was being tipped over the edge into a point of no return. 'Are you alone here?' she asked, nervously.

'At the moment I am,' he said, squinting at her with his beady eyes.

Judy instantly sensed malevolence in his answer.

He lifted up the hinged counter and opened a waist high door for them to step through. Once all three were trapped in his cage, he reversed the procedure and padlocked the door and counter shut. He led them through another door, locking that too behind him. Judy and Murray were instantly taken aback.

The room they had entered was a complete contrast to the cell they had just left, making Judy's vulnerability melt away in an instant. Its walls and ceiling were white and the parquet floor was highly polished. Central in the room stood a double-sided mahogany Victorian desk that covered the biggest part of a traditional Persian rug. Two high-backed chairs had been placed on the side nearest to Judy and Murray. Behind the desk was an elaborate chair, which looked more like a gilded throne. Its upholstery matched the wine coloured leather inlay on the top of the uncluttered desk.

'Please - take a seat, while I clean up,' said Jimmy, unexpectedly adopting a polite manner as he left the room. Judy and Murray sat down and waited tentatively, neither knowing what to think, but before they even had the chance to discuss the situation, Jimmy reappeared, transformed. His face was clean and he had discarded his tattered clothes in favour of clean jeans and a fresh shirt. His hair was combed back so that it lay flat against his head, disguising a bald patch. So far removed was he from the character behind the front counter that Judy did a double-take. His accent too had changed from that of an East End cockney to that of someone well-spoken but still of London origin.

'I do apologise if you got the wrong impression of me. It'll all become clear as we talk. I take it from your expressions, you had no idea what or who you had stumbled across.'

'That's an understatement,' said Judy. 'And I'm guessing you're O'Flannagan?'

'I am indeed. But please, call me James. Jimmy's reserved for the shop and the layabouts I have to deal with. I was born and bred around here and privately educated. The Irish heritage is from a long way back.' He sat down on the leather chair and swivelled it from side to side, appearing quite relaxed. 'Can I offer you tea or coffee? Or perhaps all you want is an explanation?'

'Just the latter,' interjected Murray, miffed that he had been fooled and still considering that the contrast of his surroundings compared to the slum out the front were highly suspicious.

'I house items belonging to...how shall I say...to a very select group of people?' said James, noticing Murray was still trying to evaluate his surroundings.

'No different to any other vaults then,' said Judy.

'I beg to differ. You couldn't find a more unusual collection of owners.'

Judy continued. 'Your reception area, is unusual too. Quite a set up.'

'As far as I know, no other security companies in London have needed to adopted such a radical approach. Another reason we're unique.'

'So for security's sake you aim to remain invisible. I get that, but how come the police don't know about your business dealings?' asked Murray.

'They do know, as it happens detective. Scotland Yard is privy to viewing the security boxes at any time should the contents be relevant to an investigation. Of course they have to be broken into if the owner proves shall we say uncooperative?'

'And your clients still trust you knowing that?' said Judy.

'As a matter of fact, yes. It's rare that we have a problem.'

'We have a key that belonged to one of your late clients,' said Murray, holding up the one that had been entrusted to him by Mitch and Don.

'May I?'' asked James. He took the key from Murray's hand and looked at the serial number. 'Ah, now this one I have a particular fondness for. Key number 12305. Her house number at one time.'

'You must have thousands of secure boxes. How come you can recall this key number so easily?' asked Murray.

'I've imagined it as a bit of a time capsule, more so as time's gone by. It's almost a shame to open it, in case it lets out her essence,' said James, offering drama to his explanation.

'I'm not sure I follow you,' said Judy, surprised at his sentimentalism.

'Do you have children DC Phelps?' asked James.

Judy still felt fiercely protective of her loved ones since the episode by the river. 'I'm not sure the details of my family is any of your business,' she said.

'I apologise for my intrusion into your private life, but I was simply trying to explain why this particular box is so special.'

'Go on,' said Judy, curious as to what he might say that related to her in any way at all.

'If you do have children, you'll no doubt have kept items from their infancy. Does your favourite matinee jacket of theirs remind you perhaps of their first days?'

For a second, Judy's world folded inwards, as she recalled the tiny hand-knitted cardigan that her stillborn child, Poppy, had worn for a memento photograph and a final cuddle. Poppy's clothing along with a lock of hair lived in a ribbon-tied box in Judy's dressing-table drawer. Had James made a lucky guess she wondered, or was he telepathic?

We're getting off the point,' said Murray, unknowing of Judy's stillborn child, but unwittingly saving her in the moment. 'What else makes your establishment so unique?'

James stood and walked over to the window. In contrast to its intimidatory iron security bars, on its ledge was a cut glass vase filled with fresh roses, in a multitude of colours. James carefully removed a blood red specimen and looked out through the substantial bars to an impressive view of London's skyline.

'All the items in our vaults belong to those who have passed on,' he said sorrowfully. 'The main reason we are unique. For many years Joe DiMaggio left a rose of this particular variety where Marilyn Monroe was buried back in the US.' He hesitated and then turned to Murray and Judy. 'But of course, you know that the body incarcerated was not hers. It was just a ploy to fool the public.'

Judy suppressed a gasp at his knowledge, while at the same time nudging Murray's leg. 'What're you talking about?' she asked, acting dumb.

'I'm ahead of you both, so don't pretend you don't know. Not if you want my cooperation that is. I was primed for your visit. This is a very intimate business I run. I've got to know the relatives and friends of the deceased very well. Or non-deceased in this case. Marilyn Monroe still being alive, keeping her belongings here was an exception to the rule.'

'So why did you mention not wanting to open her box in case it let part of her out?' asked Judy.

'I wanted to gauge your reaction plus decide whether you were going to be open as to why you're here,' said James.

'I find myself wondering why you're happy to suggest something so ridiculous to me and my colleague,' said Murray. In his mind, Gloria had used her wiley ways on every man since Marilyn's death and James was no exception.

James placed the rose on the desk and began to put Murray in his place. 'Don't be tiresome. You wouldn't be here with that key if it weren't for your renewed interest in the case. I know stuff that would make headline news and I could've sold big stories to the tabloids about any one of my customers but haven't. And I'm not about to do so now. I've heard folks weep openly downstairs, years after losing their loved ones, while others just want to sit quietly on their own or trust me with their stories. Joe was all of those examples bundled into one. I considered it an honour to be privy to his feelings. We became very close friends. That's how I know Marilyn escaped from America.'

For a second, Murray thought the word Marilyn did not slip so easily off of James's tongue as it should. There was something about him that smacked of deception despite his slick way of delivering his side of things. He decided to listen on and hoped that James might entrap himself during the conversation.

'Did DiMaggio pay well?' interjected Judy, bluntly. 'I'm guessing there's a big price for your silence.'

'If I didn't think we were on the same side, I'd show you the door right now,' said James. But seeing as you want an honest answer, you'll get one. I consider myself guardian of one of the biggest love stories of all time. I need you on my side as much as you need me on yours, if this story is to be kept private.' He picked up the rose and caressed it. 'So in answer to your question, when Joe died, I refused further payment from his estate to keep Marilyn's things here. I continued out of respect for the man and for her. I never met her but I wished I had. Every week since Joe died, I have put a red rose like this one next to his safety-deposit box.'

'Why would you do that?' asked Murray.

'Before he died, he said to me that he resented leaving flowers for the woman who was buried in Marilyn's place. He didn't like her one bit, and he thought the burial site was too good for her. If he's up there somewhere looking down, I hope he'll know what I've done on his behalf.'

'This is all very lovely,' patronised Murray, 'but have you got records to substantiate what you've told us?'

For a second, Murray had exhibited a cold-hearted edge that Judy found questionable, but she told herself he was just keeping the investigation within normal parameters, refusing to let emotion cloud his judgement.

'Yes and I'm more than happy to show you. Nowadays everything is stored on my computer.'

Murray rounded on James. 'I'm not interested in your updated system of filing. At least not for now. DiMaggio died when there were still paper records. I'd like to see those if you still have them and, I must warn you, we will most likely need to seize those, your computer and the safety-deposit box in question.'

James appeared visibly vexed. 'I'd like to request that

you examine it all here instead. I'm happy to accommodate you or you're forensics team whenever it suits you.'

'It'll be looked after once we take it away,' said Murray.

'I don't expect you to understand, but I'd be grateful if you would at least consider what I've asked of you.'

'If you don't think we understand you, I apologise,' said Judy, cutting in, still not happy that Murray had shown no sign of sensitivity for his story. 'I'm a sucker for a good love story as much as the next woman.'

'You were right to spot I'm a romantic DC Phelps. But I'm not ashamed to say that's one of the reasons I do what I do. It feels that down in my vaults there are a lot of lost souls, hanging onto their physical remnants while keeping each other company. I watch over those precious things, which are only handled by those that loved them. I'm the gatekeeper if you like to think of me in that way.'

'I get that, don't you Murray?' said Judy, kicking him hard in the shins. She did not see James the same way that Murray did. To her, he was comparable to a welcoming cup of cocoa on a cold and rainy night.

Murray winced at the force of her pointed shoe. 'Let's see the records first, and while we're verifying DiMaggio's part in using your facility, I'll give your request some thought,' he said, in order to appease both James and Judy.

James stood up and went over to a tall fridge in the corner of the room, next to which sat a table home to an electric kettle, mugs and a selection of teas and coffee. He opened the fridge door and removed the entire front section of shelving. Much to Murray and Judy's surprise, on first glance what had looked like nothing more than a well-stocked fridge turned out to be nothing but shelves of synthetic duplicates of food. The back of the fridge was stacked from top to bottom with endless piles of ledgers with their spines facing outwards for easy reading. James made a selection and brought a couple of ledgers back to the table.

'Like I said, this is a rough area so I've had to box clever. I'd like to think if someone were to break in, they'd not consider my fridge contents worth stealing. If you take a closer look you'll see that most of the fake food looks mouldy and out of date, so even a vagrant would probably turn their nose up at it.'

'That's nifty,' said Judy. 'Tricks like that are normally reserved for Hollywood movies.'

James continued. 'These paper records are priceless as far as I'm concerned, even though I've transferred the details to my hard drive. Where would you like to start?' he asked.

'When DiMaggio first came into your life,' said Murray. 'As a matter of interest, when did you first meet?'

'Way back, just before he brought Marilyn over from the States. I'd been recommended to him by a close friend of mine. At first, it was to keep some things Joe had managed to get out of the States before the police tore her place apart. He had it flown over disguised as pharmaceuticals.'

'Do you have any of those items now?'

'I've no idea what's in there. I never have. I have the master key and the client keeps another. Both need to be used at exactly the same time. Joe added a lot of items over the years but he didn't share those sorts of details. He'd come and go and that was as much as I knew.' He selected one of the ledgers and turned its pages.

'How come they're in such pristine condition?' asked Judy, noticing there seemed to be no fading, tearing or curling of pages.

'They haven't seen the light of day for years. I transferred all the data back in the late nineties and I've kept them at the back of the fridge since then.'

James continued to turn pages until he came to the first entry regarding Marilyn and Joe. It was signed by Joe DiMaggio. 'There was nothing to record on his first visit. That was just a quick visit to check the vaults were to his specification. But his second visit as you can see here, is proof of my connection to him. He deposited her personal belongings on that occasion.'

Judy could see why anyone would be caught up in the romance of such a love story, but Murray was having none of it. It made the reason he remained unmarried more obvious to Judy.

'Let's see what you've got,' said Murray, in a matter of fact way.

'I'd like to be present when it's opened,' said James.

'That's fine, isn't it Steve?' said Judy, more as a statement than a question, blocking the opportunity for Murray to display more insensitivity.

James led them through a maze of corridors and doors, which belied the size of the premises, before leading them down a metal staircase. The solid metal door of a vault blocked their way to another world. James was silent and positioned himself so neither Judy or Murray could see the combination he was to use, as he began to turn dials and listen for clicks. Murray exhibited no emotion to suggest that he was intrigued, adopting instead as usual, his code of professional practice. Judy however, was aware of the butterflies in her stomach.

James pulled on the door. 'Come on my beauty,' he said, talking to it as though it possessed a life-force of all the souls he had mentioned. 'I promise you these people are friends,' he said to his invisible tenants.

Judy imagined that the door was resisting James's efforts in order to protect its secrets, whereas Murray looked to her for confirmation that James was more likely unhinged. In Murray's mind, he had spent too much time under the streets, with nothing but echoes of the past to keep him company.

Nevertheless, as they entered, it was as though the exposed vault let out a long soft sigh. Judy was emotionally floored for a few seconds. James's reference to souls keeping each other company, resonated with her.

The vault was roughly the size of a squash court. It was lit by a single strip light but its furthest confines stretched away into near darkness. The only sounds were the low hum of an alarm system and air-conditioning ducts. The door to each security box was stainless steel as was the ceiling. The floor was solid concrete painted black.

'So you're always in here when they open their box?' asked Murray, testing what James had already said.

'That's right, but then I leave them alone. Like I said earlier, I never see the contents. When they've finished, they ring a bell which alerts me upstairs. Then we lock their door together, and they sign out. It's simple but an effective process. Their entrance and exit is upstairs, out the back, so they're never seen on the street at the front of the shop.'

'How long do they get to stay down here?' asked Murray.

'It's generally an hour long slot that's prearranged, but if we're quiet I keep it flexible. There's never more than one client at any one time. And if you're wondering about Joe - he spent hours down here. Sometimes afterwards, we'd go for a beer, but more often than not, he'd go off looking like he'd lost his last dollar on a bet.'

'Which one's his?' asked Judy, hoping her intuitive nature would come into play as she ran her hands along the fronts of vaults nearest to her. Her fingers were beginning to tingle, but it was nothing to do with the cold metal. Suddenly she drew closer to a rose that had been threaded through the handle of a stainless steel door at waist level. The rose was clearly fresh and in full bloom. 'You've been down here already today,' she said, touched by his sentimentality.

'Yes, first thing,' said James.

Murray approached the door of the security box and hesitated. 'So since Joe died back in the late nineties, no one has opened this? Not the Gator brothers, nor anyone else associated with him?'

'Not a soul. I swear,' insisted James, making the sign of the cross on his chest.

'What about cleaning? Who does that?' asked Judy.

'Me but because of the nature of the place it doesn't get dusty, so I only give it the once over very rarely.'

'We're doing this all wrong Jude,' said Murray suddenly. 'I want the door dusted before we even take a look at the contents.' He looked at his phone and quickly realised there was no phone service to be had in such a place. 'Let's call in forensics immediately. You said you're owed a few favours Jude. Get onto it, will you?'

As they climbed the stairs back to James's office, Murray reflected on how he had felt when they first arrived. It had not gone unnoticed by him that Judy was unhappy with his apparent cold-hearted attitude. While she made the call, he stood by the barred window while James made tea, rebuking himself for showing so little consideration to the souls that James believed resided more than a hundred feet below street level. It occurred to Murray, that the constant drone of passing traffic made the silence of the vaults below seem all the more eerie, but he had not yet experienced what James, and now Judy seemed to sense. He wished he were more open-minded, and that he could adopt a more spiritual outlook on life, but being that way eluded him. He needed to change. With such thoughts whizzing round in what was a normally ordered mind, he was surprised when Judy appeared so soon from the back of the premises.

She whispered in his ear. 'Forensics are on their way.'

'How the hell did you pull that off so quickly?' he asked.

'I took a gamble and gave a teaser to Martin about the case,' she said, still keeping her voice lowered.

James had slipped out into an adjoining room. They began to argue about the rights and wrongs of police procedures.

'What did you say to him?' asked Murray, concerned she may have said too much.

'I just asked what he'd do if a dead celeb were to suddenly turn up alive and kicking.'

'I suppose that's not so bad. He's got plenty to pick from,' said Murray.

'Exactly. It was the thought of something exciting going on, that made him shift a few things around.'

'That's all very well, but depending on what's in the vault, they'll guess who we're investigating straight away.'

'Martin knows better than to open his mouth to the wrong person. He's bringing Brenda to take photographs. She's been working with him for donkey's years, so she can be trusted.'

James appeared with a carton of milk and finished making drinks.

Forensics are coming down straightaway,' Murray said to him.

'It's a delicate and lengthy procedure,' said Judy. 'I guarantee everything will be handled with great care.'

James looked slightly forlorn, as though he had been Marilyn's lover and was the only person with the right to handle her more intimate belongings.

A while later, he was leading the way once again, only this time Murray and Judy followed behind Martin and Brenda. As before, the vault seemed to let out a sigh. Trusting that women were more receptive than men to all things unexplainable, Judy looked to Brenda to see if she had picked up on what she had just told Martin, but her lack of reaction suggested otherwise.

As Martin began to lay out his equipment watched with interest by James, Judy whispered to Murray. 'If what James said is true, why do you want the door to the security box dusted? DiMaggio's prints will be long gone, so there'll be no prints but James's.'

'Just a hunch,' Murray said in her ear. 'In case James is lying and has been showing someone else around. Don't just assume he's compassionate Jude. He's running a niche business here.'

'But they wouldn't have access to the box anyway if there's only one key.'

'Well we'll know that for sure if Martin finds no other prints than James's,' said Murray.

Before the rose was removed by Martin's latex gloved hand, Brenda took a series of pictures with the rose in place. In Judy's mind the contrast between the red rose and the stainless steel door was a piece of art in itself. Martin dusted the door for prints, using a specialised torch to examine for any residual sweat or grease that might have been left behind by fingerprints. Brenda photographed the area then Martin removed the rose in double-slow motion so as not to allow the petals or stem to pollute what he had already done. For a second, Judy sensed him going the extra mile as his hands seemed to possess a tender touch more befitting of a man in love. He repeated his initial process, dusting any area he had not been able to reach in the first place. Judy realised she was holding her breath in anticipation. The butterflies in her stomach were gathering in intensity. She wondered whether Murray was feeling something similar or whether men like him were simply not wired in the same way as her.

Martin worked quietly, occasionally asking Brenda to step in again and photograph what he had found, while everyone else kept well back. From time to time, Judy looked to James. There was nothing about his body language that indicated he was nervous as to James's findings. His expression suggested that he was intrigued by the lengthy procedure. Martin had began to apply rubber tape to areas of the door, swiping the edge of a short metal ruler across it to remove any bubbles. Finally he peeled off the prints, covered them and wrote on the back of each.

Murray stepped forwards. 'Is there anything of consequence?' he asked.

'It's impossible to make any judgements until I've taken a look back at the lab. I've got some really clean prints though.'

At that point, Judy knew that Murray had bitten. He

would normally have sat back and waited until the lab sent him the results.

'Okay, carry on,' said Murray.

James instructed Martin on the procedure for using both keys. In Judy's mind, it was as though the door resisted, the sound of its hinges opening sounding like a squeak of protest. DiMaggio had selected one of the larger of the security boxes. Inside was a black metal box, that once dusted, on careful removal appeared to be the size of a small suitcase. Martin lifted it from its housing as carefully as though he were about to diffuse a bomb. The table that ran half the length of the centre of the vaults had been prepared like an operating theatre for him to lay out his findings. He laid the box on a sterile sheet and dusted the sides he could not reach when it had been inside its housing. Then unusually for someone of his nature, who would normally be unfazed, he stood quietly and looked down at the box deep in thought. All of a sudden, he beckoned Judy and Murray to one side so he could keep their conversation private.

'Whose belongings are in it?' he asked, unexpectedly.

'Marilyn Monroe's,' said Judy.

Martin's mouth dropped open. 'Wow, in that case I almost want to leave it as it is. I do feel pretty privileged though.'

'Both you and me then,' noted Judy. 'But I didn't know you were a fan.'

'What man isn't?' whispered Martin. 'Coincidentally, I wrote a piece on her death for my final dissertation,' he added. 'The cover up was pretty damning.'

Judy suddenly felt guilty. She was not sure how Martin would react if the case blew up and became the front page news story she suspected it would. He would no doubt feel wounded by her keeping the magnitude of the case from him.

He continued. 'She died before I was born. Right now I feel like I'm one of her lovers, touching things that touched her skin.'

'I never knew you could be so poetic Martin,' said Murray, sarcastically, trying to ground the conversation.

'A discovery like this warrants it, don't you think Steve? I get now how the archaeologists must've felt when they discovered Tutankhamun's tomb,' said Martin.

Martin was one of the best forensic scientists that Judy knew, plus in her mind, his interest in Marilyn meant he could be entrusted with her belongings.

She watched closely as he stood back, as though to admire his handiwork. Then he used minimum contact in order to lift the lid.

At that moment. Murray's phone bleeped. 'That's strange. We've no signal to speak of,' he said, reading a text. Suddenly he pocketed his phone and turned to leave, a sense of urgency apparent on his face. 'I've got to go. Jude you stay on and see this through. Call me when you're done.'

He climbed the stairs two at a time.

Chapter 24

Under London

Murray slammed the door as he left O'Flannagan's and checked it was secured, as there were several dubious-looking customers from earlier, watching him as he prepared to head off. The refuse lorries had departed, but the odour of foul-smelling rubbish still lingered. He walked to the nearest taxi rank and soon was en route to Huntley Manor, his driver willing to leave London knowing he would pick up a decent fare. Murray called Frank. He was clearly bereft and told Murray why.

The situation was serious. By the time Murray had reached Huntley Manor, an hour had already passed. An hour was too long as far as he was concerned, the first minutes being the most critical now that Norma had gone walkabout again, but this time not been found. He paid off the driver and waited for him to disappear into the distance. Two agents were manning the gates, both talking frantically on their phones and pacing backwards and forwards, suggesting to Murray that Norma was still missing. The gates swung open and the men gestured for

Murray to jump in the car that was parked just inside. There was a big security presence. It seemed that Frank had called for his own backup while waiting for Murray to arrive, but in Murray's opinion, there was an overkill of activity. The grounds were teeming with men combing the bushes and tracking across the grass in a uniform line while the estate's dogs hoovered the ground with wet noses. It was immediately clear to Murray that all evidence had been contaminated. His initial concern for Norma was replaced with anger at such carelessness. To call in his forensics team suddenly seemed like a complete waste of time. As he was thinking this, all of a sudden, Frank stepped onto the drive waving his arms wildly in the air to the driver to stop. He braked hard, almost collecting Frank up.

Frank jumped in the car, out of breath and saturated in sweat. 'Thanks for getting here so quickly,' he said to Murray.

'Fill me in,' said Murray. He had already decided that a dressing down for messing up a crime scene could wait until a more suitable moment.

'Nothing like this has ever happened. Not only is she missing but someone's ransacked her room. Whoever gotten in must've got hold of the codes. Everything's gone down.'

'How do you mean?' asked Murray.

'The house alarm, electrified fences, CCTV cameras, you name it. It doesn't make sense. They're all independent systems, totally unreliant on each other. Whoever did this must've gotten hold of inside intel. Worse than that, we don't know if they found her and have taken her off the premises by now.'

'Has everywhere been searched since we spoke?' asked

Murray.

Frank began to falter. 'Not yet. I've just sent several men to the old swimming pool... and to the lake.'

'Stop the car,' shouted Murray. The car skidded to a halt for the second time. 'Shouldn't that have been one of the first places...'

'We did an initial sweep,' interrupted Frank. 'There were no fresh footprints or anything to suggest someone's been that way.'

'You do know I have to call for backup,' said Murray.

'When I couldn't get hold of you, I called Austen. He's on his way,' said Frank, suddenly turning pale. 'He's already organised divers,' he added.

Murray jumped from the car with Frank so close to his heels that he thought he might be tripped. Both men sprinted into the house and up the stairs two at a time. The doors that gave access from the galleried landing into Norma's lounge and bedroom were wide open as were her windows. 'Who's been in here since you raised the alarm.'

'Anyone and everyone,' said Frank dejectedly. 'It's chaos I know. We were unprepared for such a breach of security.'

'So when your careful planning was tested, you panicked,' said Murray, trying to hold back his anger. He peered into the lounge from its threshold. 'But we can't worry about your cock-up for now.'

It was as Frank had said, in chaos. Lamps and chairs had been upturned, pictures hung crookedly on walls and broken ornaments littered the floor. It was windy and the full-length lace curtains were torn and flapping as they beat against the leaded lights.

Murray moved along the landing rather than

contaminate the scene further, and studied an equal mess that littered Norma's bedroom. Similarly to the lounge, chairs had been upended, as well as the pillows and eiderdown pulled from her bed. The drawers to her dressing table and bedside cabinets had been ripped out, their contents strewn everywhere. His photographic memory kicked in allowing him to store everything he had just seen. 'How long until Austen's here?'

'Half hour tops I'd say,' said Frank.

'Once your guys have finished by the lake and the pool, tell them to come back to the house. We'll use the drive by the front steps as a meeting point. It's doubtful Norma would have been taken out that way.'

Suddenly Frank snapped. 'For fuck's sake Murray. If for no one's sake but hers, can you call her Marilyn from now on? Show the woman some respect in her last days.'

Murray looked deep into Frank's eyes. He was broken and beyond repair. 'As you wish,' he said, with no intention of doing so when Frank was out of earshot. 'Now go and organise your men.'

Once he was sure Frank had gone, Murray closed his eyes and took a few deep breaths. He had already envisaged Norma having tripped and fallen into the swimming pool or lake, but for some inexplicable reason his instinct immediately told him that such a scenario seemed unlikely. Nevertheless, he sensed that she was nowhere close by and that Frank's fear that she may have been taken, might be a distinct possibility.

He descended the stairs, studying every inch of carpet, even though muddy prints indicated several pairs of shoes had been up and down since Norma had gone. He concentrated on looking for anything out of the norm, such as fibres from her slippers suggesting she had not gone out alone for a stroll but been dragged out unwillingly.

When he reached the hall, he stopped. He had a keen nose. There was a separation about the air, one that manifested itself in contrasts. Not only was there the sweet scent of flowers, but there was also something else indefinable that reminded him of incense sticks. He was quick to realise that there was little chance of detecting Norma's perfume for sure due to the huge display of chrysanthemums that graced the central round table but even so, the vague scent of patchouli began to tickle his sense of smell.

He took the back entrance that she generally used when on her way for a stroll. The patchouli scent followed him there. Frank's men were already converging from all directions and making their way round the side of the house to the front. To lessen the impact of any more needless contamination whilst he was carrying out his own search, Murray took a route slightly to the side of the path, checking for shoe prints in the flower borders immediately below Norma's suite as he went. He stood for a few seconds until the voices of the men were nothing but a distant murmur from the front of the house. The dogs were silent, having been penned and given a treat for their efforts.

As he reached the orangery he took a closer look at the steps that led up to it. The gardener was normally diligent in clearing the pea shingle and any mud that might have dropped from the soles of people's shoes, as any debris left would make it treacherous for Norma when she was out and about. However, it was impossible to tell whether he had carried out his normal routine as a trail of mud and leaves had been left from the steps to the inside, indicating the orangery had been searched thoroughly.

Murray walked on to the places that Frank feared had claimed Norma, quickly ruling out that she had tumbled into the swimming pool. The stagnant water was undisturbed, resembling a perfect carpet of crushed green velvet peppered with dead insects and twigs.

He moved onto the lake and began to skirt around it, this time ignoring his compulsion to go anti-clockwise so that he could see everything from a different perspective. The memory of the Satanic ritual from his dream began to flit through his mind, but he cast it out quickly and studied the plants that hung over the path, realising that someone had rushed along, snapping them as they went. Large footprints and the imprint from a stick used to clear the way confirmed his suspicions. He had gone some distance, when he noticed a distinct change in the path, in the sense that it narrowed and undulated, making it difficult to negotiate. The boot marks stopped here and turned in the opposite direction, indicating that whoever had been searching for Norma had already decided that there was no way she could have walked further on such an uneven terrain.

He continued on, but this time ignored the ground beneath his feet, looking out to the right and left in case she had fallen into the undergrowth. He decided to try and meet up with where he had stopped the day before.

He was almost three quarters of the way round the lake to where he had first set out in the rowing boat, when he spotted a building nestling in the trees that he had not been told about. It stood pale and bleached by the sun and was fashioned in the style of a Grecian folly. It occurred to him that every time he visited Huntley Manor it was as though he had stepped inside a giant glass bubble that protected hidden treasures like the folly, only this time the bubble had been smashed and things would never be the same again.

Very quickly he was approaching the folly's steep steps. He climbed onto its round stage, which resembled a bandstand. He was offered a spectacular view of the entire lake and the main house in the distance. Had circumstances been different and finding Norma had not been of paramount importance, he would have chosen instead to have lingered a while, but not allow himself to be lulled to sleep by the sun. He listened for the sound of unwanted visitors thinking how something about Norma's disappearance did not add up, but he could not put his finger on why he felt that way. Finally, satisfied that there was nothing more to see, he retraced his steps, all the time looking for tell-tale signs.

By the time he had done a complete lap and was back at the house, it was painfully clear to him that the chaos that had gripped Huntley Manor had succeeded in panicking absolutely everyone. Round at the front of the house, Austen was deep in conversation with Frank. Both men turned to look at Murray. Just as he was thinking about what to do or say, his phone rang. It was Judy.

'Jude, how's it going?' he asked.

'I'm almost glad you weren't at the vaults in the end,' she replied. 'You'd have laughed at me. I got emotional when Martin opened DiMaggio's box.'

'So did you process her belongings?'

'All photographed and the box resealed. It's back at the lab.'

'James didn't put up a fight about you taking it?'

'Surprisingly no, in the end. He knew it'd be safer with us.'

'I'm surprised. What was in it?'

'Listen, I'm nearly at Huntley Manor. Should be there in five. I'll tell you more when I see you, but there was something significant in...'

'Murray,' said DI Austen, immediately cutting short Murray's conversation. 'What do you think? Where is she?'

Murray ended the call and scanned Frank and Austen's faces, at the same time frustrated that Judy was about to tell him something compelling. Frank's face was ashen. And Austen was clearly deeply concerned. There was no red fire in his eyes this time. For the first time in the whole investigation, Murray began to wonder whether there was any subterfuge in either of them.

Finally he spoke. 'Despite the clumsiness of your men Frank, I can say with a hundred percent certainty that Marilyn is not at the bottom of the pool, and I'm positive about the lake too, but use the divers to check I'm right.'

'How can you be so sure?' asked Austen.

'It's a fucking big lake,' said Frank, losing all sense of decorum. 'How can you of searched it so thoroughly single-handed?'

'I've just got a hunch,' said Murray.

'A hunch? Are you telling me that's all you've got?' asked Frank, angrily.

'You'll have to give me more than that Murray,' said Austen, calmly. 'If she's not still on the estate, who do you think would have taken her?'

'I reckon I'll have the answer in an hour or so,' said Murray economically, leaving Frank and Austen open-mouthed. He headed for the front steps of the house. An important clue had been staring him in the face.

Chapter 25

It's All in the Detail

Murray had barely reached the top step when Judy's car pulled up by the fountain. He waited for her to join him before entering the house.

'What's going on? Is this why you had to leave O'Flannagan's in such a hurry?' she asked, flummoxed as to why there were so many suited men and a police presence.

'Norma's gone awol. Worse than that, she may have been taken.'

'Jesus. That makes my news somewhat insignificant. Any ideas as yet?'

'We'll talk inside,' said Murray, casting a lengthy look over the men congregated on the drive impatient for fresh orders.

'Do you think it's an inside job?' Judy suggested, quietly, not failing to notice the significance of Murray's scrutiny.

'Take a look at those guys, then you tell me if it's an inside job.'

Judy subtly manoeuvred him around, so that she could glance casually across his shoulder while still talking. 'Is this a test?' she asked, trying to keep her glances matter of fact and brief.

'Not at all. It's just I'm beginning to care what happens to Marilyn,' he said.

She laughed. 'You? I don't believe it for a moment.'

'I'm not a heartless bastard all the time,' insisted Murray.

'And did I hear right? You called her Marilyn,' teased Judy.

'Only on Frank's request, so forget I made that faux pas. What really bugs me is that I'm becoming emotionally involved and it's going to cloud my judgement.'

'You could try being a bit more positive and look at it another way,' suggested Judy. 'You know as well as me that passion's at the route of most violent crime. Maybe if you stop being such a cold fish and feel it for yourself, it'd make you a better detective.'

'Are you saying I'm not a good one?' asked Murray, realising that Judy was trying to lift his spirits.

She pushed him towards the front door. 'I wouldn't dare suggest such a thing but your girlfriend might. How is she, by the way?' she added, knowing the answer.

'I haven't seen her for days. Or is it weeks?' said Murray, realising that being so wrapped up with the goings-on at Huntley Manor had caused him to lose all sense of time.

'My point exactly. You need to make more effort or you'll lose her.'

'Anyway, moving on, let's get on with the business in hand,' he said, changing the subject as they entered the hallway. 'So, what do you think about the guys outside? Any of them behaving out of the ordinary?'

'Not that I could see,' said Judy. 'They're all running around like headless chickens, shitting themselves in case Frank sacks each and every one of them.'

'That's my opinion too, but what about Frank himself and DI Austen?'

'Are you asking me whether the guv is in on it? How about a big no in capital letters? He's as clean as a whistle. And as for Frank, his face is so white he resembles the living dead. He's beside himself.'

'My thoughts exactly. While they don't know if they're coming or going, let me show you around upstairs.'

'Something's bugging you. What is it?' asked Judy, following Murray up the stairs.

'I want your take on things,' he said. 'Then I'll comment.' He stopped Jude on the threshold of Norma's lounge. The forensics team were in full flow but he asked them to leave.

They filed out obediently and stood attentively as close as possible to hear Murray and Judy's words of wisdom. Although she could not adopt Murray's peculiar way of honing in on his senses, Judy stood stock still and took in the scene before her. After a few moments considering what had taken place, she stepped across to Norma's bedroom door and did exactly the same. She said nothing while she was looking or forming an opinion, but at last she spoke. 'I've seen enough. Let's talk downstairs where it's quiet.'

A unilateral sigh of disappointment went up from the forensics team, as they realised they were not to be party to Judy's usual eagle's eye analysis or Murray's "Sherlock" instincts. As it was, the team had not been told just who was being investigated because of the levity of who it was that was missing. They filed back in, knowing better than to butt in and ask.

Downstairs, Judy pulled Murray by the hand into the library and closed the door. Immediately she went over to one of the book shelves that housed an impressive display of vintage leather-bound books. Silent and thoughtful, she ran her finger across their gold-embossed spines, then felt the tops of each for dust, before turning to speak to Murray.

'Well, what is it Jude?' he asked, curious but loving her unusual way of approaching what was in question.

'Marilyn's life story is - coincidentally just like any one of these books,' she said.

'I'm not getting you - what do you mean?'

Judy plopped herself down in an ancient worn armchair and gestured for Murray to join her on one opposite. A puff of dust plumed into the air as he sat down, suggesting to him that the library was little-used.

'This is how I see it, so bear with me,' said Judy. 'When I read a really good book, I always hate coming to the end, especially when the story has gripped me from the beginning and ends with an unexpected twist.'

'I don't see where your analogy lays,' said Murray.

'Well, there's no doubt that Marilyn's life is an epic story,' said Judy. 'And it would have been more so, that is, if JFK had lived, stepped down from the presidency and they had lived happily ever after in England.'

'But they didn't,' said Murray.

'Exactly. So Marilyn's story ended when he was assassinated. Her life after Jack is irrelevant in her mind, with the exception of raising Mary. I've no doubt that she never got over Jack, so the rest of her life has been just like the dust gathering on the top of those books.'

'I see the comparison. You're even sounding poetic in

your old age.'

Judy smiled broadly. 'That's praise coming from you. But joking aside, her early life is a bestseller up with the classics. It immortalised and stopped her from growing old. Exactly how she wanted the public to remember her.'

'So you think she could still be alive?' asked Murray, just about following Judy's take on things.

'Maybe, but she wants to die quietly. Like an old cat that's crawled into its cosy basket in the corner of its owner's home. She doesn't have that sort of privacy here so she's chosen to disappear and be at one with nature. No one's taken her.'

Her last sentence jolted Murray back into the moment, away from him trying to interpret her reasoning. 'Well if you're so sure, where the fuck is she then?' he asked, frustration by his own lack of intuitive guidance at that precise moment.

'Who - Marilyn or Gloria? Have you noticed how we've both started believing? You used to call her Norma, almost without fail, but that was the first time you called her Marilyn today. You're convinced.'

'Maybe I am - maybe I'm not,' said Murray, refusing to acknowledge the possibility.

'Oh don't be so cussed. Marilyn is on the estate somewhere. The suits have been looking in the obvious places and not understood the thoughts of a dying woman. And anyway, Steve, you surprise me. Didn't you notice her stick was missing?'

Murray thought back to scanning Norma's suite and how he had logged the contents in his mind. He revisited his photographic memory and scanned the lounge and adjoining bedroom in case she had discarded it elsewhere, but he could not locate it. It angered him to have missed such a critical detail. 'You're right,' he said.

'Did you find anything else strange about her room?' asked Judy, wishing there was more time to tease him instead of joining the search party.

'You're one step ahead of me on this occasion. What have you spotted?'

'Well her suite was upside down for sure, but then I realised that there was no muscle behind the mess. Apart from a few smashed ornaments everything was not far from its original place. The pictures and shelves that were higher up on the walls are still untouched, so the person that created all the debris was neither tall nor strong. It's a woman's work, though I hate to suggest all women are weak. I think she lost it for a few seconds. Who wouldn't, death staring them in the face?'

'Surely Norma couldn't have done it,' said Murray.

'Why not? Nothing heavy has been upturned.'

'She'd have been heard surely.'

'Maybe she unintentionally picked a time when all the men were out of the house and Geraldine was in the kitchen. If she listens to a radio while cooking, she wouldn't have heard the commotion upstairs.'

'I'm such an idiot sometimes Jude,' said Murray, suddenly remembering a very important point. 'And you're a genius. I do have something to add to your amazing theory though. Norma's still on the grounds, and I can prove which way she was heading. Let's hope we're not too late.' He leapt from the chair.

They both rushed from the library to the entrance at the back of the house, with Judy running behind, still proud of her epic detective work. She was trying to stay upright on the highly-polished hall floor. 'Don't you want to tell the others?' she asked.

'Absolutely not. If she's alive, the shock of us all converging on her will finish her off.'

'Where are we going?'

'You'll see,' said Murray, walking briskly across the lawn, choosing not to sprint so as to conserve his energy for what he might find. Judy kept pace, glancing behind from time to time to check that no one had cottoned on to the fact that they were onto something significant. After tracking the route he had taken earlier, Murray stopped suddenly, causing Judy to nearly crash into the back of him.

He bent over to catch his breath. 'Look Jude. What do you see?'

Judy looked down at the ground where Murray had first noticed that it narrowed and undulated. She brushed aside a tuft of grass and took a closer look. 'Footprints. Two sets. The ones to the side of the path, I'm guessing was you, protecting the evidence. Size nines?'

'Yes, spot on. The others?' asked Murray.

Judy looked again. 'Much bigger. A heavy male judging by the depth of the tread in the mud. Could be her kidnapper, but I think not. He wasn't in a hurry.'

'How do you know?' said Murray, testing her, but already having come to the same conclusion.

His prints are perfect and level. Even weight on back and front of shoe. They stop here and turn around back the way we came. He was simply looking for her,' said Judy.

'And that means?' asked Murray, pressing her for more.

'One of the suits and he gave up the search.'

'What about these marks?' asked Murray, pointing out a trail of holes.

'Could be made by a bird's beak, digging for worms,'

suggested Judy.

'If it had been random, then perhaps you'd be right. But they're all equal distance apart and too big for a bird's beak? They're the result of Norma's stick,' said Murray, triumphantly.

'You're right, but they could've been there a while, from before she was taken ill,' said Judy, knocking him back.

'Think harder Jude. Her being so frail, the pressure of her stick wouldn't have left deep imprints in bone dry soil. A week ago we'd had no rain for ages. These holes are deep and still full of rainwater. They're very recent. The water's not had time to drain away.'

'You're good,' said Judy, congratulating him. But what's this,' she added, kneeling down on the grass to take a closer look. 'There's a third set of prints.'

Murray knelt down on the grass next to her. At first he could see nothing more than what they had discussed, apart from disturbance by insects and the fresh bit of evidence of Norma's stick. But after a few seconds he began to hone in on the vaguest of patterns, which looked like the faint crisscross weave of a flat sole.

'Norma usually wears kitten heels but this time she came out in her slippers,' said Judy. 'That's why her footprints are so faint. She was still alive awhile ago.'

'How did she manage to get this far unaided?' said Murray.

'Just like that cat I mentioned. She's looking for somewhere to die alone and undisturbed.'

Murray gulped. He looked thoughtfully to where the temple peeked coyly out of the trees. Instantly his heart began to thump. He imagined Judy could see it against his chest wall. 'There's only two places left to search,' he said. 'The island, but the boat's on the bank still. And the temple. But I was there earlier. It's clean.'

'Let's take another look,' said Judy, marching on ahead, but this time keeping to the grass that bordered the path.

'There's nothing here Jude,' said Murray as they reached the temple. 'Only what you can see. Just this circular stage and a few Grecian style pillars.' He stood next to her and looked out towards the manor house for the second time that day.

'It's worth a look, just for the view,' said Judy, appreciating the same panorama that he had witnessed shortly before. 'Bit off the beaten track. Wonder what it was used for.'

'Nothing in particular. Most likely just the work of an architect stretching his creative muscles. Lots of country estates are littered with buildings like this.'

Judy adopted a pose of an actor in full flow and began to spout lines from a well-known nineteenth century play, while dramatically waving her arms in the air to an imaginary audience.

'This is serious business Jude. Probably not the best time to be clowning around,' said Murray, scolding her.

'You're right of course. Sorry - let's take another look around, just in case,' she said.

'Like I said, this is it,' said Murray, still staring at the house in the distance. His mind was empty of any more options of where else to look. He turned to speak to Judy but she was nowhere in sight. 'Jude, I thought I told you to stop clowning around.'

There was no reply apart from a complaining flock of geese flying overhead as they headed off to the west. Murray went to the edge of the stage and circumnavigated it to see if Judy was hiding behind a pillar planning to jump out. His patience was taxed. 'Come on Jude.

Enough's enough. Let's get back.'

'Pssst,' came a voice all of a sudden from the undergrowth.

Judy was ten feet below him, having climbed down a flight of crumbling brick steps that he had not noticed earlier on. They disappeared into a tangle of brambles and nettles. She gestured silently but eagerly to him, holding a finger to her lips. He pushed the undergrowth to one side and dropped the last few feet to the grass beside her, protesting under his breath at every thorn that pierced his suit trousers. The folly towered above, framed by an azure sky and the occasional fluffy white cloud. The steps joined a paved path that disappeared into an untended section of the estate, prolific with crowded trees and young saplings fighting their way up to sunlight.

'What have you found?' he asked. 'There's no way she could manage those steps.'

'Keep your voice down and listen,' said Judy. 'There's something in the bushes.'

'It'll just be rabbits,' said Murray.

'Maybe, but look at that,' said Judy.

Murray followed her gaze. There was a lower level to the folly that at first glance seemed to just be its foundation stones, packed tightly behind the undergrowth.

'Someone's been this way. More than once,' said Judy, pointing out an intermittent well-trodden path that circled the rear section of the temple. 'That's more than a path made by animals. It's been flattened.'

'Groundsmen putting out traps perhaps?' suggested Murray.

'Maybe.'

'Let's take a better look then. You go the other way Jude, and we'll meet in the middle,' said Murray.

They split up but he had only gone a few yards when the path stopped abruptly, blocked by more brambles. He was immediately taken back by the sight of a stone arch beneath the stage. It housed a pair of doors that were at one time decorated with colourful stained glass in the upper section, most of which was now scattered around on the ground. Shards of rainbow colours crunched beneath his feet as he approached to take a better look.

Suddenly Judy caught up with him. 'There's nothing round the other side,' she said, stopping dead in her tracks. 'Wow, what do you think's in there?'

'I'd be guessing but probably nothing.' Murray took a tissue from his pocket, wrapped it around his hand to protect evidence and tried the left hand door, which was swollen with moisture due to rain expanding the rotting woodwork. The door resisted his attempts when he tried to open it beyond a few inches. He and Judy exchanged looks, more in keeping with kids that had just imagined there was hidden treasure beyond.

Chapter 26

Twenty-One Again

Daylight was beginning to fade prematurely, retreating as menacing shadows began to morph into long and distorted shapes. It was as though nature was slotting in an especially short day to its calendar to suggest that it was in mourning and that Norma might be dead after all. Aware that time was of the element, Murray knew that it would be nigh impossible to search efficiently once it was dark. He took hold of the handle again, pulling slowly so that it would not come apart in his hands. 'It won't give,' he said, knowing he should show respect in case he was battling with a building of historical importance.

Judy hung back as she watched the sun dip behind tall forest trees. 'Shouldn't we call for backup?' she asked.

'There's no time. I've no phone signal and by the time one of us gets back to the house it might be too late.'

All of a sudden, the door gave into Murray's efforts and sprung open. Judy nestled up behind him as they stepped inside. After a few seconds of waiting for their eyes to adjust to the lack of light, a curved wall mirroring the circle of the stage floor above, came into view. Stained glass arched windows were dotted at equal distances around the walls of the chamber. Diluted sunlight peppered the walls and floor creating a myriad of rainbow colours. It seemed an ill-fitting tomb for anyone apart from rabbits and mice.

'This place gives me the creeps,' said Judy, switching on her phone torch and shining it into the darkest corners.

'It would've been a great place for a kid's den before it got into this state,' said Murray. 'I bet Mary played here when she was a child.'

Out of the blue there was the slightest of movements from the shadows.

Judy jumped backwards and cowered behind Murray. 'What was that? It'd better not be a rat. I hate them.'

'They're good on toast with a bit of salt and pepper,' said Murray, trying his best to humour her.

'You're disgusting, do you know that?'

Murray picked up a garden fork from the floor and began to poke around among paraphernalia, no doubt stored there years ago and forgotten about. At any moment, he expected something to scuttle out and make Judy scream.

He took his phone from his pocket to double up the light from her phone. Their combined beams brought the details of the chamber into focus. There was a water-damaged table on which was sat a single fat candle. Full sacks of logs had been stacked around the edges of the chamber, interspersed with threatening looking farm implements and barbaric animal traps. The latter had rusted away through years of being kept below ground level in a damp environment.

'Can you hear the voices?'

'You won't scare me that easily Jude. I'm not a cissy like you.'

'I didn't say anything,' said Judy.

'Quit messing about and look for evidence.'

'No seriously, I didn't say a word. There's someone else here,' said Judy, her voice an octave higher due to her fear.

Immediately Murray noted the unexpected scent of patchouli.

'It's me,' said a fragmented voice from the darkness. 'Is that you Jack?'

Judy and Murray both stepped backwards in shock.

Murray spoke first. 'Norma, don't be frightened. We've come to help.'

At last, a stooped figure stepped out from the darkness, leaning heavily on a stick. 'They followed me all the way from the house,' said Norma.

'Who did?' asked Judy softly, taking Norma's other arm to steady her.

'Oh I didn't see anyone because they're so clever at hiding. Even you wouldn't spot them. I just knew they were following me. I heard them calling my name from the trees. I was so frightened.'

'I'm sure you were,' said Judy, going along with Norma. 'But how did you get this far, and why hide in such a horrible place?'

'I come here with Mary - she's my little girl you know. She's only five. It's our special place. We have secret tea parties and sometimes my fiancée Jack joins us. He's the president of the United States.'

Judy and Murray exchanged nervous glances, but said nothing, a silent message passing between them that Norma needed gentle handling while in her make-believe world.

Completely oblivious that she was not of sound mind, Norma turned away and rummaged in a wooden crate. After a few seconds of talking to herself and impatient rustling with various objects, she pulled out several pieces of a child's porcelain tea set and held it lovingly to her chest. 'So rude of me,' she said, starting to lay the water-damaged table with the broken things she had found. 'Would you like a cup of tea? I know you English people like it.'

'I'd love a cup of tea,' said Murray, opting to humour Norma in her delicate state of mind.

'Sugar? she asked, spooning nothing from a cracked bowl with an imaginary spoon.

'Have you any biscuits?' asked Judy, beginning to formulate a plan. 'Only I skipped breakfast and I'm really hungry.

'Oh dear, I don't think I have,' said Norma, digging deep in her pockets. 'The president ate the last one.'

'We can't have tea without biscuits,' said Judy cleverly, pleased that her gamble might just pay off. 'But I know where there are some delicious ones. Yummy shortbread, my favourite. Shall we go to the tearooms and buy some?'

'How lovely. I'd like that. Is the car outside?' asked Norma.

A deep sense of sorrow seemed to fill the chamber as Murray and Judy witnessed Norma's rapid mental decline.

'It'll be here soon,' said Judy. 'Let's wait outside in the sunshine until it arrives.'

They eased Norma into daylight before she could cotton onto their deception, talking to her all the time about what was waiting at the tearooms, while reversing the route they had taken to find her. She seemed so switched off that she was unperturbed when lifted over obstacles and carried up and down steps. Judy laid out her jacket on the folly's stage so Norma could sit and lean back against a pillar with the last of the sunlight on her face. She continued to humour Norma with stories of her own childhood tea parties while Murray used a sudden burst of phone service to call Frank.

Twenty minutes later a small entourage had arrived, Frank struggling to contain his relief that Norma although lost in a world of her own, was alive and that she recognised him. The folly was in an impossible place to call for air assistance to land, so she was carried back to the main house on a stretcher that they had thought to bring with them. Murray, Frank and Judy tailed behind, Murray telling Frank about the voices that Norma had mentioned.

He seemed unperturbed. 'This isn't the first time as you already know. But the last episode was years ago, when she first arrived in England.'

'But nothing recently?' asked Judy.

'Not a sniff of it,' insisted Frank.

'Judy and I'll update Austen, while you do what you need for Marilyn,' said Murray as they finally reached the main house.

'I like the fact you call her by her real name at last,' said Frank, following the stretcher bearers inside.

Murray chose not to rebuke himself this time as he and Judy made their way round to the front of the house. He knew in his heart as did Judy, that no matter what his viewpoint might be, he was still intrigued and he doubted he would ever deal with a case so unusual again. One thing he was sure of however, was that the only person who could possibly convince the world that they were Marilyn, apart from the icon herself, was Gloria. There was a lot in it for her and as a younger woman, she had been conniving by all accounts. She had eluded recognition in life, but in death it might still be waiting for her.

Murray looked up to the sky, sensing for the first time that there was more to life than what he could see. Why he thought that, he did not know as he had no religious beliefs. The sky offered up no shaft of sunlight or the sounds of angels playing harps. It was once again a deepening shade of blue, now that Norma had been found alive, with no trouble brewing in the form of grey storm clouds. If the failing woman on the stretcher was Gloria, the fruits of her story splashed across the front page of next week's tabloid newspapers, his hunches would be proved to have been right all along. He wished so much that he was wrong.

When he and Judy reached the front of the house, police cars and vans were parked bumper to bumper around the fountain. The dogs were still in the handlers' vans, barking in frustration due to being kept pent up for the last hour or so. On hearing Murray and Judy approach, Austen turned from his conversation with senior colleagues.

'Good work team. I knew you'd look after her.'

'Thank you Sir. Is an ambulance on its way?' said Judy with one eye on the proceedings.

'Ambulance? No, she'll be treated here,' said Austen.

'Surely she...' said Murray.

'Surely nothing,' said Austen, interrupting him. 'She's a good team on hand and we don't want any smart-arsed journalists sniffing around. Now this is settled, we can close this down,' he added, turning to walk to his car.

'The case isn't closed. The foren...'

'Shut it,' said Judy, kicking Murray hard in the shin. 'He doesn't know about forensics. It's strictly a personal favour remember?'

Austen began to dismiss the other officers and seated himself in the front passenger seat. He wound down his window, nodding approval to Murray at a job well done, then he instructed his driver to move off. Murray watched his car disappear down the drive until it was out of sight.

'What is it?' asked Judy. 'Are you still doubting it's Marilyn.'

'Until proved otherwise. That's your only failing Jude. You're gullible and a romantic. I don't believe a woman of ninety-one could've done what she just did. The effort would've killed her in my opinion,' said Murray. He hesitated. ' Gloria was younger than Marilyn wasn't she?'

'About eight years younger. Not enough for the difference to be noticed back in the sixties, but now of course it would stand out,' observed Judy.

'Exactly Jude, there's still a margin of possibility a woman of eighty-four, especially one who had looked after herself, could've made her way to that hell-hole under the folly.'

'Oh my goodness, you're right. I'd never even given it any thought. So you'll be interested in the contents of the vault then.'

'That had completely gone out of my mind. You were itching to tell me about it,' said Murray.

'Back at our rooms. I've checked and they're not bugged. I'll tell you all then.'

By the time they had got back to the guest quarters it was dark. Judy kicked off her shoes and flopped down onto her too soft mattress. For a few seconds it undulated like a boat on a smooth sea and made her feel that at any second the tension of the day might dissolve away and that she would fall asleep.

Her room was a mirror image of Murray's; chintzy and fussy and the wallpaper too busy. It played tricks on her eyes, so much so that each time she glanced at its pattern, she imagined another pink flower had bloomed. She dismissed the illusion as a symptom of her tiredness and closed her eyes. Amoeba-like dots were dancing across the surface of her eyes like tiny tadpoles.

'You look knackered. I don't need to tell you though that time's against us,' said Murray, removing his jacket and hanging it on the back of a chair in his usual way to prevent it from creasing. He sat on the end of her bed, keeping a respectful distance between them and turned to look at Judy. She was fast asleep. He covered her over with a duvet knowing it was useless to try and rouse her. He would have to wait until morning for her exciting news.

Chapter 27

Caught in the Act

Judy was asleep the following morning when Murray
knocked at her bedroom door. It was still dark outside,
but he had already been awake awhile, pacing his room
as he tried to put the pieces of the jigsaw together. Judy
on the other hand had been thinking the case through in
her sleep.

'Come in,' she said, at the sound of his knock. She was
wide awake and excited about starting the conversation
they should have had the night before.

He put his head around the door. 'Too early?' he asked,
immediately scolding himself for having given her the
option to nod off again. 'I come bearing gifts,' he added,
presenting her with a tray of coffee, fruit juice and
croissants. He knew the way to get the best out of her at
any time of day.

'You're a star,' said Judy, plumping up her large hotel
type pillows and sitting up.

'Norma's rallied,' said Murray. 'I couldn't believe
it when I went over to the main house. She was in the

breakfast room, dressed already at this hour, chatting to Frank. Unbelievable.'

'Sorry about last night. Don't think just because I crashed out I'm not excited,' Judy assured Murray.

'You can fill me in now, especially as you've had waiter service,' he replied.

Judy laughed. 'You know Steve, back at the vaults I felt like a kid on Christmas Day. Once Martin was satisfied with his procedures, he asked Brenda to fetch something from his van. I guessed he did that so we could talk freely. You've no need to worry Steve. I said nothing about us investigating Marilyn being alive, though I bet he'd be thrilled if he knew she was.'

'Might be alive Jude. Never lose sight of the facts,' Murray pressed home.

'Come on - are you still harping on about Gloria? Well I'm not buying that theory and I'm pretty sure you're not either.'

'Let's just say I haven't decided which horse to back as yet. So let's get back to what happened at the vaults.'

'Of course - the box. Martin was impressive as always. Such a delicate touch. Like he was holding a newborn baby,' said Judy, dragging out the suspense for maximum effect.

'That's his job.'

'You're such a cold fish Steve. I despair sometimes.'

'That's my job. To be cold, calculating and more importantly - detached. As you should be too Jude, instead of seeing everything through rose coloured spectacles.'

She dismissed his pretence of being heartless and continued. 'Everything in the box was wrapped in pink tissue paper tied with ribbon. Clearly done by a loving hand,' she added, as an afterthought. 'Among other things there were some nice pieces of jewellery: engagement and wedding rings and a fine gold chain with a heart locket. The locket had two photos in. One was of JFK, which I'm surprised DiMaggio didn't dispose of. The other photo was of a woman we need to do some digging about. It could be her mother I suppose?'

'I'm more interested in the rings if it was Marilyn who came to England, as we don't know if she married again, but we don't have that sort of detail about Gloria as yet.'

Judy sighed. A wistful look, which was becoming the norm, crossed her face. 'Another mystery to unravel. If we're talking about Marilyn, maybe she married JFK in secret.'

'He'd have to be a bigamist. The rings would more likely have been a gift from DiMaggio.'

Judy ignored his reluctance to embrace her romantic notion and continued. 'There was also a well-used beaded clutch bag. Beads and sequins were missing, so it must've been a favourite. When Martin opened it I felt like the cat that got the cream. I don't expect you to understand why it affected me so much.'

'Let me guess why you think that. Because I'm a man?'

'That and, because you're you, more-like,' said Judy lightly. 'But how shall I put it to you? Do you remember the Titanic documentary about the retrieval of artefacts from the seabed? It was just like one of those moments. Like I'd stepped back in time.'

Murray rolled his eyes. There was no getting away from their different slant on things. Nevertheless, he was unusually riveted to her drawn-out explanation. 'Please put me out of my misery and get on with it.'

'I'm trying, I'm trying - really I am,' said Judy, breakfast done and chin butter-free for once. 'Inside were a number of items; a powder compact, a comb and bright red lipstick. I had the strongest of urges to use the lipstick, being it was her lips that it touched last. But there was something else far more significant,' she added, her eyes glazed as she looked out of the window.

'What?' asked Murray, impatiently.

Judy hesitated as though to tease. 'A pocket-sized diary from nineteen sixty-two, her name in the front and full of entries.'

'Fuck me,' said Murray, suddenly realising that swearing was becoming part of his regular vocabulary. 'For once the lack of technology doesn't matter.'

'How do you mean?'

'Well think about it Jude. If this story were happening now instead of back then, daily info would be stored in a mobile phone. We'd identify the owner by their phone contract. But a handwriting match is just as good and exactly the sort of evidence you were hoping for.'

Judy grinned an all-knowing grin. 'I would've liked to have read her texts to and from JFK if that technology had existed. They'd have been steamy to say the least.'

The problem is though Jude, all this proves is that DiMaggio deposited things of Marilyn's at O'Flannagan's. And I do want to know more about it all. We need to pin down the likely manufacture date of the diary. But it doesn't bring us any closer to who we are dealing with at Huntley Manor. There may be no connection whatsoever.'

Judy ignored his scepticism. 'I'm one step ahead of that request. Without giving the game away, I had one of the team on it while I was en route here. I sent them a photo of the cover and an empty page showing the typeface used for days of the week. It was manufactured in the US sometime around nineteen-fifty-seven, by a company that was in production right up until the mid sixties. When we get back I'll get a handwriting expert on it so they can compare it to some proven handwriting of Marilyn's.'

'Was there anything else in the box of consequence?'

'There were a few items of clothing. Gloves, satin underwear, stockings. But probably most importantly, there was a silk suit. A beautiful cornflower blue. Martin said it had been worn a number of times as there were face powder marks around the collar and perspiration marks on the underarms. I guess deodorants weren't so effective back then.'

Murray sensed there was more to tell. 'What are you holding back?' he asked, now rattled that he had not been there to witness the unveiling.

'I saved the best until last. I've been so desperate to tell you, which is why I can't believe I crashed out like I did last night. As well as the diary, Martin found blonde hairs on the small brush as well as the suit collar.'

Murray's heart began to pound like the familiar African drum that presented itself to him on exciting moments such as these. 'Get Martin down here, straightaway. We need hair samples from Marilyn while she's still with us.'

'Marilyn or Gloria?' asked Judy, sarcastically, making the call.

'I reserve judgement. As should you.'

She ended her call after a brief conversation. 'He's on his way,' said Judy, in reference to Martin.

'Can he be trusted?'

'Are you kidding? You're riddled with doubt about practically everyone. You're fighting your demons again. What is it with you?'

'There's something about this case, that's all,' he

said, wondering whether enemies were closer than he expected.

'Well forget it. It's bull shit. Don't you want to hear more about the diary?'

'Of course.' He was quietly amused by her enthusiasm. She was bubbling over like a champagne bottle that had been vigorously shaken and uncorked.

She took her notebook from her pocket. 'Martin wasn't keen on me taking photos on my mobile, so savour what I'm about to tell you Steve. Obviously I don't have the diary. I wasn't allowed to handle it, but he held open a few pages with his instruments for me to see a sample so I could give you the gist. Marilyn hadn't tried to hide what she was doing, but as it was a pocket diary, space was limited. This might convince you finally. She made mention of people whispering down the phone, being followed and the such-like.'

Murray's logic was pushing and pulling him. 'That confirms what Frank was telling us about and what we've witnessed first hand.'

'One thing's for sure from her entries, she was avoiding Bobby Kennedy like the plague, so much so that she was actively encouraging Gloria to take him off her hands. There's mention of a romantic date she had set up between them and she mentions her relief to have dumped him on Gloria.'

'Any mention of JFK?'

'That goes without saying - on almost every page that I saw. She had the habit of doodling hearts and kisses next to his name. She was definitely seeing him regularly right till the end, despite the media thinking otherwise.'

Murray went to the window and peered through a gap in the blinds. 'So it'd been going on for years. No wonder there were some who wanted her dead. Maybe he did too.'

'You're still doing it. Dismissing anything that's remotely connected to the heart. Since seeing these excerpts, I'm convinced he loved her as much as she loved him. I think they would have found a way to be together if he hadn't been assassinated.'

'On the other hand, if she was hearing things and imagining she was being followed like we witnessed at the bandstand, who knows what else she might kid herself about?'

'So are you beginning to believe it's her or not?' asked Judy.

'Celebs turning up from beyond the grave is so far-fetched.'

'Doesn't mean it can't happen.'

'Have you ever known it to happen?' asked Murray, sure of the answer.

'No one springs to mind, but I'm always hoping Richey Edwards will walk into a police station one day.'

'That's my point exactly. I'm taking it you're a big fan of the Manic Street Preachers and you believe he's still alive.'

'As it happens I do,' she admitted. 'If he just went awol, then just embrace the possibility that this case might just be the same. I'm also thinking about a different aspect altogether. With what we've found out about Gloria's character, I don't think she would have been happy to remain holed up at Huntley Manor for the rest of her life, do you? She loved the limelight, whereas Marilyn was running away to hide. Wouldn't Gloria have milked the story to an inch of its life to make money out of it while she was young enough to enjoy it?'

'True, she might have sat on it for a while until the time was right,' said Murray. 'She stood to make a lot of money by releasing the facts. She might also have pretended she was Marilyn if she thought that she could make more money that way instead of owning up to just being her body-double. With no postmortem results, she might have considered it easy. Though she hadn't counted on the fact that Marilyn had a half-sister who's still alive.'

'That would've been a good reason to wait on its own. If the half-sister were to die of natural causes, there would be no one to challenge her identity. The trouble with the half-sister, would she be able to positively identify Marilyn after all these years?'

Murray left the window and sat on Judy's bed again. 'There is absolutely no way we could go to her and ask for a DNA sample. The shock would kill her.'

'What about Aileen?' continued Judy. 'We seem to have put her story to one side altogether.'

'Strangely I trust her evidence more than anyone's. No one pointed me in her direction. It was a random search on the internet back at the Yard that led me to her. If Frank or any of the others had given me the details of her whereabouts I might have dismissed it as yet another part of the scam. She was well clued-up about Gloria, who has until now been forgotten about by just about everybody.'

'You'd think, back in the States Gloria would've been as vulnerable as Marilyn. She knew too much just by watching Marilyn come and go. Good enough reason for her to chicken out of the original deal.'

'Now perhaps you understand why I've been taken with either possibility. Every time I think I've just about made up my mind, something turns up to scupper it. While we're waiting for Martin, let's take a look at the photographs again. I'll go and get them.'

Murray left Judy for a few minutes, during which time she closed her eyes and tried to slow down all the thoughts that were racing around in her mind. Steve was right. She wanted the frail woman in the big house to be Marilyn and it was affecting her judgement. She was trying to manipulate him into thinking along the same lines and that was not helpful to either of them.

As Murray opened the door to his room, he had already made up his mind for the third time in a week. Judy would not be pleased to know that he was gambling that it was Gloria eating breakfast with Frank and, that probably she had a string of descendants who would benefit from her successful scam. But it was true to say that there was a shift in his feelings. He clearly wanted Marilyn to be the one that was alive in preference to gold-digging Gloria. He was in love with the memory of Marilyn as a vital young woman. She was a fantasy figure that seemed able to conjure herself up even from beyond the grave and leave her mark on everyone. He was still thinking this as he entered his room to collect the photographs but did not expect to see the housekeeper, Geraldine. In his mind, she looked nervous and she was feverishly pretending to dust the top of his dressing table.

'That won't be necessary,' he said. 'The room's clean enough.'

'As you wish,' she said, backing out of the room.

Murray stood still and listened to the tone of her footsteps. She was scurrying, like a mouse running away from a hunting cat. He honed in on the room. She had been busy, but not with cleaning. Every drawer and wardrobe door had been opened and not put back to how it had been when he was there last. The blinds had been pulled up as though she had been checking for anyone turning up that might disturb her snooping. He went to the window and examined her line of sight. She was still crossing the lawn with her yellow duster flapping in her hand as she broke into an occasional jog. He wiped a finger across his dressing table to confirm his suspicions. There was the lightest layer of dust. She had come with no intention of cleaning. He had disliked her from the start, but now he disliked her even more.

He knelt down and poked his head under the bed. He had arrived in time. His briefcase packed full of photographs lay undisturbed, a long blonde hair against the edge of the case representing its original position. An old trick, but it always worked. Murray picked up the hair, wrapped it in a tissue and put it in his wash bag, momentarily thinking of his ill-suffering girlfriend whose hair it was. Taking the briefcase back to Judy's room, he shelved the thought temporarily that Geraldine might be something other than what she was employed to be.

Chapter 28

Camelot

Murray was still thinking about Geraldine when he and Judy were crossing the lawn to the main house a few moments later. By the time they had reached the orangery, they had chosen after lengthy debate to include Martin in their findings as they were about to ask him for a speedy forensic favour.

Martin was already waiting in the library when Judy and Murray entered, down on his hands and knees, examining the faded Persian rug. He stopped his inspection and jumped to his feet and began instead to fiddle with his kipper tie. In Murray's opinion, Martin was a typical geek and his out of date clothing when not in his white coat or protective gear, compounded that fact.

'Thanks for coming so promptly,' said Murray.

'Try keeping me away - this is some place isn't it? I feel trapped in some sort of time warp.'

'I can see why you might think that,' said Murray.

'Not sure I could endure living here for long. It's creepy

to say the least, what with all those ancient skin cells floating around in the air or imbedded in cracks in the walls,' added Martin, pulling a ghoul-like face.

'Enough of the kidding around. At this point in the investigation, all we need to know is that we can completely trust you,' said Judy, knowing the answer, but making a point anyway. She watched for Martin's reaction to her bluntness.

His expression suggested that he was hurt rather than angry. 'Jesus, not like you to be so up front with your feelings. It was Steve earlier. If this carries on I might take offence.'

Murray made an attempt to soften Judy's comment. 'Jude and I have never come across a case quite like this. Can't have any Chinese whispers going on back at the Yard.'

'That why we're telling you to keep tight-lipped Martin. You're one of us,' added Judy, cementing the three of them together and attempting to make Martin feel important.

'Think no more of it,' said Martin, generous with his forgiveness. 'So now it's clear we're on the same page, why am I here? Something pretty big I presume.'

'Drink?' asked Judy, uncertain of how to break their silence regarding Marilyn.

'That's a bit irregular, but hey, don't mind if I do.'

Murray rang a bell on the wall and waited, seating himself in a chair directly facing the door to the entrance hall. A few minutes passed until there was a gentle knock. Geraldine entered. As soon as she spotted Murray she shrunk back like a flower starved of rainwater.

'Seeing as it seems the norm for certain staff to behave inappropriately, we'll do the same Geraldine,' said Murray icily. 'Fetch us a decent bottle of red and three glasses.' He looked her straight in the eye, which only added to her nervousness.

'Yes Sir,' she said, bobbing up and down in an attempt at a curtsey. Then she backed out of the room in her usual submissive way, as quickly as she could,.

'What's she done to upset you?' asked Judy.

'I found her nosing about in my room when I went to fetch the photos. She'd been taking a good look at all my stuff.'

'Anything missing?'

'Not that I could see. I disturbed her in time. Nevertheless, I'd bet on a tenner she's up to no good.'

For fear of being reported to Frank, Geraldine reappeared quickly. Murray made a point of halting the conversation while watching her arrange glasses on the coffee table. The near silence created a vacuum that seemed to suck the air out of the room. Once she had left, Murray listened like he had when she left his room as her hasty footsteps faded away. Satisfied that he had been served a decent vintage, he uncorked the bottle and poured it. He savoured its aroma, while considering the sensuality of its ruby colour. It was a sexy wine, which conjured up instantly a flash of Marilyn as a young woman. She sashayed past him in a body-hugging sheath of a gown, embellished with blood-red gems and sequins, then evaporated as quickly as she had appeared, in a cloud of red glitter.

'So why have I been called out a second time?' asked Martin.

His direct questioning jolted Murray back from the scarlet-lipped Marilyn to his question. 'I take it you haven't done any work regarding O'Flannagan's?' he asked.

'I've not had the time seeing as you've got me running here, there and everywhere.'

'Before we tell you why you're here, you might want to take a swig of that wine. You're going to need it, so get it down you fast,' said Murray.

Judy seemed more appreciative of the respect owed to the vintage, as she sipped slowly. 'Your visit to O'Flannagan's is connected to this place,' she said.

Martin glanced around at the ancient bound volumes that filled every available shelf. A word of warning seemed to be directed at him from the beady ebony-detailed eye of an eagle that had been carved into the intricate walnut fireplace. The bird's outstretched wings created the illusion that it was in full flight and in attack mode. Not easily spooked, Martin dismissed its threatening posturing as well as the rest of his antique surroundings. He was no closer to guessing the connection that Judy had hinted at.

'You know you said you were a fan of Marilyn Monroe?' she said, suddenly.

'Absolutely. She was a one off. I don't buy all that crap that she killed herself, do you?'

Judy could feel a snigger coming on, despite the gravity of the situation. Mischievously, she decided to hit him with the facts so that it would have the maximum impact. 'Well, the thing is, we need you to come upstairs with us... to take a sample of Marilyn's hair to compare to what's in the safety deposit box.'

Martin had been half-way through drinking his wine as suggested by Murray when Judy hit him with the big reveal. He coughed violently as the wine went down the wrong way. 'What the...?'

'She's ninety-one and quite unwell,' interrupted Judy,

taking great pleasure at witnessing his reaction to her remarks. 'So you might want to get a move on before she pops her clogs.'

'What is this - some sort of joke?' asked Martin. He put down his glass, pulled out a tissue and wiped the front of his shirt, which was now peppered with red wine spots.

'There really wasn't any other way to tell you, but Judy's not messing about. It could be Marilyn upstairs,' said Murray.

Judy frowned at Murray's relentless denial. 'If it's not Marilyn, I'll never be allowed to forget my mistake,' she said, forcefully.

Martin emptied the the remaining contents of the wine bottle into his glass and downed it. 'Can we backtrack a bit?' he asked, finally, composing himself. 'You're saying Marilyn Monroe is upstairs, in this very house - alive?'

'At last you've got it,' said Judy. 'So get that down you and chop chop.'

Murray intervened. 'Whoah there Jude. It's one of three people remember. Marilyn, her previous body double or a doppelganger,' he said, making any chance of Martin making sense of his words nigh impossible.

'Listen, you don't need to know all the ins and outs right now. We'll fill you in as we go,' said Judy.

Half an hour later, a dazed Martin had tenderly removed a few strands of hair from Norma's head while she was sleeping peacefully. He could see nothing of the screen idol he so revered. As he descended the front steps, he was met by Judy, lolling against the side of his car, with her arms crossed. A big smile was etched across her face. 'Biggest and best case you're ever likely to work on I bet,' she said, opening his driver's door for him.

'You're telling me.' Still visibly in shock, Martin slipped

out of his white protective all-in-one, bagged it, and threw it in the boot of his car along with his other forensic kit.

'Now don't forget, keep your visit between the three of us. I know it's exciting, but don't blab to anyone,' said Judy.

'Mum's the word. But I'm going to wake up tomorrow morning pinching myself, just in case I'm dreaming.'

Judy watched bemused as he drove away, then she joined Murray who was on his way down the grand staircase. They returned to the library for a second time. 'You've nothing to worry about as far as Martin's concerned,' she emphasised again.

'I hope you're right,' said Murray. He was seated at a semi-circular table that fitted neatly into the space created by a large bay window. Partially distracted, he was thumbing through the photos surrendered by Aileen.

Judy seated herself opposite him and began to browse at the photos he had piled up between them.

Murray continued to sift through images. 'It's taken me awhile, but I realise now why I can't connect the two as being the same woman. The middle bit of her life makes her seem like she was in limbo.' He began to lay the images out in a time line, trying to make sense of their hidden story.

Judy scanned all four corners of the room as though checking there was no obvious mechanism to record their conversation. She was drawn instead to an unusually large cobweb, which was attached between the central ceiling light and its ornate ceiling rose. The silvery web pulsated backwards and forwards like a rhythmic heartbeat, despite the windows being closed and there being no breeze to assist it. A large black spider was centre stage in the web, in the process of deftly wrapping its wriggling prey. Judy likened the dying fly to Marilyn losing her struggle with life and the challenges it had laid at her feet.

She joined Murray while he began to shuffle the images of Marilyn like a deck of cards as though by doing so he might deal himself a good poker hand. Metaphorically speaking, in Murray's mind, Marilyn was the Queen of Hearts, outnumbered by the four kings; JFK, his brother Bobby, Joe DiMaggio and Frank. What of Gloria then? There seemed to be the absence of a card to fit her guile. The Joker came nowhere close in reflecting the evil she had carried around. A tarot pack was more suited to someone of her cunning as well as for all the characters in the planned destruction of Marilyn fifty-five years previously. These ominous spectres resided in their castles immune to the outside world, unlike mythical Camelot, which tumbled and fell through Guinevere's treachery with Lancelot.

All of a sudden, the word Camelot, resonated deep in the corridors of Murray's mind. The first thought to surface was that it had no significance, but rather than dismiss it, he allowed his intuition to kick in. For a few moments, he exercised some mindfulness by meditating, to see if it would give him any clarity. The symbol of a triangle materialised at the front of his mind, most likely because of the love triangle within the original story. But a triangle was also symbolic of something much darker. Something he cared not to mention out loud in case by the very mention of its name he would inadvertently conjure up its malevolent dynasty. It was as though its symbolic shape burned his forehead and would leave a permanent scar if he were to not cast out the darkness.

Then he had it: the significance of Camelot. Jackie

Kennedy had used the word in order to shape a lasting memory of her husband's administration. After his assassination and as decades passed, the romanticism attached to the Arthurian myth would only increase tenfold when applied to John F. Kennedy. There was a message in Murray's confusion, but the more he tried to break it down the more he became tied in knots. The answer would most likely come in his sleep or when he was looking elsewhere.

Chapter 29

Falling Like Flies

Judy realised she had left her phone on the silent setting. 'I've two voice mails,' she said to Murray, cross with herself for missing calls.

Anything we need to prioritise?' asked Murray, still deliberating about the significance of Camelot.

'The first is from the original DC that was dealing with this case. He's on his way here now.'

'That's a bit odd. He's not called me. Who's the other message from?' asked Murray.

'Shit. It's from Aileen. She's been burgled. I'll call her straight back. Do you think we should encourage her to get out of Ireland again?'

'Absolutely. You'd best get back to the Yard so you can organise a flight. Oh and pick her up from the airport. I think it's about time she met up with our lady anyway.'

Judy made ready to leave. 'I'll get on it straight away. Let me know what DC Taylor has got for us.'

Once she had gone, Murray held up the empty wine bottle to the light to check if Martin really had emptied it. To his disappointment, it had been drained dry. If he could have ignored his profession and his dedication to being the fittest that he could, he would have continued filling his glass well into that night. Drinking himself into oblivion might make him see things from a different viewpoint and aid him to unravel Marilyn and Gloria's lives. He began to reflect on the last few weeks. His mistrust in those around him seemed to be diminishing. He wondered why he had imagined that Austen specifically, had been dancing with the devil. Perhaps instead, the devil had been waltzing with him instead. Black magic seemed to flit in and out of the equation, but Murray could not ascertain whether it lived only in his imagination or in the very fibre of the grand house and its darkest corners.

He was soon shaken from his satanic thoughts when Geraldine showed DC Taylor into the library. Murray was taken back at his appearance. He had already formed the opinion that he would be out of touch with men's fashion being so far removed from bustling London as he was. It took him by surprise therefore, to see that Taylor was sharply dressed and sported a manicured beard and hair. Murray scolded himself for having prematurely painted a picture of a tired and bored middle-aged man who dealt with nothing more than small time crime. Little did he know however, that the DC Taylor that Olivia had encountered, had smartened himself up for the occasion of meeting someone from Scotland Yard. That aside, Murray was certainly unready for the spark in Taylor's eyes.

'Thank you for coming out to the back of beyond. Sorry we missed your call,' said Murray, smoothing his own hair down and buttoning his suit jacket, so as not to feel outdone.

'Things are quiet at the moment so it's no trouble,' said Taylor.

His comment confirmed Murray's original suspicion that provincial police work might be far less challenging than what he was used to.

'However I had an interesting call yesterday,' added Taylor. 'Nothing that couldn't wait, but as I can't make any sense of it I thought I'd swing by and meet you in person.'

'Have a seat,' said Murray.

Taylor continued. 'How's the case going? I'm a bit off the radar since it was passed to Scotland Yard.'

Murray toyed with what he should say to Taylor, bearing in mind him having very little involvement. 'It seems you were right to pass it on to the Yard.'

Taylor seemed taken aback. 'Am I allowed to know anymore while the case is still ongoing?'

'I don't know much more than you,' said Murray, bending the truth as though he were flexing a piece of bamboo to breaking point. For some reason Taylor made him feel that competition existed between them, but to anyone who might see them together, both men could only be considered as very polished. He straightened his tie and continued. 'It seems the old woman you met is probably of some importance after all. Unfortunately, she's now at death's door, so we haven't proved her identity one way or another. We do think however that because of her status, that's why she's been privy to so much security.'

Taylor found it easy to naturally trust Murray. In his mind, he oozed both experience and sophistication. He assumed therefore that he was probably not only highly respected but also considered to be the golden boy at Scotland Yard. He keenly examined the cut of Murray's suit and expensive suede shoes, quickly making up his mind that he was a man most likely obsessive about detail. He did not feel the threat of competition like Murray did and was more interested in the possibility his information could be of use. At that moment, he all of a sudden aspired to learn from Murray and one day switch his desk for one at Scotland Yard. 'I'd like to know the outcome when you've closed the case.'

Murray avoided making such a promise. 'So what is it you wanted to tell me?' he asked, sensing that Taylor was in awe of his pedigree. He did not like to be put on a pedestal, but Taylor made him feel that he was doing exactly that. 'It'll be good to pool our resources until my partner returns,' he said generously, but with no intention of revealing too much more.

'The young woman who brought this place to our attention called me at the station out of the blue,' said Taylor, flicking quickly through his notes. 'Said she'd suddenly remembered something. She was worried she'd get in trouble for missing it out of her original statement.'

'So what did you manage to get out of her?' asked Murray.

'I've yet to get her to come to the station again but the gist of it is, that she remembered the old woman saying that her secrets could be found at the Birdhouse. She also told Olivia not to forget that point, as it was important.'

'Which is exactly what she did,' said Murray, irked. 'Could be key information,' he added, taking the time to think it through. The thought that Marilyn had been entangled in one of the key places in London's underworld when she set up home in England, did not add up. It seemed more fitting for the devious and conniving Gloria to frequent such a place as the Birdhouse in order to attract monied men. On the other hand it was one of DiMaggio's haunts, and where he hung out, Marilyn might have hung out too. DiMaggio knew no one there would have dared reveal her identity either back then or since, as they would risk being dumped in the Thames by the Gator brothers or their successors. And why would DiMaggio shield Gloria if Marilyn were dead? By all accounts, he hated her. Olivia's simple addition to her statement seemed to add nothing fresh to the case. All it had done was cause his beliefs to swing backwards and forwards like a giant pendulum once again. He was disappointed.

'The Birdhouse?' he asked innocently, testing Taylor's detective skills.

'That's right, but I haven't got a clue what it means. Sorry I can't help you out more,' said Taylor.

'When Miss White comes into the station, let me know if she thinks of anything else,' said Murray, relieved that Taylor had not asked him the relevance of the Birdhouse. Had he done so, he would have wanted to keep it under wraps. It was a dangerous place for naive detectives to visit, especially those who were not known to Mike Higgins. Taylor might be one of those young detectives who put curiosity before being prudent. 'Have you been to the smoke recently?' he asked, with the Birdhouse in mind.

'No, not for a couple of years. Why do you ask?'

'It's not all its cracked up to be you know,' he continued, down-playing his position, having picked up on Taylor's dreams for the future. In his mind, Taylor had spent the last five minutes with a look that resembled a doting puppy.

'Well isn't London where everything happens?'

'Only in TV dramas. We depend on good detectives like you to bring in useful leads,' continued Murray, schmoozing Taylor and standing to indicate that the meeting was over.

'I don't feel I've given you anything useful,' said Taylor, shaking his hand.

Murray patted him on the shoulder then held the library door open to hurry his departure. He watched him walk briskly across the capacious hallway to the front door. Although self-assured, he seemed in awe of his surroundings, as he glanced up at the grandiose stairway and oversized oil paintings. Murray reflected on when he had been young and eager. Sometimes it seemed that he had been in service a lifetime, a thought that his ever-suffering girlfriend shared and never failed to mention.

He closed the double doors to the library, this time turning the key in the lock to keep everyone out while he did some deep thinking. He was more confused than ever. He had been so certain about Gloria's part in the mystery and he could not place her with DiMaggio. The possibility of them having any sort of relationship was on the surface unquantifiable, unless, DiMaggio had seen something in the younger woman that reminded him of Marilyn when he had first married her. Was Gloria that good an actress and DiMaggio that desperate to be with Marilyn that he began an affair with Gloria to keep his memories alive?

The time had come for Murray to call up his greatest gift, and he knew that he must not be disturbed for it to work successfully. He began by resuming his position by the window, making sure he was comfortable while looking for clues in the photographs. He had no name for his implausible gift. It was somewhere between where sleep meets wakefulness, in a place where he could imagine he was part of any scene that he selected. He concentrated on his breathing until it had become slow and regular. The sounds of the ticking clock and burning logs retreated into the distance as he began to enter a meditative state.

He had selected the scenario he would manifest. It was the president's birthday party that Marilyn had attended and sang to him from a lectern. It was like plunging from the great height of a waterfall as the scene opened up to him.

Marilyn was among party-goers. She was dressed in a dress that was so tight and semi-transparent that she appeared almost naked. Her hair was streaked with shades of ash and tones of golden wheat. Her male admirers pressed close to her in order to occupy her space.

'Oh my, I can hardly breathe,' she said. 'Catch me if I faint fellas.'

The men laughed at her humour while hanging onto her every word, turned on by her way of making a normal situation seem sexual. They were dressed like a colony of penguins in tuxedos and chattered over each other as they tried to get her undivided attention. There were also females in the room, standing back as they watched their partners flirt. A few women were wearing expressions of disdain but most looked on in awe, wanting to be Marilyn and possess her power.

As quickly as the crowd had formed, all of a sudden and with no cue to do so, it parted like two opposing magnets. A hush overcame the room as a man walked towards Marilyn and took her gloved hand in his. He raised her hand and kissed it, all the time looking straight into her eyes. It was the president of the United States: John F. Kennedy.

Even though he was manipulating his own imagination, Murray gasped out loud, imagining that had he actually of been there as a ghost, everyone might have heard him. Meanwhile, Marilyn was returning the president's gaze. The crowd seemed to take his presence as a signal to leave, immediately dissolving into thin air rather than leaving the room.

'D'you think they know about us?' asked Marilyn, in a soft fragmented voice.

'So what if they do. It won't matter soon.'

'When will I be your First Lady?' she asked JFK, her slender fingers gently stroking the cloth of his suit.

'There's been a change of plan,' he said.

'How do you mean sweetie?' she asked, deferring the usual respect required when addressing a president.

'It's not safe for you in LA anymore,' he said.

All of a sudden, Marilyn looked scared. Her lips began to quiver.

With no warning, Murray felt nauseous and he was sucked from the scene prematurely. He was breathless and angry that he did not possess the ability to materialise and comfort Marilyn and to find out what danger JFK was in. On top of that, someone was pounding on the library door.

'DC Murray, are you in there? The doors stuck. I can't get in,' came Geraldine's voice.

'Go away. I'm busy,' he barked, trying to hold onto the conversation between Marilyn and the president.

'It's important Sir. You're needed on the phone.'

Murray went to the door and opened it. Geraldine backed away in her usual manner and pointed to the phone on the hall table. Murray locked the library door behind him, pocketing the key in full view of her. 'That'll be all,' he said, curtly.

She melted away.

'Murray,' he said, as he picked up the phone, still angry with Geraldine for disturbing him at a such an important moment. It was Judy calling from her car.

'Steve, I've just had a call from Martin,' she said. 'All the evidence has gone. Every last shred. He's beside himself.'

'You've got to be kidding me. Maybe it's just been moved by one of his team.'

'He's been through the store room twice over. It's not there.'

'Has he asked his team whether it's been moved?'

'He can't do that remember. This is unofficial. A favour he owed me.'

'How long till you're back there?' asked Murray, twirling the library door key between his fingers.

'Forty-five at a push.'

'Do you reckon you can narrow down a time frame for when it went missing? Talk to Martin. Check the log of forensics staff movements.'

'I'll do better than that. I'll check CCTV footage before I start to raise the alarm.'

'Good call. I'm on my way,' said Murray, gathering his evidence from the library.

Chapter 30

All Is Lost

Murray burst through the office door with such force that it swung back on its hinges causing its handle to smack against the wall. The commotion made his nearest colleagues jump. Documents fluttered to the floor like sycamore keys from normally ordered desks, causing detectives and civilians to scramble on their hands and knees as they fought over jumbled-up pieces of paper. Oblivious to the pandemonium he had caused, Murray continued on through the open plan office, leaving a ripple of disgruntled whispers behind him. A hand reached for him through an open door and pulled him in.

Judy glared at him. 'I thought we were trying to stay under the radar. You've just ruined any chance of that.'

Murray peered through a chink in the venetian blinds and realised immediately that he was solely responsible for the carnage left in his wake. 'Ooops.'

'Now everyone will want to know what's pissed you off,' said Judy.

'Where're we at?' asked Murray, sidestepping Judy's anger. 'This is going to be on Martin's head for sure.'

Judy grabbed Murray's arm and forced him to face her rather than look out at the pandemonium still continuing in the outer office. 'You're being a bit harsh. He wasn't even there when the evidence went walkabout.'

'He's head of his department so whichever way you look at it Jude, he's still responsible. And frankly, him letting his eye off the ball could cost us the case.'

Judy humphed and logged onto a computer. 'Before you judge him, you might want to take a good look at this. The thief's been caught on CCTV.'

Murray turned and fixed his attention on the grainy footage on the screen.

'There are two bits to show you, the first being the removal of the security box from the building. All I've retrieved for now, is external footage from cameras on local buildings,' said Judy.

The low resolution footage twitched and distorted, making it hard to identify a young female walking from New Scotland Yard along the Victoria Embankment.

'Whoever it is, they're clearly carrying something heavy. Shame it's in a plastic bag. Makes it harder to be certain it's our evidence,' said Murray.

Judy switched to different footage. 'I recognised the beige raincoat. It's the new forensics girl, Amanda.'

Murray watched again. This time Amanda was picked up on camera adjacent to passing traffic. A black Sedan had slowed to walking pace next to her and the front passenger window had been lowered. Amanda had slowed but also increased the distance between herself and the car. She appeared to be talking to whoever was inside, but the window was not wound down enough to allow the camera to pick up on anyone's features.

'Did you run a check on the number plate?' asked Murray.

'Nothing registered. It's a fake,' said Judy.

'Have you told Martin it's Amanda?'

'No, I wanted to tell you first,' said Judy. 'If he confronts her, she might panic and do a runner.'

'Get her in here - straight away,' said Murray. 'But don't let Martin see you extract her from the lab.'

A few moments later, Judy had returned with Amanda. This was the first time Murray had seen her up close. She was pale, uninteresting and scared. Her physical features mirrored those of a small rodent plus she looked as though she expected at any second to be cornered by a cat. She shot nervous glances backwards and forwards between Judy and Murray.

'Do you prefer to be called Mandy or Amanda?' asked Murray, starting his interrogation.

'Either Sir,' she whispered.

He waded straight in. 'Do you know why you've been called in to speak to me Amanda?'

'No Sir. I'm afraid I don't,' she said.

'Sit down,' said Judy, authoritatively.

Amanda sat and wrung her hands together, looking down into her lap to avoid making eye contact.

'Let me make it easier for you. Look at the screen,' said Murray, replaying the footage. 'What did you remove from the forensics lab?'

Amanda burst into tears. 'Am I going to lose my job?' she asked.

'You'll definitely lose your job if you don't tell me the truth. I want to know everything, from the moment that car stopped, to when you removed important evidence and handed it over to its occupants.'

'They made me. They said they knew where I lived and if I didn't do what they asked, I'd be sorry,' garbled Amanda.

'Who's they?' asked Judy, in a slightly softer tone than Murray's.

'I don't know. I didn't recognise them.'

'Can you tell us anything about them? Did either of them have an accent?' asked Murray.

'I didn't really notice. I was so frightened all I could think of was getting away.'

'What else did they say?' asked Judy.

'One of them told me to meet them a bit further down the road when I finished work. Without fail, and he told me what to bring with me.'

'And what was that?' asked Judy.

'A black metal security box. They told me the date it was deposited and I wasn't to look inside, just deliver it in a plain carrier bag so I wouldn't be spotted.'

'So how did you know you were removing the right box?' asked Murray.

'There was only the one box fitting their description and I cross-checked when it was logged.'

Murray looked to Judy.

'I'm really sorry. What's going to happen now?' asked Amanda.

'Nothing,' said Judy. 'But for your peace of mind, is there somewhere you can stay for a few days, with friends or family?'

'I live with my brother in Croydon. We commute up to London everyday together.'

'Good, that's settled then,' said Murray. 'Travel in with him as usual but ask him to accompany you right here. It's unlikely anyone will approach you if you have company. We'll let you know what disciplinary action will be taken when Phelps and I have discussed it further.'

'What if my brother asks why I need a chaperone?' asked Amanda.

'I'm sure you'll think of something,' said Murray. 'After all, dishonesty doesn't appear to be alien to you.'

Amanda scurried off, having appeared to have shrunk a few inches in height, her light footsteps only compounding Murray's initial mouse comparisons.

'You can't leave it like that. It should be instant dismissal, or suspension at the very least,' said Judy.

'So exactly how do I go about that, Jude? It's not my place to fire people, plus Austen will get to hear of it. Then what do you suggest I say to him?'

'When you put it like that Steve, I'm not sure.'

Murray plunged into the possible scenario. 'Oh Sir, by the way we've been continuing a covert investigation going way beyond what you had agreed, without informing you of how much police money we have ploughed into it. Evidence has been collected without your permission Sir, and now it has been passed over to God knows who in an unmarked car.'

'Point taken, but it's her or us,' said Judy. 'Or maybe both.'

'Not if we crack it and get that evidence back quickly.'

Judy seemed to deliberate for a few seconds before speaking again. 'Steve, how did the men in the car know when the security box was deposited?'

'That's a very good question Jude. Why didn't I think of that?'

'I've got a theory,' said Judy. 'Only the Gator brothers and their heavies knew we were going to the vaults.'

'So? They were willing for us to have DiMaggio's key,' said Murray.

'Let's assume just for a second that James wasn't a fan of theirs. He might not have been willing to let them get to the contents. Maybe they got us to do their dirty work for them.'

'But the Gator brothers worked for DiMaggio. They wouldn't double-cross him.'

'Maybe they consider they were next in line to inherit,' said Judy. 'Marilyn's belongings are priceless. Who knows how much they'd fetch.'

'They're only priceless once proved to be hers, and Martin hadn't got that far,' said Murray, instantly bursting Judy's bubble.

She slumped down into the office chair. 'Who wouldn't want the truth out I wonder?'she asked, head in hands on the desk.

'Gloria,' said Murray.

Chapter 31

The Luck of the Irish

A s Aileen stepped onto British soil once again, she breathed a sigh of relief. She had never been a massive fan of the English, but on this occasion she was happy to put aside her prejudices for the sake of the chance of witness protection. She had travelled light, leaving room in her rucksack for her prized photo albums that Murray would be ready to hand back for her return journey. The burglars who had ransacked her home had taken nothing related to her novel and she was beginning to wonder whether their presence had anything to do with it at all.

Crossing London made Aileen jumpy. Unable to resist checking for unwelcome company, every minute or so she checked over her shoulder, trying to retain the memory of any individual that was with keeping pace for more time than seemed natural. Judy had got held up in traffic and had instructed her to mix up her journey, by using the DLR light rail system from City Airport and change to the northern line. From there she was to leave the underground at Angel and walk the rest of the way to

Duncan Terrace. Using the tube worried her. It made more sense to use a taxi but she was not about to argue in case she got caught up in a car chase like Murray had done. At the best of times she struggled with confined spaces and avoided them wherever possible. Her anxiety levels had been made worse more recently, by her unexpected flights to and from Ireland and London.

The light railway was packed with early evening commuters. Aileen gave herself a proverbial pat on the back for being so brave under the circumstances. However, when she ventured into the tube station at Monument, she began to feel agitated, sandwiched between other commuters travelling downwards. Others had been forced to use the same route as her, due to scheduled engineering work on adjacent lines. She gripped the escalator handrail to prevent herself from being tripped from behind. The platforms were busy and she had missed a train by seconds. Lack of punctuality irritated her so with minutes to spare until the next one, she tried to position herself to avoid the crush and be one of the first to board.

The platform was continuing to fill and seemed fit to burst. It was as though Aileen had been forced to abandon ship and was being carried along helpless on a choppy sea along with other survivors. She had started off by being somewhere in the middle of the platform, but had been nudged to the far end. She was so close to the tunnel that she could taste and smell the gritty breeze created by the coming and going of trains. Her mouth began to feel dry and she could feel the start of a panic attack rising in her chest.

She recalled when she had travelled to London to see the Millennium fireworks and had become trapped by other revellers on one of London's bridges. The anticipated spectacle of the show had faded into insignificance as her and her friends had protected their children by lifting them above the surging crowd onto their shoulders. A lasting reminder of the occasion had etched itself in her mind, that of a pushchair having eventually been trampled underfoot.

She held no great hope in her current situation that anyone would come to her aid. In her experience, people were selfish at times of danger and looked out for themselves. Thinking she could stand no more and with her heart thumping in her chest, she made for a gap and squeezed through into a spot not yet swamped by others still spilling onto the platform. The digital overhead board displayed one minute until train arrival. She counted down seconds under her breath, trying to distract herself from feelings of claustrophobia by studying the billboards on the opposite wall. Compared to her state of mind, the advertisements seemed indulgent in their nature, all wasted on her cynicism. She tutted at the offer of eternal youth dished up in the form of cosmetic procedures or by the trowelling on of layers of makeup. She moved on from such adverts and studied the intricate routes on the underground map. Suddenly, she was shoved from behind.

In a split second, her recent life played through her mind faster than the train approaching the platform. In blind panic she called out, but the scream remained lodged in her throat as nothing more than a rasping noise, as though she were choking on a piece of apple. She had been pushed way beyond the yellow warning line and was teetering on the edge of the platform. The draft from the tunnel indicated the train was imminent.

Despite the sensation that she was about to dive headlong onto the rails, she rallied and from somewhere, found her balance, but just when she thought she was out of danger, she received another violent blow between the shoulder blades. This time the impact knocked the breath out of her. As she fell forwards she began to see stars and the metallic glint of the rails rising up to meet her. Helpless she waited for the train to hit.

Just as all seemed lost, the straps from her rucksack suddenly went tight around her shoulders and she was plucked from behind by a strong pair of hands. She instantly likened the sensation to the memory of her parachute opening when she had done a sky dive years ago. She was jolted back to the present by an argument behind her.

'What the fuck are you doing man?' said her protector to another man.

Her attacker pulled the peak of his cap down so that he could not be seen easily on CCTV and made a hasty retreat by fighting his way through commuters, using his elbows like battering rams. Men and women began to fall like skittles as he aggressively barged his way through.

The man who had saved Aileen, helped her to her feet. 'Here, sit down,' he said, helping her to a bench. 'I'll call the transport police.'

'Please don't trouble yourself. I'm sure it was an accident and...'

'I saw it all,' he interrupted. 'That loser deliberately pushed you.'

'What use will it do to call the police. He'll be long gone by now, plus I've got to be somewhere in the next half hour.'

'But...'

'I'm so grateful,' continued Aileen, interrupting again. 'I'd be dead for sure if you hadn't intervened.'

'Well...if you're sure you're okay, I can't stop you, but I'm still going to report it. He's a complete nutter.'

'Tell you what, take my number. If you get a result with the police, give them my details so they can call me,' said Aileen. She reached into her pocket, pulled out a business card and handed it over. 'And thank you again - from the bottom of my heart.'

The next train pulled in. Still feeling disorientated, she boarded. She had not thought until that moment to study the man who had rescued her. She looked out of the window. He was a skateboarder, dressed in shorts, T-shirt and scuffed trainers. His strength under pressure belied his lean build. He bore no resemblance to how she imagined a superhero would look.

As she came out of the station at the other end of her journey, she was presented with an even busier scene than beneath London's streets. The pavements were clogged up with multiple bike racks and tired people leaving offices or closing up shops for the day. To add to this, her onward journey appeared to be hindered by stop start traffic, its progress impeded as much as hers by priority bus routes and a complicated network of traffic lights.

Her back and shoulders still ached from her ordeal on the platform, making it hard to concentrate on her next section of her route, but she distracted herself by joining London's hustle and bustle. She consulted a piece of paper on which she had scribbled Judy's instructions, trying to make sense of her bearings. She wished at that moment that she was more au-fait with phone apps, which may have been more efficient, but then she remembered the latest trend in scooter thieves snatching valuables.

It seemed later in the day than it was, due to a heavy grey blanket that hung in deep folds over London's skyline. It bulged ominously and threatened a deluge at any moment. Knowing that her nerves were jangled, Aileen tried to adopt a stoic expression and a confident stride in case she was being followed. To show her heightened sense of fear might alert whoever was tailing her to prey on such vulnerability. Fortunately, her route was not to be as she had initially feared, that of darkened alleyways and unlit streets.

She turned right from the station and right again to find herself immediately out of the crowd that was cramming the pavement outside the tube station. The only passers by held no menace. Taking one quick glance behind, she realised that as yet, no one was in pursuit and everyone was too busy to notice she had broken ranks. Striding on, she took time to familiarise herself with her surroundings in case she had to pass this way again. She noted that offices and shops had been left behind on the main road, in favour of three and four storey period properties, most of which had been divided into swanky flats.

In no time at all she was approaching the park where she was to meet Judy, sandwiched within a square of houses very similar to those that she had already passed. It was that time of day when day and night are separated by a thin veil of dusky grey making it hard to pick out detail. Streetlights were beginning to come on.

As she turned into the park she was alerted by her intuition warning her that there was danger close by once again. There was the sound of hurried footsteps coming up behind her. Due to her earlier ordeal, she was unsure as to whether she should turn round to square up to the person or simply increase her pace. She opted for the latter knowing that Judy was in the vicinity and at any moment would greet her. Suddenly a hand touched her shoulder causing her to jump. She turned in anticipation of a beating, with nothing to use as a weapon.

'Hi Aileen,' said Judy. The man who had been closing in on Aileen, swept past, taking evasive action so as not to crash into both women.

'You scared me,' exclaimed Aileen.

The stranger pulled the peak of his cap down, which immediately camouflaged the upper part of his face. He did a complete about turn and in seconds had left the park and melted into the distance.

'Thank goodness it's you,' said Aileen. 'I'm sure that man was following me. Did you see the speed he made off at as soon as you appeared?'

'Are you sure you're not imagining things? After all, it is rush hour. Maybe he's just in a hurry,' suggested Judy.

Aileen went on to tell her what had happened on the underground as they made their way to their meet-up point with Murray in a small cafe close-by. As they walked, Judy considered how she was going to break the news to Aileen that all of her photos had gone missing and that all that was left was Steve's photocopies. Knowing that they were Aileen's pride and joy, she decided not to mention their theft unless Aileen were to raise the subject regarding their return. She concentrated instead in keeping her talking, so as to distract her from repeatedly glancing over her shoulder as they walked.

Daylight had departed as quickly as the stranger had done, trampled underfoot in Aileen's mind by an invisible heaviness that spoke of shorter daylight hours. Judy felt differently however. The case regarding Marilyn Monroe was hotting up and made her forget that it would soon be the time of year that she usually found depressing. As they approached the welcoming orange glow of cafe lights, both women felt instantly relieved to be away from danger. Once inside the cafe that Judy had chosen, the waitress took their coats and showed them to the table that Judy had thought to reserve.

'Bit better than the Birdhouse,' said Judy, trying to draw Aileen out of her thoughts. 'You won't see any unsavoury characters in here, 'she added, with a broad grin.

Aileen was still studying the other diners. 'Let's hope you're right,' she said, her tone lukewarm.

'Do you really believe someone was after you? Believe me, London can seem somewhat intimidating at the best of times.'

'I'm not imagining things. The guy that saved me from the track seemed to think I'd been pushed purposefully.'

'Well if the underground's CCTV shows anything up, I'm sure we'll get to hear about it, one way or another.'

'A lot of good that would do if they were having to scrape me off the rails right now,' said Aileen, sounding beaten and depressed. 'What do you think it's all about?'

'Look, you're here now, and Steve and I will look after you twenty-four seven,' said Judy, sidestepping. 'Try and relax and take in the atmosphere. This is one of our favourite haunts when we're trying to unwind.'

Aileen looked around for confirmation that Judy had made a good choice. She had been so distracted by sinister thoughts that she had failed to notice that they were now seated at a window overlooking the park. Multicoloured fairy lights were strung artistically through the park's trees, painting out Aileen's recent scare with a vivid splash of colour. She considered that although Christmas was months away, the reds, greens and yellows gave the area a truly festive feel, casting a cheery light on people passing by.

'You're right. It's a nice place to sit and watch the world go by. Excuse me for being so on edge.'

Judy changed the subject. 'Steve told me about the burglary,' she said, deciding not to discuss Aileen's assault on the underground until she had consulted Murray.

'Would you rather I wait until he arrives to tell you about it?' asked Aileen.

'Get it off your chest over your hot drink,' said Judy, relieving their waitress of two mugs brimming over with cream and pale pink marshmallows and a dusting of chocolate sprinkles.

'The burglar or burglars made a point of targeting my femininity, not that a woman of my age has much of that left. They went through my underwear drawer and my perfume bottles had been emptied. A message had been scrawled on my dressing table mirror with one of my lipsticks. Bright red. I haven't used it for years, but never got round to throwing it away.'

'What did the message say?'

'We're watching you. That's all,' said Aileen. 'Listen DC Phelps, I live in a quiet little village. Nothing ever happens there. At least not until now. Only weeks after I publish my memoirs about Marilyn Monroe and only days after your lot have been sniffing around, I get burgled. There has to be a connection.'

'Clearly there must be,' agreed Judy.

'I want my photos back if you've finished with them, and I want protection. And, more than that, I want you and DC Murray to tell me what's going on.'

'Ah, about your photos,' said Murray, appearing silently

and sitting down opposite Aileen and next to Judy.

'What about them?' asked Aileen, a frown crossing her face.

'Sorry about the circumstances you find yourself in, but it's good to see you again. Yes, the photos. This one to be precise,' he said, avoiding Aileen's question as he pulled a photocopy from his inside pocket. It was the image of Marilyn or Gloria in the silk suit. 'The originals are in safe-keeping,' added Murray, trying to look genuine and hating the fact that he was lying.

Judy kicked him under the table and he tried not to wince. It was a habit of hers that was all too familiar to him. 'Do you remember anything about this photo?' asked Judy, taking over.

'How could I not? She looked beautiful as always. From memory it was a day she was getting ready to see the president.'

'You can remember specifics like that?' asked Judy.

'Only because I was there on that occasion and she had given me a fashion show so I could help her decide on what to wear. It was before things went sour I'm sure of it. By that, I mean, before Gloria got to be a problem. In fact, it must've been quite a while before as I remember her being happy all the time.'

'Can you remember the colour of the suit?' Judy threw in suddenly.

Aileen picked up the black and white photo and studied it. 'That's a big ask. She was always so stylish. Looked good in everything. Her favourite colour was green, but I don't think this outfit was green.'

'Can you try a little harder?' asked Judy, crossing her fingers under the table.

Aileen picked up the photo again. 'Is it significant in

any way?' she asked.

'Could be,' said Murray, economically, praying that Aileen would say that the suit was blue.

Aileen remained silent for a moment while she took the time to consider the smiling face in the photos once again. 'I'm sorry I can't be of more help. I'd just be guessing if I fired a colour at you.'

'Not to worry,' said Murray, cleverly masking his disappointment as he swept the photo from the table and placed it back in the inside pocket of his coat. 'If you remember later, tell me then.'

Judy gave him a beaten sideways glance as she picked up the menu to order. 'I'm ravenous. There's nothing more we can do tonight. Let's eat and then head off.'

Chapter 32

Nothing to Go On

The following morning Aileen made her way downstairs with Murray and Judy. 'This is a beautiful hotel. Thank you for organising it.'

'It's the least we can do. Did you sleep well?' asked Judy, making polite conversation.

Aileen looked around the foyer for unfriendly company. 'I'm afraid not. I think I was expecting someone to burst in at any moment.'

'It'll get easier I'm sure. A few days and you'll be right as rain,' said Judy, trying to reassure her.

While Murray talked to a uniformed officer who had been posted overnight, Judy checked Aileen out at reception. As they left through the revolving door at the front of the hotel, Murray kept a watchful eye on passersby.

'Where are you taking me?' asked Aileen, as they descended the steps.

'For a ride to take your mind off things,' said Judy. 'And to show you how our countryside compares to Ireland's.'

'Give me more credit than that DC Phelps. I'm sure you've more in mind than just sightseeing.'

'You're right of course, but let's discuss it en route,' said Murray.

Judy's car had already been brought round the front from the hotel's private car park and was being minded by a smart doorman dressed in top hat and tails, a glorious brocade waistcoat and highly polished black shoes. As was customary, he held the passenger door open. With one last look around, Murray seated himself in the back next to Aileen.

'Do you normally drive yourselves about?' she asked, somewhat surprised that Judy was at the wheel instead of a police driver.

'Not always. But on this occasion it suits us to not draw attention to ourselves,' said Judy, locking the doors as a precautionary measure from inside. 'Plus it's much easier to talk openly being as it's such a sensitive case.'

'I'm not sure what this case is exactly. You've not giving much away,' said Aileen, feeling that she was going to get nothing from either of them. She sat back in her seat and began to look at what London had to offer that was different to Dublin.

All the time they were in the city, Judy felt reassured that they would not be followed or apprehended by a third party, due to the volume of people providing a buffer against hostility. Nevertheless, she found herself shooting an occasional glance in her rear view mirror in case they were being tailed. It was not long before she noticed that she had been wise to do so, as there were two scooters a few cars behind that had followed their route for sometime. The riders were dressed in black from head to toe. Rather than alarm Aileen, Judy took a hard left and made discreet eye contact with Murray in the rear view mirror. Already having sensed there was something wrong by her last minute manoeuvre, he gave her a nod. Small enough to say that he knew something was amiss, but not so obvious that Aileen would notice.

'So now we're on our way, exactly where are we going on this mystery tour?' Aileen asked.

Murray turned so that he could make eye contact with her and at the same time take occasional looks behind. 'It'd be pointless for me to lead you up the garden path Aileen. You're clearly an educated woman, so I'll keep it simple.'

'There's no need to butter me up detective.'

He laughed. 'Was it that obvious?'

'Extremely - but go on. I'm all yours,' said Aileen.

'We're investigating Marilyn Monroe's life - since nineteen-sixty-two,' he said, being mischievous with his response.

This time Judy fixed him with an amused look in her rear view mirror.

Aileen took a few seconds to absorb what Murray had said before she spoke. 'Can you run that by me again, but this time more slowly?' she asked.

Murray repeated his statement word for word, noticing that in between Judy keeping an eye on the men on scooters, that she was still enjoying his method of storytelling.

Aileen was trying to process Murray's words. 'So let me get this right - you're saying she didn't die in August, nineteen-sixty-two?'

'Might not have died,' said Murray. 'There are still other possibilities to consider.'

'Not that I believe a word of what you've just said, but

if she survived that awful night, when did she die?' asked Aileen.

'Well that's what we're trying to find out. We're taking you to see someone. A ninety-one year old woman who claims to be her.'

Aileen's mouth dropped open and for a few seconds it opened and closed making her look like a cartoon goldfish. 'She's still alive?' Her face began to colour up. She took a small vintage fan from her bag and began to wave it in an effort to cool herself, much to the amusement of both Murray and Judy.

Judy turned her attention to whoever was following them. She began to make a few tricky manoeuvres but Aileen was still too much in shock to notice.

'She gave me this fan,' continued Aileen, her face now beetroot red as she continued to fan herself. 'Do you really think it's her then? How wonderful that would be.'

Judy chimed in, forgetting police protocol and treating the investigation lightly. 'We're almost at the stage of taking bets on it. I'm more convinced than Murray. He thinks it's a scam.'

'So you're clearly hoping I can identify her to prove it either way. If it is her, who do you think died instead that night?'

'If not Marilyn, then possibly the character Gloria that you told us about. Or someone else altogether, who wouldn't be missed,' said Murray.

They were close to leaving central London but Judy noticed the scooter riders were now right behind. The lights were against her as they approached a junction. She gripped the steering wheel tightly, ready for a fast getaway as she slowed to a stop still in gear. Both scooters came up alongside and their riders looked into the car, but their faces were hidden by tinted visors. They revved their engines so as to intimidate.

'What's their problem when they're at home?' asked Aileen, oblivious to the fact that they might be posing an imminent threat.

'They're just admiring my new car and challenging me to a race,' said Judy, making light of their body language. 'It is a bit of a beast and I could see them off no trouble.'

As she said these words, the scooters moved slowly forward so that they were in front, blocking her from accelerating away. She looked to Murray for a hint of what she should do. He nodded to the left so she flicked on her indicator and began to creep forward turning her wheels slightly to show her intent. As the lights changed to amber then green, the scooters began to make the turn, but Judy accelerated hard and took a hard right turn, causing the cars alongside her to brake and hoot their protest. The scooter drivers were left sandwiched between traffic, with no space to do a quick about turn.

Judy watched as arguments started at the crossing, with a vague smile crossing her face. She was as good as any police driver.

'Were they following us?' said Aileen, having finally realised that things were not as they should be.

'Probably,' said Murray. 'They would've been checking us out to see if we're minted so they could snatch something,' he lied. 'It happens all the time. That's why Judy locked the doors.'

What Aileen did not know, was that although he may have been right, there was also the possibility that the men had other instructions that came from higher up. It was only when outer London turned into suburbia, followed by green fields, that both he and Judy realised there was no sign of a tail. By then, he had filled Aileen in on the need-to-know elements of the case without divulging anything that was too sensitive.

'I feel like I'm dreaming and that at any moment you'll tell me it's all a joke,' Aileen said when he had finished.

'I'm not surprised,' said Murray.

'You mentioned that this old woman feels someone's out to get her.'

'That's correct,' agreed Murray.

'Gloria was a vicious individual. So jealous of Marilyn's talent and success. Maybe she's alive somewhere and if this woman is Marilyn, she's after revenge for never fulfilling her potential.'

Murray thought for a second. 'She'd be in her eighties now if she were still alive. I doubt she'd have the stamina or the know-how.'

'Maybe she hasn't got the stamina, but what about children if she ever had any, or grandchildren. Maybe she's on her deathbed too and it's her last chance to exact revenge through them.'

Judy chuckled. 'Have you ever thought about becoming a detective?'

'Police work isn't for me. I prefer to stick to writing about the craft of sleuthing,' said Aileen, laughing too.

Murray felt bruised by Aileen's cleverness. While Judy and Aileen continued to chat, his mind began to clear. He realised at that split second that throughout the case he had viewed the evidence surrounding Marilyn Monroe with tunnel vision. Doggedly, he had considered Marilyn to be the likely corpse in Westwood Village cemetery and the woman at Huntley manor to be Gloria or a simple scam artist. Suddenly he remembered something from Olivia White's preliminary statement to DC Taylor. She had mentioned that Norma had mistaken her at first for JFK's granddaughter Rose, coming to exact revenge on behalf of her mother Jackie.

He glanced out of the car window and noticed they were passing a barren brown field. Its crops had been harvested too soon in his opinion. In the centre was a single oak tree, stripped bare of its leaves and braced for winter prematurely. The solitude of the tree in such a vast field reminded him of whoever lay at Huntley Manor; all their friends and most of their relatives having passed already. The only difference was that the oak still had many more years ahead of it. Time was of the essence and he needed to find answers. The paths of possibility were beginning to divide and he and Judy, along with the help of Aileen, had much to unravel in a few days.

Whereas he was elsewhere in his thoughts, Aileen was still reeling with the revelation of Murray's big reveal. She was turning the possibilities over and over in her mind. She pondered over what it would be like to meet Marilyn. As the car swept unchallenged up the gravel drive to Huntley Manor, waved on by men in suits, she felt as though she were about to meet with royalty. However, such an exciting thought was instantly quashed due to the body language of everyone she passed on the way in. They seemed to be prematurely in mourning.

When Aileen eventually came face to face with the frail woman dwarfed by a king-sized bed, she began to understand why other people on the estate looked morose. She was meeting with nothing more than an empty shell and not only was she instantly filled with sorrow, but she was uncertain as to whether the person who lay before her was indeed Marilyn.

The woman's skin was peppered with liver spots and

deep creases and her eyes were closed. The slightest twitch of her eyelids suggested that she was dreaming. Aileen hoped that if it were Marilyn, that she was imagining being wrapped in John F. Kennedy's arms.

'Well?' said Judy, suddenly, interrupting Aileen's train of thought. 'Is it her?'

Aileen searched her own memories of Marilyn for any identifying mark, as she continued to look down with a sense of pity at the body before her that was caught between this world and the next. 'I don't know,' she said simply. 'I can't even see her famous beauty spot. She must've had it removed.'

'Take your time if need be,' added Murray, picking up on what she had just said as being an important point that he had overlooked.

Aileen's disappointment was overwhelming. She had hoped to swop stories with Marilyn, and in so doing, prove without doubt who she was. 'I'm sorry. I can't help you,' she said, wiping a solitary tear away. 'Whoever this is, they might as well have crossed over.' She turned away and went and stood by the window. Unexpected tears began to fall freely.

Chapter 33

The End of an Era

On the next occasion that Murray and Judy visited Huntley Manor, they had said little to each other on the way. This time they had entered by an unfamiliar route, via a gatehouse at the back end of the estate, similar in architecture to the others that punctuated Huntley Manor's vast acreage. The drive was narrow, unlike the main entrance, which boasted of wealth. The grass either side was dappled with random patterns created by dancing sunlight filtering through the trees. In Murray's mind, the sun was attempting to brighten the event he and Judy had been invited to. He glanced over his shoulder at a regimental line of other unmarked black vehicles following behind, realising that no amount of good weather could reduce the solemnity of the occasion.

The news that Norma was dead had reached those with a need to know. It was no secret that Frank had wept openly as had most of the female staff as soon as the news had filtered through the household. It should have been as simple as that, but Murray was attending a funeral out of respect only, as he was still not convinced of the truth. Judy on the other hand, was certain that Marilyn had escaped Hollywood back in the sixties and was at last at rest.

Murray had decided first thing that morning, that he would keep his professional opinion to himself and would try to address Norma's spirit instead as the screen icon she had claimed to be. After all, apart from on the days where she had been as confused as him as to her identity, she had insisted she was one and the same. Now he could no longer sit and talk to her about her real or imagined past, he felt empty and wanted nothing more than to close her file for the last time. However, he was impeded by the fact that until every piece of evidence had been sifted through thrice over, he could not move on to something fresh. The trouble was, in his opinion, that until forensics came up with something, the story might never make a big splash in the tabloids. More likely it would make a small column in the local newspaper.

As his car passed by some of Frank's men, he noted that they were walking silently with heads down as they patrolled the grounds with dogs in case locals were curious about the volume of people arriving. The crunch of gravel under tyres jolted him back to what was to come. It was the first time that he had seen the chapel they were approaching, even though he considered that he had explored the estate from one end to the other. Instantly it annoyed him that he had missed yet another a detail as he had with the folly, but it soon became clear as to why. Segregated from the rest of the grounds by impenetrable shrubbery and densely planted forest pines, the chapel's existence had been obliterated by nature taking over. For this particular occasion however, the original path to the front entrance had been cleared of weeds and leaves to allow mourners access to the main entrance.

Murray stepped out of the car. He watched as the procession continued to snake down the hill, considering whether the chapel was a grand enough choice to celebrate someone as famous as Marilyn Monroe even though she had been lost to the world for many years. In the eyes of the general public, she might be seen to deserve nothing more than a discreet burial. The chapel was on the other hand, too good for the devious woman who may have mimicked Marilyn. Murray tried to console himself that if he were wrong and Judy were right and Marilyn had indeed hidden herself away for fifty years, there would soon be a sea of bouquets left at the front gates to elevate her memory and the occasion of her death, much like when Princess Diana had died.

Frank was already waiting at the open chapel doors. He had aged ten years. He took Murray's hand and shook it firmly as though offering the sincere hand of friendship. 'Thank you for coming,' he said. 'Marilyn would've wanted you here. You made her life interesting and at times fun again. Some of her last words were to tell you that the truth would come out.'

Murray gulped, lost for what he should say in response. He had thought that he would have been regarded as nothing more than a nuisance.

In contrast to the subdued chatter inside the building, the chapel was awash with colourful garlands and flowers. Bunches of red roses tied with shiny ribbon were attached to the end of pews and seats had been labelled to indicate who was to sit where. Murray's inner voice told him he deserved to sit at the back, because he had not cracked the case before Norma had died. His feelings of being heartless were compounded as he looked to the back row for his allocated chair, only to find that he had been placed right at the front. He took his seat next to Mary and Judy. The chapel was already packed with mourners, none of whom he recognised. Most were dressed in black and a few women were clearly trying to hide their identity behind mesh veils attached to elaborate hats, making it impossible to see if any of them were famous. Murray wondered whether some were celebrities, who had also faked their deaths to live in isolation, and that to do so might be more common than he imagined.

He bowed his head and clasped his hands together, feeling he should pray out of respect. However, he was not a religious man so he hoped that if he cut himself off from his surroundings, he could pretend such a sad occasion was not about to happen. Instead of conversing with the others, he sat silently waiting for the service to begin, studying the enlarged photographs of Marilyn Monroe that had been carefully placed at the front of the pews on easels. Most had been taken during her years of stardom. He willed her to wink at him as some sort of spiritual sign.

'How are you feeling?' whispered Judy, sensing he was understandably downbeat.

'Rubbish to be honest. I wish we'd found out the truth one way or another.'

'It didn't matter to her,' said Judy. 'I think she enjoyed you not believing. It was like a game and she made it her mission to tantalise you with the truth.'

Murray realised the logic behind Judy's statement, but before he could comment, classical music began to play. The pallbearers, one of whom was Frank with his head bowed low, walked slowly up the aisle. As the coffin was placed on a plinth, Murray noticed that it was small, a sure indication of how frail the woman within had become. It was topped with a cascade of highly scented red roses, which spilled over the sides like a waterfall.

He could not detach himself from the shared grief of those around him. The rest of the service was a blur of eulogies led by a rotund vicar and members of the congregation. Mary and Frank were too traumatised to speak, so their words were spoken by Mary's daughter whose existence Murray had never been aware of. It occurred to Murray instantly, how at thirty, she bore a diluted likeness to Marilyn Monroe, which made him feel even more guilty about his scepticism. He turned his mind instead to how he imagined Marilyn would feel if she were looking down from on high. He imagined that most likely she would have wanted to skip this depressing performance. She would instead want to get on with the party in the sky as she sat above the chapel on a white cotton-wool cloud, sipping from a glass of Dom Perignon and blowing kisses at the congregation below. As Murray conjured up the image, he imagined each kiss magically transforming into a red rose petal, fluttering down and coating the chapel roof and the adjoining graveyard in a thick carpet of red snow.

The service was lengthy, but once it was over, the congregation began to file out to make its way to the house for the wake. Frank and Mary remained while the coffin was carried out. Murray had been primed that its final resting place was somewhere in the gardens and a secret to all apart from a select few. He hung back, not wanting to invade Frank and Mary's privacy, but placing a bet with himself that Norma wished to be buried on the island in the centre of the lake where she had spent so many lazy summer days as a younger woman.

Frank noticed Murray lingering and approached. 'I'd say you could come with us but...'

Murray put a hand up to stop him mid-flow. 'I'll see you at the house in a while.'

As Frank turned away, Murray felt a pang of pity.

Judy took his arm, noticing that he seemed unwilling to accept comfort. He seemed locked in with his thoughts. 'Are you coming? You've got to eat you know. You've already skipped breakfast.'

'You go ahead. I'll join you soon. I need a bit of head space.'

'Don't be long, or I'll come looking for you,' said Judy. She walked off briskly to catch up with the rest of the funeral party.

Murray began to follow from a distance so that he would not be dragged into casual conversation. Soon the long line of mourners were out of sight. He ambled with no real intention other than trying to make sense of everything he had been told or uncovered over the last few weeks. To fill the unexpected void in his heart, he began to sift through texts and emails that he had flagged up, aware that he had ignored too many over the last few days. After having read a few, he noticed a message from DC Taylor, which he had not got round to reading, containing the new addition to Olivia White's statement. He read it once and then again to be sure he had not misinterpreted it. His heart began to pound. He broke into a jog and had soon caught up with Judy. He pulled her to one side.

'What is it? We *are* officially off duty and I need at least one stiff drink.'

Murray began to drag her away from the other

mourners. 'Jude, I've been such an idiot.'

'Tell me something I don't already know,' she said, fearing her high heels would dig into the grass and cause her to fall flat on her face.

Murray released his grip and took off across the grass at speed, while Judy removed her shoes and did her best to catch up with him in stockinged feet.

Chapter 34

Double Meaning

By the time Judy had caught up with Murray, he was already on the grass under Norma's balcony, bent double as he tried to get his breath back.

She pulled up next to him. 'Alright Usain Bolt, what's this all about?'

He passed her his phone. 'Read the email I've just opened. I can't believe I let this slip by.'

She read the email several times over. 'I don't get what's exciting you so much,' she said. 'What have you picked up on that I'm missing?' When he failed to answer, she looked up, but he was nowhere in sight. Finally, she suddenly spotted him.

He was behaving most oddly as he foraged in flower beds with his bare hands. Eventually he retrieved a long stout stick and waved it at her. 'What does the word Birdhouse mean to you Jude?'

'The same as it means to you. It's the cafe we've been to a few times. Only I'm not so keen to hang out there as you are,' she added.

'All that's true of course, but what about the other birdhouse?' asked Murray.

'Now you're acting weird. I hate it when you turn all cryptic on me.'

Murray pointed upward with his stick, watching for a reaction from Judy.

She looked up at the white dovecot that hung next to Norma's balcony and then back at the email. Murray was already stabbing at the bottom of the dovecot with the stick.

'I didn't get it at first either,' he said. 'I read the word Birdhouse and just like you, all I could think about was the cafe. But Olivia's much more specific. She mentions the old woman's secrets being where the dove's roost. Birdhouse or bird house - they're one and the same. Norma's secrets are here. I'm sure of it.'

Judy's excitement kicked in as she realised the possible implication of what Murray had just said. 'Oh my God. I can't believe you've stumbled across such a thing on today of all days. It's like she waited till now to send us the most important clue.'

'No one's looking - let's get this done,' said Murray, wishing he had a stepladder. 'Get on my shoulders.'

'But we can't. Not like this. If we just crack it open, all the evidence will be contaminated,' insisted Judy, holding him back.

Murray looked for a something to stand on. 'It doesn't matter now she's dead,' he said, losing all professionalism.

'But it does. Don't be rash. Just wait while I call Martin,' said Judy.

By the time Murray had found enough logs to stack, Judy was speaking to Martin. In no time at all, he was walking towards them trying to adopt a casual stride so as not to raise suspicion in anyone in the funeral party.

'Now I know why you're not a detective,' said Judy as he approached.

He ignored her playful sarcasm. 'What's so important that I've had to walk away from the bar and bring my kit in such a hurry?'

Judy humoured him. 'You're not the only one who fancies a drink. I'd kill for a double right now.'

Murray filled Martin in on Olivia's statement and their interpretation of it.

'I'm glad you didn't get stuck in without me,' said Martin, looking upwards while working out the best way to attack the problem.

'We need to get a move on before we're spotted,' said Murray, pacing backwards and forwards.

Martin chose to ignore Murray's impatience and put on latex gloves. He laid out a large sterile cloth on the grass then picked up the stick that Murray had used. Mounting the logs, he tried to detach the bird box carefully from the tree, but just as he had hooked it from the branch, the bottom came away.

Carcasses of dead insects and the box's contents rained down, followed lastly by a cloud of pink confetti, which fluttered down like thousands of sycamore keys. Most of it drifted off in the breeze but there was a light dusting across the lawn.

Murray and Judy fell to their knees, eager to inspect their treasure, finding it nigh impossible to take notice of Martin who was trying to reign them both in.

He was silent as he took photos and dropped various items from the birdhouse into plastic bags with tweezers, numbering each bag as he went.

Murray watched intently. 'What do you make of the

confetti? Whose wedding was that for?' he asked.

Martin shrugged. 'Let's hope this turns up something,' he said, holding up a well sealed plastic bag that was approximately the size of a bag of sugar. He turned it over and over to try and find a clear section that might show him what was inside.

'This might be your only chance to redeem yourself, if you don't lose the evidence this time,' said Murray to Martin.

Martin began to defend himself. 'Ah, about that. I haven't had the opportunity to tell you...'

'Tell us what?' said Judy and Murray, interrupting him in unison.

'The evidence never went missing after all,' said Martin.

'What the...are you telling me you just mislaid it?' asked Murray.

'It would be really nice if just for once you had a bit of faith in me. The powers that be had me examine the evidence outside the Yard. I had a few hours to do it in another lab before it was put in a secure place that only Austen knew about.'

'Why the hell would they ask you to do that?' said Murray. 'And what about Amanda? She was so upset.'

'She does amateur dramatics in her spare time, so it was rigged,' said Martin. 'But I'm guessing they also thought we had a mole and that the story would be in the papers in no time.'

'The whole thing stinks,' said Murray. 'It'd better not be me or Jude they suspect.'

'Well we'll have to look into that later. Now's not the time,' said Judy, trying not to get angry.

'I'll take it to the top,' said Murray, defiantly, feeling

bruised at being shut out from a very early stage.

'Erm... the top is where it came from in my opinion,' suggested Martin. 'You might just have to forget about it.'

Murray began to pace backwards and forwards once more, which was something he always did when something was getting the better of him. 'If you think I'm going to be a puppet...'

'No I'm dead serious,' said Martin. 'You and Jude taking on the top ranking officers of Scotland Yard? I don't see where that will lead you.'

'He's right Steve, ' said Judy.

'Forget about it,' said Martin. 'After all, you've more important things to think about, such as the cine film I've had processed,' he added, with a broad grin on his face.

Murray looked at him in disbelief. 'What cine film?' he asked.

'From DiMaggio's security box.'

'Jude, you didn't tell me there was cine film,' said Murray, accusingly.

'Don't have a go at Jude,' said Martin. 'We didn't examine the contents in detail at the vaults.'

'What was on it?' asked Murray.

Chapter 35

The Truth of the Matter

Finally, Judy and Murray were seated in a media suite back at Scotland Yard with Martin, their anticipation heightened by having been delayed. It had been impossible to remove themselves from the funeral wake, as not only would it have been disrespectful, but their impatient behaviour might have been picked up on by senior officers. Knowing this, they had lingered until late afternoon until other guests had begun to depart.

'I still can't believe you kept the existence of the cine film quiet until the day of the funeral,' said Murray to Martin.

'I was in an impossible position,' said Martin. 'My hands were tied so to speak.'

Murray humphed.

'The footage has been restored and enhanced in a hurry, so it still needs some work,' continued Martin.

The colour film flickered into life, transposed to a different format to protect the original's delicate state.

'The constant temperature in O'Flannagan's vaults

preserved the content far more than had it been in someone's loft,' added Martin.

Instantly Judy let out a gasp at the sight of what was on the screen. She wanted to speak but was mesmerised by a view of Marilyn's swimming pool, framed by palms and borders in her garden. Marilyn was clad in a bikini and talking to a younger Aileen, who was dressed in a simple shift dress. Marilyn put on her sunglasses, lay back and closed her eyes. It was clearly a beautiful sunny day. Her sandals had been kicked off and lay on the ground next to an empty wine glass and a bottle.

The camera operator was clumsy. A change of light hit the lens momentarily, bleaching out the image. Marilyn seemed oblivious to the fact that she was being captured on camera and continued to rest as the operator moved around the pool's edge. Soon the camera operator was standing over Marilyn, casting a shadow across her semi-naked body. The cooling effect on her skin caused her to sit up suddenly. The dialogue was fuzzy but audible.

'Hey, shut that thing off why don't you? You know I hate people sneaking up on me.'

'Aw - don't be like that. I'm just doing my homework,' answered a woman.

'Turn it off I said,' demanded Marilyn.

The second woman left the camera rolling but returned to the bungalow, the world appearing topsy-turvy as she carried the camera. A few seconds later everything was the right way up again as it continued filming from its original vantage point somewhere just inside the house. The second woman walked into shot, turned fleetingly to pose for the camera. Dropping her chiffon garment, she sashayed towards the pool and dived in.

'It's Gloria,' said Murray, his heart beginning to race.

She surfaced the other side and pulled the top part of her body onto the side of the pool. Unexpectedly an argument ensued between the two women, but the camera's technical specification meant that clear sound at distance was patchy. Marilyn was agitated and was waving her arms in the air. She plucked the dark wig from her head and threw it at Gloria who in response struck a provocative pose.

'They could be twins,' said Martin.

'I've been told about this little scenario but I didn't know it was captured on camera,' said Murray. 'Marilyn was pissed off Gloria was wearing her favourite swim wear.'

The scene played out much as it had been told to Murray and he waited for Gloria to return to the bungalow to deal with the camera. Instead a hand accidentally passed across the lens before removing it from its vantage point.

'A third person's involved,' said Judy.

'Maybe not. Maybe they were just mad at what Gloria was doing,' said Murray.

The film flickered for a few seconds as a new scene opened. It focused on a man's face. It was Joe DiMaggio. He began to speak.

'For the record, that broad Gloria is dangerous. I don't know what she's up to, but I reckon she's up to no good. I could destroy this film, but I figure it might be useful. Gotta go, someone's coming.'

The camera was picked up and hurriedly placed back on the window ledge, filming ad hoc the garden and Marilyn out or range. A conversation ensued.

'Hey Joe, I didn't know you were here,' said Gloria, unaware that her voice was being recorded.

'Hey, Gloria, I only just got here,' said Joe.

'Who let you in?' asked Gloria, in a tone that suggested she was not happy he was there.

'I have a key remember. I come and go as I please,' said Joe, defiantly.

'That'll have to change, now I live here permanently,' said Gloria, her tone changing to that of a slithering snake. 'You know Joe, Marilyn and me are just two beautiful actresses trying to keep the same secret. The more folks come and go, the more risk the whole caboodle will get out.'

Joe's voice became more forceful. 'You've been useful so Marilyn can have some sort of private life, but I can see right through you. Your work here's done.'

'Oh really. More like her work's done,' said Gloria.

'What do you mean by that?'

Gloria was beginning to use her sexuality to get Joe on side whereas he was building a script for his own purpose.

'Wouldn't you like a younger version, Joe honey,' she said with a soft growl.

'No I wouldn't. You're nothing like her and never will be.'

'I can pretend. She's pathetic, allowing men to use her for the chance of love.'

'She's wonderful. I should've seen it years ago. Now we've a second chance, you'd best butt out if you know what's good for you,' said Joe, warning her off.

'Aw Joe honey - don't be like that. I can be anything you want me to be baby. Role playing is my speciality. That why I'm gonna become her.'

'You crazy broad. You're not that good an actress. You're nothing but a cheap too bit chorus-girl. You're finished. Pack your stuff and get out.'

'Like hell I will,' screamed Gloria. Her voice faded away as doors were slammed, indicating she had left the room.

Joe turned the camera to face him again. 'Something's gotta be done. Tonight.'

The camera was switched off.

The viewing room was silent as Martin, Murray and Judy sat, stunned, at such an accurate and fortuitous snapshot of history.

'I don't believe it. Is that all of it?' asked Judy, wishing it were a feature length film.

'That's it,' said Martin.

'We still can't be sure of who was bumped off, probably that same evening,' said Judy.

'But we can,' said Murray. 'This verifies that DiMaggio was not taken in by Gloria. He was in love with the real thing and not the slightest bit tempted by some cheap copy. He was going to get her out of the way that very night.'

'That's as maybe,' said Judy. 'But we have no concrete evidence that he achieved it.'

'I have the DNA results back regarding the lock of hair,' said Martin. 'The good news is that the sample from the vaults is a match to the samples I took from Norma.'

'And the bad news?' asked Murray.

'There were hairs from several individuals,' said Martin. 'It must've been tried on by several people.'

'Does that matter?' asked Judy. 'It proves it was worn by Marilyn.'

'Or Gloria,' said Murray.'

Judy's shoulders visibly dropped. 'But there's a picture of Marilyn wearing that suit.'

'That's not to say that Gloria didn't borrow it,' said

Murray.

'We got so close and now we might never know,' said Judy, totally disheartened.

'There is one more thing,' said Martin. 'Items found recovered from Marilyn's birdhouse contained letters on White House headed paper. I got good prints off of them from whoever read them. Then I cross-referenced them with the contents of the items in the clutch bag in the vault.'

'Well?' asked a wide-eyed Judy.

'A definite match.'

Judy looked to Murray for an indication that she might be right after all, but instead, he nodded his head as if to say that there was still nowhere near enough evidence.

'You might want to know what one of the letters said,' teased Martin, throwing drama into the mix.

Murray lifted the blinds and opened the window to feel fresh air on his face so that he could cope with what was about to be said. 'Hit me with it,' he said, fearing the worst.

Judy closed her eyes and tried to control the unpleasant feeling that was rising up through her abdomen and into her chest, suggesting that Steve as usual had been on the ball and that she had been wrong all along. At that moment, she hated the fact that he was right.

Martin unfolded a photocopy, Murray and Judy feeling that he was dragging out the truth to add tension to their already jangling nerves. 'This one's just a quick note but it sums things up pretty well,' he said, somehow managing a deadpan face. 'It was written by JFK, dated the week before he was assassinated.'

'My darling Marilyn, I hope you're still doing okay in England. I think about you and Mary every moment of every day, despite being busy trying to run the country.

Everything's in place though. You know what I mean by that. So I guess I'll be with you both in a couple of weeks, if all goes to plan.

Keep safe, and remember to destroy this once you've read it. Yours. Jack.'

Murray suddenly felt a lump in his throat and he closed his eyes to try and hide his emotion from the others. He knew instinctively that Marilyn would have read the note a thousands times over through the years, knowing full well Jack would never make good on his promise to come to England. It was a small consolation to Murray that the evil that was Gloria had been stamped out.

Uncharacteristically, he put one arm around Judy for a few seconds. She was close to tears. At the same time, he watched as an airliner approached City airport, wondering fleetingly whether it was carrying another celebrity trying to find a place to hide away from the paparazzi and the rest of the world.

It was just as he was thinking such a sombre thought, that a single red rose petal spiralled down from the sky, which was the bluest of blue and laced with cotton wool clouds. The petal drifted lazily in through the window and came to rest on the window ledge close to where Murray was standing. He reached out slowly to gently pick it up, but a soft breeze snatched it away and back out into the open air. He watched as the petal floated away until it was out of sight.

THE END

ABOUT THE AUTHOR

Born in London, Sally has moved around the UK, enjoying the hustle and bustle of London, a quintessential English village in the Midlands and the Hampshire seaside. She currently lives where the work takes her and has no intention of ever retiring.

She has fond childhood memories of heady summer days in her parents' garden, seated at a table learning to draw and paint. It was this period that would eventually mould her career.

Sally's mother, an accomplished seamstress, taught Sally to knit and sew, so that by the age of thirteen Sally was able to make her own clothes.

After leaving grammar school, Sally trained to be an engineering tracer and detail draftsperson and ran her own company employing several tracers. She also designed record sleeves and was a layout artist for Marvel comics while raising three children. Subsequently, she was offered the chance to design costumes for an established ballet school.

Her father encouraged Sally's creative skills: his persuasion gave her the final push to go back into full time education. She studied Fashion and Textiles and later obtained a BA and MA in Costume Design.

As well as writing, Sally is still a Costume Designer. She is also writing screenplays and will be directing for the first time sometime soon.

Printed in Germany
by Amazon Distribution
GmbH, Leipzig